Staging Words, Performing Worlds

The Bucknell Studies in Latin American Literature and Theory
Series Editor: Aníbal González, Pennsylvania State University

Dealing with far-reaching questions of history and modernity, language and selfhood, and power and ethics, Latin American literature sheds light on the many-faceted nature of Latin American life, as well as on the human condition as a whole. This series of books provides a forum for some of the best criticism on Latin American literature in a wide range of critical approaches, with an emphasis on works that productively combine scholarship with theory. Acknowledging the historical links and cultural affinities between Latin American and Iberian literatures, the series welcomes consideration of Spanish and Portuguese texts and topics, while also providing a space of convergence for scholars working in Romance studies, comparative literature, cultural studies, and literary theory.

Titles in Series

Silvia N. Rosman, *Being in Common: Nation, Subject, and Community in Latin American Literature and Culture*
Patrick Dove, *The Catastrophe of Modernity: Tragedy and the Nation in Latin American Literature*
James J. Pancrazio, *The Logic of Fetishism: Alejo Carpentier and the Cuban Tradition*
Frederick Luciani, *Literary Self-Fashioning in Sor Juana Inés de la Cruz*
Sergio Waisman, *Borges and Translation: The Irreverence of the Periphery*
Stuart Day, *Staging Politics in Mexico: The Road to Neoliberalism*
Amy Nauss Millay, *Voices from the* fuente viva: *The Effect of Orality in Twentieth-Century Spanish American Narrative*
J. Andrew Brown, *Test Tube Envy: Science and Power in Argentine Narrative*
Juan Carlos Ubilluz, *Sacred Eroticism: Georges Bataille and Pierre Klossowski in the Latin American Erotic Novel*
Mark A. Hernández, *Figural Conquistadors: Rewriting the New World's Discovery and Conquest in Mexican and River Plate Novels of the 1980s and 1990s*
Gabriel Riera, *Littoral of the Letter: Saer's Art of Narration*
Dianne Marie Zandstra, *Embodying Resistance: Griselda Gambaro and the Grotesque*
Amanda Holmes, *City Fictions: Language, Body, and Spanish American Urban Space*
Gail A. Bulman, *Staging Words, Performing Worlds: Intertextuality and Nation in Contemporary Latin America Theater*
Anne Lambert, *Crating the Hybrid Intellectual: Subject, Space, and the Feminine in the Narrative of José María Arguedas*
Dara E. Goldman, *Out of Bounds: Islands and the Demarcation of Identity in the Hispanic Caribbean*

http://www.departments.bucknell.edu/univ_press

Staging Words, Performing Worlds

Intertextuality and Nation in Contemporary Latin American Theater

Gail A. Bulman

Lewisburg
Bucknell University Press

Associated University Presses
2010 Eastpark Boulevard
Cranbury, NJ 08512

The paper used in this publication meets the requirements of the American National Standard for Permanence of Paper for Printed Library Materials Z39.48-1984.

Library of Congress Cataloging-in-Publication Data

Bulman, Gail A., 1957–
Staging words, performing worlds : intertextuality and nation in contemporary Latin American theater / Gail A. Bulman.
p. cm.
Includes bibliographical references and index.
ISBN-13: 978-0-8387-5676-8 (alk. paper)
ISBN-10: 0-8387-5676-X (alk. paper)
1. Spanish American drama—20th century—History and criticism. 2. National characteristics, Latin American, in literature. 3. Theater —Latin America. I. Title.
PQ7082.D7B85 2007
862′.609328—dc22 2006027656

PRINTED IN THE UNITED STATES OF AMERICA

For Peter—lover, friend, research assistant

For Jerry, Michael, and Laura—the reasons for everything

Contents

Acknowledgments

THIS PROJECT WOULD NOT HAVE COME TO FRUITION WITHOUT THE support of many colleagues, friends, and family members. I am indebted to my colleagues in Latin American theater—Sharon Magnarelli, Jacqueline Bixler, Laurietz Seda, Priscilla Meléndez, Amalia Gladhart, Stuart Day, Elsa Gilmore, Francine A'Ness, Georgina Whittingham and Sandra Cypess, among others—who continue to inspire me through their own scholarship in the field. Thank you especially to George Woodyard, whose mentoring, leadership, and words of encouragement have impacted me greatly and have provided a model for all of us.

Along the way, I have been fortunate to be able to communicate with many Latin American playwrights and their insights have been invaluable in the drafting of this book. Pedro Monge, Raúl de Cárdenas, Eduardo Rovner, Néstor Caballero, Matías Montes Huidobro, Rafael Spregelburd, Myrna Casas and Inés Muñoz Aguirre have shared with me their great ideas along with copies of their latest works. I also appreciate the support of my friend and colleague in Latin American literature, Gisela Norat. Her words of wisdom, "No te rindas" (Don't give up) kept ringing in my ears.

I am grateful to many colleagues in the Department of Languages, Literatures, and Linguistics at Syracuse University. Erika Haber and Margo Sampson, for their friendship, their warmth, their inspiration, and their professionalism, deserve special mention. I also appreciate my colleagues in Spanish who have worked closely with me on service, teaching, and research projects. Among them, Kathryn Everly, Dennis Harrod, Alicia Ríos, Myrna García, Lara Walker, and Pedro Cuperman stand out for their collegial spirit. Catherine Nock and Silvia Figari worked tirelessly editing my translations from Spanish to English and I am thankful for their careful reading, their broad knowledge and keen intuitions in both languages, and their sharp sense of linguistic style. Awa Diop, my former student, helped me with the translations from French. Another Syracuse University student, Libby Hemming, deserves credit for her artistic design and for completing it during her graduation week. Thank you also to my department chair, Jaklin Kornfilt, to Associate Dean Gerald Greenberg, and to the College of Arts and Sciences for the professional and financial support of my work.

The editors of Bucknell University Press, especially Aníbal González and Greg Clingham, made important contributions to this project and I am grateful to them as well as to the editors and staff at Associated University Presses, most notably Julien Yoseloff, but also Christine Retz and Maryann Hostetler for their guidance and attention to detail.

My college friends—Claire, Jane, Reills, Ruth, and Betty—have supported my professional life for more than twenty-five years. I am deeply indebted to them; their wittiness and sense of fun have sustained me. My friends Mary Ellen Gilbert and Christine Praino have provided a refreshing perspective and good camaraderie along the way. I am very grateful to the entire Bulman clan for their moral support through the past decades. My sister Sandra Brackett and her husband Andy moved me forward with their inspiring words, their generous vacation offers, and their frequent displays of kindness and understanding. I am especially grateful to my parents, J. Gerard and Susan Goguen, and my sister Lisa Hamel, for believing in my talents and for constantly encouraging me. I am indebted to my father and late mother, Arlene Sharp, who sacrificed greatly so I could explore the world in my early years.

Finally, this book would not have been possible without the unconditional backing of my immediate family. I express my gratitude and my love to my husband, Peter, who willingly cooked, cleaned, and did laundry all along the way so that I could spend countless hours alone with this manuscript. He read my book as often as I did and provided many creative ideas for which I am also appreciative. Special love and thanks go to my children, Jerry, Michael, and Laura, who have grown up hearing about Mom's book without complaining. Their goodness and their love continue to overwhelm me.

I wish to formally thank the following granters of permission for use of material in my book:

"Staging Exile: The Search for Self and Nation in Pedro Monge's Theater" in *Gestos: Teoría Práctica del Teatro Hispánico*, 35 (April 2003): 87–103. Permission granted by Juan Villegas, editor.

"Martí, Monologue, and the Metaphorical Dawn in Raúl de Cárdenas's *Un hombre al amanecer*" *Latin American Theatre Review* (Special Issue on Caribbean Theatre), 37.2 (Spring 2004): 95–113. Permission granted by George Woodyard, editor.

"Paradise Lost? Rewriting Exile, Breaking the Silence with *Las Hetairas habaneras*" *Ollantay Theater Magazine*. Jackson Heights, N.J. Vol. XI No. 21 (2004): 141–51. Permission granted by Pedro Monge, editor.

"With a Little Help From My Friends." © 1967 Sony/ATV Tunes LLC. All rights administered by Sony/ATV Music Publishing, 8 Music Square West, Nashville, TN 37203. All rights reserved. Used by permission of Lacey Chemsak, Sony/ATV Music.

Hieronymus Bosch (c. 1450–1516). Consignment: COA0043083 (Position: 1) Seven Deadly Sins. Museo del Prado, Madrid, Spain. Photo Credit: Scala/Art Resources, NY Permission granted by John Benicewicz. Photo provided by Alicia Fessenden.

Staging Words, Performing Worlds

Introduction

NATION IS AN ELUSIVE CONCEPT. WHO OR WHAT GIVES THAT WORD meaning? The bloody boundary wars in the Middle East and Asia, the ethnic wars in Rwanda, Sudan, the former Soviet Union, and the former Yugoslavia, the attacks on the United States, Spain, Great Britain, and other sovereign nations by transnational terrorist groups in the name of religion, all challenge any notion of nation as a stable geographical space and question ethnicity or religion as national markers. Globalization, with its far-reaching political, economic, cultural, and technological implications, further complicates definitions of nation.

Most Latin American nations have been relatively stable during the past hundred years; no new countries have emerged and, in spite of violent factions within some spaces, the nations themselves have remained intact. However, defining nation and one's place in it is becoming increasingly difficult. In 1999, for example, amid civil unrest and oppositional attacks, Venezuelan president Hugo Chávez renamed his nation the Bolivarian Republic of Venezuela to commemorate and extend the national discourse of nineteenth-century patriot, Simón Bolívar. Economic problems in Argentina, political tensions in Chile, Ecuador, Colombia, and Peru, indigenous uprisings in Mexico, an indigenous-led government in Bolivia, the Cuban diaspora, Dominican transnational communities, and statist debates in Puerto Rico threaten cohesive definitions of individual nations in Latin America.

Though unstable, nation is, more than anything, a linguistic concept, for it is language that defines both the territory and those who belong to it. Moreover, as Simon During suggests, "Nationalism is . . . quite specifically, the battery of discursive and representational practices which define, legitimate, or valorize a specific nation-state or individuals as members of a nation-state" (1990, 138). Nation is configured through linguistic combinations, and as such, nation is a text, which, like other texts, does not exist in isolation. As texts refer to, recognize, or incorporate other texts within their boundaries, so too does the concept of nation depend on other national texts and contexts to define it.

Highlighting nation as a text, this book explores intertextuality in contemporary Latin American theater and shows how the incorporation of a precursor text into a play-text can rewrite a national discourse, a discourse that may not be apparent without such an intertext. Theater offers a unique medium to examine both textuality and nationality because, as E. J. Westlake (1998) argues, there is a need to perform the nation, and the theater offers a public venue to fulfill this need. Westlake suggests, "Those who count themselves as citizens gather at a national theater to publicly approve or disapprove of the images presented to them" (111).

Focusing on Latin American plays that deliberately refer to and incorporate other texts, I examine the intertextual construction within the play-texts and analyze the functions of those intertexts within their new (con)texts. In the plays selected, I argue that intertextuality is a multifaceted structure that enriches both the precursor text and the new text, broadens the reading of the play itself and of the culture that it represents, and is "written" and "read" by both the playwright and the reader/spectator. Through their connections to the intertext(s), the texts under consideration further serve to expand the discourse on nation and provide new insights into national identities. In these plays, intertextuality foregrounds aspects of nations, which would not necessarily be addressed or highlighted if the intertexts were omitted. In other words, without knowledge or recognition of said intertext and comprehension of how it functions within each given play, national questions would be addressed differently, if at all.

The present study analyzes plays from four Latin American nations: Argentina, Cuba, Mexico, and Venezuela. While analysis of other plays and/or other countries may indeed extend and support the premises, it would be impossible to include all Latin American countries or every play about nation. I choose these plays because they include different genres of intertexts and provide varied examples of how intertexts function within a dramatic text. In addition, these works demonstrate how playwrights might interweave texts to represent their ideology of nation.

In these plays, I identify the major intertext(s) in each work, recognizing that, if every text is a "network of quotations," as Roland Barthes suggests, not all sources, influences, or citations can or should be recognized or determined (Worton and Still 1990, 19–20). Once each major intertext is articulated, I then suggest an origin for the intertext in question and discuss it to the extent that it may shed light on our reading of the new text. The heart of the study begins when I examine the way in which the intertext is worked into the textual fiber, through the language of what Polly Hodge calls the "present text" (1999, 99). Sometimes the intertext becomes part of the spatial script, embedded and encoded into the didascalia in such a way as to impact performance. In other cases, it is used to explore a theme or to represent a style of writing.

Once the intertext is recognized, its origin marked, and its structure in the present text examined, I analyze both the dramatic and the ideological functions of the precursor text within the new play-text, recognizing, as does Juan Villegas, that "the functionality of these relationships is connected to the political and cultural transformations of cultural systems, and consequently it varies in different historical moments" (2000, 102).

My purpose is to determine how these intertexts, through their connections with the precursor text(s), inform the concept of nation in each text. How are the nations defined in each case? How might the insertion of these other texts impact the interpretation of nation or national ideology through these plays? The intertexts in question rewrite an image of nation for the playwrights and their receptors in these works. Ironically, by incorporating the other texts into their plays, these playwrights delineate a clearer perspective on their own nation and national identity.

This study does not mean to imply that all intertexts in theater speak to issues of nation. Sometimes intertexts serve other artistic or ideological functions and may reveal very little about nation or nationality. Indeed, as I will discuss, texts can be a mere dialogue between texts serving to reveal new knowledge about one or the other text or to pay homage to a precursor text or its author. More often, however, intertextuality moves the text beyond a dialogue between texts and expands other meanings.

Intertextuality as a defined term has a long and complicated history. Julia Kristeva used the word in the 1960s; however, the idea behind it had been previously articulated and acknowledged by French linguist Ferdinand de Saussure and Russian formalist Mikhail Bakhtin (Allen 2000, 2). Saussure's theories of the relational function of language, that all language functions within a system and that it can never be separated from that system, form the basis of Kristeva's theories on the interconnectedness of texts. For Saussure, "signs are arbitrary, possessing meaning not because of a referential function, but because of their function within a linguistic system as it exists at any one moment of time" (Allen 2000, 8). Saussure's description of the tension between the synchronic (one moment in time) and diachronic (language that evolves through time) planes, and his distinction between "langue" (the system) and "parole" (what is produced as a specific act of linguistic communication), foreshadow new ways of reading textual relations as well. Language only exists in relationship to the larger system and meanings produced within language are always relational; "they depend upon processes of combination and association within the differential system of language itself" (Allen 2000, 9–10). Similarly, texts, too, are intimately tied to literature, as a system, and to the corpus of texts that comes before them.

Bakhtin (1981) broadens Saussure's concept of linguistic relationships both by extending them to literature and by expanding them to include the social contexts in which words are exchanged. Bakhtin's theory of heteroglossia, "the base condition governing the operation of meaning in any context," insists that, "at any given time, in any given place, there will be a set of conditions—social, historical, meteorological, physiological—that will ensure that a word uttered in that place and at that time will have a meaning different than it would have under any other conditions" (428). For him, the meaning of all words, all expressions, depends on their context and on what comes before them.

Another contribution of Bakhtin, dialogism or the idea that "everything means, is understood, as part of a greater whole," proposes that neither word nor text exists in a vacuum (426). His insistence on the dual nature of the word itself, and on the idea that the interpretation of all utterances depends upon a reciprocal relationship between speaker(writer) and listener(reader) points to the complexity of both linguistic and textual relationships and provides fertile ground for the invention and analysis of future theories of intertextuality.

Bakhtin's many theories, including that of carnival, further enrich interpretations of intertextuality by suggesting that the dialogic can be played with and subverted to question authority and to undermine the predominance of any one "official" story or worldview (Allen 2000, 20). Thus, this dialogic relationship within texts, the connection between texts and other texts, and between texts and the social context, can be manipulated to express the author's will and to prioritize certain "voices" over others.

While neither Saussure nor Bakhtin employ the term intertextuality, Julia Kristeva rereads and revises their theories and from this constructs the term. Kristeva believes that every text is, "a permutation of texts," and, as such, a text is "the space in which several utterances, taken from other texts, intersect and neutralize one another" (ibid.). For Kristeva, the "individual text and the cultural text are made from the same textual material and cannot be separated from each other" (Allen 2000, 35). Her idea is that intertexts are not mere sources or influences; rather, they express the ideological structures found in society. Intertextuality embodies otherness and disrupts the possibility that any text is a stable entity. Texts are unstable because they relate to both the symbolic (social) sphere and the semiotic (instinctual, prelinguistic) plane. In this way, Kristeva adds a psychological dimension to Saussure's linguistic and Bakhtin's social analyses of texts, by connecting her reading of intertextuality to a description of the tension between conscious and subconscious forces that drive language production and utterance.

Kristeva's psychological interpretation of language and hence, intertextuality, allows her to articulate other theories of the dichotomy/multiplicity/polyphony within texts. For her, no text is original; no text is stable. Within each text reside both a *phenotext* (that part of text that connects to her idea of the symbolic) and a *genotext* (related to her definition of the semiotic) (1984, 5). This conflict within the split text is displayed through language; the phenotext can be read through the superficial textual language, and is manifested in "strictly linguistic structures" (1984, 91). On the other hand, "even though it can be seen in language, the genotext is not linguistic . . . It is, rather, a *process,* which tends to articulate structures that are ephemeral (unstable, threatened by drive charges)" (1984, 86). Every text includes these two forces that, together, make up the actual (communicative, grammatical) language of the text (phenotext) and manifest the process (drives, impulses) behind it, within it (genotext).

A further psychological dimension of language and texts that Kristeva elaborates reinterprets Freud's concepts of "condensation" and "displacement," two "fundamental processes in the work of the unconscious" (1984, 59) and applies them to the construction of texts. Condensation, where one sign collects into itself a host of meanings, and displacement, where one sign from another area of signification stands in for the real content, form the basis of her theory of intertextuality and lead her to label it *transposition* (Allen 2000, 54). According to Kristeva:

> If one grants that every signifying practice is a field of transpositions of various signifying systems (an inter-textuality), one then understands that its "place" of enunciation and its denoted "object" are never single, complete, and identical to themselves, but always plural, shattered, capable of being tabulated . . . We shall call *transposition* the signifying process's ability to pass from one sign system to another, to exchange and permutate them; . . . Transposition plays an essential role here inasmuch as it implies the abandonment of a former sign system, the pas-

> sage to a second via an instinctual intermediary common to the two systems, and the articulation of the new system within its new representability. (1984, 60)

Transposition explains how texts within texts are employed, transformed, and take on new meaning within a new text. As a precursor text is referred to and then incorporated into a new text, it abandons its former meaning, becomes an intermediary with elements common to both texts, and ultimately articulates a new system. In these plays, I argue, this transposition unmasks a new perspective on nation.

Beyond these theories of polyphony, the split text, and transpositon, arises the question of authorship. For Kristeva, the position of the "writing subject" is multiple and mobile (1984, 91). Kristeva's mentor and colleague, Roland Barthes, has articulated a theory of the death of the author that also has great implications for the development of theories of intertextuality. Barthes argues that "writing is the destruction of all voices, all origins . . . From the moment the event is recounted . . . the author enters into his/her own death, the writing begins" (1994, 491).[1] He maintains that the idea of authorship is a completely modern concept and that, in early societies, "the story is never put into motion by a person, but rather by a mediator, a shaman or storyteller, whose 'performance' one can necessarily admire but not his/her 'talent'" (491).[2]

Alongside the dead author emerges the collaborative reader, who participates in the textual creation. Barthes's theory further argues that both the reader and the writer are "intertextual sites." Therefore, "the 'I' is never 'innocent,' but always a selection of other (inter-) texts, so that the subject becomes as 'plural' and 'open' as the literary text" (Morgan 1989, 257). In his own work, Barthes confirms, "The text can be read without the father's guaranty; the restitution of the intertext, paradoxically, abolishes its heritage" (1994, 1215). Neither author nor reader can escape intertextuality and, like in Kristeva, "the subject is projected into a vast intertextual space where he or she becomes fragmented or 'pulverized' into an unending series of exchanges between his or her own and others' texts" (Morgan 1989, 260).[3]

Contrary to Kristeva's more psychoanalytical approach, Harold Bloom's *The Anxiety of Influence* (1973) posits intertextuality as an ever-present, but disturbing, element of literature that tugs and pulls at the (new) authors, as they struggle to both recognize and reject their sources. Bloom outlines a six-point theory of intertextual relations in which the poet (1) swerves away from the precursor text(s);

(2) recognizes and "antithetically completes" the parent-text; (3) "moves toward discontinuity with the precursor"; (4) minimizes the uniqueness of the earlier work by opening him/herself up to the "power just beyond" the precursor text; (5) moves toward self-purgation which leads to purgation of the parent-text too; and (6) "kills" the author of the precursor text by "rewriting" the text as if it were his/her own (13–16). Bloom's theory highlights the battle between the "new" writer and the "parent" writer, between new text and precursor text, and suggests that it is impossible to escape this intertextual love-hate relationship. Ironically however, Bloom argues that in spite of this necessary and ever-present anxiety, "poetic influence need not make poets less original; as often it makes them more original" (7).

Different from Bloom but similar to Kristeva's theories on genotext and phenotext, Michael Riffaterre's theories of intertextuality posit the act of reading as a dynamic process that entails two stages of understanding: linguistic and literary. Modifying Peirce's concept of the "interpretant" ("a sign that translates the text's surface signs and explains what else the text suggests"), Riffaterre sees intertext as the interpretant or mediator between text and precursor text (Morgan 1989, 263).[4] Morgan suggests that "intertextual traces guide interpretation" and argues that the text "pushes the reader toward correct interpretation by marking the path with intertextual 'traces.'" This triangular relationship marks both *explicit* intertextuality (the easily traced down quotation) as well as *implicit* intertextuality (the more elusive allusion) (Morgan 1989, 262–65). Thaïs Morgan sees contradictions in Riffaterre's theories, and suggests that the latter vacillates in his view of the reader's role by positing the reader sometimes as a "powerful sleuth who hunts down" intertextual meaning and at others, as a "stubborn resister" who "refuses to play its idiolectal language game, and continually seeks 'relief by getting away from the dubious words back to safe reality'" (1989, 265).

The contradictory role of the reader is parallel to Kristeva's view of subjectivity. In her theory of the subject-in-process, Kristeva (1977) reveals a new understanding of the "I" that involves a dynamic of both destruction and creative identity leading to the reconstitution of a new plurality. She sees a subject-in-process, "attacking all stasis of a unified subject" and postulates that this subject-in-process does not eliminate or diminish subjectivity but, rather, opens up the subject, rendering it multiple (61–65). Her theory of the "rejets" of identity, with the implicit tension between destruction (to reject) and growth (to recreate the flows/a rebirth), sheds light on intertextuality as a love-hate relationship within and between the writing/reading subjects and within and between the texts.[5] This split textual tension, in the case of the plays in question, often highlights a similar love-hate relationship with regard to nation. Moreover, intertextuality in these texts posits dialogues with the past, the present, and the future, and sheds light on national identity as it is formulated from within national borders and outside of them.

Further expanding readings of intertextuality, Gérard Genette's theory of palimpsests shows the complex but constant presence of intertextuality in literature and establishes that all texts "hover between originality and imitation" (Morgan 1989, 270). For Genette, "each literary or aesthetic text produces a palimpsest, superimposing several other texts which are never completely hidden, but always hinted at" (Morgan 1989, 271). Genette (1997) believes that *transtextuality,* "the textual transcendence of the text," is the very subject of poetics. In *Palimpsests,* he defines transtextuality as, "all that sets the text in a relationship, whether obvious or concealed, with other texts" (1). Dividing his idea of "transtextuality" into five categories, Genette develops a literary theory of relationships between texts. He marks his first category, intertextuality, as the most concrete of transtextual relationships, citing that it is, "a relationship of co-presence between two texts or among several texts, . . . typically as the actual presence of one text within another" (1). Intertextuality includes quotation, allusion, and plagiarism.[6] Genette's other categories include para-, meta-, hyper-, and architextuality.

Genette's terms and their definitions are extremely useful to this analysis of theater's intertextual relations with other genres. Beyond intertextuality, his paratextuality, "a less specific and more distant relationship which binds the texts," allows us to use the new texts' title, subtitles, prefaces, forewords, or epigraphs as markers or "pacts," which receptors must recognize. He believes that paratexts "provide the text with a (variable) setting and sometimes a commentary, official or not" (3). As another form of transtextuality, metatextuality "unites a given text to another, of which it speaks without necessarily citing it, in fact sometimes even without naming it . . . This is the *critical* relationship par excellence" (4).[7]

Hypertextuality, the category of transtextuality most developed by Genette in *Palimpsests,* will, perhaps, be of the most use to my study. The *hypertext* comments on, incorporates, revises, modifies, imitates, or transposes the *hypo*—or precursor—text. Genette determines that "what I call hypertext, then, is any text derived from a previous text either through simple transformation, which I shall simply call from now on *transformation,* or through indirect transformation, which I shall label *imitation*" (7). Genette's idea of imitation refers to a "way of arranging words" and leads to his definitions of caricature and pastiche. My study focuses more on Genette's ideas on transformation, rather than imitation, because I see, as he suggests, that "serious transformation or transposition, is without any doubt, the most important of all hypertextual practices" (212).

For Genette, "there is no such thing as an *innocent* transposition: i.e., one that does not in one way or another alter the meaning of its hypotext" (294). Two types of transpositions form the basis of his argument: formal and thematic. Formal transposition, including translation and versification, affects meaning and, though it is inevitably an imperfect imitation, it attempts to "say the same thing" as the hypotext. Formal transposition entails "a change of mode, but not a change of genre" (277). While formal transpositions may give the hypotext a new form, they ultimately do not transform the theme.

The intent of a thematic transposition, on the other hand, "appears to be more complex, or more ambitious than in formal transposition," since it "adds both text and meaning to the same story" (Genette 1997, 294). Thematic transposition can be divided into two categories: diegetic transposition, designating the spatiotemporal world delineated by the text; and pragmatic transposition, consisting of a modification of the events or actions in a plot.

Other theorists discuss the differences between intertextuality and intratextuality, where meaning is construed within the text itself, as it makes itself and creates its own system of meaning (Altman 1981, 41). Charles Altman discusses the murky boundary that separates inter- from intra textualities and writes that "a constant tension exists between . . . coded intertextual meanings and the text's never-ceasing ability to form its own language through intratextual rewriting" (46). Each text establishes its own intratextual code, but, as Altman argues, "it is the transfer of intratexual meaning to another text that I am terming intertextual meaning" (46). These complicated processes of meaning-making, perhaps, become more apparent in theater, as the intertextual becomes intratextual when the precursor texts are worked into the spatial script (through the didascalia), the dialogue, or the very fabric of the play, thus creating their own sign systems that function on both the dramatic and the ideological levels.

In essence, my chapters examine how intertextuality moves from language, to structure, content, and ideology in these plays. Other concepts of intertextuality will further inform my study, such as Lucien Dällenbach's theory of "autotextuality" or "mise en abyme" (1976, 1989). Rather than look at the distinction between intra- and intertextuality, Dällenbach, among others, distinguishes between general or external intertextuality (relations between texts) and restrictive, or internal, intertextuality, which he classifies as the relationship of a text with itself (1976, 282). This theory is especially relevant to my analysis of Argentine playwright Eduardo Pavlovsky's *Poroto* (1996, 1999a) plays and their relation to their "mirror-text" *Dirección contraria* (1997). Different from theories of intratextuality, Dällenbach suggests that through autotextuality a text reflects upon itself, both structurally and in terms of content, and establishes dialogues within itself through internal repetition. This specular process questions whether, by doing this, the text ceases to exist and recreates another "self" (1976, 283). After querying whether autotextuality "massively amplifies the redundance of the work," thus closing rather than opening the text, Dällenbach argues that, on the contrary, by confirming the literary game of the text, autotextuality does indeed open the text. He writes that mise-en-abyme affirms "I am literature, I and the story that encompasses me" (1976, 285).

Based on Dällenbach's mise en abyme, on Levi-Strauss's "bricolage," and Derrida's idea that every utterance is an "interweaving of signifiers," Thaïs Morgan argues, "the text itself is an unstable process of illimitable intertextual transformations" that need to be interpreted by the receptor.[8] The notions that both author and receptor do their part to decipher the text and that every text is unstable have greater meaning in the theater, where performance, as Amalia Gladhart reminds us, "is intrinsically contingent and unstable" (2000, 14).[9] Moreover, the idea of repetition is encoded in theatrical texts, as they are intended both for reading and for multiple performances (Gladhart 2000, 221).

Intertextuality, when it is obvious in theater, can be found in multiple locations within the play-text; it can be discovered in the play's title, in epigraphs, in the didascalia, and/or in the dialogue itself. Whether as reference to another written text, to music, to painting, or to culture, intertextuality adds to the script's tension by encoding it to a pre-text or pre-texts in rhizomelike fashion. However, as Jonathon Culler (1976) suggests, intertextuality is a way for a text to release new energy and reveal new knowledge. It is this new knowledge about nation that this book examines.

In releasing new knowledge about the texts in question, one needs to recognize the multiple directions into which the new knowledge can pull the reader. The new information speaks simultaneously to both precursor text and new text, to their structures and to the contexts they delineate. John Frow establishes that "What is relevant to textual interpretation is not, in itself, the identification of a particular intertextual source but the more general discursive structure to which it belongs. This has implications for the kind of knowledge we should expect to be relevant to the reading of texts" (1990, 46). In intertextuality, Frow argues, what is important is "the ability to reconstruct cultural codes which are realised (and contested) in texts" (46). In most cases in these plays the cultural codes established through intertextuality are ironic in that, by pointing the text in question to another text, the script is directing the reader's attention both inside and outside the national context.

These vacillating definitions of intertextuality show that it destabilizes the notions of language, text, reader, and author, and lead one to wonder whether all texts are necessarily intertextual. Referencing Barthes, Judith Still and Michael Worton affirm that "a text may appear to be the spontaneous and transparent expression of a writer's intentions, but must necessarily contain elements of other texts" (Worton and Still 1990, 19).[10] Kristeva, too, maintains, "every text is under the jurisdiction of other discourses" (Worton and Still 1990, 9). She further suggests that each quotation of a precursor text is a metaphor that speaks of that which is absent, by pointing to what the precursor/quoted text simultaneously is and is not in contraposition to the text it is quoted in and their relationship.

If intertextuality is necessarily present in every text, why examine it? Because it is in the degree of presence and the function of that presence where tension is created and new meanings are construed. The weight of emphasis that the playwright places upon the intertext, as well as the intertexts' dramatic and ideological functions (Villegas 2000, 101) within the present text, create a new text and context, which, in these cases, transform images of nation and national identity.

In addition, Heidegger argues that "Every work of art says something other than the mere thing itself" (Worton and Still 1990, 12). For this reason it is necessary to perceive the intertextual connections in order to interpret a work. Moreover, as these intertexts reveal new knowledge about nation, so too will they enhance perspective on the dramatic text(s) in question. Jonathan Culler would seem to agree when he writes of "presuppositions," present in every text, which "open an intertextual space which can easily become ironic" (1976, 1390). Moreover, Culler maintains, "It is of considerable importance which propositions a work chooses to assert directly and which it chooses to place in this intertextual space by presupposing them" (1390). The intertexts that playwrights choose to weave into their works have a thematic and structural fiber that highlights the themes and structure of the new text and reveals a unique ideology.

Intertextuality in Hispanic tradition has a long, successful, and well-delineated history. In the first "modern" novel in the world, Miguel de Cervantes masterfully intertextualizes medieval sources and contemporary texts and contexts, as well as *his own first volume* within the covers of his two-volume masterpiece *Don Quixote.* Later painters and writers from Velázquez to Galdós follow suit, producing some of the most interesting and "baroque" artistic texts in Hispanic tradition. More recently, Jorge Luis Borges revolutionalizes intertextuality when, in works like his short story *Pierre Menard, Author of the Quixote* (1977) he plays with the concepts of text and intertext, reader and author, by highlighting the *differences* between Cervantes' *Quixote,* and that of his fictional author, Pierre Menard.[11]

Works like those of Cervantes and Borges underline the intrinsic tension in intertextual relationships and, at the same time, depict that tension as simultaneously binary and multiple. On the one hand, some theorists affirm the relevance of the author, the text, or the writing itself as integral to intertextuality, while others establish the priority of the reader and/or the reading in their discussions of the concept. The fact is, as Riffaterre affirms, intertextuality is neither; it is a relationship between the reader's response and the "textual elements that we're *obliged* to perceive" (Worton and Still 1990, 24). Intertextuality is far from a binary concept; it is not a dialogue between two texts, but rather it focuses on tensions and presuppositions directly established in or implied by the referencing of one text within another. Borges and others have argued, too, that the new text actually invents the precursor text. Which text comes first depends on the reading.

Polly Hodge writes of the great number of Hispanic plays in recent years that dramatize or refer to other literary texts and proposes that intertextuality can function at various levels in theater (1999, 97–98). She maintains that the key question in examining intertextuality is to determine, "How does the present text communicate with the previous texts, the intertexts, and what meaning does this dialogue have in the cultural sphere of the present moment?" (100). Among the many functional levels, Hodge suggests that an intertext: (1) pays homage to the precursor text and highlights its role and cultural significance; (2) functions as a metatheatrical mechanism, which emphasizes blurred boundaries between genres;[12] and (3) serves "as a mode of transmission of a social or cultural comment from a histrionic perspective" (98). Thus, intertextuality has specific functions on both textual and ideological levels.

Juan Villegas also emphasizes the importance of the "function" of intertextuality on these two levels. He writes that "the analysis will consist of showing the functionality of the constituents of the text with respect to that social imaginary and that image of the world" (2000, 31). He further determines that any valid analysis of intertextuality must show both its dramatic and its ideological functions (101–2). In other words, why does the playwright use certain intertexts and how do they function with regard to both the text and its political/social/ideological context?

Villegas further argues that theater, like all artistic texts, "is understood as a 'creation' or 'production' of language" (11), recalling the Saussurian origins of intertextuality. He, too, sees that intertextuality directs attention toward receptors because they recontextualize the play's meaning. Villegas highlights the importance of the receptor when he writes that "each cultural practice involves the competence of the potential receptor to decipher the message" (30). He further maintains that "the danger of intertextual analysis is to emphasize the similarity between texts and not to question their differences, the ideological signification of the new versions, nor their meaning for the new receptors within the new contexts of communication" (104). An analysis of intertextuality must do more than study the similarities between texts; it must emphasize their differences, open reflection on both texts, establish unique ideological meaning within the new text, and create "new" contexts for the receptor(s) of those texts.

Recognizing these new contexts and meanings through intertextuality can give pleasure to the audience as Aristotle had theorized (Worton and Still 1990, 5–6). Beyond pleasure, however, new knowledge is gained through intertextual connections. As Jeanne Brownlow and John Kronik argue, "Just as chaos is no longer a tumultuous state or condition but a revision of order, so is intertextuality no longer a formalized contract between two distinguished and distinguishable parties but a wide-ranging instrument of relevance retrieval whose function is the accrual rather than the immediate exchange of knowledge" (1998, 12).

The new knowledge revealed through intertextuality in these plays functions to establish unique definitions of nation and to depict national identities, while, at the same time, it creates a literary game that highlights both texts, thus uncovering new artistic meanings as well. Intertextuality moves these dramatic texts beyond dialogue, and establishes multiple dialogues with the past, present, and future, with other cultures, with other nations, or with multiple paradigms within self and nation. In this way, the plays reflect on their own national context. Intertextuality, here, continues to echo back to Bakhtin's "dialogic," which then opens up to the polyphony and heteroglossia of literary, critical, and cultural meaning. By opening these scripts to intertextual interpretations, the nation is foregrounded.

As I have proposed, definitions of nation, like the structures of texts, are impossibly unstable and incohesive.[13] Homi Bhabha argues that "to write the story of the nation demands that we articulate that archaic ambivalence that informs modernity" (1990, 294). Though each citizen embraces a unique notion of nation, on some level, nation is a collective "script." Like theater, which is rewritten in each performance and by playwright, director, actors, and spectators, nation evolves in each individual and collective articulation of it. Nonetheless, theater can be used to rewrite definitions of nation. According to Marcela Sosa and Graciela Balestino de Adamo, "Rewriting, in the case of Latin American dramaturgy, is the best way to affirm identity" (1997, 142).

Through written and performed theater, Latin American dramatic texts have explored the construction of nation since pre-conquest times. Adam Versényi (1993) determines that, in those early years, Aztec, Andean, and Mayan rituals dramatized the interstices between politics, religion, and nation through the use of music and dance. Versényi argues that "Theater and spectacle were an integral part of the maintenance of Empire" in those early years (15). Moreover, during the colonial period, theater became a prevalent tool for the evangelization of the indigenous people and for their indoctrination into Spanish political ideology. Plays like *El güegüense* (Nicaragua), *El Rabinal-Achí* (Yucatan peninsula), and *Ollantay* (Andes region) consider the construction of nation, the imposition of colonialism, and the nation's relationship with its citizens. By the end of the eighteenth and beginning of the nineteenth centuries, theater was the preferred means of spreading political ideology. Indeed, Versényi notes, "As the late eighteenth and early nineteenth centuries continued, the theater increasingly became the preferred arena for political discourse. This was true both for those yearning for independence from strict obedience to what they now perceived as a foreign power, and for those who strove to maintain, or impose, their authority throughout the colonies" (46).

Nineteenth-century dramatic texts naturally interrogated notions of nation and national identity as an extension of the political, ideological, and philosophical discussions within the emergent nations. For both the marginalized and the ruling classes within each new geopolitical demarcation, important issues arose that became the theoretical framework of novels and theater alike. The question of civilization and barbarism in the Southern Cone; the theme of "South American" unity enunciated by patriots like Andrés Bello, Simón

Bolívar, and Joaquín Olmedo; the issue of Cuban patriotism expounded by José Martí, José María Heredia, Gertrudis Gómez de Avellaneda; and the topic of Mexican national identity in voices like Joaquín de Lizardi and Federico Gamboa became blatant themes in the theater of these and other nineteenth century writers.[14] For nineteenth-century playwrights, nation was a problematic construction as they struggled to define their identity and their homeland during and after the difficult years of independence.

Theater in the early twentieth century further queries the construction of nation(s) and begins to turn its attention to the social and political concerns of the new republic(s). Through the use of *costumbrismo* in the early 1900s, theater vividly depicts national life and conflicts. In Argentina and Uruguay, for example, Florencio Sánchez's gauchesque plays "treat country and city, the middle classes and the slums" (Dauster 1996, 552) and highlight the ongoing tensions between immigrants and citizens at the beginning of the century. Additionally, Uruguayan political leader Gregorio de Laferrère scripts satirical comedies "about the superstitions and foibles of the urban middle class," while in Mexico and Central America a regional Mayan theater was developing (Dauster 1996, 552). During the middle part of the twentieth century, though, reflections on nation turn to a preoccupation with theater itself and to its relationship to art in general. Brechtian concepts, theater of the absurd, and vanguard tendencies dominate the stage throughout those years, reflecting a return to European tendencies and the art of the "other" to mask national instabilities and doubt.

During the 1960s, 1970s, and beyond, however, Latin American theater is forced to turn back to the preoccupation with nation, as its violent governments exploit the rights of its citizens and push patriotism to its limits. The Cuban Revolution, the Argentine, Chilean, and Uruguayan Dirty Wars, the civil wars in El Salvador, Guatemala, and Nicaragua, are some examples of the political unrest that mark the last half of the twentieth century. In most countries, theater clandestinely stages national conflicts and often provides a cathartic outlet during those years of terror.[15]

The idea of nation, which began to emerge in Latin America in the nineteenth century, is problematic in any context. Homi Bhabha contends that "The very concepts of homogenous national cultures, the consensual or contiguous transmission of historical traditions or 'organic' ethnic communities—*as the grounds of cultural comparativism*—are in a profound process of redefinition" (1994, 5). Benedict Anderson has argued, "Nation is an imagined political community—and imagined as both inherently limited and sovereign" (2003, 7).[16]

Anderson further establishes that nation is "imagined as a community, because, regardless of the actual inequality and exploitation that may prevail in each, the nation is always conceived as a deep, horizontal comradeship. Ultimately, it is this fraternity that makes it possible, over the past two centuries, for so many millions of people, not so much to kill, as willingly to die for such limited imaginings" (7).

National sovereignty, however, also becomes a questionable process. As James Gow argues, "Certainly, the meaning and content of sovereignty will often change according to the will of a particular government at a particular time—it is a plastic term which means that governments can justify almost any action, whether assertive or contrite, in terms of exercising their sovereign rights. Essentially, this means a government has the autonomy to decide for itself what it would like to do" (1974, 463). Sovereignty, then, gives a nation the apparent "power of action without being bounded unto others" (Pocock in Gow 1974, 464). Equally problematic is the issue of nation as an "imagined community." Ernst Renan (1882) suggests that there is an inherent duality in that vision when he argues, "A nation is a soul, a spiritual principle. Two things, which in truth are but one, constitute this soul or spiritual principle. One lies in the past, one in the present. One is the possession in common of a rich legacy of memories; the other is present-day consent, the desire to live together, the will to perpetuate the value of the heritage that one has received in an undivided form" (Bhabha 1990, 19). For Renan, the past/future image of nation shapes citizens' identity with regard to their place within that imagined community. The tension between the past bonds of its citizens and the imposition and need or desire to accept and be part of the same future, "imagined" community, influences writing about nation. Moreover, in order to imagine nation, citizens have to break through the barriers that others have imagined for them and sometimes that entails forgetting the pain of the past. Seamus Deane declares that "In the attempted discovery of its 'true' identity, a community often begins with the demolition of the false stereotypes within which it has been entrapped. This is a difficult process, since the stereotypes are successful precisely because they have been interiorized" (Eagleton 1990, 12).

As a community tries to "read" itself and (re)construct its own image, it is continually battling the identity that is constantly being imposed upon it by the outside "other." Hernán Vidal discusses the notion of otherness as it relates to ideologies of nation in Latin America and argues that "After more than a hundred years of apparent political independence we are direct heirs of the Liberal project of the early nineteenth century towards the formation of strong, independent nation-States, based on the material progress gained from participation in the rising international capitalist market" (1991, 31). He explains that, nonetheless, "during the twentieth-century this project showed its contradictions when these very same national master narratives . . . became obstacles in the Liberal utopia of a free world circulation, accumulation, and transfer of capital" and that, "throughout recent decades these trends have evolved into a deeper awareness about the disintegrating effects of an unrestrained transnationalized economy on national policies" (31).

As Latin American nations try to modernize while still maintaining their cultural, political, and economic autonomy as well as their ethnic diversity, they are caught in a tug and pull between past and present and between autonomy and economic prosperity. Vidal describes some of the tensions at issue in the self-definition of modern Latin American nations when he writes, "The foreign symbolic capital circulated by the media and the educational systems, the accumulation of master narratives of national identity, the persistence of pre-Columbian and African folklore and the massive migrations of the populations throughout the national territories and beyond, according to economic fluctuations controlled from abroad, generate forms of creolization which fuse together all kinds of expressive elements in complex patterns of cultural syncretism" (1991, 32). All these tensions influence notions of the national self and form differing perspectives on nation.

Moreover, while nation may be a tangible geographic space, delineated by set boundaries and imagined by a certain "national" community, the nation also "lives" inside each national citizen, whether or not that national being resides within the nation's borders. How do exiled individuals and communities imagine their nation and to what extent is the nation embodied and defined within those individuals and communities? According to Michael Peter Smith and Luis Eduardo Guarnizo, "The term 'transnationalism' has reached particular intensity at the end of the twentieth-century" (1998, 3). They argue, "Transnationalism refers to the development and consequences of transnational practices linked to the processes of mass migration, economic expansion, and political organization across national spaces" (4). However, as Ulf Hannerz suggests, "There is a certain irony in the tendency of the term 'transnational' to draw attention to what it negates—that is, to the continued significance of the national" (Giles 2003, 6). How is nation defined within transnational communities? For example, what is Cuba to Cubans forced to live in exile? How does this "Cuba," defined from the diaspora, manifest itself in Cuban theater written outside Cuban borders? As Heidrun Adler establishes in her prologue, "since two Cuban societies exist, one in Cuba and the other in the United States, . . . the political framework within which Cuban theater developed after 1959, necessarily led to the politicizing of theatrical discourse" (Adler and Herr 1999b, 9).

Whether its impact on individual or national identity is positive or negative, there is little doubt that transnationalism, in its many manifestations, is reconfiguring national discourses. Some argue that it is "the transnational system itself that menaces national autonomy" (Jameson 1998, xv), while others take an opposing perspective, suggesting that it is a creative force, offering new hope for otherwise powerless nations. Smith and Guarnizo, for example, maintain that "far from withering away in the epoch of transnationalism, sending states once presumed to be 'peripheral,' are promoting the reproduction of transnational subjects; and, in the process, reinventing their own role in the 'new world order'" (1998, 8).

This new world order is further redefined through globalization, a reality that embodies similarly contradictory potential for nation-states. Whether cultural or economic, globalization has begun to erode the concept of nation, yet, at the same time, through mass media, communication, and technology, it may offer creative possibilities for the empowerment of underdeveloped communities. As George Yúdice argues, it is these things, "from migrant circuits to multinational networks and supranational regional integration agreements such as NAFTA and MERCOSUR that are rearticulating the imagined community" (2001, xxix). Moreover, through these processes and the consumerism that undoubtedly results from them, García Canclini envisions that "the political notion of citizenship is expanded" because consumption becomes not just "a mere setting for useless expenditures and irrational impulses, but a site that is good for thinking" (2001, 5).

Globalization shifts thinking from classic identities based on geography, nation, social class, or ethnicity to new identities established through communication technologies and consumption (García Canclini 2001, 5–6). While some argue that the emphasis on globalization creates tension within these entities because of the rift between the global and the local as the local attempts to define itself rather than be defined by the imperialist other, Lola Proaño-Gómez maintains that "In this way the local and the global are converted into specular images of the same" (2001, 60). On the other hand, she argues that the local "loses its exceptional character to transform into a sign consistent with the globalization model" (60). While tension certainly exists between the global and local, Paul Giles affirms that "the power of global capitalism resides in the way it avoids becoming attributed to any specific locality" (2003, 65). In isolating itself as the new ideology and in affirming new ways of imagining community, globalization encourages new means of empowerment.

While globalization may have its positive impact on conceptions of nation, it is marked by polarity and tension both within nation-states and between them. In his attempt to define the term and the forces behind it, Fredric Jameson sees "globalization as an untotalizable totality which intensifies binary relations between its parts—mostly nations, but also regions and groups—which, however, continue to articulate themselves on the model of 'national identities' . . . Such relations," he suggests, "are first and foremost ones of tension or antagonism, when not outright exclusion; in them each term struggles to define itself against the binary other" (1998, xii).

While tension has always marked constructions of nation and national identity in Latin American theater, in contemporary theater the political tensions revealed are far less binary. Tensions are not between a right and a leftist perspective, between bad government and good citizens, or between immigrants and nationals; rather, tensions are simultaneously within, in favor of and against self, and within, in favor of and against nation. Ironically, it is within this ambiguous space called nation, the space of the struggle, where both nation and nationality attempt to be defined.

In theater there is also an inherent tension in the text on many levels: most notably the tension between the written play-text and the performance. As Kirsten Nigro argues, "the vast majority of play-texts have been and still are written to be staged, a fact which somehow must be reckoned with" (1987, 102). She views the play-text as "likened to a symbolic notation for the live *presentation* of these (fictive) activities" (102). Juan Villegas, as well, emphasizes that "the dramatic text and the theatrical text (are) different cultural products and . . . even the same text, read or performed, constitutes differentiated cultural objects" (2000, 200). However, as Anne Ubersfeld proposes, the theatrical text is always present within performance as a "voice." As such, it both precedes and then accompanies performance (1999, 8). These considerations, which, according to Villegas, have been argued since Aristotle's time, might lead us to question whether the incorporation of certain intertexts within a play would have a different impact on readers of the play-text than on spectators of the live performance. The way intertexts are woven into the textual fiber, either in the didascalia or in the dialogue, will also show that they function as ideological metaphors for nation in both the written and the intended or actual performance text.

Theater can be an important vehicle to transmit the multifaceted identities of the contemporary nation. In his article, "De globalización y teatro latinoamericano" (On Globalization and Latin American Theater), Pepe Bablé argues that Latin American theater is a powerful medium through which to express the conflicting forces of globalization. He determines that "The world has been suffering economic and polemical crises, but not intellectual or cultural ones. Now, faced with this knowledge of homogenization that we suffer, sheltered under the concept of globalization, we have to once more ask for social, ethical and aesthetic transgression through the artistic vehicle of the theater. And if diversity creates conflict, we have to defend it by all possible means; and here Latin American theater has a lot to say" (2001, 238).

Theater and the texts and voices it incorporates can be an effective way to help articulate the national. However, this study does not suggest that nation is a homogenous concept for Latin America. Far from the South American nation imagined by Simón Bolívar in the nineteenth century, this book reads nations in Latin America as unique, independent, self-defined constructs configured from the inside out. Theater written within and about these nations and by citizens of said nations will help us define each "imagined community."

The imagined communities that playwrights postulate through intertextuality are quite different from each other and, in some cases, lean more toward transnational than national configurations. However, nation continues to be an important construct. As Paik Nakchung suggests, "the nation-state . . . no longer enjoys the same authority in the current age of globalization . . . nations and nation-states (or remnants thereof) will continue to be a material presence, and nationhood a going concern . . . no effective action then, whether to adapt oneself to this modernity or to abolish it and arrive at a genuine postmodernity, will be possible without coming to terms in some manner with the reality of nations and nationhood" (Jameson 1998, 219).

Examining the nation through the lens of intertextuality raises questions and suggests oppositions within texts, intratextual relations, which, in these cases, open up possible new interpretations of notions of nation in Latin American contexts. This book attempts to examine these connections and the questions about them and to propose ways in which intertextuality can inform readings of nation and national identity. Through the use of theories of intertextuality and the play-texts themselves, I discuss nine plays written in the last three decades from four Latin American countries.

Since intertextuality is a broad and complexly defined term, it has the danger of referring to anything in a text. In order to avoid that pitfall, discussion on intertextuality will be limited to intertexts that are directly referenced and not to those that simply evoke (no matter how strong the allusion) a (con)text. But, as Juan Villegas argues, in the direct referencing of another text, there lies a context, since intertextuality points to both dramatic and ideological functions.

Examining how specific play-texts communicate with the precursor text referred to by the playwright will allow a richer reading of that playwright's conception of nation. How does the playwright's use of intertextuality display a unique national ideology? How is nation staged and what does that mean to Latin American citizens at the end of the twentieth century and in the beginning of a new one? We will see new ways to address nation and, conversely, as Akhil Gupta suggests, we will witness that "nationalism as a distinctively modern cultural form attempts to create a new kind of spatial and mythopoetic metanarrative, one that simultaneously homogenizes the varying narratives of community while paradoxically accentuating their difference" (Vertovec and Cohen 1999, 511–12).

Chapter 1 takes a macroview by looking at the "master narratives" that are the foundation of Mexican culture and then showing how reworking specific texts within the master narratives might ultimately change the whole national script. Víctor Hugo Rascón Banda's *La Malinche (Malinche)* (2000) subverts the Malinche narrative by rewriting it in many forms throughout his text. Though he is clearly dramatizing the Malinche story, Rascón Banda fills his play with at least eighteen other texts. He is so indebted to these intertexts that he lists them at the end of the printed version of his play under the heading "Sources, Fragments, and Quotes" (145–47). These books, chronicles, songs, newspaper articles, poems, and Internet texts move the Malinche script into the present and rewrite her and her nation's image. On the other hand, Maruxa Vilalta's *En blanco y negro: Ignacio y los jesuitas* (*In Black and White: Ignatius and the Jesuits*) (1997) rewrites the other major Mexican master narrative, religion, once again through a fusion of other texts that the playwright painstakingly inscribes into her play through footnotes and intertextual references. The intertexts, however, expose the textual lies and in a spiral-like game of textual hide-and-seek, Vilalta plays with religion, history, and "antihistory," and their role in Mexico and Mexican theater.

Chapter 2 examines César Rengifo's *Un fausto anda por la aven-*

ida (A Faust Walks Down the Avenue) (1979) and Néstor Caballero's *Con una pequeña ayuda de mis amigos (With a Little Help from My Friends)* (1983), and argues that these Venezuelan playwrights use intertextuality to show the difficult relationship between Venezuela and the United States, a relationship that began to assert itself earlier in the twentieth century but remains influential and problematic in the nebulous "present time" that the later play cites. Rengifo rewrites *Faust* and places him on the streets of Caracas to subtly expose Venezuela's own role in the "pact" with the U.S. devil, a pact that threatens the country's economic, social, and political wellbeing. On the other hand, the Beatles' song in Caballero's play ironically questions whether "friendship" between individuals or nations is possible when the imbalance of power forces subservience and exploitation.

The following chapter, "Texts without Exit: Rewriting Argentina's Labyrinth," looks at Eduardo Pavlovsky's three versions of *Poroto* (1996, 1997, 1999) to show how text-making and identity-making are parallel processes. I examine how Pavlovsky moves his texts back and forth between theater and narrative and keeps them in the blurry boundary between genres through shifts in narrative voice and point of view. Moreover, as the texts are transposed into new versions, so too is the title character transformed; he is becoming Argentine for through his title character Pavlovsky shows a fragmented and split national subjectivity. Similarly, in Rafael Spregelburd's *Heptalogía De Hieronymus Bosch: I, II, III* (*Heptalogy of Hieronymus Bosch: I, II, III*) (1999), I look at ways in which the playwright manipulates and subverts portions of Bosch's fifteenth-century painting, *The Tabletop of the Seven Deadly Sins,* and I suggest that by modeling Bosch's style, Spregelburd, ironically, makes his play postmodern. However, beyond a discussion of the postmodern in theater, I argue that Spregelburd's subversion of Bosch's themes exposes a new ideology of nation.

In the final chapter, I show how the playwrights use intertexts to highlight exile and its impact on the transnational Cuban community. In each text, José Corrales's and Manuel Pereiras's *Las hetairas habaneras* (*The Courtesans of Havana*) (1976–77), Raúl de Cárdenas's *Un hombre al amanecer* (*A Man at Dawn*) (1988–89), and Pedro Monge's *Otra historia (Another (Hi)Story)* (1996), I demonstrate how the playwrights subvert other texts to show the tragedy of exile, to draw parallels between the intertext's or their author's similar situations and their own, and then to recontextualize their own exiled status by breaking the silence imposed on the exile through the creation of a new text. In each of these texts, intertextuality rewrites exile and the nation and opens a unique path for their interpretations.

An analysis of intertextuality in contemporary Latin American theater permits both an examination of the presuppositions behind the concept of nation and an interpretation of new constructions of nation on the contemporary stage. Intertextuality exposes the tensions within and beyond the play's space by examining the complex relationships between dramatic text and precursor text, dramatic text and dramatic theories, as well as between author and texts, reader and texts, and author with self, culture, and nation. Theater permits the development of more potential tensions than any other genre in that, above and beyond the tensions mentioned above, in theater there are always the added tensions between play-text and performance, between dialogue and didascalia, and between playwright, director, actors, and spectators. All these tensions make intertextuality an even more powerful tool in the theater.

Still and Worton argue that "the analysis of intertextuality . . . is inevitably political in its assertion that—at the very least—the 'textual' and the 'extra-textual' inhabit each other, or that,—more radically—the 'extra-textual' is another kind of text" (Worton and Still 1990, 33). In Latin America, the relationship between artist and nation, too, is always political. The tense relationships that playwrights (and other artists) have faced with their national governments in many Latin American countries during the last half of the twentieth century are parallel to the tensions inherent in a discussion of intertextuality. In a sense, what is being examined in these plays is what Roland Barthes refers to as the space "outside the sentence," which he describes as "words, syntagms, bits of formulae and no sentence formed," but relevant to receptors because it passes through them nonetheless (1994, 493). What is "outside the sentence" in my study, takes on a double meaning, for it concerns intertextual references found both inside and outside the play's dialogue (in the title, the stage directions, or established in the play's extradiagetic space) and outside the text (in the precursor text). Yet it is not totally extra-textual either. It is both the space and place of "interstices and discontinuities" (Barthes in Morgan, 258–59), but it may be the grand signifier of these plays.

As Akhil Gupta argues:

> We need to study . . . processes by which certain spaces become enshrined as "homelands," by which ideas of "us" and "them" come to be deeply felt and mapped into places such as nations. On the other hand, we need to pay attention to those processes that redivide, reterrito-

> rialize, and reinscribe space in the global political economy. Only then can we understand why the naturalized divisions and spaces that we have always taken for granted become problematic in certain circumstances, and only then can the "problem" of nationalism be posed adequately. (Vertovec and Cohen 1999, 516)

Intertextuality is configured within the space of the text, yet it is outside that text. So, too, is nation defined within and outside its borders. This multiple vision—a look toward both past and present, both inside and outside, both self and other— interpreted through intertextual relationships in these plays, rewrites the script of nation and its relationship to citizens in modern times.

1

Unraveling National Threads: Redirecting Mexico's Master Scripts

> The elections (of 2000) were of course preceded by significant political developments beyond the realm of electoral politics, and the election of Vicente Fox should thus be set against a dynamic backdrop that includes, for example, the continued political tensions in Chiapas, the strike at the National University of Mexico, and the ongoing effects of transnationalization on Mexico's economy and culture . . . It is tempting to subsume the recent events in Mexico within existing political and historical critical paradigms, whether to confirm assumptions about globalism or Mexico's internal historical and cultural processes. Nonetheless, the dethroning of the world's oldest political dynasty poses unique conceptual challenges to cultural and political discourse and invites a rethinking of critical assumptions.
>
> —Carl Good, *Discourse: Journal for Theoretical Studies in Media and Culture,* introduction to special issue on *Mexico in Transition: Art, Culture, Politics*

THE POLITICAL AND ECONOMIC SITUATION IN MEXICO AT THE END OF the twentieth century has created a difficult environment for the development, production, and staging of Mexican theater. Hugo Salcedo argues that "the panorama in which end-of-the-millennium dramatic authors exercise their craft has perhaps been the most discouraging and iniquitous that Mexican dramaturgy of the twentieth century has known" (1997, 86). The Mexican crisis, which, according to Jacqueline Bixler (1999), began in 1968 with the events that led up to the bloody Tlatelolco massacre, has had serious economic, political, and social implications in a country whose profound distrust of authority impacts all realms.[1]

According to Ronald Burgess, economic and political crises in the nineties affected Mexican theater in various ways: raised theater ticket prices, lowered attendance rates at local productions due to street violence, allowed fewer women's productions to be staged, and sometimes impacted the total number of plays staged in a given year (1997, 68–69). Nonetheless, it is certain, Burgess argues, "that interest in Mexican theater is growing, along with the number of new plays and playwrights; that while an established group of successful dramatists exists, there also exists a new openness that can encompass other points of view; that economic, social, and political considerations drive much of the thematic content; that a new group of writers may be on the verge of creating new influences; and that, with so much activity, anticipating the future is harder than ever" (61).[2] Timothy Compton, as well, notes that, even though "the level and type of governmental support always varies from administration to administration," it is clear that "Mexican theater is sufficiently vigorous, creative and mature to continue producing for many years" (2001, 162).

Perhaps one important reason why Mexican theater remains so healthy, in spite of political and social obstacles, is its ability to thematically recapture its own history in technically innovative and experimental ways. As Bixler argues, history takes on a new form in postmodern Mexican drama. In an article on Sabina Berman, Bixler shows that "rather than resurrect these historical episodes simply for 'the record,' Berman postmodernizes history to foreground its representation and to remind her audience that events from the past acquire not their existence, but their **meaning** thanks to their representation, whether it be on the pages of a text or on the stage" (Bixler's emphasis 1997, 45). The same holds true for many other contemporary Mexican playwrights as well.

History is taken as just one more "master narrative" that playwrights continuously and "defiantly question" (Bixler 1997, 46). These playwrights purposely combine and present intentionally contradictory points of view in their work, thus "undermining history and calling attention to its representation and concomitant ideology" (Bixler 1997, 47). In essence, Bixler suggests, current Mexican playwrights highlight the assertion that history, too, is a text, and as such they do not portray it "as an absolute truth, but rather as a narrative, created, repeated, and modified to fit the ideological desires and needs of the moment" (57).

Among the ways in which contemporary Mexican dramatists destroy, mock, and show irreverence toward their country's history and political situation, Armando P. Tayzan notes the use of anachronisms, humor, parody, virtual reality, and intertextuality (1997, 93–95). In the past, he argues, intertextuality was not a conscious process (91). Now, however, Mexican dramatists like Vicente Leñero, Sabina Berman, Jesusa Rodríguez, and Victor Hugo Rascón Banda, among others, incorporate earlier texts into their own works to play with, subvert, question, and destroy writing and textuality and to satirize, parody, or comment on the historical or cultural messages of those pretexts.

In the following two sections I examine how two contemporary Mexican playwrights rewrite and subvert master cultural narratives (the Malinche and the religious text), as well as concrete texts about those master narratives, and other contemporary texts, to create a new message about the turn of the twentieth-century Mexican nation and to present new kinds of dramatic texts.

Víctor Hugo Rascón Banda's *La Malinche:* Metatheater, Performance, and Myth

> I believe that the playwright should not be more than that: a witness and informant. Why? So that the audience, the spectators, have a window to other worlds, to other universes, to other dramas, to other points of view about what is happening in society, because seeing the news on television or in the newspapers is not the same as seeing it as an artistic act, as a dramatic and theatrical phenomenon, that is art. First it is art, it is metaphor, and then it is denunciation.
>
> —Víctor Hugo Rascón Banda, interview with Stuart Day (2005), 32

Born in 1948 in the northern Mexican town of Uruachic, Chihuahua, Víctor Hugo Rascón Banda fits neatly into what has come to be known as the "New Mexican Dramaturgy" (Dauster 1998, 88).[3] The more than fifteen works he has published and staged since 1977 have been variously classified as realist, hyperrealist, documentary, subversive, and contestatory (Dauster 1998, 88, 93).[4] Recently Rascón Banda has dabbled in narrative as well. His first book of short stories, *Volver a Santa Rosa* [*Return to Santa Rosa*], was published in 1998.[5]

La Malinche, staged in 1998 and published in 2000 in a volume that includes the *bitácora,* a logbook bearing a detailed description of the initiation, evolution, rehearsals, and staging of the project, is, in some ways, just one more among the numerous Malinche plays published and staged during the past forty years. Sandra Cypess's seminal study, *La Malinche in Mexican Literature* (1991), began to classify and categorize the colonial woman's importance in contemporary Mexican literature and theater. Cypess's analysis of the Malinche shows how language and texts combine and work off each other to transform cultural content, and she proposes, "thus the sign 'La Malinche' functions as a continually enlarging palimpsest of Mexican cultural identity whose layers of meaning have accrued through the years. With each generation the sign 'La Malinche' has added diverse interpretations to her identity, role, and significance for individuals and for Mexico" (5). Cypess shows how this linguistic sign, "La Malinche," becomes a text that is continuously altered, transformed, and incorporated into other texts. In this way, she notes, "intertextuality offers a way of reading that places a text or sign in a discursive space, relating it to other texts and to the codes that operate in that space" (5).

As Cortés's interpreter and mistress, mother of the first Mexican/Latin American, La Malinche is an important and powerful figure in representations of the conquest. Her power and status, however, have diminished through the centuries, as she changed from "great lady to terrible mother" and was transformed into an instrument that "serves the particular historical needs of a complex society in change" during the post-independence period (Cypess 1991, 9). In *El laberinto de la soledad* [*The Labyrinth of Solitude*], Nobel Prize laureate Octavio Paz explains how that one woman has become the symbol for a culture that betrays itself to foreigners at every turn. Cypess notes that Malinche's image as a traitor is based on the Battle of Cholula where she is said to have betrayed her own kind by standing alongside the Tlaxcalans and by revealing the Cholula Indians' plot to attack Cortés's group, thus saving the Spaniards (34–35). Moreover, Malinche is also said to have rejected an Indian suitor, preferring instead to marry Spaniard Juan Jaramillo.[6]

As Cypess explains, *malinchismo* today means favoring the foreign over the native. In his book, Octavio Paz (1959), as well, shows how the inferiority complex that has become part of Mexican culture and whose origins lie in Malinche's betrayal continues today in Mexico's relationship with the United States. Moreover, Paz asserts, the whole Malinche complex explains Mexicans' fiery personality, as Mexicans view themselves in explicitly sexual terms as either the Chingada (the violated) or the Chingón (the violator).

Various Malinche stories have been told through Mexican theater; Cypess discusses many of the most relevant Malinche plays in her book. She notes the differences in the perspectives on the Malinche figure in Rodolfo Usigli's *Corona de fuego* (*Crown of Fire*) (1960), Salvador Novo's *Cuauhtémoc* (1962), Celestino Gorostiza's *La leña está verde* (*The Firewood is Green*) (1958), and Carlos Fuentes's *Todos los gatos son pardos* (*All Cats are Brown*) (1970), and shows how in most of the plays, the battle between two opposing cultures is configured as a clash between sexes (100). Moreover, Cypess confirms that, because of her double role as interpreter and mother, Malinche "has been divided into two parts—a voice and a womb" and these body parts serve as synecdoches for the whole Malinche. Cypess argues that "Since woman is allowed to be a womb, that aspect of her role is converted into a positive force; but the references to her voice are always negative" (102). Cypess further shows how "the body of La Malinche serves as a synecdoche for the land that will produce offspring/fruit fashioned in the image of Mexico" (103) and thus she expands interpretations of La Malinche to signify the Mexican nation.

La Malinche's fragmented body—her womb and her silenced voice—as symbols for a frustrated and handicapped Mexican nation continue to be themes in Malinche plays of the late 1970s and 1980s; however, these postmodern plays are filled with humor, exaggeration, parody, satire, metatheatrical devices, and a heightened use of technology and virtual reality to "demonstrate that the accepted cultural conventions are as artificial and as destructive as the imaginary technology they invent" (Cypess 1991, 124). As Cypess aptly shows, in plays like Rosario Castellanos's *El eterno femenino* (*The Eternal Feminine*) (1975), Willebaldo López's *Malinche Show* (1977), and Sabina Berman's *Aguila o sol* (*Eagle or Sun; Heads or Tails*) (1984), the characters are aware of their history and their entrapped place in it, and humorously but tragically represent their stereotyped images in an effort to break with that mythical past. Through the exposure of these stagnant Malinche images, the playwrights hope to display them as false and worthy of correction, thus attempting "to create new myths, symbols, paradigms by deconstructing the institutionalized ones" (Cypess 1991, 124).

Interestingly, the latter three plays, especially *Aguila o sol,* extend intertextuality beyond the Malinche cultural myth by incorporating other Malinche texts into the play as well. Berman's play, for example, works off León-Portilla's *La Visión de los vencidos* (Translated as *The Broken Spears* [1962]) and Octavio Paz's poem *Aguila o sol* in an effort to postulate the written/performed text as a way to subvert history. By reworking these other texts, playwrights focus on text-making as an ever-evolving process, which, like history-making, does not reveal absolute truths and should thus be considered alterable.

Moreover, humor factors largely in the above-mentioned texts. Referencing Bakhtin's theories on the function of humor, Cypess notes, "laughter has the remarkable power of making an object come up close . . . Laughter demolishes fear and piety before an object, before a world, making of it an object of familiar contact and thus clearing ground for an absolutely free investigation of it" (134). Through their use of humor, playwrights make the Malinche figure more approachable, less threatening, and thus render her more likely to be accepted as a sympathetic figure trapped in a false (hi)story.

Priscilla Meléndez (1996) argues that techniques such as humor or intertextuality question history but also call into question the art forms that represent it. In her study of Sabina Berman's *Aguila o sol,* she writes, "the fact that Berman turns to a disparaged genre such as farce and other forms of popular theater—to street theater and the circus tent—becomes a way of questioning traditional, institutional, and even ideological theater" (32).

Rascón Banda's *La Malinche* adopts many of these same strategies to reveal its dramatic message but it also adds some important new twists to the Malinche myth through the fusion of past and present and through the use of many other actual intertexts from both past and present. Staged in 1998 amid much controversy, the play's thirty-seven scenes present the psychological conflicts of Malinche as she tries to make sense of her history and her role in contemporary Mexico and a global world.[7] Characters are taken from both past and present. Hernán and Martín Cortés, Moctezuma, Cuauhtémoc, Bernal Díaz, among others, replay "historical" scenes, often in humorous and anachronistic fashion, while the president, the psychoanalyst, Chiapas Indians, and the deputies play their roles at the turn of the twenty-first century. Most of the scenes allude to an intertext, at some times more obviously and directly than at others. Although the playwright lists his "Sources, Fragments, and Quotes" at the end of the play and often notes certain references at the end of the scene that includes them, he sometimes plagiarizes the exact wording from the intertext without even including quotation marks. In other words, sometimes Rascón Banda's characters repeat the referenced intertext verbatim.

In this section, I examine seven of the intertexts that Rascón Banda weaves into *La Malinche* (2000) to show how he manipulates the intertexts to open a new reading of contemporary Mexico. The seven intertexts include a song, two indigenous versions of the conquest presented by León-Portilla, two contemporary essays about the Malinche (Bolívar Echeverría and Octavio Paz), a newspaper article by Carlos Fuentes, and Chiapas revolutionary subcommandant Marcos's essay, *The Winds from Above.* In each case, I discuss the "original" source's text and then show what Rascón Banda does to it in his play, how he reworks it to extract a key meaning for his reader/spectator. Before revealing how the intertexts change the meaning of the Malinche and thus posit a new path for Mexico's future as a nation in a global world, I will first examine the roles of the three Malinche characters to show how Rascón Banda unravels Malinche's image to rupture the possibility of a static perspective of her and her nation.

Rascón Banda's play presents an image of an unstable, split Malinche; concretely, she is divided into three or more images, even though she is really the (one) Malinche. Interestingly, he also presents an image of modern Mexico divided within itself; specifically, the play opens in the Chamber of Deputies with members of the three major political parties, the PRI (Institutional Revolutionary Party), the PAN (National Action Party), and the PRD (Democratic Revolution Party), fighting among themselves. The political parties fight over everything, from Malinche herself to the origins of their country and their plans for it. Malinche, then, is reincarnated in the present-day in the perpetually divided Mexican nation yet, ironically, as her psychoanalyst suggests, "They represent the nation, not you" (27). From the outset, the psychoanalyst presents the problem; Mexico has transferred the blame for its problems and its image onto someone else.

Along with intertexts, Rascón Banda uses his three Malinche characters to disrupt any possible duality with regard to the woman or her nation. These three characters work with the intertexts to fuse past and present in the very fiber of his play; scenes alternate between presenting the memory of the mytho-historical Malinche and portraying the present-day context and setting, where Malinche, as a representative of the marginalized indigenous people of her nation, comes to the Chamber of Deputies, to plead their and her case. Besides the fact that she is, clearly, a figure from the past, the "traitor" marked by her history, many flashbacks in the play (re)present scenes from the conquest.[8] The entire play is a series of vignettes of past and present Mexico with virtually no separation between the time frames. Malinche appears in both eras, sometimes as the Old Malinche, sometimes as the Young Malinche, sometimes as the Adult Malinche. These three divided Malinches have distinct characteristics; however, occasionally, they are fused into the generic Malinche, and, although she is not listed as a character unto herself (so she could be portrayed by one of the other Malinches), she is a hybrid being that floats between past and present and attempts to illuminate both time periods.

Adult Malinche's role in the play is to confront Malinche's terrible historical past and its impact on her present life and on the life of her nation. She knows what has happened to her, explains it to the psychoanalyst, and strives to make sense of it. At the same time, she attempts to assert her rightful place in Mexico's contemporary mindset and culture. Her efforts are constantly thwarted because her past image is too rigid, and she continues to be abused now while working to liberate herself from the image imposed upon her.

Adult Malinche opens the play; she has the first speaking part in the entire play. In the first scene she takes the stage in the Chamber of Deputies on behalf of her people for the sole purpose of correcting a grave historical oversight; she wants to add her name to the list of those recognized in the formation of her homeland. In her speech to the deputies she affirms, "There are the men and women who gave us our homeland. Those who showered the ground of our country with their blood so that we would have the most precious thing a man has: the homeland" (16). Her image of the homeland as sacred and precious explains why she herself and the controversies surrounding her myth are so important to Mexico and Mexicans today. She stands in front of the deputies in the Congress and demands respect for herself and her people, but she is laughed at and abused, both physically and verbally. After her beating in the Congress, a bruised and battered Adult Malinche visits the psychoanalyst to try to make sense of the situation. The analyst, however, immediately blames the woman for everything stating, "you were to blame . . . you put yourself there, no one called you . . . you provoked them" (27). Adult Malinche does not understand why she is guilty or why they will not show her the respect she thinks she deserves. She feels angry and lost and begins to explain her history to the psychoanalyst (27).

Adult Malinche continuously asserts her innocence and presents her side of the story. Again with the psychoanalyst she affirms, "I didn't have anything to do with it. I didn't denounce Cuauhtémoc. I only translated what those who spoke to him were saying. I don't know if it was true or if it was a game. I don't know" (83). She emphasizes her role as the "voice" and continues to try to make her present-day voice heard in an effort to set the story straight.

In her final scene, she continues to speak for the indigenous, this time for her people from modern-day Chiapas; nonetheless, now she wants the agreement in writing. The *licenciado*, however, will grant no such thing and chooses instead to differentiate between subtle meanings in words as a way to circumvent their meaning and deny the Indians what he had apparently promised to them (127–30).

In contrast to Adult Malinche, Old Malinche seems to have a lesser role than the other two; however, in each of her four appearances she presents blatant facts and functions as a conscience or interior voice to the other characters. Her first appearance is with the psychoanalyst where she talks about her first deception, the Battle of Cholula. This important event, which, as Cypess notes, is perhaps the reason for Malinche's negative reputation and character in Mexican history, was a key moment in the conquest. In the scene called "My First

Deception," Old Malinche explains her side of the story arguing that she did not hear or translate any part of the betrayal.

> *Cortés.* They were conspiring against me.
> *Malinche.* Who said so?
> *Cortés.* The Tlaxcalans came to warn us.
> *Malinche.* I didn't hear that! I didn't translate that!
> *Cortés.* I found it out through another source.
> *Malinche.* They're killing them right there, without any reason!
> *Cortés.* They were traitors.
> *Malinche.* It's not true!
>
> (46)

Her revelation that she did not hear any of the conspiracy in Cholula and that she never translated any of the plot for Cortés, as well as his quick admission that he heard it from someone else, presents the story as false from the outset, the need to question the original text. In the rest of the scene, Old Malinche argues with Cortés over the "facts" and exposes him as a liar. At the end of the scene she denounces him totally, though he attacks her to silence her.

> *Malinche.* Now I know you. You are cruel.
> *Cortés.* Like your people.
> *Malinche.* You enjoy spilling blood.
> *Cortés.* Like your gods.
> *Malinche.* You are not a god. You are not a god. You are not a god.
> *Cortés approaches Malinche furiously and squeezes her neck with his hands, choking her.*
>
> (48)[9]

Besides standing up against Cortés, Old Malinche also serves as the conscience and advisor to Young Malinche. Distressed and desperate, Young Malinche sees that "the humble people are full of fear" (55). She is confused and does not understand why the gods do not intervene on their behalf. Wiser and more experienced, Old Malinche repeats, "Flee, Malinche, Flee!" (55), advising her to escape this terrible situation before it is too late.

Finally, in scene 24, Old Malinche and Adult Malinche show how the plagues brought over by the Spaniards are equivalent to the new plagues brought over by the new foreigner, the United States. After listing the seven plagues, mostly diseases, which the Spaniards brought over to the New World, they determine that "but now there are new plagues that are killing us" (98). The new plagues, all related to capitalism, industrialization, globalization, and imperialism, specifically by the United States, are killing Mexico, its culture, and its traditional national values.[10] They affirm:

Adult Malinche. Halloween kills the Day of the Dead.
Old Malinche. The mall kills open-air markets.
Adult Malinche. Harvard kills the Autonomous University of Mexico.
Old Malinche. NAFTA kills commerce.
Adult Malinche. Woodcutters kill forests.
Old Malinche. Ozone kills Mexico City dwellers.
Adult Malinche. A lot of smoke everywhere.
Old Malinche. Mist.
Adult Malinche. Fog.
Adult Malinche and *Old Malinche.* Everything is dark.

(98)

Not surprisingly, Young Malinche's role is the most frequent and the most unique because, for the most part, she is ignorant of any past and naive in her conception of herself and her history. More importantly, she is largely an incredulous observer, a spectator of both past and present, denying any constraints placed upon her and attempting to understand and react to the performances before her in an appropriate way. Often, she is both actor and spectator of the performances of the conquest and this emphasis on performance highlights that history is just that, a performance that is watched and interpreted. As a spectator, Young Malinche often expresses shock and fear over what she sees. Her reactions to the scenes before her give spectators new possibilities for interpreting those historical events as well.

The play highlights performance and shows that performance permeates all realms.[11] In other words, no matter how hard one tries, it is difficult to change one's cultural and political script. Everything is performance in *La Malinche.* Just as Malinche is locked into her role as Indian woman (who must be abused), interpreter, and mistress, the president's role is to call for order in the chaotic Chamber of Deputies. Similarly, the script of the various political party members in the Chamber dictates their disagreement with each other.

Moreover, many flashbacks are interspersed throughout the text; sometimes they are separate scenes that flow from the conversation, at other times they represent a break in the dialogue and serve to demonstrate what the characters had been discussing. The flashbacks from the colonial texts are performances within the performance; they attempt to act out the texts and portray scenes that spectators and readers are already familiar with. When Adult Malinche first goes to her psychoanalyst, for example, she expresses her anger and frustration over her history and explains some of that history to the therapist. As she reveals how she and the other young Indian girls were beaten and tortured by the Spaniards, the stage directions mandate a performance of the scene she describes:

> *Another area of the stage is illuminated. A group of frightened young Indian women appears, besieged by Spanish soldiers. They try to protect themselves by banding together; they back up, they try to flee. Little by little the Spaniards surround them and impede them from escaping. Some run away. The Spaniards catch them and subdue them. Terrified, the women scream, kick, bite the Spaniards who throw them to the ground. The men jump on them, slap them, and restrain them. There is a collective rape. Young Malinche remains before the psychoanalyst in a state of shock.*
>
> (30)

The dramatization of this incident repeats what readers/spectators already know, that Indians, especially indigenous women, were abused and tortured by the Spaniards during the conquest and thus, Adult Malinche repeats it and it is shown as a matter of course. This play within the play that both spectators and actors (Adult Malinche, the psychoanalyst, and Young Malinche) watch, presents history as a text that we all know and accept. However, Young Malinche's reaction to the scene, which spectators, Adult Malinche, and the psychoanalyst also see, suggests that our reaction to these events is out of line. Rather than accept these actions as normal, we, too, should share Young Malinche's shock. Moreover, the receptor can assume that the characters of the play within the play (the Spaniards and the abused indigenous women) are also witnessing young Malinche's shock. Since even the protagonists themselves register Malinche's shock over what they are experiencing, the reader/spectator is urged to do the same.

Even though there are three Malinches with slightly different levels of consciousness about their history and their contemporary position, all really serve the same function and represent similar points of view. Sometimes the text's stage directions do not distinguish between the three women; occasionally just Malinche comes on the stage and, again, because Malinche is not listed as a character in her own right, a director could choose to have the Young, Adult, or Old Malinche play her role at any given time. However, this hybrid or generic Malinche clarifies Malinche's stand. Although there are differences in the three Malinches' approaches to the characters and their roles in both the past and the present, they more or less embody the same spirit and philosophy; they all place the blame elsewhere.

Others in the text continuously analyze them, yet, ironically, they rarely examine themselves. Why then does Rascón Banda include three different Malinches in his play and then sometimes include a fourth, ageless figure?

The three Malinches are parallel to each of the three main political parties in contemporary Mexico, the PRI (Institutional Revolutionary Party), PAN (National Action Party), and the PRD (Democratic Revolution Party). Each of the three parties is present from the beginning of the play and none of them get along. Symbolically, then, Rascón Banda proposes with this that, even though these parties appear to have differences, they all embrace malinchismo and have completely sold out to the foreigner. Or perhaps he is suggesting, through his choice of and use of the intertexts, that none of the parties has found the solution to Mexico's crises because they continue to place the blame on the foreign other and the past texts, rather than look toward internal solutions, their own texts. The intertexts bring forth this message.

Through his inscription of intertextuality into his play—the intertexts he chooses and the way they function—Rascón Banda's play presents the possibility that the three Malinches, similar to the three political parties, do not really represent three different perspectives, but rather they share one, somewhat limited vision of Mexico's present and future articulation, and that is precisely the problem for the nation. When Adult Malinche is at the microphone in scene 1, the PRI politicians hit her while the Perredistas try to help her. In the next scene, however, a member of the PAN party takes the microphone and pronounces that Hernán Cortés is "the true father" of Mexico. This begins another battle in which all parties participate. Although they have different views on their history, it is really the same old story, and none of the three politicians proclaim independence or autonomy, either in the past or in the present. As Young Malinche reveals in a monologue, "I am afraid. Something tells me that a tragedy is going to occur. They are going to encounter the others. Who will discover whom?" (44). While she is definitely alluding to the conquest, her words forecast a tragedy from this constant preoccupation with the other.

On the surface, Rascón Banda's three Malinches, like the three predominant political parties in Mexico, would seem to suggest multiple internal positions on Mexico's relationship to foreigners, whether the Spaniards of the conquest or the United States today. Deeper analysis, however, shows that the "three" all really express the same vision. Rascón Banda then uses intertexts, mostly from Mexican sources, to open up the text, suggesting that, rather than blame the foreign other, Mexicans need to look more explicitly at their own script, their own role in the development of their nation. Each intertext presents a unique perspective on the Mexican nation and points the reader/spectator back toward the Mexican self as the subject who can alter the text.

Intertextuality takes on a new form in this play because, at the end of the published version, the author lists eighteen intertexts he incorporates into his play. The many intertexts include Hernán Cortés's and Bernal Díaz de Castillo's different writings on their versions of the conquest, León-Portilla's *La visión de los vencidos,* his *Fifteen Poets of the Aztec World,* and Angel María Garibay's *Historia de la literatura náhuatl* (*History of Nahuatl Literature*) (1953), two contemporary songs, fragments of writings from Vasco de Quiroga, from Cortés's son Martín, from Fray Bernardino de Sahagún, from the subcommander Marcos of the 1990s Chiapas Revolution, and from Octavio Paz, as well as newspaper articles by Carlos Fuentes and David Márquez Ayala.

A quick assessment of the numerous and diverse intertexts Rascón Banda employs reveals that they present multiple perspectives: past and present sources; indigenous and nonnative voices; written, oral, and musical expressions; "real" historical texts and "opinion" essays. This diversity alone, of course, speaks volumes about the polyphony Rascón Banda is attempting to dramatize. Against the backdrop of his primary (cultural) intertext, the Malinche text and context, these intertextual points of view serve to question, subvert, and present a unique portrayal of the contemporary Mexican nation. Why does the playwright incorporate so many specific intertexts of varying types into his play? How do these intertexts function and what new text(s) and message(s) do they create?

The intertexts reinforce malinchismo as an illness of the present but also add new information about Malinche, contemporary Mexico, texts and intertexts. Examining the intertexts in *La Malinche* exposes the difficult political climate in present-day Mexico and proposes a way out, through a rereading and rewriting of the old scripts. Though published in the year of Vicente Fox's presidential victory, the play was performed before the PRI was ousted after seventy years of rule. Nonetheless, the real problem with Mexican politics, perhaps, does not lie in the parties' differences, but rather in their similarities around one important point: their relationship with the United States foreigner.

The intertexts move the play forward dramatically and ideologically, while both paying homage to and diminishing the importance of the "original" source-text and the new Rascón Banda text. Ideologically, they expose Mexico's tough role in a globalized world, link it to a cyclical vision of history, and suggest the potential for self-empowerment by creating an "interpreter's utopia" and looking inward, rather than outside, for answers. Dramatically, the intertexts mark a forward progress in the new text by ironically and continuously looking back to the sources. This game empowers Rascón Banda's dramatic text as another artistic source, which ironically is as capable of making history and changing images as *any* text. Moreover, the "dialogue" that Rascón Banda establishes between each intertext and his new text destroys any possibility of a binary reading. Each intertext posits multiple views of both text and nation. Texts are not read as one or the other, but rather the emphasis is on rearticulating them to empower the new text they create. Similarly, Mexico's contemporary position is not tied exclusively to an indigenous or colonial past, nor to a new indigenous or foreign present.

Throughout the play, the time frames flip back and forth between two defining moments in Mexico's history: the Spanish Conquest and the present. Early in the play, in scene 2, Gabino Palomares's song, *La maldición de Malinche (The Curse of Malinche),* helps form a bridge between these two times; the song describes the atrocities of the conquest and their impact on present-day Mexico by exposing and condemning the blatant malinchismo that exists today in Mexican culture.[12] As the song suggests, malinchismo is an "illness of the present" and, in scene 30, entitled "The Interrupted Party," Rascón Banda shows how that illness manifests itself in contemporary Mexico. The song of scene 2 is echoed much later in the play; in this way the play moves forward dramatically as well.

In that scene 30, a generic Malinche, not defined here as Young, Adult, or Old, is at a dance to celebrate a historic day. The licenciado announces, "This is an historic day. Today we are entering the First World. We are beginning to speak to the gringos and the Canadians in a familiar way" (118–19). The licenciado is visibly distressed because indigenous activists have infiltrated the celebration to voice their demands. When Malinche is finally allowed to lead the Indians in, the licenciado tries to dismiss them and their requests quickly. They speak to him in an indigenous tongue, nonetheless he tells Malinche not to translate for him. The licenciado pretends he understands their concerns and in an effort to appease them and dismiss them quickly he agrees to their demands. He lies to them outright in English and agrees in English that he will sign a pact; however, he and his receptors know full well that no written agreements will be signed.

The song, then, is sung once in scene 2, but then its content is dramatized later in the play. Both "performances" weave past and present and expose the government's lies as an impediment to progress and a precursor to violence and destruction in both times. Another intertext, in scene 11, "Moctezuma Receives Cortés" (57–59), is based on a fragment entitled "The Informants of Sahagún" from Miguel León-Portilla's *La visión de los vencidos* (xvii–xviii). In the Rascón Banda scene, Young Malinche plays the role of interpreter. Curiously, when Cortés speaks to her in English, she answers him with a "yes" but soon she switches back to Spanish even though he continues to use English. Moreover, Young Malinche tries to explain to Cortés the beauty of Moctezuma's language stating, "That is how their language is. Like a song, like a poem" (58). Later, when Cortés interprets Moctezuma's kind words as an invitation to take possession of indigenous land, Malinche explains, "Don't get confused. It's a courtesy. That is the way Mexicans talk. 'My house is your house.' That is what they say. They say 'your house' and they talk about their house" (59). Attempting to do her job as a thorough interpreter, she also warns Moctezuma about language's potential to construct mixed messages stating, "Be careful, words have double meanings" (59). Malinche recognizes the double meaning of words and explains how miscommunication and misinterpretation can lead to disaster. She herself manipulates language and controls its interpretation, thus using the double meaning of words to attempt to divert the real hostility between the men.

The fact that Cortés and his men are Americans and that Cortés speaks English to Malinche in the Rascón Banda scene only serves to reinforce that the new invader/conquerer is the United States and that the invasion is not only material, but also linguistic. Interestingly, the pre-text that Rascón Banda sends us to is significant: first, because *it* is not an original text either, and second, because its function is to explain just how distant from actual fact each interpretation is. The highlighted excerpt from *La visión de los vencidos* presents Sahagún's versions of the conquest by focusing on how removed that author was from the actual written texts. León-Portilla (1961) explains, "following the 1528 text in importance and antiquity is the much broader narration of the Conquest that, under the watch of Friar Bernardino de Sahagún, various indigenous students in Tlatelolco wrote in Nahuatl language, taking advantage of reports from old Indians, witnesses of the conquest" (xvii–xviii). This extremely important 1528 text, attributed to and directed by Sahagún, was already twice removed from him; indigenous students wrote down what they heard from their elders. Even more importantly, however, that text, which was supposedly completed around 1555, was destroyed: only a second draft remains, also in Nahuatl, completed some thirty years later, but according to Sahagún himself (says León-Portilla), it too was altered. León-Portilla writes, "according to Sahagún, several corrections were made of the first, since in that text some things were written that were badly written and others were silenced that were badly silenced" (xviii). This lost and later revised text, "constitutes the broadest testimony left by the Indians about it" (xviii).

Significantly, Rascón Banda does not even send us directly to this second draft of this great indigenous testimony but rather he directs us to an explanation of how far removed even those lost *original* texts are from the actual events. The chronicles of the conquest, especially that of Hernán Cortés, are continously questioned in terms of their historical accuracy. They by no means present the total picture. Rejection of the Spanish versions of the conquest often leads to a blind acceptance of the indigenous texts, yet as León-Portilla, and thus Rascón Banda, reminds us, the indigenous sources are also questionable. Though the conquest is history, *all* interpretations of it are fiction, subjective pieces often far removed from their authorial source. The Sahagún intertext emphasizes the nebulous "facts" in the sources. If the sources are so unreliable, then so too are the roles they have cast.

Beyond encouraging readers, spectators, and performers to question the images of history presented in the ever-questionable sources, Rascón Banda's play continuously presents Malinche as a woman aware of her role, a self-conscious character. She is caught in the middle of two cultures, two worlds, and as such she makes conscious choices. Another scene, "Invention of the Truth" (scene 23), based on Bolívar Echeverría's "Malintzin, la lengua,"[13] in Margo Glantz's *Malinche, sus padres y sus hijos* (*Malinche, Her Parents and Her Children*) (1994), uses intertextuality to highlight Malinche's impossible but powerful and self-conscious position as interpreter between two incompatible worlds.

Scene 23 rewrites that article and its point of view. Here, modern-day Malinche reveals to her analyst the dilemma of the position she had been placed in, stating, "They were two languages. They were two worlds. No. Two universes. So far apart, so opposite, impossible to unite and make into just one" (95). Caught between these two distant universes she was asked to make sense of them and to translate each one into the "other's" terms. Echeverría notes that her task was nearly impossible, "Malintzin had before her the most difficult case that an interpreter could possibly imagine; she had to mediate or reach understanding between two discursive universes constructed around two histories whose kinship seemed null" (1994, 132). Recognizing her insuperable assignment, Echeverría suggests that Malinche used her power and her privileged position to create what he calls an "interpreter's utopia": "A utopia that presents the possibility of creating a third language, a bridge language, that without being either of the two in question, and being in reality a lie for both, is capable of recounting and connecting together elemental symbolizations of their respective codes; a language woven of coincidences improvised from the condemnation of misunderstanding" (1994, 131–32). Because Malinche was aware of both the incompatibility of these two worlds and her difficult position between them, Echeverría shows that, under the circumstances, Malinche's intervention was admirable:

> And she dared to introduce that communicative alteration; she lied to one and the other, to the right and the left, and she proposed to both the challenge of converting into truth the great lie of understanding: precisely that two-faced lie that allowed them to live together without starting a war for a whole year. Each time that she translated back and forth between the two worlds, from the two histories, Malintzín was inventing a truth made of lies; a truth that could only be such for a third party which was yet to come.
>
> (134)

Demonstrating Echeverría's theory, in Rascón Banda's representation of this intertext Malinche reveals her difficult position to her analyst, and she confesses that because of this she made a conscious decision to lie to both sides. She affirms, "The conquerors would never reach an understanding with the conquered. They were so different. And I became courageous. I dared. I lied to both of them. I changed the words. I proposed to convert the great lie of understanding into truth" (95). She used her power and privileged position as an interpreter to manipulate the facts and then she asserts "I do not regret it" (95).

Through her necessary lies Malinche created a "truth" that has implications in modern times; worlds will continuously collide and ever more profound chasms will grow between them because of globalization. How we interpret and negotiate that chasm will determine our present and future course. According to Echeverría, Malinche's existence and an awareness of her most difficult role shed light on many complex questions of modernity. Globalization is a type of modern-day conquest and as such it marks an intense conflict between universal and local interests. Yet, should the universal always be prioritized over the local? Echeverría asks, "Is it necessary then to place a limit on this unifying 'will,' to disobey the 'market wisdom' and defend cultural singularities? But if so, should we do it with all or, only with the 'best'?" (136). The Mexican crisis with its economic and political ramifications is intensified because of globalization. Economically, programs like NAFTA, oil exploration and exploitation, trade, unemployment, and technological modernization create a rift between their local implementation and the global benefit. Mexico's political situation has been recently uprooted as well, for better or worse. Ironically, as Mexico becomes more "modern," so too do its local indigenous voices speak louder and with ever increasing force.[14]

Moreover, Echeverría argues that "The defeated figure of the historic Malintzín emphasizes the misery of the conquerors; the cloistering in one's own, original, authentic and inalienable was for Spain and Portugal the best route to disaster, to the destruction of the Other and to self-destruction" (137). By destroying a culture, destroying a world, who really wins? For Echeverría, "mixture is the true mode of the history of culture" for in that blending positive and powerful identities can be formed. The mythical Malinche is an ambivalent figure still being constructed and defined in Mexican national consciousness; R. Salazar Mallén argues that Malinche is an image that "tries to overcome the nationalist image of 'Malinche, the traitor'—she who scorns her own people, because of their inferiority, and who humbles herself before the superiority of the conqueror" (Echeverría 1994, 137). Plays like this expose Malinche's impossible position of the past in an effort to work through some of the pressures of modern times. Through Echeverría's text on the Malinche, Rascón Banda proposes questioning the "position" of the conquered and the conqueror and suggests that these binary images of winner and loser will not function in a global world.

Among those pressures is the issue of how one deals with difference without ceding to imperialism. Who is the other and how do we deal with him/her in the twenty-first century? Mexico, like so many other modern cultures, "perceives the ambivalent need for the Other, its contradictory and complementary character, its threat and its promise" (Echeverría 1994, 137). Although the Malinche myth has focused on her role as traitor and on her surrender to the other, by emphasizing the latent power of her privileged position, the difficulties she faced, and her potential as a manipulator of both sides, this and other texts attempt to vindicate her and offer a more positive self-image of a Mexico largely living in between two distant worlds, the indigenous and the foreign. Modern-day Mexico is the Malinche, not the Malinche traitor or the self-loathing "Chingada," but rather the Malinche in the interpreter's utopia, caught between two other cultures existing within Mexico's borders. If Mexico is "La Malinche" then she too can create an "interpretor's utopia" by rejecting the discourse of the other, which has now become part of her own national discourse. Similarly, Rascón Banda's use of this intertext prioritizes his own text as this utopic space destined to rewrite the script and "interpret" the "real" scene.

As the Echeverría intertext revises the Malinche/Mexico's political space and new role between two cultures, scene 12, "The Women of Chalco" (61–66) uses fragments of a Nahuatl poem by the same name, found in León-Portilla's *Fifteen Poets of the Aztec World* (1992), to further modify the female/national image and to posit the powerful role of artistic texts in revising the national story. According to León-Portilla, the Nahuatl poet Aquiauhtzin wrote *The Song of the Women of Chalco* in approximately 1479.[15] The woman in this seemingly erotic poem seems to possess many of the same qualities and characteristics of the mythical Malinche; she is a prostitute longing for sex, a type of indigenous Eve who admits, "I brood sadly, I desire evil" (León-Portilla 1992, 275). Though she desires sex and is willing to give herself over to her lover, she knows that her people "are ashamed I have become your mistress" (278). Even with this knowledge however, she continues her erotic adventures and affirms, "I am an old whore, I am your mother, a lusty old woman, old and without juice" (279). Her sexual desire and her willingness to give herself fully to her empowered lover, coupled with her knowledge that she is being judged harshly for doing so, put her in a parallel place with Malinche's image in Mexican myth.

Nonetheless, *The Song of the Women of Chalco* is more than an erotic poem. León-Portilla suggests that the poem's underlying message redirects it toward a discourse on nation. He argues that the poet "seeks with this song, in the guise of a subtle challenge, for a new way to increase the benevolence of Axayacatl (the enemy ruler) toward the conquered nation" (256). The Chalcans had been a subjugated people, but in approximately 1483 a war began in which the warriors from Mexico-Tenochtitlan defeated the Chalcans. *The Song*'s poet had probably participated in that war, and he used the love poem to disguise his real intentions: to write a poem that described Mexico-Tenochtitlan's battle against and defeat of the Chalcans. León-Portilla portrays how, in the seven sections or movements of the poem, "Here the women of Chalco are seen as precipitating a war. The poet has them challenge the lord of Tenochtitlan to a battle in which only the most highly sexually endowed could hope to win. The war is transformed into an erotic siege, with the opposing armies closing in on one another, symbolizing the sexual act with all its foreplay" (256).

Rascón Banda's scene "The Women of Chalco" (61–66) repeats some of the exact verses, symbols, and metaphors of the original poem and also imitates the Nahuatl poem's tone and style. For example, the reiterated "the flowers of water and fire" highlights that, in spite of the seemingly erotic intent, both texts, Rascón Banda's and the Nahuatl poet's, are explicit poetry about war. Some subtle differences in the two versions, however, give new meaning to Rascón Banda's version through his manipulation of the Nahuatl poem.

In the Nahuatl version, one woman speaks for all Chalcan women and invites only one extremely powerful man, the ruler/conqueror, the Lord Axayacatl, to have her. Moreover, though referring to an actual ruler, the man in the indigenous poem symbolizes the nation, and as such he has no voice; the entire poem is written from the woman/women's seductive perspective. She wishes to possess the man/ruler/nation and in the end she encourages him to "slowly, slowly surrender to sleep, rest, my little son, you, lord Axayacatl" (León-Portilla 1992, 280).

In Rascón Banda's scene, many prostitutes, La Malinche among them, invite any man on the street to be with them, although Malinche directs her seduction toward Cortés. After Malinche calls him repeatedly, Cortés approaches her and they make love, even though the stage directions contradict that by telling us that "*Cortés goes to one side, impotent*" (63). Nonetheless, they continue to try to possess each other; first she on top of him ("*Malinche lies down on Cortes and obliges him to possess her*") and then he on top of her ("*He possesses her frenetically*") (64). Finally, though, "*Cortes separates from Malinche, horrified. She has transformed into an old woman with a skull face*" (65).

Although both the Nahuatl woman and Rascón Banda's Malinche are transformed into old women, the woman in the ancient poem is vibrant, alive, powerful, and exciting; she is capable of arousing the lover/nation and then of putting him to sleep. Rascón Banda's Malinche, on the other hand, metamorphoses into a grotesque figure that drives her lover away. At the end of the play, "*Cortes screams with fear and leaves horrified. Malinche laughs macabrously*" (66).

The use of this Nahuatl poem as an intertext once again highlights the questionable, mythical role of the Malinche as a woman and a seductress and exposes a certain love/hate relationship between a people and their nation. As the Chalcan women try to seduce their new ruler and entice him into a war they cannot and will not win, so too does Malinche try to playfully and powerfully seduce Cortés in this scene, as her role dictates that she did. Rascón Banda's revision of this intertext suggests that Malinche/Mexico has missed her opportunity to transform her ambiguous position into the forceful, powerful, creative conqueror of the other, the dominant, vibrant woman of Chalco. Instead, she has allowed herself to become a powerless, pathetic figure, used and abused by others and herself.

However, León-Portilla emphasizes, as did Angel María Garibay before him, that it is important to understand the function of the Nahuatl poem; it was a dramatic poem whose purpose was *to entertain* the ruler Lord Axayacatl. Garibay argues that the poem was "an example of the 'mimetic production of the Nahuatl world'" and León-Portilla states: "I agree with Garibay that the text itself could have given rise to later forms of dramatic or mimetic presentations, and we now have proof, thanks to the chronicler Chimalpahin, that the poem was originally conceived to be accompanied by music and sung as a sort of challenge in the presence of the lord of Mexico-Tenochtitlan. It is indispensable to have this in mind in order to understand and evaluate its more profound meaning" (1992, 263).

As in the Chalcans' time, Rascón Banda's play and his use of intertexts show how a poem about the sexual desires of one woman can also describe and express the defeat of an entire nation. At the same time, the poem, like his own play, can serve both a didactic and an artistic function. Hence, Rascón Banda empowers his own text; his play about that one woman, Malinche, reworks the many national texts, to open up a new view of nation. Yet the playwright accomplishes this through the intertexts he chooses to highlight and the way he and his receptors rework them. He pieces together those texts to show his complicated view of Mexico and its place in the twentieth/twenty-first century. The intertexts function to reveal the process of creating a unique national identity and of empowering the woman/nation. Because these texts also symbolize the Mexican nation, the national image can also be reworked by rewriting the script. Though difficult to recast, nation, like woman, can also be rewritten and rethought by remodeling the text.

However, Rascón Banda uses these past texts to write a play, and thus the intertexts have an important dramatic/artistic function as well as an ideological one. As León-Portilla reminds us, "Poems and songs were, in themselves, the only thing of lasting value that a man could hope to leave on earth" (1992, 265). These and other poems, songs, and texts about Malinche have lasting value. If that were not so, Malinche would have died long ago. Because her image is created and repeated through artistic texts, the only way to change it is to rewrite the script. Through his text, Rascón Banda attempts to rewrite Malinche texts and thus revise her image by forcing his reader/ spectator to reread those texts through his lens. This not only rewrites Malinche's role but also empowers Rascón Banda's own text and ensures its "lasting poetic value" as well. Because his play is unique, humorous, and fun, spectators are also entertained by it. As Cypess suggests, this humor helps readers/spectators let down their guard, "thus clearing ground for an absolutely free investigation" of the messages presented (1991, 134). In addition, because of the artistic text's "lasting value," there is hope that these innovative images of the Malinche will replace the old stagnant ones and turn her into the vibrant Chalcan woman who can recast her nation.

In another intertextual rewriting, one of the episodes between Malinche and her psychoanalyst (111–13) is based directly on a fragment from Octavio Paz's *The Labyrinth of Solitude* (1959, 77–78). In scene 28, the psychoanalyst repeats Paz's condemnations of Malinche and blames her for all the identity problems and conflicts within contemporary Mexican culture. The analyst contrasts Malinche to the Virgin Mary, again converting her into a type of indigenous Eve, a violated and abused mother. Moreover, she accuses her of being a passive traitor and repeats Paz's words that "this open passivity to the exterior makes her lose her identity; She is the violated one. She loses her name, she is no one. And, nonetheless, she is the atrocious incarnation of the feminine condition" (112).

In addition, the therapist argues that these statements must be true because "The Poet said it" (111). Ironically affirming the authority of Paz's text as THE TEXT because "This is our great poet. Our Nobel prize," the analyst simply repeats Paz's words and takes them at their face value. On the other hand, Malinche forcefully denies all these accusations and she questions the authority of Paz's text. She argues, "Poets do not always tell the truth. Sometimes they lie" (111). When the analyst accuses her of not having offered resistance, Malinche questions, "He says that? And was he there? Did he see it all when the Spanish soldier forcefully grabbed me, when he fought me?" (112). Like Sahagún's text, repeated by León-Portilla, which questions the texts and their sources, this scene reinterrogates the validity of texts about and interpretations of Malinche's image.

Furthermore, this scene uses irony to make its point. What makes Paz's text so "noble"? Who is this great poet who has become the voice of authority on contemporary Mexican culture, basing his argument on other texts and readings of the past? Malinche refuses to accept this image that has been pinned upon her, yet, ironically, she cannot break free from it either. At the end of the scene she screams, "Oh, so I am a traitor? Oh so they do not forgive me? Fuck the mother of all of them!" (113). She repeats this common Mexican denouncement, which ironically refers to her own stagnant image;

she is the mother that she is cursing. In an effort to discredit past texts that formed and shaped her negative image, Malinche herself cannot escape from the bind they have placed upon her.

For the most part, Rascón Banda's play interrogates past texts as a way to question the stagnant images they have scripted; however, in other cases, the playwright shows that even some of the more contemporary scripts need rethinking. The playwright's reference to Chiapas revolutionary leader subcommander Marco's speech in scene 31, "Not even the air belongs to us," is possibly the most important intertextual reference in the play; the excerpt not only concretely moves the context and themes of Rascón Banda's play from the conquest to present-day Mexico, but it also defines the contemporary issues in the play and in modern-day Mexico and shows them as parallel to those of the conquest. The 1994 revolution in Chiapas and its ongoing impact and manifestation in present-day Mexico demonstrate how very little progress Mexico has made in five hundred years, socially and politically, and also functions as a backdrop against which Rascón Banda can display the powerful role of language and text in the articulation of national consciousness.

The Chiapas Revolution began when the Zapatistas launched a ten-day uprising in the state of Chiapas on New Year's Day 1994, demanding greater rights for the indigenous, who make up the majority of Chiapas's population. More than 140 people were killed fighting against Mexican army forces. According to Molly Moore of the *Washington Post,* "A partial accord was signed in February 1996, giving Indians greater rights but the initiative died when the administration of President Ernesto Zedillo failed to submit enabling legislation to Congress" (1998, 2).

Although the Chiapas conflict seems to have a concrete starting date as mentioned above, Rascón Banda's play, among other sources, would suggest that it is a mere extension of the conquest, in that it posits the indigenous native as "other" against both foreign and internal imperialist powers. Moreover, regardless of which political party holds power, the conflict continues in contemporary Mexico with no apparent end in sight; thus reinforcing what Rascón Banda has already suggested through his three Malinches and three political parties, all really expressing the same vision. Specific events in the Chiapas conflict repeat colonial history, and some of those incidents (the Acteal massacre, for example) are also rewritten and cited within Rascón Banda's play.[16]

Rascón Banda recasts the Chiapas conflict and its continuing manifestations and connects it to Malinche and her role in the conquest to display a larger image of the controversies and conflicts in contemporary Mexico. Even though it seems that the Chiapas issues are a battle between two opposing sides—the Mexican government and the marginal members of the EZLN (the Zapatista National Liberation Army led by the mysterious subcommandant Marcos)—the situation is far less binary and much more complicated.

Adolfo Garza argues, "Mexico is among the world's most corrupt nations, according to watchdog Transparency International" (2000, 2). Even though some had hoped that corruption would lessen if not end with the final days of the seventy-year rule of the PRI, President Vicente Fox of the PAN's decisions to increase Catholic Church involvement in government as well as his questionable handling of the Chiapas conflict have caused some to wonder whether Mexico's government will ever be on the straight and narrow path.[17]

However, the Zapatista's relationship to the Mexican government is not the only problem in Mexico; too many factions exist on both sides to even begin to resolve the conflicts. As the licenciado points out in scene 32 of Rascón Banda's play, "The Chiapas Indians are not all the Indians in Mexico. Who authorized them to speak in the name of all the tribes in the country? The Tarahumaras, the Pimas, the Yaquis, the Coras, the Mazuhuas were not in San Andrés. What right do we have to harm them by imposing on them decisions made by others?" (129). Although clearly the licenciado is using the many indigenous voices as his excuse to stall the peace process, there is much truth behind his words in Mexico's actual political and social situation. A May 6, 1996, article entitled, "Armed Group Attacks Peasants in Chiapas State" describes an attack by the Chinchulines, an indigenous gang in the Chiapas region associated with the PRI, on a group of peasants associated with the Democratic Revolution Party (BBC Monitoring 1996a, 1–2). Interestingly, these factions are indigenous, but also connected to specific political parties, suggesting that there is involvement in this conflict at every level and that the lines between the "two" sides are not clearly delineated.

Moreover, the Chiapas conflict is not isolated geographically anymore either. A *La Jornada* article from August 1996 explains how in the state of Veracruz, "some persons are recruiting youths for Zapatist forces that split from the EZLN due to their disagreement over negotiations with the federal government" (BBC Monitoring 1996b, 1). Constantly recruiting new members, the EZLN also includes many disparate factions. "In addition to the Huasteca area of Veracruz bordering with Hidalgo, the presence of convoys and military camps has also intensified along the Tezonapa mountain range, bordering with Puebla and Oaxaca, after the appearance of the Revolutionary People's Army (EPR)" (BBC Monitoring 1996b, 2).

Although some have argued that this EPR is a splinter group of the EZLN, in 1996, Subcommander Marcos openly rejected any connection between the two groups, arguing that the EPR would have to earn its legitimacy just as the EZLN had earned its own rightful power. Furthermore, Marcos writes in an open letter to the EPR published in *La Jornada* in 1996, "I wanted to point out that political leaders (even guerrilla leaders) do not give legitimacy to a movement" (BBC Monitoring 1996c, 2). He insists that the EPR is different and separate from the EZLN, and he attempts to discredit the splinter group.

The many different groups on both sides of the conflict along with the numerous factions within each group are exemplary of the complex political situation within Mexico at the end of the twentieth century and the beginning of the new one. Rascón Banda includes those many factions within his play through his use of multiple intertexts as well as through his split characters, namely the three Malinches at different stages of maturity and the representatives of Mexico's three main political parties.

The inclusion of Marcos's speech as an intertext underscores these ill-defined, multifaceted factions and adds a new level to Rascón Banda's themes and message. On the one hand, Marcos's text presents many of the economic, political, and social problems in contemporary Mexico by highlighting exploitation of the indigenous people both by foreigners and by the Mexican government. On the other hand, the whole Chiapas Revolution, along with its leader, has been questioned. Who was this powerful subcommander Marcos? This mysterious figure was accused of being a foreign student who, out for personal power and gain, was himself exploiting the natives. Moreover, Marcos's text contains two other important components that illuminate Rascón Banda's message: its tone is totally ironic and it, too, uses intertextuality to set this tone.

Marcos's 1992 speech is printed on the EZLN Web site. According to the Department of Press and Propaganda of the EZLN, the speech is reproduced, "To shed light on the thirst for knowledge about the Chiapas situation . . . to raise the consciousness of those who might consider joining our fight" (Marcos 1994, 1). In a sarcastic and ironic tone, the five chapters of Marcos's two "Winds," "The One Above" and "The One Below," describe the impoverished condition of the Chiapas region and its indigenous people and blame that poverty on foreign-based governmental exploitation of Chiapas's land, natural resources (electricity, gas, oil, coffee, animal life, water), industry, and education. Marcos basically accuses the government of "bleeding" Chiapas to death and of stealing its natural wealth. Moreover, he argues that the government promotes tourism in the region while ignoring the basic needs of the area's inhabitants. Marcos affirms, "There are about seven rooms for every thousand tourists, while there are 0.3 hospital beds for every thousand Chiapas' residents" (1994, 5).

In addition, Marcos's document goes beyond presenting what he views as the terrible facts; with it he attempts to incite a revolution in the region. He writes, "Ah! And another thing. It will not always be this way. Another Mexico? No, the same one . . . I am talking about something else, like other breezes are beginning to blow, like another wind that is picking up" (6). He then directly criticizes the Mexican government by stating, "Jails and barracks are the principal works this governor has produced in Chiapas. His friendship with landowners and powerful businessmen is no secret to anyone, nor is his ill will towards the three dioceses that regulate Catholic life in the state" (6). Even when the local government attempts to address some of the inequalities and injustices and the poverty in Chiapas, it is sidetracked by corruption and nepotism at the national level and by its relationship to the powerful, but unhelpful Catholic Church.

In the play, the two scenes that flank scene 31, "Not Even the Air Belongs to Us," serve as a preface to what Cuauhtémoc, Marcos, and Malinche discuss in scene 31 and further exemplify some of the ideas presented in Marcos's speech. In those two scenes, the indigenous group, led and mediated by Malinche, attempts to express its perspective to the government, in this case the licenciado, and tries to negotiate for its rights. As Marcos explains in his speech, the indigenous forces are asserting their power, fighting against the wind from above, the government: "This wind from below, that of rebellion, that of dignity, is not only an answer to the imposition of the wind from above, it is not only a brave reply, it carries within it a new proposal; it is not only the destruction of an unjust and arbitrary system, it is above all a hope, that of the conversion of dignity and rebellion into freedom and dignity" (Marcos 1994, 9). Marcos suggests that what the Indians are proposing is not only the destruction of an unjust system; they are not just answering to their past, but rather they are articulating new ideas for their future. In the Rascón Banda scene prior to "Not Even the Air Belongs to Us," the licenciado attempts to appease the Indians by having Malinche tell them that they will receive food, clothing, and education. The indigenous reply, "We do not want that. We want to live according to our own practices and customs . . . to live freely" (120). Here, Rascón Banda's characters reiterate the plan and ideology that Marcos had outlined for the Chiapas Indians.

As mentioned above, the licenciado lies to the Indians in an effort to get rid of them and continue with the celebration. In the scene following "Not Even the Air Belongs to Us," called "The Disagreements of San Andrés," Malinche and the licenciado again talk about the double meanings of words by discussing some of the language of the Constitution and of the "Agreement of San Andrés." As Rascón Banda's title of the scene suggests, the "Agreement" was really a "Disagreement," as nothing was ever resolved or agreed upon. Both sides see the same picture differently; each group accuses the other of exploitation and of collaboration with the foreigner.

Although Rascón Banda's scenes sometimes simply reiterate Marcos's views in the mouths of the different Indians and the licenciado, at other times, the play deliberately exploits Marcos's speech and twists its intention, subverting it and giving it the completely opposite meaning. For example, at one point, Marcos's words are expressed in the play by the Indians' nemesis, the licenciado. Whereas those in power have been condemned because of their betrayal to the foreign other, in this scene the licenciado suggests that the Indians themselves are the traitors, a direct allusion to the Marcos controversy and, of course, the Malinche's accepted role. The licenciado states, "There is petroleum and electric energy there. Behind the Indians there is a mafia-like network of dark interests, foreign interests that follow the natural resources" (128). His perspective is the complete opposite of Marcos, who in his speech accuses the Mexican government, backed by foreign capitalistic interests, of destroying Chiapas and its natural resources. Moreover, when Malinche tries to remind the licenciado what he had promised to the Indians, the latter argues, "the words are blown away by the wind." His statement is a repetition of the words that Indio 2 had expressed in scene 30 and a direct subversion of the winds that Marcos describes in his speech. Rascón Banda reiterates and alters the very content of Marcos's speech, parodying its intent and placing its arguments in the mouth of the licenciado rather than the Indians. The playwright takes Marcos's powerful "wind from above" (soon to be replaced by the indigenous "wind from below" of the ensuing rebellion) and turns it into the wind that blows away the words and documents of the "agreement" and erases all traces of compromise.

But, beyond this subversion of Marcos's speech and the bonds between it and Rascón Banda's play, certain stylistic connections give a burlesque tone to both, indigenous and governmental, points of view. Like Rascón Banda's text, Marcos's speech also attempts to be intertextual; each chapter is prefaced by a summary paragraph that imitates the style and tone of earlier semihistorical documents, most specifically that of Bernal Díaz del Castillo's *La historia verdadera de la conquista de Nueva España (The True (Hi)Story of the Conquest of New Spain).* These summary paragraphs not only explain the content of the chapter to come, but the language Marcos or his editor uses in them borders on archaic, imitating colonial discourse.[18]

Besides parodying the intertexts and in an effort to give his indigenous rebellion more force, Marcos uses history to promote his cause. He does this to reinforce the connection between past and present. In his address, Marcos calls Governor González Garrido, "the viceroy's apprentice" and refers to him throughout the text as the viceroy. Moreover, his allusions to Zapata's return are hauntingly similar to the colonial myth of Quetzalcoatl's return. He professes, "The eldest among the elders of the communities tell that there was a certain Zapata that rose up for his people and that his voice sang more than screamed, 'Land and Liberty!' And these elders tell that Zapata has not died, that he shall return" (9). In an ironic twist of the myth, Zapata will return to aid the indigenous in their "re-conquest." Zapata is the godlike figure who, contrary to Quetzalcoatl in colonial myth, will miraculously bring the Indians their victory.[19]

A more glaring connection between Marcos's speech and Rascón Banda's text is the sarcastic tone employed in the former. Irony is an important element in both texts, but Marcos uses sarcasm and negation to reinforce his argument. After vividly and sarcastically describing the economic and political bleeding of Chiapas by the imperialistic government, Marcos states "Welcome!! . . . You have arrived at the poorest state in the country: Chiapas" (4). In another paragraph, he uses the famous ironic "no" of empowerment, so skillfully employed by Sor Juana Inés de la Cruz, to paint his picture of the impoverished state of Chiapas. He writes, "Right now it is a school, it is 11:00 in the morning. No, do not come closer; do not look inside, do not see those four groups of children overflowing with worms and lice, half naked, do not see the four young Indians who pretend to be teachers for a miserable pay that they have to collect after walking the same three days that you walked; do not see that the only division between one classroom and the other is a tiny hallway" (5). Here, Marcos meticulously employs the "tricks of the weak" for the double purpose of painting his picture of the poor conditions and that of emphasizing the estrangement between those who should look but do not. In other words, by repeating "No, do not come closer, do not look inside, do not see," he highlights the perpetual "hands-off" attitude that has widened the rift between those in power and the marginalized in the first place.[20]

The Marcos intertext, then, shows the modern-day indigenous

"problem" as a continuation of the conquest. Rascón Banda uses the Marcos text to expose the ambiguous role that every Mexican citizen has played. Moreover, lack of trust impedes all progress; in the play, both sides blame the other, Indians blame government, the government blames the Indians, and each suspects the other of betraying the nation and ceding to foreign interests. By incorporating Marcos's text into his play, Rascón Banda highlights the irony of the situation; it is impossible to move forward if placing the blame is the nation's only focus.

The final intertext I discuss in this play comes from an April 20, 1998, article in the newspaper *Reforma* by Mexican writer, journalist, historian, and critic Carlos Fuentes. In it Fuentes argues that since Mexico asserted its independence from Spain in the nineteenth century, Mexican culture has turned its back on "the multicultural, indigenous, African, and Iberian heritages, with the goal of becoming, as soon as possible, 'modern'" (1998, 1). Examining the relationship between Carlos Fuentes's article, "After Neoliberalism" and its repetition and transformation in Rascón Banda's scene that bears the same name (scene 34), offers some interesting comments on Mexican national identity and its self-image and expression on the contemporary political stage.

Fuentes's article repeats many of the same themes as Gabino Palomares's song *La maldición de Malinche* referred to above; however, Fuentes adds an important twist to the development of the malinchismo argument. Rather than always blame the foreigner, he suggests, "We find it hard to admit that we ourselves are our own Devil and that, as in William Blake's poems, we ourselves are the door to our own hell and our own paradise" (1). He argues that, even when the problems take on an international or global dimension, Mexicans themselves need to find the solutions (1).

In a vote of support for the "Latin American Alternative" plan articulated and expounded by Jorge Castañeda and Roberto Mangabeira Unger (Fuentes's own intertext), Fuentes repeats some of the major arguments of their plan and adds his own dimensions. He uses his general argument against Mexicans always looking to the outside other to reiterate Castañeda and Unger's proposition on the need to increase internal savings by creating a "capitalism, savage or well groomed, it doesn't matter, that does not recognize borders or laws that are superior to its own Market dynamic" (1). Fuentes agrees that by investing in itself and supporting itself through taxes that affect every Mexican, the nation can build a strong, democratic, global, but autonomous economy from the inside out.

Fuentes does not hesitate to expound upon the political problems in Mexico that impede this autonomous economic system and these political problems are variously represented in Rascón Banda's text and the other intertexts, as well. Namely, Fuentes argues, "It is true, there cannot be a credible tax policy in Mexico and Latin America without exemplary punishment for evasion, but also not without eradicating corruption, dishonesty and inefficiency" (2). As Marcos had criticized corruption in the Mexican government, so, too, does Fuentes argue that, unless corruption can be stopped, no progress will be made. But Fuentes goes one step further when he optimistically posits that "The child, the future citizen, will be the author and the actor of Latin American democracy" (2). Through education, the young can break the cycle of violence and corruption in Mexico and attempt to escape from the "Malinche cycle": an endless repetition of crises that, rather than address the causes instead focuses on where to put the blame, always placing it on an outside other rather than on the Mexican self.

In his article, Fuentes adds little new to Castañeda and Unger's argument; he more or less repeats and rearticulates the ideas of his source-text. Similarly, in scene 34, "After Neoliberalism," the three Malinches in Rascón Banda's play repeat Carlos Fuentes's words and ideas verbatim. The words express the possible social and economic implications of turning one's back on one's indigenous roots; the women repeat the assertion that they live in fear of globalization and savage capitalism and that they are their own worst enemy. However, all three Malinches express these views, not together, but one after the other, suggesting that, from any perspective, it is not the over-valuation of the foreigner (malinchismo) that is the problem, but rather, the de-emphasis of Mexico's own role in its history, present and future, that has caused the crises.

As demonstrated above, Rascón Banda includes a variety of intertexts in his play, and he refers to them in each scene and again at the end of the play.[21] Beyond the Malinche cultural intertext, during different scenes Rascón Banda foregrounds many other specific intertexts, and though it would not be possible to analyze every one, their important role within the text is undeniable. The above examination of some of the intertexts shows how Rascón Banda repeats them, sometimes alters and subverts them in his play, and expands upon their meaning to question the meaning of texts and to expose his own view of the modern Mexican nation to his public.

Rascón Banda's play questions many national issues and highlights some of the complex tensions in contemporary Mexico such as NAFTA, the Chiapas uprisings, the role of the party system and the corruption surrounding it. The play presents these delicate and complicated modern issues within a long-standing historical context that displays them as almost impossible to resolve, unless the texts are rescripted and exposed as the fiction that they are. Moreover, it raises profound philosophical issues with regard to the nation. Framing the question of "autonomy" within the Chiapas rebellion, for example, the licenciado explains to Malinche, "I would take out that about 'guaranteeing their autonomy.' That is where they went crazy. Do they want to be autonomous like the Basques? Do they want us to go around killing each other like the Serbians and the Croatians? We are not Czechoslovakia nor Ireland. What do they want autonomy for? To separate, to form another country?" (128). The licenciado recognizes that autonomy is a myth in a globalized world. There are no separate and independent states in Mexico or anywhere else in the modern world. Like texts, nations are necessarily interconnected.

In addition, all the intertexts Rascón Banda foregrounds are also highly intertextual; each, in its own way, highlights or refers to other texts and focuses on the difficulty of determining textual origins or meaning. Moreover, the intertexts largely fuse past and present sources, as does his play, rendering the nation dependent upon its past for the interpretation and articulation of its present and future.

The connections between past and present in the play have been demonstrated above and are manifested in the past flashbacks, presented in the form of performances of the characters from the past, mostly for one of the modern-day Malinches and the psychoanalyst. The function of this layering is to demonstrate just how very little has changed since the conquest. As Adult Malinche tries to understand the reasons behind the turmoil, chaos, and fighting in the Chamber of Deputies with her analyst, Young Malinche watches a similar scene of violence and miscommunication that may have occurred during the conquest. As Malinche explains, "The messengers spoke Mexican and the soldiers spoke Spanish. They did not understand each other. They made signs to each other, as if they were mute, and they did not understand each other at all. They looked like the mimes of Coyoacán" (31). Anachronisms like these make an obvious connection between past and present in an effort to poke fun at the present and take some of the historical burden and "blame" off the past. Cortés and Moctezuma spoke different languages just like today's Mexican politicians, in a vicious cycle of selling out to the "other," are unable to communicate and move forward.[22]

Rascón Banda, like many of his peers, uses humor to present some of these serious themes. From the image of Bernal Díaz reporting from Veracruz to the king via cell phone (41) to the portrayal of an exaggeratedly greedy Cortés who can only be cured by gold (35),[23]

Rascón Banda shows how language and text can manipulate tone, structure, and meaning by incorporating subtle and intentional transformations into their own structures.

Moreover, the number three is significant in Rascón Banda's play; three Malinches, three political parties, three or more perspectives, open up new, nonbinary paths for interpretation. The intertexts expose this because each intertext that Rascón Banda chooses is not just one text but the fusion of or the revision of many texts, a plurality of texts. The texts show that a Malinche struggling with and moving beyond her highly constructed good or bad binary image, posits a Mexican nation that needs to break out of the positive or negative imprints in which it is entrapped, by creating a new text, an "interpreter's utopia," a space for growth and change in a future where neither the foreign nor the stagnant image of present-day Mexico reigns. This idyllic possibility for a globalized world postulates nations as border spaces where neither one nor the other, neither the imperial nor the "subordinate," the foreign or the local cultures dominate.[24]

In addition, in the "interpreter's utopia" the playwright/author cedes some of his control to the reader/spectator. Like Young Malinche, we are part of the play, but simultaneously we are viewing it, interpreting it, and rewriting the script. Rascón Banda's choice of intertexts and their incorporation and manipulation in *La Malinche* attempts to dramatically mimic this interpreter's utopia. Extracting said pretexts from their contexts, highlighting them as already altered and nonoriginal, unofficial sources, and then replacing them and rewriting them within his own play-text, he expands their meanings and recreates their image. No longer the texts they address, they are reinscribed and redefined as scenes in a new play, whose performances will continuously rewrite them and the history they attempt to project.

Through his three stagnant Malinches, the playwright shows a nation locked in a monotonous, unproductive cultural script. He uses intertextuality to attempt to expose that script and rework it. Through the intertexts he selects and what he chooses to emphasize, repeat, or alter from the past texts, he (re)presents them and demonstrates that there are other potential scripts and roles that could emerge from them, depending on the reading and rewriting. Rascón Banda reminds us that there are many other textual sources to look at, and the texts we choose and how we look at them can rewrite our role and our history. Mexicans must move beyond that one Malinche script and look to other Mexican sources for a new interpretation. Moreover, though the intertexts are pasted together in the play like a collage of Mexican history/fiction, by examining each "piece" of the collage, the reader/spectator can see just how very deep and complicated each image is.

All the intertexts chosen show that no text is a simple string of innocent words offering a single interpretation. All texts are multilayered, polyphonic constructions whose artistic value and thematic expression are open to multiple interpretations. Texts are powerful artistic and ideological tools.

Rascón Banda rewrites these texts as theater, as a play, because he sees that, from these different genres of fictional or historical texts a script has emerged. This script has created a role for Malinche and for Mexico. Theater is prioritized in the intertexts even though they are not plays and so, as Polly Hodge reminds us, Rascón Banda shows us how all texts have a dramatic essence. These nontheatrical intertexts have created Malinche's role, written her script, and moved her forward on the real stage of history. Rascón Banda demonstrates that the most powerful and effective way to (re)present her role is through theater. By placing her on a new stage and having her and her new creators recast her role, her image can be renewed with every staging. Since her script has locked the nation on a certain stagnant course, rewriting the script also restages the nation.

At the same time, however, intertextuality does not only have an ideological function, it must also have an aesthetic one, as Villegas postulates. Rascón Banda highlights some of the Mexican sources and turns them back on themselves. The intertexts come alive in Rascón Banda's script, and each new (re)presentation of them entertains reader/spectator with their new story. Rascón Banda's play reflects both on these texts and on his own text, whose power, as theater, can rewrite the story of both the woman and the nation. By doing this through theater, Rascón Banda further marks the reciprocal properties of narrative and fiction and, at the same time, empowers his own play as the new authoritative source that includes all others.

History and Text, History as Text: Maruxa Vilalta's *En blanco y negro: Ignacio y los jesuitas*

> Ever since Shakespeare, playwrights have been struggling with their lack of positive religion . . . I know that civilization needs a religion as a matter of life and death.
>
> —George Bernard Shaw, *Back to Methuselah* (in Usigli 1965, 9)

> Our literature is a substitute for religion.
>
> —Rodolfo Usigli 1965, 9

During her more than four decades as a powerful force in Mexican theater, Maruxa Vilalta has masterfully created and combined different dramatic styles to explore and criticize important social, political, and humanistic themes of her time. Howard Quackenbush describes Vilalta's earlier existentialist theater and affirms that "it sometimes incorporates chaotic, antisocial, or pathological elements of expressionism and serves as a bridge between expressionism and the theater of the absurd, but its message is more evident and has a more traditional form than the theater of the absurd" (1974, 49). Whether in her earlier absurdist or existentialist works or her later religious or political plays, one constant remains; Vilalta's theater is richly poetic. Tamara Holzapfel sees poetic symbols in much of Vilalta's work and shows how her *Nada como el piso 16* (*Nothing Like the Sixteenth Floor*) (1978) "combines a genuine dramatic poetry with social commentary" (1981, 17). Vilalta's theater combines contradictions in a unique and interesting way, never losing sight of the fact that drama is an art, and as such, it must be poetic.

Luis de Tavira, as well, affirms the rich network of contradictions that Vilalta ably weaves together in her plays and he believes that this allows her both to present the innate violence within individuals and society and to speak out against it as a form of protest (2002, 137). In his introduction to *Una mujer, dos hombres y un balazo* (*A Woman, Two Men, and a Gunshot*) (2002) in Vilalta's *1910,* Tavira argues, "Maruxa Vilalta's theater reencounters itself in the violence of a protest against structures imposed on the individual by society, through a methodical and contradictory theatricality that presents a truth by means of an exaggerated emphasis on the extreme opposite" (2002, 137). Vilalta's works of both the past and the present display the problems of their time within a unique context and they portray them using dramatic styles, which, though not always totally postmodern, incorporate various new trends in an interesting way. Moreover, her plays are also largely psychological, attempting to portray the profound psychoses of individuals, nation, and sometimes the human race.

According to Sharon Magnarelli, "Maruxa Vilalta (born in Barcelona, 1932) is the author of more than a dozen dramatic works, most of which have been collected in four volumes and published by Fondo de Cultura Económica (Mexico)" (1998, 23).[25] Her earlier works show both psychological manipulation of characters and the sharp criticism of society through what Carlos Solórzano (2002) calls "didactic expressionism." Solórzano describes how Vilalta's plays of the sixties and seventies, such as *Esta noche juntos, amándonos tanto (Together Tonight, Loving Each Other So Much)* (1973),

Nada como el piso 16 (1978), and *Historia de él* (*The (Hi)Story of Him*) (1980) use existentialism, theater of the absurd, and Brecht's epic theater as a way to show a lack of communication between individuals and to connect that with problems in the world in general (12–14).

While Vilalta's earlier works seemed to fit within a certain absurdist, existentialist, and/or epic tradition within world theater, her plays since 1990 offer a new style and perspective. With few exceptions (*1910* being one very important one), Vilalta's plays of the last decade of the twentieth century center on religious figures and themes and do so within a methodically researched, text-based, historical context.[26] As Solórzano suggests, these plays, *Una voz en el desierto: Vida de San Jerónimo* (*A Voice in the Wilderness: The Life of Saint Jerome*) (1990), *Jesucristo entre nosotros* (*Jesus Christ Among Us*) (1995), *Francisco de Asís* (*Francis of Assisi*) (1993), and *En blanco y negro: Ignacio y los jesuitas* (*In Black and White: Ignatius and the Jesuits*) (1997), "mark a definite rupture with the *costumbrismo* that has poisoned our theater for so many years and they lead us to the true essence of an experiment that culminates in the discovery of a unique reality: that of theater, with all its deceit and its profound truth; the game, the gratuitous dynamism, the power of the author to show us various contrasting aspects, not just the one preferred by psychologism, of human beings" (2002, 12).

Vilalta's most recent plays deserve a closer look not only because their (mostly religious but also historical) traditional themes are so radically different from both her earlier works and from the more recent works of other Mexican playwrights, but also because she incorporates these seemingly traditional themes into a dramatic framework that is unique and revolutionary. Most of her new plays include more than ten, sometimes as many as twenty characters; this is in stark contrast to Latin American and Mexican theater trends of the late twentieth and early twenty-first century, which lean toward a cast of as few characters as possible.[27] The fewer character plays and even the large number of monologues produced in Latin America have largely been in response to economic concerns; there are simply not enough funds to support large productions. Vilalta's works, somehow, are still staged, though, and the playwright seems to get around that problem by scripting that a few actors (seven or so in most cases) will play multiple roles. In her later plays, as Carlos Solórzano argues, actors change identities and, interestingly, they often do this without using masks. In analyzing *1910,* for example, Solórzano tells us:

> The demand to change identities has been accentuated in this work since its own nature no longer requires the use of masks, but rather it asks actors to change identities solely through the power of their acting, a difficult task to thoroughly accomplish, as Brecht himself would verify, but that has a very specific meaning; that of giving us the impression that we are before a community in which all individuality has vanished, to open the way to the "popular face" similar to the graphic arts of the Soviet Revolution.
>
> (2002, 14)

This technique has implications on the thematic content of the plays as well as on the dramatic function.

Additionally, Vilalta's recent plays offer an interesting new style of theater based on religion or history; the playwright incorporates extensive research on the protagonist, his life, and his writings, into her script, seeming to focus on piecing together actual historical documents as a way to rewrite a life. Vilalta's methodology is thorough and rigorous and, at the end of each play, she includes a comprehensive bibliography of the sources she cites and refers to within her play. Her sources vary from historical texts, religious texts, newspaper articles, paintings, and dictionaries; sometimes she cites directly from the intertext and sets it apart in her play-text with quotation marks. At other times, she places the pre-text's words in the mouth of one or another character in the play, rendering it difficult to determine whether or not she has taken the quote verbatim or "translated" or "transposed" its theme or tone into her new text. Ironically, however, her plays include so many intertexts, and they refer to the intertexts so thoroughly, that it is extremely difficult to question them or to trace them back to their original source.

Vilalta creates a new type of theater, rare because of its emphasis on religious figures, its inclusion of extensive historical documentation, its collagelike overlapping of intertexts, and its use of multiple characters played by few actors. In this section, I look at one of her recent plays, *En blanco y negro: Ignacio y los jesuitas (In Black and White: Ignatius and the Jesuits)* (1997), to show how Vilalta uses her historical intertexts to give life to her protagonist and then to move him out of his past context and into present-day Mexico, making her work more about Mexico than about its non-Mexican protagonist. Moreover, by examining how she combines "history" and "antihistory" in this play, I argue that, with this and other recent plays, Vilalta is, in essence, returning to and reinventing a uniquely Mexican theatrical style that has the capacity to penetrate the most deeply felt traumas of the national psyche.

In a sense, with this theater centered on a religious figure, Vilalta is returning to two important traditions in Mexican theater: religious theater, whose origins were in the conquest, and the antihistorical play invented and developed by Mexican master, Rodolfo Usigli. Usigli himself wrote his own religious antihistorical play, *Corona de luz (Crown of Light),* which dramatizes the essence of Mexico's patron saint, the Virgin of Guadalupe. By looking at these two traditions and the space in which they merge with Usigli, I hope to show that, just as Usigli used his antihistorical (and religious, in this case) plays to highlight Mexican national consciousness and conflicts, so too does Vilalta use a play about Saint Ignatius and his teachings to present important messages about the Mexican nation.

First staged in 1997, *En blanco y negro: Ignacio y los jesuitas* travels through the life of Saint Ignatius of Loyola, the founder of the Society of Jesus, otherwise known as the Jesuits. As in her other works of this type, Vilalta pieces together some of the most important moments in the saint's life by citing directly or referring to information found in certain biographical, religious, and/or historical texts written about him. Carlos Solórzano describes this same technique that Vilalta also uses in *Una voz en el desierto: Vida de San Jerónimo:*

> The life of the saint is seen in various connotations by means of a theatrical procedure that allows, with only seven actors and four actresses, who in one of the acts change their mask according to the situation of the drama, to travel from the moment in which the central character, locked in his cell, devotes all his energies to an attempt to obtain an almost physical proximity to God. The change of direction that Maruxa Vilalta has made with this work is notable, even though her religiosity had found a noble expression in a previous work dedicated to *Saint Francis of Assisi.* But what needs to be pointed out in this work is the existential firmness of the saint who refuses to participate in any liturgical pomp in which the Catholic Church is invested.
>
> (2002, 12)

No masks are donned in *En blanco y negro,* but each actor (except for the one who represents the saint himself and the one who plays the contemporary journalist) and the one actress do play many different characters. Moreover, we learn about the important moments in Ignatius's life and the important teachings of his most relevant text, *The Spiritual Exercises,* as we move through the many other rewritten texts that Vilalta pieces together. Her sources for *En blanco y negro* include works allegedly written by the sixteenth-century saint himself, both historical and contemporary texts written about him, his life, and his teachings, books on the Spanish Civil War, three articles written by her father in defense of the Catalan separatists, an entry from the 1961 and 1966 editions of *Webster's Third New International Dictionary,* and entries from the *Diccionario enciclopédico UTEHA* and the *Diccionario de la lengua española.*[28]

In his prologue to the play, Héctor Azar (1997) suggests that repression is the central theme because of many contradictions woven into its content. Moreover, he believes that in the work, "Vilalta finds the present indicative of Ignatius of Loyola and of Jesuitism and, at the same time, the position of the clergy in the fratricidal war (which war is not?) of Spain, in 1936" (11). Saint Ignatius is the central character of the play and the playwright skillfully fuses his image as a historical figure with a suggestion that he still lives in the present. Moreover, the Spanish saint's location in his homeland, some references to the Spanish civil war, and the inclusion of the references to the articles written by Vilalta's father, certainly do seem to locate this play in the Spain of both the past and the present. However, as I show, Spain is not the only context of this play and of this saint's life, nor is religion the only theme.

Henrique González Casanova (1997) also suggests another reference—spatial/historical/political—for *En blanco y negro,* which is indeed closer to my own. He argues that the play includes both religious and political themes and that "The drama is about the Jesuits, about our time, the relevance of the past, flesh and blood history at the end of this century" (13). Taking the connection between this seemingly "Jesuit" play and Mexico one step further, González Casanova affirms that in this play "It is Ignatius and it is Chiapas. It is the liberal thought of the author and her denouncement. It is the assassinated Jesuits and the guerrillas, it is Liberation Theology, it is the defense of the republican premises that do not compromise with the dictatorship; it is the fight for liberty, for justice, and for life" (15). Yet, I suspect that the play is not just about Chiapas or Liberation Theology either. As I will show, *En blanco y negro* uses texts about a religious figure to postulate a national position and the rewriting of it. Certainly González Casanova is right when he affirms that "a single reading is impossible because the direct style implies a multiplicity of references" (14).

En blanco y negro is a complicated play. There are clear indications in the work, such as the inclusion of the contemporary journalist as a protagonist, that Vilalta's themes extend beyond the borders of both the sixteenth-century Jesuit and his life and the Spain that was his nation. Yet, even though Vilalta moves this saint back and forth in time through his dialogues with the journalist and through her use of anachronisms that modernize the themes and content of the piece, it is the way in which she incorporates and manipulates intertexts that transforms the play's meaning, time frame, and context. Even though Ignatius's spirituality does exemplify the values and ideology of Liberation Theology and even though many Jesuits around the world today embrace the liberal, active Catholicism that works with the poor, ministers to the sick, and welcomes women into the Church, Vilalta's play does not paint such a "black-and-white" picture of spirituality today. This Ignacio and his followers are men of conflict. Through these intertexts, Vilalta shows how Ignatius embodies the spirit of a contemporary figure, caught in the gray space between past and present, between religion and politics, between the national and the global.

Similarly, her predecessor, Usigli, chose the Virgin of Guadalupe for his *Corona de luz* because she is the patron saint of Mexico, and as such she symbolizes both the Catholic Church and the Mexican nation. So important is the Catholic religion in Mexico that, as Usigli explains, "The Virgin of Guadalupe is not a theme of reflection in Mexico since she is an element of *respiration.* You cannot think of her objectively, just as you do not think about the blood that circulates through your body; you simply know that it is there" (1965, 17).

Since the Catholic religion is and has always been an important part of Mexican culture, it is no surprise that Vilalta, too, would return to plays about Catholic saints or about Jesus himself as a way to reinforce contemporary messages. Moreover, as Iani del Rosario Moreno (1996) describes in her analysis of Vilalta's *Jesucristo entre nosotros,* even though the Catholic Church is still strong in Mexico, many changes have occurred in the past forty years that open a space for discussion and questioning. Significantly, Moreno relates *Jesucristo entre nosotros* to Liberation Theology, a movement within Catholicism that "different from traditional [Catholicism], it places much emphasis on the idea that to achieve salvation, oppression and poverty must be eradicated from this world" (82). The central figure in Liberation Theology, Jesus, is also the protagonist of *Jesucristo entre nosotros* and that Vilalta play revises both Jesus's image and the contemporary view of Catholicism for the turn of the twenty-first-century spectator (Moreno 1996, 84). What stands out, however, is a contradictory, conflicting image of both Christ and his Church, and as Moreno explains, "At times his image and personality resemble that of the traditional Christ, and at others, that of a twentieth-century Mexican person" (84).

En blanco y negro portrays similar religious tensions by highlighting the life, the philosophy, and the teachings of Saint Ignatius of Loyola, the sixteenth-century founder of the Jesuits. Born in 1491 in the Basque province of Guipúzcoa, Spain, Ignatius was the last of eleven or more children. At baptism he received the name Iñigo de Oñaz y Loyola, probably in honor of the Benedictine Iñigo de Oña. Though his father wanted him to enter religious life, he first sent his son "to receive basic formation as a gentleman and a courtier" and then as a soldier, where he valiantly tried to defend the Spanish town of Pamplona from French invasion (Bangert 1972, 3–4).[29]

Saint Ignatius is best known for his spirituality and for his leadership of the Society of Jesus. During his early years he is said to have seen an apparition of the Virgin Mary, followed in later years by numerous other religious visions. He made a pilgrimage to Jerusalem and several trips to Rome, but the turning point of his spiritual life took place in a small town near Montserrat (near Barcelona), Spain, called Manresa (Guibert 1972, 27, 41; Bangert 1972, 7). In this provincial town, Saint Ignatius "gave his gentleman's clothes to a beggar, and then, garbed in his pilgrim's robe and with staff in hand, prayed through the night before the Blessed Virgin's altar" (Bangert 1972, 7). Thus renouncing "all worldliness of his past life" he began begging from door to door and soon became known by the local children as "old man of the sack."

It was also in Manresa where Ignatius began to take notes and formulate ideas for what was to become his greatest "text" and the foundation of Jesuit spirituality, *The Spiritual Exercises,* published in 1548. This simple but important doctrine "is a series of practical instructions on methods of prayer and examination of conscience, on ways to arrive at an unbiased decision, on plans for a variety of meditations and contemplations, all aimed at helping an exercitant discover God's will for him and to carry it out with vigor" (Bangert 1972, 9).[30]

The Spiritual Exercises affect both the life of the individual and the life of the community since it is concerned with the interior life of the person and his/her manner of directing others. As Guibert suggests, "in most instances the spirituality of the group will have for its starting point the spirituality of some one person, a founder or teacher; and the nature of the spirituality will be what results from his life, his teachings and his practice, his writings, or from some treatise which in the living tradition of the group is considered to establish a norm" (1972, 2). Hence the importance of Saint Ignatius to the Jesuit order.

Though it is clear that Ignatius was synonymous with spirituality, as Guibert reminds us, there will always be divergences in the spirituality of a group. He argues:

> As a matter of fact, however, just as the spirituality of the group will not remain something congealed but will inevitably undergo adaptations and developments, so too this same word "spirituality" will become able to designate increasingly more realities which are quite different—either a certain number of spiritual principles, or forms of prayer or of asceticism, or sometimes even a complete system which the group imposes on its members and considers fundamental for them and practically sacrosanct.
>
> (2–3)

Vilalta highlights these rifts and factions of spirituality in her play, making them the starting point for the questioning and reflection.

On the other hand, spiritual life cannot be easily separated from everyday actions since one of the most important aspects of Ignatian spirituality is that it fuses the spiritual with the practical. Guibert tells us, "Jerónimo Nadal, one of the men who knew Ignatius most intimately, thinks that his special grace was 'to see and contemplate in all things, actions, and conversations the presence of God and the love of spiritual things, to remain a contemplative even in the midst of action'" (45).

In *En blanco y negro* Vilalta includes many "real" scenes from Saint Ignatius's life, such as his vision of the Blessed Virgin, his conversion in Manresa, and his transformation into the Old Man of the Sack, reference to his time in Jerusalem, his encounters with the various women in his "real" life, and his unanimous election as general of the Society of Jesus. She also dramatizes his time at the University of Alcalá when "he and the companions who joined him at Barcelona all dressed alike, soon became popular in the city for their ability to discourse movingly and effectively on spiritual topics" (Bangert 1972, 12) by showing the various Ignacio clones and portraying their conversations with him (scene 2).

From the beginning of the play, we are "reading" images of the saint, texts about him, both verbal and visual, and this is continuously emphasized by the many footnotes of textual sources that Vilalta sends us to throughout the play. In the opening scene, the journalist encounters the saint in his study and, even though the receptor has already seen Ignacio (in the character onstage), the journalist describes him, "Dressed in black. The white neck open at two small lapels, of an irreproachable taste. Narrow face and a big nose. Big forehead with craggy temples. A small mustache and scant beard" (24). First, then, the audience sees the Ignatius character and then the journalist describes him. Interestingly, however, the journalist's description comes directly out of other texts, for at the end of this description, Vilalta documents her sources in a footnote; the journalist's words are revisions of other texts, and, ironically, those texts are reworkings of the descriptions found in still other texts.[31] This technique forces reader/spectator to be suspicious from the outset; we see an image/read a description of the person before us, but it is immediately revised for us in someone else's words (the journalist's/his sources, and the texts on which those sources are based). Moreover, we cannot trust those words either because they too are extracted from other texts, texts that have also been rewritten and revised in an endless game of intertextuality.

The journalist repeats the textual image of Saint Ignatius that he is familiar with, and he, too, recognizes that the image comes from classic iconography. He states, "Ignatius of Loyola. I cannot believe it, you are in front of me. Just like you are painted in classic iconography" (24). But then, when Ignacio questions whether the journalist is familiar with a portrait of the saint, the newspaperman decides to slightly alter Ignacio's image in this representation:

> *Journalist.* Of course I am familiar with your portraits; everyone knows them . . . It is not true that your eyes are hard . . . At least they don't look that way right now, with your death approaching, when you are hardly here at all.
>
> (24)

Modifying what he knows about Ignatius from the other texts, the journalist revises those texts slightly. Nonetheless, the audience sees yet another image before them: an image that is related to the past texts and to the journalist's text, but which they too must "read" according to their own perspective, in order to choose from among all the images presented.

Religious and historical texts are not the only intertexts that Vilalta cites or alludes to. Even though there are no footnotes directing us to them, she also refers to books of chivalry (so important to the real Ignatius's formation according to Bangert) and, more importantly, textual interpretations of them, for example, their presentation in Cervantes' *Don Quixote.* In scene 3, Ignacio has just been converted at Manresa into the "man of the sack." He describes to the journalist his encounter with the Virgin and the penance he chooses to participate in for "his lady."

> *Ignacio.* Before Our Lady of Montserrat I kept vigil over my weapons all night, always standing, with my staff in my hand, and sometimes

kneeling. Before her altar I hung my dagger and my sword. Now I am free.

Journalist. Free of what? Or for what?

Ignacio. To live exclusively for love and to serve my Lady and my God. (45)

Even though the Virgin is Ignacio's "Lady" here, certainly, the very words of this scene connect this Ignatius in some way to Don Quixote. Alonso Quijana's excessive faith in the texts of chivalry transformed him into a knight in shining armor. This Vilalta scene evokes the night when Don Quixote kept vigil in the patio of the inn, guarding his arms to be free to devote himself to his Lady (Dulcinea).[32]

En blanco y negro is not only rereading texts on Ignatius the individual; the Jesuits too are presented as a text taken from various sources. We know that, historically, the Jesuits were expelled from many countries around the world in the eighteenth century.[33] As the Ignacios of Vilalta's play list the dates and places of the Jesuits' expulsions, the stage directions tell us that "*a plastic representation of the exodus is formed while* The Ignatiuses *say their lines*" (40). The multiple Ignacios are meant both to indicate the many followers of Ignatius (the Ignatius clones throughout the world) and the many images presented of Ignatius by the different textual representations of him. Vilalta manipulates multiple texts here; expulsion means movement, yet she presents the expulsion as a plastic, visual image, static in this "translation." Moreover, she juxtaposes this "new," static image of the expulsion against the journalist's words, which focus on the past caricature of the expulsions that were presented in the newspapers of that time.

Journalist. They are taking this like a tragedy. By contrast, in the newspapers of the period they were an object of caricature. (*He laughs*) The Jesuits run out, rolling up the sleeves of their cassocks. (*But the laughter freezes on his face before the seriousness of Ignacio*). (40)

The movement suggested by the word "exodus" and the movement that the actors engage in after this scene as they take their expulsion literally and run away from the journalist, are juxtaposed with these two static images ("the plastic representation of the exodus" and the Jesuits as an "an object of caricature") to exaggerate the contradictions presented by textual images. Our idea of the Jesuits conflicts with what may have been their reality. However, we will never know what they really were since all images left behind of them are textual.

Because the journalist highlights the contradictions between the Ignatius texts and the image of him presented here to readers/spectators, he plays an important role in this play; he is an intermediary, who, like the reader/spectator, both reads texts and rewrites them. Describing his own role to Ignacio, the journalist affirms, "I am trying to establish a dialogue between you and the audience. I am the audience" (27). As audience he "reads" the texts, both the past ones that Vilalta incorporates here, and the new one (the Ignacio character) in front of him. In an effort to try to fix the text, make it static and "truthful," he records everything on his omnipresent tape recorder. Yet even this attempt at the truth fails.

> *Journalist.* We have to talk about all this. We will use the tape recorder. (*He takes it out of his pocket. He will maneuver it during the whole course of the play*). I never separate myself from it; it is a very useful invention . . . the bad thing is that, sometimes, tape recorders lie.
> *Ignacio.* What do you mean?
> *Journalist.* A sentence taken out of its context no longer means the same thing.
> *Ignacio.* And are you planning to take what I say out of context?
> *Journalist.* It won't be necessary. Others have already done it.
> (28–29)

The journalist hears and sees everything. Thus, even though he is an actor in this play, he is also a spectator. He brings the tape recorder wherever he goes, in an effort to record the words, the texts, the stories. Nonetheless, the texts, like the texts that Vilalta includes in her footnotes, are taken out of context and thus the images that they present will necessarily be manipulated and re-expressed in new contexts. Like the journalist, it is our role as reader/spectator to record the images presented and rewrite them into our own script. This process forces the receptor to acknowledge that there is no truth, for it too is fiction. All texts can be twisted and manipulated; all language can be taken out of context and distorted. Ironically, Vilalta herself is among the "others who have already taken Ignatius's words out of context" and this is part of her textual game. By including fragments from other texts as part of her image of Ignatius, his world, and our world, and manipulating them as she wishes, she is creating a new text, which in some cases, is the opposite of the "original" texts.

Humor also helps to highlight the discrepancies and contradictions between the different versions of the Ignatius story. For example, as the Ignacios list their expulsions and the reporter records them, the journalist reminds Ignacio that the pope expelled them. Those very words make Ignacio immediately leave the scene, in the middle of the interview:

> *Ignacio.* We are leaving.
> *Journalist.* Why?
> *Ignacio.* We're obeying. We have been expelled. (*He leaves.*)
> *Journalist.* But Ignacio, I still have many questions to ask you. Wait! (*To the Ignacios*) Many questions.
>
> (41)

In this humorous scene, the journalist chases after these "obedient" servants of the pope so that he can find out more about them.

Sometimes, the humor borders on satire. In the scene with the friars (scene 4), Calixto explains why he does not have a coat. He remarks, "I used to wear a black cloth cloak. But when it got hot I gave it to a poor priest" (52). Fraile Uno's response satirically questions such works of charity, "Bad idea. Charity begins with one's self" (52). The satire does not end there, however, for the way in which Vilalta footnotes this text both directs us to page 66 in the *Autobiografía* text and, at the same time, criticizes this notion of charity. What exactly is she taking from the pre-text? This first friar is not even a character in that precursor text and surely no clergy of the period would so twist the idea of charity and turn it into a selfish concept. Here, the footnote seems to direct us to no text; even though the playwright lists the autobiography and includes a specific page number, it is clear that the information expressed in her text will not be found there.

Other examples of humor in the text question the idea of "saintliness." In scene 7, Ignacio meditates in the belfry prior to his election as general of the Society of Jesus. His fellow clergy, his disciples, are arguing with each other over whose town is better. The juxtaposition of this image of Jesuit serenity (Ignacio) and this trivial bickering presents a humorous questioning of the scripts. Moreover, the whole scene parallels another Catholic script, that of Jesus in Gethsemane, praying peacefully while his disciples doubted and Judas plotted to betray him. Furthermore, Ignacio lies to them about his whereabouts. When they ask him where he was he replies, "At home. I was at home" (80). He is then elected unanimously as general, but it takes three elections and a session with his confessor to convince him to accept the post.[34]

The focus on the texts and their revisions is further emphasized through metatheater in the play. Parallel to Sharon Magnarelli's analysis of metatheater in *Una voz en el desierto,* here too, roles and role-playing are paramount (1998, 27–36). Both the journalist and Ignacio are aware of their roles. At one point the journalist asks Ignacio, "Do I seem aggressive to you?" and Ignacio replies, "You are playing your role" (74). At the end of that scene, Ignacio decides that he has fielded enough questions and he walks out on the journalist. The journalist reminds the saint that his conduct does not coincide with his role, "Listen Ignacio . . . leaving halfway through the interview is not the conduct of a saint" (75).

Other characters are also struggling to reshape their role and this is especially obvious with regard to the women in *En blanco y negro.* The women are presented in scene 8 and, as mentioned above, the same actress plays all four women. One by one, the women dialogue with Ignacio and through them we learn bits and pieces of his "history" with these women. The women have diverse roles in the play and in Ignacio's life, but what stands out is that each of these women is a text, which is and has been manipulated and reshaped throughout the centuries.

According to the text(s), Catalina de Austria was the object of Ignacio's affection, but because we see and read various versions of her, we realize that only Vilalta's script places Catalina in that role definitively. The stage directions tell us that "Catalina enters, young and beautiful, wearing the crown of the Queen of Portugal," and then they immediately send us to Vilalta's footnote. The footnote sends us to many other texts about Catalina. First, Vilalta describes some of the many paintings of Catalina and the other women. The receptors then form conflicting and contrasting images between the actress they see and the Catalina of the paintings. The footnote continues, however, by presenting a quote from page 103 of the *Obras de San Ignacio de Loyola.* The quote hints at the controversy surrounding this woman who was the object of Ignatius's desire but does not directly say, only suggests, that it must have been Catalina.[35] In her play scene Vilalta has once again twisted the words and expanded their message, inventing a new image of Catalina and an unsaintly relationship between her and the saint.

Vilalta's scene 8 then picks up where the original text left off, finishes the story, and presents Catalina as the woman of Ignacio's dreams. Ignacio confesses to Catalina that he could not stop thinking of her. "When I left I could not stop thinking about you . . . your big eyes, your ingenuous look. I carried them with me to the war with the French, in Pamplona, and afterwards, because of the life-threatening wounds I received, to my home in Loyola" (86–87). Catalina takes on a new role in Vilalta's play, one that had been merely suggested in the pre-text but not totally scripted.

The other women as well have their origins in other texts; however, Vilalta tells us in a footnote "I could not find a portrait of Isabel Roser" (139). Nonetheless, the playwright gives us her Isabel, inventing her script. "It is the same actress, her majesty lost, without the crown, maybe with a shawl over her shoulders, transformed into a middle-aged bourgeois woman. It is Roser, tenacious, energetic, angry, pacing from one side to the other" (88–89).

These women, rewritten in this new text, are presented to spectators/readers as self-conscious characters and their metatheatrical script brings theater to the forefront. After the fourth woman, Juana, affirms to Ignacio that she was secretly allowed to join the Jesuit Order, she also tells him that, even though she kept the secret, the word got out. Juana confirms, "I have kept the secret. But a lot of mail passes from Rome to Castile, which provokes envy and entails danger. Such that this time, I decided to converse with you *on the set of a theater* . . . Here no one will be able to see us or hear us. Don't you agree?" (95, emphasis mine). Juana's words are not only suspect, they are exposed as a downright lie, when the journalist tells Ignacio, "I was here around the corner; I heard everything. And I recorded everything. I wanted to talk with you about women, but I was afraid you would refuse. I thank you for agreeing to it" (96). Launching himself into the spectator's role, he unravels the text's lies that Juana had just presented. Moreover, by insisting that the conversation take place "on the set of a theater," Juana insists on her role as actress and brings Ignacio, the journalist as spectator, and the other spectators onto the stage with her.

The many subtle differences between Vilalta's text and her intertexts revise this script, making it about the representation, that gray area of interpretation, rather than about the character, Ignacio, or his context. Similarly, the apparent themes presented—a saint's life, Ignatian spirituality, and the Jesuits and their contexts—are redirected too; by maneuvering the script to evoke the act of interpreting, readers/spectators look inward at their own life, their own context, and interpret it. Vilalta's play starts with a religious figure and a seemingly religious context. However, the intensive emphasis on the different textual versions and the distancing that naturally occurs with each revision ironically draw attention away from the saint and his religion, the supposed subject, and pull receptors into the text, engaging them to interpret their own role and context.

A careful reading of Vilalta's text and the footnotes/intertexts she quotes and refers to in her play shows how texts can be twisted to say anything or its opposite. Receptors must determine the reading; if not, the texts will necessarily be manipulated for them. Throughout *En blanco y negro* Vilalta presents us with images of Saint Ignatius, the Jesuits, their sixteenth- and seventeenth-century world, and the journalist's reading of that world in an effort to focus on the reading, the interpretation, and our role in it as part of the text(s).

Hence, the text, the book becomes an important tool through which to read this play. As John W. O'Malley (1990) points out, the book was supremely important to the "real" early Jesuits as well. O'Malley lists some "factors that contributed to a distinctive spirituality in the early Jesuits and set them apart from other religious groups of their time," and he considers the book to be the major differentiation. This book, *The Spiritual Exercises,* "gave them a clear focus in their vision of life's journey and their mission" (16). Vilalta shows us the power of books, of texts, and demonstrates the ways in which even the most upstanding books can be subverted.

Moreover, she connects past and present by including the end of the twentieth-century reporter as a main character, by inserting many often humorous anachronisms, and by presenting all kinds of pretexts, some historical, some fictional, all from diverse places and times. Her technique not only forces contemporary receptors to be suspicious of the texts and the information presented in them, but it also urges readers/spectators to carefully (re)read the signs and texts of their own time.

Like Usigli, Vilalta chooses an important religious topic and then approaches it historically or, more accurately, antihistorically. Placing Vilalta within Usigli's antihistorical dramatic tradition allows us to focus on that purely Mexican style of theater that takes history at its original "source" and makes it a fictional text. Usigli's theory of antihistorical theater postulates that history and historical "facts" serve as a backdrop against which dramatists develop their work, and that imagination is more important than historical accuracy. Usigli maintains that "if one is not writing a history book, if one is carrying a historic theme to the terrain of dramatic art, the first element that should prevail is imagination, not history" (1965, 70). Imagination, then, becomes the cornerstone of the antihistorical play.

When he began to write the *Corona* trilogy, Usigli intended to take "a prolonged excursion through the chronicles" to nourish the plays' contents, but when time ran out for him, he realized that imagination was a more necessary component of his theater (28). History, for Usigli, simply enhances the dramatic story, giving it "a simple accent of color, of atmosphere, of the epoch. In other words, only imagination allows us to theatrically treat a historical theme" (33).[36]

For Usigli, antihistory necessarily included many historical errors since, he reminds us, "No one can be faithful to God and the Devil at the same time. No one can serve theater and history at the same time. I want to serve theater and serve history according to my criteria that history is not yesterday, but today, tomorrow and always" (33). While historical facts may form the backbone of a dramatic "story," antihistory focuses on the story, the fiction. Sharon Magnarelli argues that "Vilalta reminds us that *history* is etymologically related to *story,* fiction—a discursive creation" (1998, 25). Throughout *En blanco y negro* Vilalta manipulates history, altering the "facts," translating the text, thus writing her own story. Her story too then may be taken out of context and rescripted.

Antihistory not only revises the story; antihistorical plays present a unique perspective on historical characters by making them accessible to spectators and bringing them into their world; thus encouraging reflection on the spectator's world. The playwright accomplishes this through "a psychological closeness of the characters," attempting to revive historical figures and make them relive not as symbols, but as characters full of oppositions, conflicts, and known contradictions (Usigli 1965, 27–28). Similarly, Vilalta's Ignacio is a man of conflicts and contradictions. By presenting so many texts about this saint, Vilalta highlights these different images, prioritizes the conflicts and makes the reader/spectator reflect upon them in an attempt to resolve them and move the plot forward. In addition, as receptors interpret the different versions of Ignacio's images, they find themselves in a similar conflictive space. In this way, the intertexts in Vilalta's "antihistorical" play serve both an ideological and a dramatic function. Ideologically, they have a didactic purpose, teaching spectators about the character, his world, and his psychological encounter with it and, at the same time, putting receptors in this conflictive place. Dramatically, the intertexts move the plot forward. Priscilla Meléndez (1990) discusses similar ideological and dramatic functions in Usigli's antihistorical works. Specifically, she argues that his technique goes beyond trying to teach spectators to reinterpret historical figures or events. Meléndez sees that Usigli's antihistory brings out the self-reflective nature of history, the story, and the text. At the same time, she affirms that the antihistorical presentation helps move the play forward dramatically (36–37). In like manner, Vilalta's weaving of fiction and nonfictional sources moves the plot along ideologically and dramatically. It teaches spectators about this one man's life and allows them to question how to "write" a life, their own life. The back and forth movement between this text and the source-texts creates a dynamic that expands the text and images and calls them all into question.

Moreover, the many conflicting versions in the texts destroy the possibility of one cohesive image of the protagonist or of his history. This forces receptors to jump between time frames and spaces in search of a possible "truth," which of course does not exist. John Kronik (1977) points out that most of Usigli's plays center on this nebulous line between truth and fiction. Kronik argues that *El gesticulador,* for example, proves "the fact that the truth which is stranger than fiction is itself a fiction" (7). He further elaborates the complex but fascinating and interchanging roles of poet and historian in Usigli's plays stating, "In *El gesticulador,* the poet Usigli, inspired by history, has invented a historian who is, figuratively, a poet and who avails himself of history in order to fulfill himself as a poet. In other words, César Rubio is a historian who, in order to take his own place in history, turns poet and transcends the factual limitations of history; yet to do so, he is dependent on his detailed knowledge of historical happenings" (8). While one might say that the journalist in *En blanco y negro* becomes the poet in Vilalta's play, the abundance of intertexts referred to in the footnotes move the reader/spectator into the role of the primary poet in *En blanco y negro.* If the source-texts are taken as "history" it is the reader/spectator/poet who "reads" that history and "transcends its factual limitations."[37]

Moreover, the search for the "historical" truth forces the receptor into an active, reflective role regarding, not the past or even the present, but the future. Luis de Tavira (1992) explains how this works in Usigli's theater:

> It entails a philosophical or poetic breaking off of the events from their unique objectivity, from their unique time and their unique space that, by belonging to the past, are irremissible, but to break them off on the basis of a consciousness of truth that explains them precisely within the trajectory of time, and because of that, their truth does not stem from the fact that these events took place in the past, but rather from their reality in the future. Thus, to say that it is about breaking an objectivity based on a historical truth seems contradictory; and it is that the phenomenon converts the spectator into an analyst who takes his/her reality apart in order to gain an intuition of its complete truth. It is broken in another time and space, that is to say, one human event is carried out from another in order to explain the latter: an antihistory is made from history in order to give to the latter the intuition of another truth distinct from the human phenomenon. This identity and difference dominate the relationship between theater and history. (81)

By including history as story, both Usigli and Vilalta emphasize the fiction in both and bring the content of that (anti)history to center stage, teaching reader/spectator a history lesson and writing a new story, while at the same time moving the dramatic plot forward. Vilalta's play makes Saint Ignatius a contemporary figure, not only because she has a twentieth-century Mexican reporter interview him (as does Usigli with Erasmo in *Corona de sombra*), but also because the juxtaposition of the historical texts with this character convert him into both a different and more modern version of the saint. The inclusion of these texts makes these past documents postmodern, and even though Vilalta pretends to use them to describe her character, they stand out as history that conflicts with his image on the contemporary stage. Ironically then, the inclusion of these historical documents in her play signals both their fiction and that of their character and at the same time rewrites them as postmodern texts. Moreover, in a revision of the Brechtian model, these historical texts rendered antihistory force readers/spectators into an active role; they are launched into their own present and beyond and forced to reflect on its and their own scripts.

Sharon Magnarelli has suggested that many of Vilalta's plays are circular in structure and that they depict a concern for discourse and theatricality as both theme and technique. Magnarelli reminds us, "Her plays continually highlight the discrepancies between discourse and praxis, between what language tells us we are seeing and what we in fact see" (1998, 23–24). In *En blanco y negro* this rift becomes apparent through the insertion and revision of the many texts. Moreover, in this play, Vilalta also emphasizes the discrepancies between discourse and praxis thematically; Ignatian spirituality is unique because it, theoretically, embodies both reflective spirituality and action. Ironically, however, both Ignatius's and this Ignacio's hands are tied. The Ignatian vision was stifled and, at some points in history, completely prohibited by the pope. Similarly, Vilalta's Ignacio's role is circumscribed by the images presented in the pre-texts about him.

Vilalta often incorporates other texts, verbal or visual, into her plays, and as Magnarelli argues, the inclusion of these intertexts in her works, "underscores the theatricality of the work and indirectly questions the validity and referentiality of any artistic composition" (27). Her more recent technique of incorporating historical texts into her own initiates the reciprocal game of questioning both the fictionality of the history and the historicity of the fiction. In other words, here again intertextuality blurs the boundary between genres and contexts.

Vilalta chooses theater because, as Usigli reminds us, it is the only three-dimensional art. Theater is always in motion and defines itself for and through its human dimension (actors and spectators) (1965,

23). Though actors represent a "historical" figure, that character's connection with both the actor and the spectator of the present inevitably "modernizes" the character. By viewing "history" onstage, present-day spectators move it into their own time frame and interpret the message in their own terms. Tavira believes that for Usigli, "the spectator of theater should aspire to a greater human consciousness. In the same way that a raised curtain converts us into theatrical spectators, the reflection on history has converted man into a spectator of his own phenomenon" (1992, 79).

What is this "phenomenon" that Vilalta wants spectators to witness and how does it relate to images of the contemporary Mexican/ Latin American nation that Vilalta portrays in *En blanco y negro?* Vilalta weaves the religious figure and historical and artistic texts into an antihistorical piece for two important reasons. First, Vilalta's script rewrites the Ignatius text to attempt to bring Mexico into a discourse of the present that rejects its own image as "isolated." By turning reader/spectator into an "analyst," the intertexts and the way Vilalta manipulates them in *En blanco y negro* bring reader/spectator into the context in which Saint Ignatius was "created." As we have seen, Ignatius was a man of great inner conflict and he was, at the same time, a controversial figure in his world. The same held true for his Society of Jesus and for the times within which it flourished, and fell, and flourished, and fell again. After Pope Clement XIV dissolved the Society of Jesus in 1774, Pope Pius VII reestablished it again in 1814. Nonetheless, according to Geoffrey Cubitt, "the revived order was the replica of its predecessor. In magnifying the Jesuits' influence, early nineteenth-century anti-Jesuit opinion made much of this eerie sameness, and largely ignored the practical problems involved in the order's resurrection" (1993, 20). In every period, the problems the Society of Jesus faced exposed "the relationship between past and present antagonisms, between inherited prejudice and contemporary perception . . ." (Cubitt 1993, 21). One purpose of Vilalta's antihistorical play about this religious icon is to expose the turbulent context of the "story." Vilalta's text, like the texts she incorporates in it, is complex, composed of many texts, and, similar to the other texts, it emerges out of (con)textual conflict. The juxtaposed and overlayed images of a conflictive protagonist in a conflictive world make this figure and this text draw parallels between Ignatius's conflictive image within a tumultuous world and the receptors' equally unstable place in his/her own inharmonious context. While this Mexican play could be dialoguing with Mexican receptors, as Usigli reminds us, Mexico is not isolated from the rest of the world.

Mexico is part of this conflictive world and the reader/spectator reads these images in this context. Usigli suggested that he wrote his *Corona de luz* to show how Mexico is necessarily connected to the rest of the world. He affirms that he wrote his antihistorical religious play to combat this idea of Mexican isolation, "Maybe through the quotidian verification of our present relationships with the outside world, I came to the conclusion that in reality we have never been isolated, not even in our archeological stage, even though Western civilization might mark a culminating hour—midday—and ours a different one, but no less transcendental or climactic in its own way: midnight. Precisely, this theory of isolation is not Mexican, but Spanish" (1965, 20). For Usigli, by presenting the Catholic religious text, a text shared by much of the Western world, Mexico is united with that world and placed within it on equal footing. The image of an isolated nation comes from outside that nation; his rewriting of that shared text, that master narrative, from within the Mexican, also rewrites Mexico's script. Placing that religious text within the antihistorical play connects Mexico to the Western world and shows how all those texts depend upon interpretation and imagination. Neither religion, nor history, nor text, is black or white, but rather all reside and are formed in a gray space in between.

A second reason that Vilalta rewrites these scripts is precisely to textually expose that gray space, the meaning between the lines of every text. Truth becomes fiction as one text's images contradict the others. Similarly, presentations of gray areas emerge between binary discourses destroying the supremacy of any one perspective. The gray area between presentations of Catholic or indigenous, Spanish or colonial Mexico, Liberation Theology or the Vatican dogma, malinchismo or imperialism, or the local and the global becomes prioritized over either binary configuration. The black and white of the title of the play like the black-and-white vestments of Saint Ignatius and all priests, past and present, are but a metaphor for this gray area, this ill-defined space where individual and nation are formed.

Moreover, in Vilalta's play, receptors are paramount for it is they who must interpret the gray area, read the intertexts and images presented to them and choose the "truth." Recognizing that there is no black or white, receptors, like Vilalta's journalist, must navigate the gray area and create their own reading of the past and their present. In the play, the emphasis on the many Ignatius texts shows the many different stories about this "real" man, who was later transformed into a saint. In both the written play-text and the staged performance, Vilalta's play forces receptors to read and see between the lines of the stories. Because they are not isolated from others' scripts, if they do not read and interpret the texts in their own way, someone else will do it for them. The play makes it impossible to prioritize any one image of Ignacio. There is no one version, no black or white image, just a composite of images, a gray area in which to interpret this man and his/our context. In Vilalta's play, Ignacio is at once lover, friend, and Jesuit leader yet, at the same time, he is a caricature of all those images. In Vilalta's text, the black-and-white images of this icon fade into the gray space of interpretation.

Additionally, the black and white of the title could also refer to the printed words, the texts. Though their letters are black on the white pages, their meaning is never that clear. Depending on their context, on their connections with other texts, with other words, and with other worlds, their meaning falls into the space in between the black and white, once again, that gray area.

Finally, through its questioning of the black and white, the play suggests that nation is also a nebulous concept. Ignatius was Spanish, but his heart and spirit were in Rome, nonetheless that connection with Rome filled him with many conflicts. Moreover, Ignatian spirit had no national boundary. Through his writings and his teachings, as delineated in his texts, Jesuit understanding spread throughout the world. Once again, however, that was not without its problems; the Jesuits were expelled from most nations in the world and have been persecuted throughout history. Moreover, because Vilalta makes Ignacio both the saint and the caricature of the saint, she urges reader/spectator to question all national, religious, and other official stories presented to them.

Similarly, as Jesuitism belonged to every country and to no country, Vilalta's play shows how wars and other "national" issues extend beyond national boundaries. Her play alludes to the Spanish civil war, but as Henrique González Casanova tells us in the introduction to *En blanco y negro,* this play is about Ignatius and it is about Chiapas. Once again, the playwright shows us how similar political situations and conflicts are throughout the world because there is no black and white.

En blanco y negro also suggests that so many of these political tensions have their roots in religion and this allows her to urge us to focus on the gray space, the area of potential new interpretation, rather than to accept the black or white images scripted for us. *En blanco y negro* questions all religious texts, all historical texts, all artistic texts, and presents them, like Usigli did, as antihistory. *En blanco y negro* posits a search for something in between: a religious spirit not totally articulated in either liberal Catholicism or the institutional Church, an interrelated but totally unique and, as yet, unimagined national configuration, not totally scripted *in any text.*

The play questions the black and white, not only in the religious text, but also in every context. Receptors of this Vilalta play move out of Ignatius's conflictive past and are launched into a questioning of all binary markers. Speaking specifically of and for Latin America, and more specifically of and for Mexico, this gray space in between the black and white also refers to identity. Rather than be locked into a binary image of Chingada or Chingón, Indian or foreign other, *En blanco y negro* postulates a new interpretation of self and nation in this poetic, dramatic space where texts and contexts are constantly created and recreated.

Vilalta makes her characters live in these plays by tearing them from their context at the same time that she immerses them in it. In this way she takes history and propels it into postmodern space. As Solórzano argues, "The examination of reality is focused starting from the premise that the characters need to define themselves first as individuals disconnected from any historical context, in order to then inscribe their nature in the incidents that shape present history" (1985, 84).

Vilalta's emphasis on religion, its scripts and its texts, in the last decade of the twentieth century is important to our understanding of her work. She is perhaps demonstrating the perils that befall us when a black-and-white worldview is adopted. War, in the present and in the past, so often has religious conflicts at the root. By allowing for interpretation and thought in the gray spaces that exist, we are in a better position to understand politics, spirituality, and humanity. Vilalta's work demonstrates the pitfalls of binary thinking.

Vilalta's earlier works had focused on the lack of communication between individuals and had often extended that senselessness and alienation to the world at large. These newer plays, centered on religious/historical figures, attempt to interpret the reasons for miscommunication by showing how texts are necessarily related and can and will be manipulated to change meaning. Moreover, the protagonists' conflicts are not so unlike our own. Here, Brecht's socially committed theater takes a different form. These characters, Saint Jerome, Saint Francis of Assisi, and Saint Ignatius of Loyola, were highly committed figures, socially, politically, and religiously. In fact, Saint Ignatius was constantly persecuted for his beliefs and teachings as were all the men who followed him. Nonetheless, his spirit lives on in the many revolutionaries who continue to fight for freedom and justice in all parts of the globe. Vilalta shows us how the struggles of these revolutionary or religious men have been translated throughout history and how their roles are ever evolving.

In speaking of Vilalta's earlier theater Holpfazel suggests that "Vilalta consistently draws on two sources of poetry: attitudes for which ordinary meanings of words are inadequate and language that conveys something other than the meaning of what has been said" (1981, 16). Holpfazel extends Vilalta's manipulation of language and of poetic meaning to the question of human identity when she writes, "the question of human identity, although also related to the more social theme of individual self-determination, has a broader, more poetic meaning here" (16–17). In her later plays as well, Vilalta connects words to identities and through her manipulation of the words, of the texts and their meanings, she creates new images of national and global citizens in the twentieth and twenty-first century.

Maruxa Vilalta manipulates historical, religious, and artistic source-texts in *En blanco y negro: Ignacio y los jesuitas* to show the religious, political, and social gray area of contemporary Mexico in a global context. Usigli notes that writing his own antihistorical, religious play, *Corona de luz,* put him up against "the most difficult of the themes I have been able to address. I was not left with any divine problems, but all the human problems remained to be resolved" (1965, 22). Vilalta's religious, apparently historical, and definitely, textual portrayal of Saint Ignatius, his life, and his spirituality, is a front from behind which Vilalta brings out the tensions and conflicts of Mexican essence and identity in a global world. She shows that Mexican readers/spectators must search for their own truth, their own meaning, by rejecting the black-and-white images imposed upon them and interpreting the gray area according to their own needs and interests. Necessarily connected to other scripts, receptors must interrogate those versions and maneuver them to create the self-image they want to affirm.

Through theater, Vilalta manipulates and reconstructs language to demonstrate its flexibility and to highlight the power and importance of interpretation. In her text and in all the texts, the divine themes testify to greater secular humanity while the historical texts are exposed as the fiction they really are. By (re)presenting Ignatius's conflictive life and reading it over and over again in all its versions, Maruxa Vilalta makes her public think about and act upon the new religious, historical, national, and international texts in the making.

2

Traders or Traitors? Twisted Images and Venezuela's Deception

Cry then about your misery,
Cry about your ancient splendour
And your past glories,
For which the very sky was envious.

It is about time you lament
Your grown pain.
Venezuela, I cannot,
Myself, being Time,
Bring you relief.

—Andrés Bello, *Venezuela consolada,* 7–8

WRITTEN IN 1804, TWO CENTURIES BEFORE THE CURRENT NATIONAL crises in Venezuela, Bello's words take on a prophetic tone. Time has not healed the deep wounds in the Venezuelan national consciousness and, one could argue, that almost two centuries after its independence from Spain (1821), Venezuela is more "colonial" than ever. The Bolivarian Republic of Venezuela, as Hugo Chávez renamed it in 1999, is the fifth largest oil-exporting nation in the world, yet 68 percent of its population lives below the poverty line. According to Moises Naim, "No other country in Latin America, with the exception of Chile under Allende in the early 1970s and again under Pinochet in 1982, has experienced a greater and more rapid increase in poverty than Venezuela" (2001, 3–4). Moreover, as Judith Ewell argues, "Venezuela's historical pattern does not coincide with that of any other Latin American nation" (1984, 1). Most of Venezuela's history has been characterized by economic exploitation, poverty, and chronic civil wars. Most importantly, the oil wealth that has so deeply divided the nation since it was discovered in the second decade of the nineteenth century quickly propelled Venezuela onto the international stage but, at the same time, it fostered growing domestic problems, such as corruption, poverty, and class division. Because of oil, Venezuela has, perhaps, suffered from economic globalization for much longer than other Latin American counterparts, yet, according to the A. T. Kearney/Foreign Policy Magazine Globalization Index, "Despite the huge volume of its international oil trade, Venezuela ranks only thirty-sixth" out of "a sample of fifty countries according to their degree of interaction with the rest of the world" (Naim 2001, 7). Naim argues, "despite the cosmopolitan look of Venezuela's major cities, the fashionable appearance of its middle class, and the volume of its oil trade, the country's global integration is limited. The great majority of Venezuelans, including important segments of its elite, live in relative international isolation" (9).

The difficulty posed by Venezuela's "degree of interaction with the rest of the world" and, more specifically, by its relationship with the United States, is the subject of the two plays I study in this chapter. I argue that in both César Rengifo's *Un fausto anda por la avenida (A Faust Walks Down the Avenue)* and Néstor Caballero's *Con una pequeña ayuda de mis amigos (With a Little Help from my Friends),* the playwrights use intertexts to shed light on what the imperialist conflict means to Venezuela. Both plays signal their intertextuality through paratextuality (Genette 1997, 3), using their title as a marker or pact with their intertext. Each play focuses on rewriting that specific intertext as a way to express some of the conflicts in Venezuelan national consciousness. Ironically, by revising a foreign text, both of these Venezuelan playwrights hone in on very Venezuelan issues and, at the same time, suggest ways to rewrite the script to improve Venezuela's position in a global and imperialistic world.

César Rengifo's *Un fausto anda por la avenida*

> A nation, a country survives above all else as long as it has a strong and creative national spirit.
>
> —César Rengifo (in Suárez-Radillo 1972, 51)

> With the bubbling of the first oil well, that had sprung up in Zumaque in 1914, the myth of El Dorado returned to the Land of Grace, as Columbus called that which would later be known as Venezuela. The myth of easily found wealth, of immediate possibility, of effortless achievement, of the golden torrent flowing from all possible sources into the boldest hands, captured the minds of several generations.
>
> —César Rengifo (in Suárez-Radillo 1972, 59)

Venezuelan poet, playwright, journalist, essayist, and painter César Rengifo is, arguably, the artist who has made the greatest impact on national consciousness. Born in Caracas in 1915, he devoted himself to painting and dramaturgy at an early age when, immediately following his graduation from high school, he embarked on trips to Chile and later Mexico to study with the world's best-known muralists and plastic artists. Influenced by Mexico's Diego Rivera, José Clemente Orozco, and David Siqueiros, he returned to Venezuela to create some of the country's finest murals and mosaics. His *Amalivaca,* painted in the Plaza Diego Ibarra in Caracas in 1955–56 during the Pérez Jiménez dictatorship, reflects the frustration of those years of dictatorship and, at the same time, is a testimony of Venezuelan national identity. According to Rengifo:

> In those moments the country was beginning to deny its own identity, it was being said in all parts of the world that Venezuela had been born with (the discovery of) petroleum, and that we had not had a culture before the arrival of petroleum. I considered the urgency of making this mural a testimony that would capture what we were, a country that possessed a culture deeply rooted in its historical development, with profound roots of great value, and that would demonstrate all the spiritual riches found in our indigenous people before the arrival of the Spaniards.
>
> (Mujica 1991, 26)

The *Amalivaca* tryptic recounts the myth of the Tamanaco Indians on the shores of the Orinoco River and portrays a Venezuela already strong and well defined before the arrival of the Spanish conquerors. Moreover, it suggests a latent possibility of power and independence waiting to be acted upon in Venezuela's future.

Rengifo believed in a strong Venezuela. According to Karin Jezierski, César Rengifo "is one of the men of whom it can be said that he achieved a perfect harmony between his life and his work. This authentic humanism has one simple reason: his love for his people" (1986, 32). For his love of Venezuela and the works in which he displayed that patriotism, Rengifo was often honored. In his early years, his paintings *Los Andes (The Andes)* and *El andamio roto (The Broken Scaffold)* were awarded the Andrés Pérez Mujica first and second prize, respectively, while *El hijo enfermo (The Sick Child)* was given the Premio Popular (1953). He received further accolades in 1954 for *La flor del hijo (The Son's flower)* (Premio nacional de pintura) and *Cena en el éxodo (Dinner in Exodus)* (Antonio Esteban Frías Prize and the Arturo Michelina Prize) (Mujica 1991, 26). In later years he was also feted for his dramatic works. Among those awards, he received the Prize for the Best Play in the Third Festival of Venezuelan Theater for *Lo que dejó la tempestad (What the Storm Left Behind)* (1961) and the Rafael Guinard Prize for *La fiesta de los moribundos (The Feast of the Walking Dead)* (1967). He also won numerous awards for best playwright and for the totality of his dramatic works, including homage to him from the Theater Critics' Circle in 1974, the Ollantay Prize, given by the Centro Latinoamericano de Creación e Investigación Teatral in 1979, and the Premio Especial del Círculo de Críticos Teatrales en Venezuela, also in 1979. In 1974 he received the Premio del Buen Cuidadano for outstanding citizenship and dedication to Venezuela and its artistic interests (Jezierski 1986, 32). His lifetime achievement award, the Premio Nacional de Teatro from El Consejo Municipal del Distrito, awarded shortly before his death in 1980, marked the culmination of his career as painter, dramatist, and poet.

As a playwright, Rengifo believed that "There is no human activity that is not political and theater fundamentally from its origins to the present day has always been political theater" (Mujica 1991, 9). He maintained that "I decided then, from the first moments I started working as an artist, in the theater as well as in painting, to express Venezuela, its society with all its contradictions, and especially to leave . . . a little theater above all part of the epic of our people. And with regard to the plastic arts, to show a little about our geography, about our habitat and especially about our people in that physical environment, and also part of the conflicts that our country and our people suffer" (Mujica 1991, 10–11). As a way of revitalizing theater in Venezuela and of working toward establishing a national theater, he and others began the theatrical movement "Máscaras" (Masks) in 1953, during the Pérez Jiménez dictatorship. It was established to speak out, "against an attitude of inertia in the country and as a type of anti-imperialist revolution" (Mujica 1991, 53).[1]

In depicting Venezuela in his plays, Rengifo focuses on major defining, often traumatic, moments in his nation's history. According to Suárez Radillo, Rengifo is the most prolific of Venezuelan dramatists, and his "contribution to contemporary Venezuelan theater can be considered the most important individual contribution to the nation's dramaturgy" (1972, 52- 60).[2] Susana D. Castillo divides Rengifo's dramatic works into five categories: conquest plays, the pre-independence cycle, independence plays, the "mural" of the Federal Wars, and the petroleum cycle (1980, 66–67). Her classification essentially omits major works like *Un Fausto anda por la avenida* and *La fiesta de los moribundos.* On the other hand, Suárez-Radillo posits four categories in Rengifo's theater; his classification highlights

Rengifo's historical and petroleum plays while, at the same time, it emphasizes the diversity of his dramatic themes and style. Suárez-Radillo suggests that Rengifo's theater can be divided into historical works, works centering on marginality, satirical plays and farces, and plays of the petroleum theme. He includes the conquest plays, the independence plays, and the plays of the Federal Wars under the classification of historical plays (1972, 52). Nonetheless, in all periods, according to Castillo, Rengifo's work lucidly depicts the historical causes of Venezuela's alienation, unrest, and resistance.

Particularly poignant are his plays in the *Mural de las guerras federales (Mural of the Federal Wars)* and his trilogy *Mural del petroleo (Petroleum Mural),* written between 1954 and 1969. The latter includes the plays *El vendaval amarillo (The Yellow Gale), Las torres y el viento (The Towers and the Wind),* and *El raudal de los muertos cansados (Abundance of the Weary Dead).* It would be interesting to study the intertextuality between Rengifo's petroleum plays and several of his own petroleum paintings, among them the paintings, *Petróleo (Petroleum)* (1949), *Lo que nos deja el Petróleo (What Petroleum Leaves Us)* (1963), and *Las torres (The Towers)* (1972). Each play, like the paintings, shows petroleum and the politics related to it as a surreal source of Venezuela's anguish and national hardships. Rengifo was obsessed with the negative impact of petroleum on his country's political, economic, and social development. He affirmed that "With the arrival of petroleum, a violent change in our culture is produced . . . The subculture of imperialism, of the colonizing forces that destroy and implant other canons . . . from there come the neuroses; therefore we are a country of neurotics" (Mujica 1991, 28).

Speaking about his plays and paintings about petroleum and on petroleum in his nation in general, Rengifo believed that:

> Oil, as we all know, has given wealth to a dominant class allied with imperialism, a class that has transformed itself into the servant and the facilitator of imperialist penetration in the country, and the great majority of the people have obtained no benefit from oil; on the contrary, they have literally suffered the physical devastation and the total socioeconomic devastation that oil brought, that is to say, they have been both oil's victim and the contrasting element within that great wealth and great misery in which the country lives.
>
> (Mujica 1991, 42)

For Rengifo, petroleum was the ironic cause of *every* national woe. Mujica reminds us that his work, *Las torres y el viento* and his other petroleum plays present "the destruction that imperialism has caused in our Homeland because of oil exploitation. The total destruction of a community, and within that community there are resources, and a permanent struggle against that devastation" (41).[3] Rengifo admits that "When I wrote *The Towers and the Wind* I did not write it with joy, but with great pain, with great anguish, because I really thought that I was writing one of the most tragic chapters in my country['s history], and I still believe this" (Mujica 1991, 48).

While seemingly much less tragic than the trilogy of petroleum plays, Rengifo's 1979, *Un fausto anda por la avenida (A Faust Walks Down the Avenue),* humorously fuses space and intertextuality to explore the essence of the Venezuelan national conscience. Unlike his petroleum plays, in which he seems to blame outside forces (United States imperialism, oil exploitation) for Venezuela's hardships, this play also highlights an internal psychological conflict at the root of a Venezuelan identity crisis and as an impediment to national progress. The Faust connection and the way in which Rengifo manipulates it, allow the playwright to penetrate the Venezuelan national psyche to depict both the outside and inside forces that impede national cohesion, economic prosperity, and political stability.

As mentioned above, the playwright marks the intertext paratextually by putting the Faust name in the title, and thus Rengifo makes it difficult for the reader/spectator to ignore the connection. Because the Faust story is so internationally well known, most receptors would recognize the intertext and some of its familiar repetitions in Rengifo's play. Rengifo parodies the Faust story, the main character, and his relationship with the devil. However, as we shall see, Rengifo relocates the protagonist, details the economic, political, and social state of his context, documents his protagonist's relationship with that context and with other Venezuelan characters, adds a humorous tug and pull between the devil and an angel, and scripts a Faust who works through the forces of good and evil to come to terms with his identity and his place in a complex world. By reworking this script, Rengifo turns a universal text into the national treasure that his protagonist holds in his own hands.

According to William Rose, *Faust* is, "The story of the man who sells his soul to the powers of evil in return for material gain," yet, at the same time, it represents humans' natural instinct to probe beyond spiritual unrest to seek higher knowledge (1925, 1–26). The many editions of the *Faust* story, published widely throughout Europe from the end of the Middle Ages well into the eighteenth-century, recount the pact between a perhaps real man, John Faustus, and Mephistopheles, the Devil. Earlier versions of *Faust* emphasized the evil of pursuing higher knowledge and showed the Devil as an anti-

Christian source of temptation. Rose argues that "the publication of the wicked life and dreadful doom of Faust was intended as a warning to all who could not find peace and content in the bosom of the Church, but would seek to explore beyond, with the treacherous aid of science, which at that time, of course, included magic (Faust was accused of being a necromancer)" (26). Later versions placed less emphasis on the antireligious nature of Faust's curiosity than on his desire for power and pleasure. Although it is appropriate that, given Venezuela's strong Catholic influence, this initially pro-religious work be reinterpreted on the Venezuelan stage, Rengifo's use of the *Faust* tradition does not carry with it the religious connotations of the earlier versions. Rather, his play alludes to the dangers of abused power and, more importantly, it portrays the battle between good and evil within the individual and the national conscience.

Un fausto anda por la avenida tells the story of Fausto, a sixty-year-old Venezuelan government employee who is about to be celebrated for his loyalty and devotion to his country and his job. On the day of the homage to him, however, the award ceremony is canceled because of a national crisis. After his opening conversation with Fausto, the Guardian Angel turns to the public to warn them that "a grave event is unfolding that will affect Fausto's life" (10). Fausto and the Angel confirm that there has been a military coup and that the nation is enmeshed in a civil war. A voice over the loudspeaker announces that all public employees must report to work or consider themselves fired, and shortly an anonymous voice tells Fausto that, since he is still at home, he is no longer employed. In a matter of minutes, Fausto has moved from becoming an honored citizen and national hero to being unemployed. He is thrust into the abyss of despair and states, "I am no longer young; outside of the job that I performed in that office, I don't know how to do anything. I don't have any family, or savings. How could I save anything with that miserable salary? What am I going to live on?" (13).

The Angel, seeing Fausto's desperation, suggests that he drink some cognac to calm himself, and upon hearing this, the Devil appears, mocking the Angel for his decadent recommendation. The Devil insists, "Fausto needs me now, there is nothing like being knocked down by injustice to sow the seeds of rancor in one's breast . . . He will turn into a demon . . . ha, ha, ha. Between my advice and all that surrounds him, we will do a good job" (13). Rather than actively seek a pact with the Devil, though, Fausto attempts to forge his own path, although at every turn both the Devil and his Guardian Angel argue over who should guide him.

Fausto uses his "resources" to put himself in a better situation. He remembers some books that were left to him by a deceased co-worker. The books explain crimes committed by some former colleagues. He uses the books, filled with their dangerous "knowledge," to attempt to reverse his curse. Rengifo's Fausto is caught in the same "story" as his intertextual namesake; he seeks and exploits higher knowledge to gain power in his life. The books Fausto finds symbolize this. Fausto takes the books and the knowledge he has gained from them and goes to see one of the criminals he has discovered through them. Fausto hopes that Mazo, the criminal, who now happens to be a wealthy business owner, will offer him a job in his company. At first Fausto has no intention of blackmailing Mazo, but when the latter refuses to help him, Fausto uses the books as a way to move himself forward.

However, the criminal will not be easily defeated or destroyed. Mazo enlists the help of Margarita; he wants her to seduce Fausto and trick him into turning over all the books to Mazo. Margarita is as false and deceitful as Mazo and the Devil; she gets Fausto drunk, pretends she will marry him, and tricks him into signing over all the books and his worldly goods to her and her mother, not to Mazo. In the end, however, Fausto sees through all their plans, and, viewing a staircase rising toward the heavens, he climbs it, ignoring the calls of both the Angel and the Devil.

In addition to the books and the knowledge Fausto discovers in them, the Angel and the Devil continuously intervene in Fausto's life, thus parodying the religious reading of the original Faust stories. In Rengifo's play, the Angel and the Devil fight incessantly over how Fausto should proceed, but they offer very little real help to the protagonist. They argue back and forth, humorously trying to convince the protagonist to perform either "good" deeds or "bad" deeds, respectively.

But Fausto is smarter than all of them. Rengifo's protagonist, as a government employee perpetually affected by political and economic instability in a nation that is in constant transition, is a symbol of the Venezuelan nation, and the playwright chooses the *Faust* intertext to make a unique statement about his nation. It is significant that Rengifo's Fausto *is walking down the avenue;* he is not the Faust who makes a pact with the Devil in his home. Rengifo posits a Venezuela torn from within, struggling with its conscience, but in the end, he suggests that the only hope is for the nation to ignore the dialogue within and the "temptations" from the outside, and forge its own path, walk down its own streets independently; Venezuela must recognize its options as well as its strengths and weaknesses, and find it within itself to move up and ahead.

Through his protagonist and his context, Rengifo shows reader/spectator what the nation is like in *Un fausto anda por la avenida.* The Venezuela depicted in this play is, like Fausto, "third class. I have never been first class" (9). It is a nation that gets by because it does not ask for high status or high pay (the Angel states, "You were lucky . . . obscurity sometimes defends the small public employees." Fausto replies, "And the low salary. I was always a good guard dog selecting the most secret State documents . . . without ever asking for promotions or pay raises" [9]). Fausto, like the nation he symbolizes, sells himself short economically. He had been content to do what he was told and he never asked for what he deserved. In addition, the nation in the play also has its share of political problems: first, the coup and then the transitional government. All this is against a backdrop where the (U.S.? Colombian? Venezuelan?) planes continuously fly overhead. These things propel Fausto to state, "We live in a country of madness!" (10).

In Rengifo's play, the Devil reminds Fausto that the books in his possession could bring him the material gain and the power and pleasure he deserves. These books provide the knowledge as well as the resources that Fausto needs. With them, the protagonist reflects upon how he should use what he has to improve his situation. The Devil suggests that Fausto has wasted his life by not pursuing power and economic benefit. He states, "Fausto, I have always told you: you wasted your life behind that desk . . . Ignoring the existence of pleasure, wealth, and power. The wise and the foolish inhabit the world . . . You have been on the side of the foolish!" (14).

The Devil urges Fausto to use the books to his advantage, because, "This is your opportunity! Sometimes it only comes about once in a lifetime!" (19). He encourages the protagonist to place a high price on his treasure, "You are walking around with a treasure and Mazo knows it . . . ha, ha, ha . . . and you know it too . . . Put a price on your treasure! (*He again points to the book*)" (25). This treasure that Fausto has and Mazo wants has the potential to change Fausto's life as oil and knowledge about the resources in their possession have the potential to change the course of the nation. The Devil warns Fausto that if he does not take advantage of this situation, "Poor Fausto! You will continue to be a transient with an unknown suit and torn shoes!" (25).

The Devil is not the only one urging Fausto to take advantage of his possessions for his own gain. Margarita, too, hired by Mazo to get the books from Fausto, advises him to forget about honesty and to pragmatically pursue his necessary due. She insists, "You are in a bad situation . . . and if you want to live and enjoy life . . . You need money . . . Mazo has it and those books, . . . well. They are worth their weight in gold!" (28). She reminds him that "In business there is no friendship . . . You have to eat, change your life, dress better" (29).

The play subverts the forces of good and evil. While Mazo is undoubtedly evil, it is Fausto's recognition of Mazo's corruption that propels him to act on his own behalf. The Devil as well is customarily scripted as the evil force, but in Rengifo's version he awakens in Fausto an understanding of his own situation and a knowledge of the protagonist's latent power. The Angel is not all good either. S/he is humorously presented as indecisive, naive, and relatively ignorant of the context and content of Fausto's troubles. One of the major points of *Un fausto anda por la avenida* is the questioning of good and evil and the need to reflect upon who should define what is good for the nation. If Fausto listens to the Angel, he will be destitute. The Angel advises him to be optimistic, yet at the same time states, "You always want to fix the world by silencing and hiding its filth. And, look at how it is! Every day it gets worse!" (17). Optimism, coupled with a few good swigs of liquor, might get Fausto through this, as the Angel ironically suggests, however, it is clear that a better route for Fausto will be a more active one. Fausto must either seize the opportunity to get ahead or ignore it, because as the Devil reminds us, this Angel's advice is out of touch with reality. He states, "I have always suspected that you are an outdated little Angel! The modern dynamic demands a different type of Angel. (*Joking*) Nothing about wings, ornaments and sandals! Little bionic angels are what you need if you want to fix the world, that, as they say, has turned into a quagmire!" (30).

It is the Devil who sees that Fausto is heading for a fall in either case, no matter whose advice he listens to. He warns, "Fausto is stumbling around and he is going to fall; and the winners will be others. I see it clearly" (31). Fausto acknowledges that the Angel and the Devil each pretend to be his good conscience and his evil conscience, respectively, but, in fact, it might be better if "Fausto can reject every kind of conscience and turn into a monster" (31). The work suggests that the most powerful course for Fausto/Venezuela would be to stop wavering and decide its own destiny, become assertive about its own fate.

Fausto does, in fact, assert himself, first to the Angel by saying, "I no longer have the will to do it!" (33). He will no longer be complicit with the Angel's will. At first, though, this means that Fausto will follow the Devil's advice and pursue life, power, and love (37). But soon Fausto becomes even more evil than the Devil himself and when the Devil recognizes this he asks, "Caramba, Fausto! Who is the Devil here, you or I?" To which Fausto replies, "(*Sarcastically*) You shock me! You have turned into a pretty poor Devil! Go now!" (40).

Fausto's crisis comes when he realizes that pursuing evil—money, more deaths, and revenge—is not the answer to his troubles and he wishes to return to his past life. Rengifo's Devil speaks many a truth, and this time he affirms that everything is in Fausto's own hands. The Devil tells Fausto, "Every piece of advice will be useless to you! I laugh at those who want to advise those who have fallen into their own traps! You need to pick yourself up!!" (43). This advice is reminiscent of the very theme of Goethe's *Faust,* since, at the end of the Goethe version, Faust is redeemed because he did not *enjoy* the pleasures that the Devil gave him (Rose 1925, 54–56). If one is not fulfilled by others' advice, and one can never really be fulfilled by outside sources, the only hope is to take control of one's own destiny.

Once he has been kicked out of his office and fired from his job, Rengifo's Fausto attempts to control his destiny by moving through the streets of Caracas. From the beginning, the playwright establishes that "The action takes place in Caracas in the present day" (6). The juxtaposition of the horizontal local space of the street with the vertical pull toward heaven or hell reiterates the good versus evil paradigm but places it concretely in Venezuela. Moreover, the title emphasizes that this Faust walks the streets of Venezuela, suggesting that he is the nation and, at the same time, alluding to an impoverished nation (street person). When other spaces are portrayed, they are interior national spaces such as government offices, and they are highlighted mostly because Fausto is forbidden in them. When Fausto does see a glimpse of other Venezuelan spaces, such as Mazo's office, he recognizes that it is a place of extreme corruption. Other spaces—Fausto's residences, Margarita's room, the restaurant—are also spaces of shady deals and latent evil. The only possibility to escape from the corruption may be the climb toward heaven that Fausto chooses to make at the end of the play.

Susana Castillo (1980) sees universal themes in *Un fausto anda por la avenida,* suggesting that the work is one of the several Rengifo plays that focus on deteriorating values and show man trapped in consumer society. However, this play, like all of Rengifo's works, is specifically about Venezuela and its social, political, and economic reality. Different from other Rengifo plays, which according to William Anseume posit an ideological separation "between that 'us' (the forsaken and displaced poor) and a 'them' (the rich, powerful, oligarchs)" (2002, 61), Rengifo's Faust play optimistically shows social class, power, and status as mobile, quickly changing constructs. In one day, Fausto fell from grace; by the same token, through his own will and determination he raises himself up to the heavens. The play is a testimony to the Venezuelan spirit of resilience. Fausto is a fighter who, despite his bad luck, stands out as clever, motivated, and impossible to keep down.

Rengifo exploits the Faust intertext to show a politically corrupt and economically troubled Venezuela that is suffering from an inferiority complex. At the same time, the playwright alters the intertext to suggest a stronger path for Venezuela, one that breaks its pacts, examines its own needs, and charts its own course. Receptors can appreciate this message because the intertext Rengifo highlights is familiar to them and because of the playwright's treatment of that familiar text. Rengifo humorously alters the text; the humor makes it easier to interpret the present text because it both spotlights the differences between the intertext and the present text and it pulls reader/spectator into the script, providing the close-up that Sandra Cypess (1991) suggests. As Fausto climbs up to the heavens, receptors might also see optimistic potential for Fausto and the nation he represents. Rengifo makes the Faust text the key to his play and the way he maneuvers the story gives Venezuela a new, more hopeful future script.

Rengifo's *Un fausto anda por la avenida* humorously and sarcastically portrays a Venezuelan nation with low self-esteem, ill-defined goals, political corruption, instability, and economic devastation: a nation that is struggling within its own conscience to determine the right path for itself. But, as the two poles of its national conscience (Angel and Devil in Rengifo's play) humorously and indecisively flip a coin, bet with cards, or toss the dice to determine the best course for Fausto's future, a totally ruined Fausto affirms, "I cannot free myself from the two of you [Angel and Devil]! You will always follow me! I know it. But now I am going in search of something . . . Fausto!" (47–48). Striving to rise above his internal conflict and the injustices that have plunged him into this woeful situation, Fausto goes in search of himself.

The intertextuality in this Rengifo play is different from the collage-type documentation and revision of multiple sources presented in Rascón Banda and Vilalta's plays. Here, the playwright first uses the Faust intertext as a paratext by naming it in the title. The Faust story marks the text and orients reader/spectator to delve further into the intertext to shed light on the present text. In addition, Rengifo highlights and subverts some of the more well-known symbols of the source story, Faust's pact with the Devil, for example, to show how unproductive any pact, whether seemingly good or bad for Venezuela, is in a global context. Moreover, by humorously and sarcastically exploiting and subverting images of good and evil and power and knowledge, Rengifo presents receptors with Venezuela's own productive choice: the need to take matters into its own hands and use the resources it has before it to chart its own course. Through the *Faust* intertext, Rengifo portrays Venezuela as a nation that should examine its national conscience, break its pacts, and, in the Devil's words, "lift itself up."

NÉSTOR CABALLERO'S *CON UNA PEQUEÑA AYUDA DE MIS AMIGOS*

> I think we are a sad country that laughs and dances away its mistakes. What a huge commitment, to be a playwright, to create a universe out of a spot on the wall.
>
> —Néstor Caballero, e-mail interview, January 2002

In her introduction to Néstor Caballero's work Mireya Tabuas exposes the difficulty of publishing and staging theater in Venezuela and lauds Néstor Caballero for his success in this realm, "To write theater in Venezuela is an act of faith. A labor of barefoot Carmelites who are only in search of the grace of God, a dream of those devoted to impossible things, to navigate against the tide with only one oar. It is practically a miracle when a young dramatist finally sees his/her name in the anthologies. Néstor Caballero has achieved this miracle" (1991, 965). Néstor Caballero—playwright, director, scriptwriter, and critic—has written more than twenty plays since his first dramatic publication, *El rey de los Araguatos (The King of the Araguatos)* in 1978.[4] A former student of César Rengifo, Caballero's theatrical training has earned him numerous awards from El Nuevo Grupo, from El Instituto Internacional del Teatro, from Municipal de Dramaturgia, from UNESCO, from César Rengifo, and from Aquiles Nazoa, among others (Tabuas 1991, 966). However, it was not until the stage production of *Con una pequeña ayuda de mis amigos (With a Little Help from my Friends),* which he directed himself, that he became recognized as a mature voice of the Venezuelan stage.[5]

The play debuted in 1983 in the National Theater as part of the Sixth National Theater Festival in Caracas and was an incredible success.[6] Set in Venezuela in the 1960s, the play juxtaposes a frame of sixties music, clothing, and lifestyle (hippies, alcohol, and drugs) with an eighties time frame, when the play was written, to suggest a loss of idealism and a denial of utopian possibility on the part of its characters (Tabuas 1991, 967–69). A consideration of intertextuality in the play, however, reveals that this play is more than a reflection on the sixties or on the idyllic nature of friendship or utopia; it is a treatise on imperialism and its effect on the covertly colonized Venezuelan nation.

Con una pequeña ayuda de mis amigos juxtaposes the sixties with the eighties or with a less synchronically defined "present-day" Venezuela. At the same time, through the use of numerous intertexts, the script fuses Venezuela with the United States of the sixties as well as with the suggestion of leftist revolution associated with Cuba. Even though Venezuela is theoretically independent, in the play the nation lives in Castro's shadow, as evidenced by Castro's powerful presence in the "oniric space" scripted in the stage directions. The comic relief that the Castro scene provides, however, only serves to highlight the deep-rooted anger and hatred that the protagonists feel toward the crushing influence of North American music, popular culture, and politics.[7]

The spatial design of *Con una pequeña ayuda de mis amigos* would challenge any director who would wish to stage it. Caballero lays out the stage set prior to the first act, mandating that each of the two acts include three different juxtaposed spaces and that there be another space, this "oniric" space, which is at once a waiting room for a psychiatrist and a baroque, dreamlike space that includes Fidel Castro, Marilyn Monroe, an astronaut, Cassius Clay, and María Lionza.[8]

The two sets of three different spaces combine past (1960s) and present ("época actual") and juxtapose public and private spaces. The first set highlights Sulay's bedroom, El Tigre (her brother)'s bedroom, which is in a clandestine garage that serves as a revolutionary meeting place, and a street near a park in a Caracas neighborhood in the sixties. The second set has two present-day spaces: the Bolívar Plaza and a television studio where commercials are filmed; these are juxtaposed with the interior of a bus in the sixties.

Even though Caballero describes these different places in a way that makes the receptor think they will simply be juxtaposed, throughout the play he mixes them in such a way as to vacillate back and forth between them. For example, in the beginning the playwright establishes that El Tigre's room is a sixties space, yet, most of the play takes place in that garage, but in present time, where, after El Tigre's accidental death, Sulay and her friends from the past meet to plan a hippies' reunion. The spaces serve to fuse past with present and, at the same time, to highlight the tenuous relationship between the "friends." In act 2, as well, spaces and times become confused; La Chata, who is in the present-day television studio, slips away to the current Bolívar Plaza where she helps Sulay hang posters announcing the reunion. While she is in the plaza, the studio crew talks to her as if she were still in their space. In that same scene, Sulay and La Chata interact with Saturno from the Plaza, even though he is proselytizing on a city bus in the sixties.[9]

In addition, the space is framed by many intertexts—Beatles' music, Janice Joplin music, the film *Clockwork Orange,* Hermann Hesse's novels, Charlie Brown comic strips, the Bible, and Pablo Neruda's poetry, among others—and the intertexts work together to create a composite view of nation that moves the text beyond a dialogue with the sixties. While many intertexts are referred to and reinforce Caballero's message, the title song is by far the most significant.

"With a Little Help from my Friends," written by John Lennon and Paul McCartney in the 1960s and recorded on their *Sergeant Pepper's Lonely Hearts Club Band* album, frames the play and speaks to the many friendships around which the story revolves. The relationship between this group of friends is a relationship that began in the sixties when they were smoking marijuana, drinking too much, and professing peace, love, and revolution. However, through that same intertext and through the irony embedded in its lyrics, Caballero moves the play from a story of individual friendships to a revelation about the state of the Venezuelan nation: a condition that began in the past but continues into the present. The irony of the song becomes apparent in its lyrics:

> What would you do if I sang out of tune?
> Would you stand up and walk out on me?
> Lend me your ears and I'll sing you a tune
> And I'll try not to sing out of key.
> Oh I get by with a little help from my friends.
> Oh I get high with a little help from my friends.
> Going to try with a little help from my friends.
> What do I do when my love is away?
> (Does it worry you to be alone?)
> How do I feel by the end of the day?
> (Are you sad because you're on your own?)
> No, I get by with a little help from my friends.
> Do you need anybody?
> I need somebody to love.
> Could it be anybody?
> I want somebody to love.

Would you believe in a love at first sight?
Yes, I'm certain that it happens all the time.
What do you see when you turn out the light?
I can't tell you, but I know it's mine.
Oh I get by with a little help from my friends.
Do you need anybody?
I just need somebody to love.
Could it be anybody?
I want somebody to love.
I get high with a little help from my friends.
Yes, I get by with a little help from my friends,
With a little help from my friends.[10]

The irony surfaces upon close examination of the song's lyrics. The title and refrain posit unity and unbreakable friendship, yet each verse presents doubt and uncertainty. Written in dialogue form, the verses highlight situations when friendship might be in doubt and suggest ways of dealing with those dilemmas. When would/could a friend leave you and what would you do under those circumstances? If the singer "gets by with a little help from his friends" why does s/he repeat, "I just need somebody to love," inferring that s/he does not feel love from the friends. Ironically, this somebody to love that s/he needs could, perhaps, be anybody. The whole song, though superficially light, questions the nature of friendship and whether such a concept actually exists. A further irony is that this song about friendship was first recorded on the ***Lonely** Hearts Club* album (my emphasis). The irony and doubt that the song highlights regarding "friends" become Néstor Caballero's leitmotif in *Con una pequeña ayuda de mis amigos* and help him to suggest that same irony and doubt as the backbone of Venezuela's relationship with the United States.[11]

Like Rengifo, Caballero marks his intertext paratextually. The title, the sixties context of the play, and the hippy reunion, all force reader/spectator to recognize the intertextual connection. However, the friends' rocky relationships in the play urge receptors to reflect upon and question the meaning of both texts because, rather than the friendship suggested by the song's/play's title, betrayal overshadows the context of the play. The friends deceive each other and they betray themselves. As the friends meet in present time in El Tigre's garage, they nostalgically reflect upon the sixties—a time that initiated both their personal friendships and their nation's "friendship" with the United States. Examining the relationships between this group of friends in the text will expose how these relationships question Venezuela's national interests and its ties to an imperialistic "friend."

The six characters that form this circle of friends are disloyal to their own interests and to those of their friends. Rather than become an artist, his real passion, for example, Alvaro, became an English teacher. Abandoning his own language, Alvaro spends his life teaching the language of the other. Beyond this professional sellout, he has been a perpetual traitor on a personal level as well. In the sixties, he gave classes in the art of betrayal to his friend Gilberto; Alvaro wooed and courted all the girls in school and when Gilberto expressed interest in Sulay, Alvaro helped him attract her in exchange for Gilberto teaching him to play baseball. After becoming a better baseball player than Gilberto, though, Alvaro deceived him and stole Sulay from him (1024–25). In the present time, Alvaro continues to have an affair with Sulay, Gilberto's wife; his betrayal began before Sulay and Gilberto's marriage, in the sixties, but continues on into the present even after Gilberto and Sulay have been married for many years. During the reunion, in the present day, Sulay and Alvaro sneak away from their "friends" (her husband Gilberto is among them) and kiss in the bathroom (1004–6). In two other scenes they make love. Nonetheless, even though Alvaro is audacious enough to have such a blatant extramarital affair with Sulay, he is a coward. When Sulay finally reveals their affair to her husband and threatens to leave him, Alvaro says, "We can postpone the question until tomorrow" (1044). In an earlier scene he had also hesitated, "No, no. Wait. It is better . . . wait. Later" (1038).[12]

Gilberto, Sulay's husband, is also a phony. He had entered the guerrillas as a youth, to fight against his government. Ironically, he is now part of that government, in charge of the Brigade Against Organized Delinquency, having switched loyalties when then-president Caldera had ordered that all guerrillas be killed (1005). He had betrayed himself and his revolutionary interests to gain power; however, as police commissioner he misuses his power by publicly abusing all his friends, including his wife.[13]

Moreover, Gilberto's power as a government official should be based on knowledge of his country's history and position in the world. However, Gilberto admits that he never cared about Venezuelan history, yet he decided to join the police, the representatives and enforcers of that history (983).[14] As a police officer, a member of the government, he should know his country's history so that he can understand and enforce its laws. He pretends to do this by criticizing and abusing everyone who is not totally supportive of his or his government's ways: Saturno, Alvaro, Sulay. He blindly supports Venezuelan interests and abuses everyone who expresses dissent. Yet, even though his government supports U.S. intervention in Venezuela, he is more aligned with Fidel Castro than the United States. He is completely two-faced in every realm of his life: toward his friends, in his knowledge of his country's history and present situation, and in his "support" of his government. In a satirical, humorous scene he confesses to Fidel that he hates Alvaro, the English teacher (1022). Although he may have reason to hate Alvaro, his abuses do not end with him or with Sulay.[15] In the end Gilberto totally abuses his power: taking out his gun he terrorizes and then, perhaps, finally kills his wife Sulay. The open ending of the play does not allow receptors any certainty as to the final outcome.

Each character betrays him or herself and, even when not abused by others, the character inflicts tremendous self-abuse. Chata's self-abuse with drugs and alcohol leads her to vomit during the hippies' reunion. Even though she wishes to lead a different life, she is incapable of stopping her self-destructing behavior.[16] Saturno, too, allows himself to be stepped on by everyone. He pursues a homosexual relationship with Tigre, even though the latter kicks him out of his apartment, calls him a fag, and tries to embarrass him in front of others. The completely nude and weeping Saturno streaks through the park where Gilberto is attempting to seduce Chata (1000–1003). Ironically, however, we discover that the pathetic and two-faced Tigre had, in fact, had sexual relations with Saturno even though he denies it to both Saturno and himself (1015–22).[17] Others, too, abuse Saturno and, as in his relationship with Tigre, he lets them take advantage of him as well.

Sulay, a female character based on an actual friend and actress from Caballero's youth, is the only character that attempts to remain loyal to her past self.[18] Her main goal throughout the play is to plan a successful hippies' reunion as a way to turn back the hands of time and erase the horrible events that have taken place since the sixties. Sulay's life has been marked by death: the untimely death of her brother Tigre, who was killed in a motorcycle accident while trying to find his "América"; the tragic death of her only baby, Eva; and, finally, the death of her father, whose wake is the impetus for her to organize the hippies' reunion. Sulay dedicates herself to planning this reunion as a way to examine her friendships and to propose "the rescue of our Age" (1013). She longs to return to the sixties because it was a time when friendship seemed different and when the friends (and nation) might have made alternate choices. She believes that by defining their friendships and their choices of the past, they might see a glimmer of hope for the future.

The friends struggle to define friendship. In a philosophical moment, Saturno relates friendship to the ancient Greeks with undertones of homosexuality. Tigre, on the other hand, cannot begin to define the word. He stumbles, "Friendship . . . friendship. (*He sits, solemnly.*) Friendship is . . . for friends. One is a friend and . . . s/he's a friend" (998). The characters attempt to be "friends" but, ironically, their relationships are marked by betrayal, deceit, abuse, violence, and death. This same relationship holds true with regard to the nation. The friendship and amorous intrigues in the play are symbolic of the love/hate relationship between Venezuela and the United States. In an e-mail interview with Caballero, the playwright affirms that for him, "The hippy movement of the sixties was not a copy of the hippy movement of the north but rather a Caribbean attempt to channel the anguish that was meant to fly around a planet dominated by North American imperialism" (January 2002). The hippy reunion is a mask behind which to examine differences between the two "friends" and to express Venezuela's frustration over the United States' political, economic, and social colonization of it.

In *Con una pequeña ayuda de mis amigos,* both the intertextual relationship and the spatial construction connect past with present, suggesting that the relationships Venezuela formed in the past continue to haunt its present. At the same time, the play's spatial design suggests a multidimensional, global configuration of space that depicts the complexity of Venezuela's national identity, by highlighting the friction between local and global interests. As M. Kearney establishes, "Globalization entails a shift from two-dimensional Euclidian space with its centers and peripheries and sharp boundaries, to a multi-dimensional global space with unbounded, often discontinuous and interpenetrating subspaces" (Vertovec and Cohen 1999, 522). Caballero's spatial script depicts this problematic global spatial configuration but, at the same time, presents it as bound up within the local: the park in Caracas, a character's garage/room, a city bus. The spaces in the script move the plot in labyrinthine fashion, connecting time frames (1960s, 1980s, and the present day) but the action is stagnant, going nowhere. The characters are trapped within this space, these spaces, but they have not progressed at all.

Similarly, the song/play title and the sixties' context reinforce the playwright's message; it is a metaphor for world influence on Venezuela that continues to mark individual and nation, culturally, politically, economically, and psychologically. In the text there are both blatant and less obvious portrayals of the Venezuelan nation coupled with hints at how individual characters define their nation. The Beatles' song, a global phenomenon that had marked a universal worldview is pulled into this local Venezuelan set. Characters are torn between that global worldview and their own local self-image(s). Gilberto, for example, prefers to emphasize his country's indigenous roots; he believes that Sun and Moon control the earth. Gilberto says "(*With rage*) The tides are the ascent and descent of the water level of the sea, that is achieved alternatively and periodically by the influence that the Sun and the Moon have on the Earth . . . From that point forward, I could not learn anything else" (981). His nostalgia for an indigenous cosmology seeks a higher understanding of Venezuela's current political and economic situation in order to determine the "natural" order of things.[19] While it might seem that he is just referring to nature's pull on the tides, the fact that Sun, Moon, and Earth begin with capital letters and the "historical" context within which he expresses this, emphasize their connection to the indigenous gods of the past. Tigre, too, reflects on this link with the indigenous gods as essential to his own definition of America: "Yes, America," he states, "I am going to Jauja, to Macchu Picchu . . . to Patagonia" (1022). His idyllic homeland looks toward South America rather than North, but, tragically, in searching for his "America," he dies.

In Caballero's play, because of the Beatles' song, the sixties connection to the present does more than evoke the failed utopia of Woodstock, it also posits a Venezuela that is fearful of losing its independence and identity because it has betrayed itself and sold out to global interests. Moreover, even though the Beatles were an English group, the characters' many derogatory comments about the United States and its role in Venezuela, as well as the play's references to the similarities between Venezuela's position vis-à-vis the United States, and that of the situation in Vietnam in the sixties, present globalization in Venezuela as symbolic of U.S. imperialism. The play's sixties facade directs us to a time when, according to Akhil Gupta, between 1956 and 1961:

> There were increased efforts to forge unity among Third World countries due to the escalation of Cold War tensions and growing U.S. military involvement in places as diverse as Cuba, Vietnam, the Congo, and Laos. For Third World nation-states . . . these actions only highlighted the fragility of their sovereignty. Superpower conflict and direct military intervention were grave external threats to the nationalistic goal of preserving and consolidating their independence.
>
> (Vertovec and Cohen 1999, 505)

While U.S. military forces never actually invaded Venezuela, it is clear from Tigre's comment, "Giant U.S. planes fired three hundred tons of bombs over North Vietnam. This happens every day. We are also Vietnam," that general sentiment views the United States' interests in Venezuela as antinational (979). As Vietnam was abused and ravaged in the controversial conflict of the sixties, a conflict that marked tremendous international and national turmoil and changed the course of history for both Vietnam and the United States, so, too, Caballero's play suggests, is Venezuela allowing itself to be exploited by United States infiltration.

Ironically, though, Venezuela's relationship with the United States has, from its beginnings, been a paradoxical construct. In the 1890s, Venezuela sought out U.S. intervention in its affairs to help the nation protect its border with Guayana from British invasion and to maintain its control over the Orinoco River. But, as Judith Ewell suggests, "By no means were Venezuelan relations with the United States to be harmonious during the next century" (1984, 28). Venezuela needed help from its U.S. "friends" to secure its territory and waterways. Moreover, Venezuela encouraged U.S. investments and commerce within its borders to further counter "the traditional dominance of the British and Germans" (Ewell 1984, 29). The "friends" that Venezuela chose to help it in the past, later, ironically, betrayed its national interest through the exploitation of petroleum.[20]

The sixties' turmoil and political unrest is not the only indication of the state of the Venezuelan nation in *Con una pequeña ayuda de mis amigos.* The play suggests that present-day Venezuela is marked by exploitation, Yankee imperialism, social class inequality, and the dominance of transnational companies. In a sixties' scene in the park where Gilberto will later sexually abuse Chata, he explains to her his reasons for joining the guerrillas, "We cannot continue to allow transnational companies to exploit the increased value of our workers. We cannot continue to allow Yankee imperialism to subjugate us. That the means of production continue in the hands of a few. No, no we cannot allow it!" (994). Present-day Venezuela continues to tolerate excessive U.S. abuses and, ironically, the Venezuelan government spends more on U.S. interests than on its own needs. After attacks on General Motors, Sears, and the American Embassy, Caballero's characters mock the fact that the police and the National Guard choose to give extra protection to "such important enterprises" (982).[21] The characters see, as Gupta suggests, that "economic dependence, indebtedness, and cultural imperialism are as great, if not greater dangers to sovereignty as military invasion" and that, "the control exerted by multinational Corporations in particular sets severe limits on both the extent and form of nationalism practiced in different parts of the world today" (Vertovec and Cohen 1999, 511–13).

Oil interests in Venezuela are, perhaps, the most problematic source of tension, frustration, and national poverty, and Caballero's characters see the irony of this quite clearly. Oil was discovered in Venezuela and began to be exploited in the second decade of the nineteenth century. According to Ewell, even at that time, "the President had to be skillful enough not only to dominate the state caudillos, but also to treat skillfully with the international oil companies and their home governments" (1984, 9). This caused corruption as the president left the running of the companies and oil interests to his "friends," family, and political allies. Petroleum-related decisions made in the 1920s affected and dominated the industry for the next half century (Ewell 1984, 57). Then dictator Juan Vicente Gómez struck an oil deal with the United States in 1922 and it was called "The Best Law in Latin America" (Ewell 1984, 57). Under this law, companies enjoyed low taxes, little pressure, no Venezuelan congressional input, and no restrictions on the amount of land they could hold. The United States received most of the oil concessions in Venezuela.

As in Venezuelan history, Caballero's play suggests that there was much resentment in Venezuela over U.S. control of oil and its production and that this resentment was not only directed toward the United States, but also toward the Venezuelan government for "catering to the foreigners."[22] In the play, Tigre affirms that "Rafael Caldera, President Elect of Venezuela, asked Richard Nixon for greater access to Venezuelan oil" (982). Later, Sulay and Tigre express together that "Caldera is satisfied that Nixon is in control of the petroleum problem" (983). The language they use, with the repetition of Venezuela(n) in the first statement (Venezuelan president/ Venezuelan oil), and the idea that the government is *satisfied that Nixon is in control* of the oil *problem,* in the second, emphasizes the sarcastic and ironic way in which Venezuelans may now view the situation. Caldera was president of Venezuela from 1969–74; however, their use of the past tense in the first criticism and present tense in the second suggests that the resentment continues into the present day.

The foreigners and the Venezuelan government that backs them are not really "friends" and, as Ewell suggests, "oil exploitation contributed to a rising feeling of nationalism among Venezuelans" (1984, 65). The characters in Caballero's play are searching for a way to come together, a defining thread, hence the hippies' reunion. They continuously look back and reminisce nostalgically about an idyllic past. The passengers on the bus where Saturno is proselytizing suggest that things were better before, under General Pérez Jiménez "In General Pérez Jiménez's time, no one was walking around like a vagrant" (1030). In some ways, things were better then in Venezuela; there was marked prosperity, some growth in manufacturing, some urban development, and less dependence on oil exporting; however, during the Pérez Jiménez dictatorship censorship was high and student protests were prevalent (Ewell 1984, 114).[23] Clearly, looking back at the past, whether from the sixties toward the fifties, or from the present day toward the sixties, distorts the "real" image of the nation.

The play also includes criticism of capitalism and its senseless spending. Saturno expresses astonishment and disbelief that the U.S. government is offering twenty-five thousand dollars to stop the hijackings to Cuba. At the same time, he makes a joke of it, and one senses that he could think of other "useless" ways to throw away that money. "Twenty-five thousand dollars! Can you imagine? Twenty-five thousand dollars to those who help stop the hijacking of planes to Cuba! Twenty-five thousand dollars, with all that money I can buy myself a piece of land to start a commune" (990).

The play suggests that present-day Venezuela is suffering from a great many self-inflicted wounds that continue to impede its progress, stability, and economic growth. Most of those problems, according to Caballero's script, have to do with a flawed relationship with "friends," a colonial relationship that was cemented in the past, even prior to the sixties period evoked in the play. At the same time, however, not all the problems were self-inflicted. The earthquake of 1967 is also evoked. On a seemingly normal day in the sixties, Chata's parents had sent her to the store on a phony mission in order to secure some amorous time alone together. As they were making love and she was out of the apartment, the earthquake hit. When she returned, "the building was no longer there . . . it had collapsed . . . it had fallen down in their love" (1040). On that fateful day that changed her life, her parents died in the earthquake. As it totally ruined Chata's life and caused her to spin into an orbit of self-abuse and self-destruction, it also continues to cause distress in an already impoverished and politically unstable nation.[24]

Ironically, the friend's help is not always a contribution. Like the friends in the play, Venezuela allows the United States to abuse it. Rather than look inside themselves to fix their individual lives, they look to their "friends," yet, the friends provide no help. Their nation, too, has turned to the United States for help with everything, from Alvaro learning to build a radio from *Popular Mechanics* in English

(980), to Peter Sellers's proclamation that "marijuana is safe" (981). The nation has never firmly said "no" to U.S. intervention.[25] The Venezuelan government has seemed to support U.S. interests in the nation and, most often, citizens display indifference toward their economic and political colonization. Elías Pino Iturrieta, professor of history at the Universidad Central de Venezuela, suggests that "All this about the indifference of the majority of Venezuelans . . . forms a climate that could be troubling for whomever might wish to take interest in this society" (Petkoff 2000, 60). The friends in the play abuse each other and the abuses lead to insecurity and greater self-abuse. Similarly, Venezuela as a nation invited U.S. exploitation and promotes it with its own internal self-abuses. Along with U.S. political and military aid, North American companies came into the country in the earlier part of the twentieth century. North American industries took over oil production and never left. Oil was Venezuela's greatest hope for economic and political prosperity; nonetheless, Venezuela's government never kicked out the foreigners, nor took control of their own resources. Even after the Venezuelan government realized that U.S. control was no longer optimal, they continued to tolerate, even support, the abuse. Instead, like Alvaro's desire to postpone the discussion of his relationship with Sulay, Venezuela has chosen to postpone the difficult question of U.S. interests in the nation and chooses to avoid confrontation with the North.[26]

Caballero carries the irony through to the ending of his play. In the final scene, Tigre plays the title song, "With a Little Help from my Friends," as the friends continue to struggle with the tensions between them, caressing each other, clenching fists at each other, dancing with each other, embracing and hating each other simultaneously. Gilberto, while dancing with Sulay, points the pistol to her head and, during the final blackout, "a big shot is heard," suggesting, possibly, that he kills her (1046–47). The final words, "an epoch has died" (ha muerto una época) are in the stage directions, not articulated, except by the author. The reader/spectator might think, as do some critics, that with Sulay's death, the sixties' idealism dies too. However, irony continues to reign through the final scene. As Gilberto had expressed earlier, "I feel like I have spent my life on the same page" (983). Ironically, nothing has changed at all. The epoch of troubled friendship with the United States has not died and that is precisely the problem.

The song "With a Little Help from my Friends" is more than just a way to remember the sixties in Caballero's play. A closer look at the lyrics reveals that irony is the predominant trope. As Michel Riffaterre suggests, we should not "assume that intertexts are just themes and motifs. In terms of content and even form, intertext and theme may indeed coincide, but they differ radically from each other in terms of their impact on the reader" (1990, 74).

The irony of the song is emphasized and exaggerated in Caballero's play. The friends evoked in the lyrics are taken in an ironic sense; friends should help each other, but the play suggests that, whether on an individual or national level, these friends do not. The play searches for the meaning of friendship on the personal and the national levels. In the sixties as well as in the present of Caballero's play, these friends drink together, get high together, and yes, get by together, but their relationships are tenuous and filled with insecurities. As Teodoro Petkoff suggests, at the turn of the twenty-first century, on the national level, "It is not a coincidence that . . . the main problem . . . is that of insecurity, and insecurity generally demands an authoritarian response, that is to say, that it demands a very rough exertion of repressive power" (2000, 61). For this reason, Caballero's characters allow their friends to abuse them and they abuse themselves. Similarly, Venezuela has suffered the abuses of many dictatorships that have, ironically, been supportive of U.S. exploitation, if not on the political level, then certainly on the economic level.

Caballero uses this intertext to show that these Venezuelan friends, rather than really help each other, betray themselves and each other at every turn. He, like Rengifo, paratextually marks his intertext from the outset by making it the title of his play. The reader/spectator is then bound to acknowledge the intertext and decipher its code. On the surface, this intertext functions to highlight the nostalgia for the 1960s and the relationship between these friends. But a deeper reading of the play, one that analyzes the characters' relationships to each other and to their space(s), directs reader/spectator back to the song, the intertext, to search for a meaning that more closely parallels the play's script. The intertextual interpretation emphasizes an alternative meaning that is latent in both the song and in Caballero's play; rather than focus on the friendship, the intertext points out the betrayal at the root of these individual and national relationships. Intertextuality allows Caballero to create this twist in theme because the irony of friendship, not friendship itself, is an important part of the song.

In addition, through intertextuality Caballero shifts the focus from this small group of friends and their personal relationships to betrayal on the national level. These friends abuse each other like the United States abuses and exploits Venezuela, but both Venezuela and its "friends" allow the abuse to continue. *Con una pequeña ayuda de mis amigos* tragically and ironically posits Venezuela as a self-destructing nation, a nation that, like Sulay and her friends, deceives itself and its own interests. As Sulay posits, however, one settles for these relationships simply because, "One gets used to it."

Caballero's plays seems to suggest, as does journalist Teodoro Petkoff, that part of Venezuela's problem is that it always looks back to the past for its solutions instead of modernizing around a riskier, but more economically and politically secure future. Even under Chávez, Petkoff affirms that this looking back is caused by a Venezuelan inferiority complex. He states, "There is a human drama behind the whole business [of inferiority]—behind the idea of always looking back that turns into a political drama" (2000, 45).

Like Caballero's characters, Venezuela's political and economic relationship with the United States has been marked by insecurity, doubt, indifference, and betrayal. Nonetheless, both Caballero and Petkoff suggest that Venezuelans continuously look back at a past that haunts them. Rather than destroy that past, or use the errors of the past to improve the future, they ironically repeat the same mistakes, trying to recreate the past, as does Sulay with her hippies' reunion. As the play's ending reveals, they do not destroy the past, but rather, they continue on the same page without questioning their destiny.

Through their business ties and oil interests, Venezuela and the United States have a type of transnational relationship. Armand Mattelart maintains that "The transnationalization process creates an appeal for increasing similar, ecumenical and universal values . . . 'a new planetary consciousness,' a new 'harmony,' 'a new world unity,' and a new consensus" (Brennan 1990, 46). While that world unity, harmony, and consensus may seem possible for the domineering nations, Caballero shows us that the facade of peace, love, and unity that this "exchange" superficially presents becomes a deeply disturbing, antinational myth that rips apart individuals and nation. The sixties' intertext, with its inherent contradictions between the peace, love, and flower power cultures and those of Vietnam, drugs, and deception allows Caballero to show that transnationalism, in this sense, is far from beneficial for the colonized partner.

With this play, Caballero proposes that Venezuela has been unable to change. Gina Lambright and Nicholas van de Walle argue that "the degree to which developing countries are harmed by economic globalization depends to a large extent on their ability to adapt and respond to changes" (Aulakh and Schechter 2000, 135). The ability to change, according to these authors, is contingent upon three factors: high levels of state capacity, a low level of social fragmentation, and a state tradition of well-functioning links between various societal groups (135). With its history of ineffective dictatorships, uneven class structure, and tense social links, Venezuela has a low level of state capacity and a high level of social fragmentation; thus, as a nation, Venezuela has not been adequately able to adjust to globalization. In addition, nostalgia for a mythicized past paralyzes its national efforts to move forward independently.

As an artist, Néstor Caballero feels a sense of responsibility to raise the consciousness of Venezuelans who live in a nation filled with corruption and violence. The dangers that the average person faces just to see his plays performed inspire him as a consciousness raiser and as an artist. As a dramatist, Caballero urgently searches for a dramatic code with which to depict his nation:

> A little bit of luck, a lot of patience and an inflamed sense of nation is necessary, because it is very difficult to be a playwright in a country that, thanks to globalization, to the foolishness and corruption of national politicians, the issue that haunts us daily is survival . . . But, above all, I place myself beside that spectator who had the grand and dangerous idea to leave his/her home to see my text performed, in spite of the kidnappings, the armed robbery, the murder by some angry delinquent. Then I say to myself, please, that poor person who today risked his/her very life to come to the theater, s/he doesn't deserve this, I must write better. (E-mail interview, January 2002)

Indeed, writing and performing theater in Venezuela are acts of faith, as Tabuas suggests. Caballero's play uses intertextuality to skillfullly depict a nation struggling against itself to enter into modernity and to create a play for a "national" theater that is working to do the same. Like his teacher César Rengifo before him, Néstor Caballero voices awareness of the profound tensions and serious shortcomings of his people and his nation, along with a firm belief in the latent power residing within them.

These two Venezuelan masters, each in his own way, highlight a foreign intertext to rescript and restage the problems, the practices, and the potential that dwell within their own national story.

3

Texts without Exit: Rewriting Argentina's Labyrinth

ARGENTINA HAS EXPERIENCED GREAT NATIONAL TURMOIL IN THE past thirty years. The Dirty War from 1976–83, the resultant censorship and forced national forgetting, and economic problems that began in the post-Proceso years but resurged and imploded in the late 1990s, have all destabilized the Argentine in the last three decades. Jean Graham-Jones (2000) and Diana Taylor (1997), among others, have described some of the political and cultural changes in Argentina in those years and have discussed the evolution of Argentine theater toward the end of the twentieth century. The plays in this chapter, written in the late 1990s, use intertextuality to combine a vanguardlike questioning of the aesthetic with a concern for the impact of national trauma on individuals and nation. Alicia Aisemberg and Adriana Libonati argue that, like their peers, these playwrights:

> are authors who distance themselves from the dominant formulas of realist-modern theatricality and their dramaturgy is tinted with an aesthetic tonality of postmodern intertext. Their texts place direct causal logic in a state of crisis; they fracture narration, they present broad self-reflective zones, they separate themselves from the psychological-realist verisimilitude in relation to characters, and they produce an unmasking of their intertextual character. They unbalance their semantics, which produces an increase in ambiguity, behind which appear oblique, obtuse, and multivoiced meanings.
>
> (2000, 77)

The intertexts these playwrights choose and the new directions in which they take them make their own plays revolutionary, both aesthetically and ideologically. The plays highlighted in this section create intertextual links not seen in the Mexican collagelike treatment or in the paratextual presentation of foreign intertexts marked in the Venezuelan plays. In one Argentine case presented here, that of Eduardo Pavlovsky's *Poroto* texts, I will show how the playwright creates, works off of, and rewrites his own intertexts and texts, each time revising the script, transforming the protagonist, and (re)presenting the national interpretation. On the other hand, Rafael Spregelburd's paratextual inscription of a medieval painting in his three plays of the *Heptalogía de Hieronymus Bosch* (*Heptalogy of Hieronymus Bosch*) only serves to shatter the receptor's potential grasp of the relationship between text and intertext. Unlike the Venezuelan scripts that pull reader/spectator into the (inter)texts in order to better understand the present text, Spregelburd's play uses the intertext to highlight what is absent from text(s), and to focus on the individual and the nation at the turn of a new century. Through the singularity of their language (Dubatti 2000, 7), these playwrights create unique intertextual connections to invent innovative dramatic modes that present an "objective" view of Argentina at the end of the twentieth century.

Point of View and the Becoming of Pavlovsky's Porotos

> What the actor interprets is never a character . . . it is a theme.
>
> —Eduardo Pavlovsky, *Estética de la multiplicidad* (*The Aesthetics of Multiplicity*), 205

> To become the spectator in the very action in which one participates presupposes a work whose protagonist becomes the reader of his/her own adventure enacted by him/herself.
>
> —Lucien Dällenbach, *The Mirror in the Text,* 90

Eduardo Pavlovsky has a long history of theatrical production in Argentina, beginning with the publication of his first work, *Somos* (*We are*), in 1962. Since then, he has published more than twenty plays, included in three volumes of his complete works, and tomes of theoretical writing about theater. His work as an actor has also molded Argentine theater. Along with director-friend Norman Briski and actress Susy Evans, Pavlovsky has performed many of his plays' key roles. His only novel to date, *Dirección contraria* (*The Opposite Direction*), stands out as well, because of its theatrical qualities, as I will show.

Pavlovsky's work as a psychologist has impacted both his theatrical and theoretical writings. He is one of the world's foremost authorities on what has come to be called psychodrama, a theory and practice that uses drama as therapy to help "real" traumatized patients and also uses therapy in drama on fictional characters.[1] Jorge Dubatti, too, sees the reciprocal role between theater and psychoanalysis in Pavlovsky and argues that "On various occasions Pavlovsky has affirmed that it was not exactly psychoanalysis that came to influence his theater; rather it was theater that came to indicate to him a therapeutic possibility in dramatizations" (1997, 48). In *Psicodrama: Cuándo y por qué dramatizar* (*Psychodrama: When and Why to Dramatize*) (1985), Pavlovsky adheres to a philosophy of using theatrical techniques to cure patients, by proposing that "real" patients imagine characters with whom they can identify and then invent spontaneous dialogues with them. He argues, "It is proposed that the participants imagine characters with whom they will tend to identify. Each member (of the therapy group) invents or creates his/her character. It is a true challenge to the imagination. After a prolonged period of five or ten minutes in which each participant works out his/her character, they are asked to interact spontaneously, creating improvised dialogues" (1985, 31). As I will show, the playwright uses similar psychoanalytical strategies in his theatrical texts as well.

Pavlovsky's theater extends psychological analysis to the Argentine cultural and political situation and many of his plays include metatheatrical comments on traumatizing historical situations, mostly pertaining to the Argentina of the pre- and post-Proceso years and of the Dirty War itself (1976–83). Plays such as *El señor Galíndez* (*Mr. Galindez*), *El señor Laforgue* (*Mr. Laforgue*), and *Telarañas* (*Webs*) inscribe the mechanisms of power, violence, and oppression into the fabric of the play-text.[2] Other works, like *Pablo, Potestad* (*Power*), and *Paso de dos* (*Two Step*) place their emphasis on the capriciousness and evil residing within human nature, whereby the abusers mask their evil behind normal facades.

Pavlovsky's more recent theater continues to incorporate these psychoanalytical and political tensions. However, these tensions become a backdrop against which he plays with questions about the nature of art and the essence of textuality and intertextuality. Critics have shown that *El cardenal* (*The Cardinal*), published in 1992, was not represented as such; Pavlovsky rewrote it and published it as *Rojos globos rojos* (*Red Red Balloons*), which premiered onstage in August 1994.[3] Like the works in question here, *El cardenal* was already intertextual before the author went on to create his own linking intertext (*Rojos globos rojos).* According to Dubatti, "*El cardenal* originates in a collaborative project with Miguel Dao in relation to Francis Bacon's painting" and it also has explicit relationships with Shakespeare's *The Tragedy of Coriolanus,* with Beckett's *Endgame,* and with certain scenes from Ionesco's *The Bald-Headed Soprano* (1997, 34). In his earliest theatrical texts, Pavlovsky had displayed an interest in and awareness of intertextuality, but the *El cardenal/Rojos globos rojos* connection marks the first time that the playwright creates and plays off his own intertexts.[4] The three Pavlovsky texts in my study follow and expand on this tradition.

In his introduction to *Poroto: Historia de una táctica* (1996), Pavlovsky questions his own text's genre.[5] On the one hand, he writes, "*Poroto* was visualized by me . . . I realized that it was not a theatrical text—but rather a literary one—almost a short story." On the other, he argues, "I PERCEIVED theater in the literary text—but I had the feeling that I was never going to know who was speaking this text that I was sketching" (3). My own first experience with this "text," however, was clearly theatrical. As part of the small, but filled to capacity audience at the Teatro Calibán in Buenos Aires in August 1999, I, like the other spectators that evening, wondered what I was watching. Aware of my role as spectator because of the layout of the theater, the proximity of the actors, the velocity and intensity of the actions before me, and the noise(s) that engulfed me, I struggled to interpret what I was witnessing. Was this a monologue or a dialogue or some combination of the two? Was Poroto, the title character, actually the protagonist, or were the actors (or the playwright) playing some sort of game?[6] The vertiginous performance I viewed raised more questions than answers for this spectator. Nonetheless, there was no doubt; this was theater!

Pavlovsky, however, complicates this text and any interpretation of it when, in the introduction to the written text, he reveals his indebtedness to intertextuality, by admitting that, as unique as his text may be, *Poroto* is an amalgam of other texts and contexts. Miguel Angel Giella explains further intertextual relationships between *Poroto* and Pavlovsky's *El cardenal* and relates intertextual connections in Pavlovsky to performance because "the uniqueness of each representation" makes the actors, "through their very corporeal movement, modifiers of the text" (1998, 148). Amalia Gladhart, too, has theorized that "performance is intrinsically contingent and unstable, and citational in the widest sense" (2000, 14). As texts inadvertently or intentionally incorporate other texts so too does each performance "rewrite" earlier versions of text(s). Through performance the pre-text(s) are linked, modified, and transformed in each show.

Yet, above and beyond these intertextual links Pavlovsky creates his own intertexts to the *Poroto* play: a novel, *Dirección contraria* (*Opposite Direction*) (1997) and another play, *Poroto: Nueva versión para el teatro* (*Poroto: New Version for the Theater*) (1999), based on the performance script. Published after *Poroto: Historia de una táctica* (1996), these two works are both a repetition of the original and an expansion on it.[7]

Pavlovsky's introduction to his written text points out the transgression of genre that marks this work and, at the same time, questions the blurry boundary between narrative and theatrical discourses in general. Additionally, the emphasis on creating the text, signaled by the author's reflections, questions the authority of the playwright and accentuates the role of reader/spectator in the creative process. By dialoguing with his own (play)texts, Pavlovsky creates a metatext, through which he begins to interpret his text and demands that the reader/viewer do the same. The receptor then analyzes the textual transformations and extracts both formal and thematic meanings that are obscured in each individual text. Of course, not every receptor will know about or understand the connection between these three texts. Not every reader/spectator will be aware of or study the intertextual connections between the three. Although one can certainly understand the play on some level without awareness of these links between the three texts, reading the texts against each other and charting their differences opens up a new reading on Argentina and the Argentine, which does not necessarily surface without this intertextual knowledge. As I will show, Pavlovsky's three texts evolve from the story of a fragmented individual to the story of a collective fragmentation, which includes the receptor. As characters and receptor (who also becomes both a witness of and an actor in the "story") are presented with real events from Argentina's past, they struggle to interpret those events and witness first their individual, and then their collective, fragmentation.

In this section, I analyze how intertextuality works in Pavlovsky's *Poroto* texts and I interpret its function. I examine why Pavlovsky first questions the genre of his "play" *Poroto: Historia de una táctica,* and then later rewrites it in "narrative" form (*DC*) and then again in "dramatic" form (*Nueva versión*). Pavlovsky's intertexts serve both dramatic and ideological functions (Villegas 2000, 102) in that they force the reader to reflect on the very nature of textuality. They question what makes up a text and what constitutes narrativity as well as what it means to be articulated as a dramatic text. Second, Pavlovsky's "play" serves a profound ideological function, which is revealed through these intertextualities. While it seems like *Poroto* is about a man, an individual on the border of madness, struggling to find himself, the changes between the three texts reveal a national subject in the making. In other words, as the texts are transposed into other versions, Poroto (the title character) is also transformed; he and his receptors are becoming aware of what it means to be Argentine.

(Inter)textuality and the Poroto Texts

The three texts are very different but, at the same time, they are quite similar. Each tells a story of Poroto, his friend Leo, whom he has not seen for many years, and Willy (virtually absent from *Historia,* Willy is the waiter in the *Nueva versión* only). *Dirección contraria* is the most unique of the three texts in that it expands the story, adds new episodes, includes new characters, and gives a deeper perspective on Poroto and his friends. Even though it reads like a novel, however, it opens with the *Poroto Historia* text in its entirety. If *Poroto Historia* is theater, then how does *Dirección contraria* differ, since it begins with the entire "play"? On the other hand, *Poroto historia* could be narrative. If so, then how does it relate to the "play" *Nueva versión?*

While the introduction to *Historia* comments on the text, the intertextual relationship between the three versions of *Poroto* does not serve as a commentary; rather, it expands, amplifies, and rewrites the text. In other words, as I will discuss, there are places where the texts are reproduced verbatim. For the most part, when there are changes between texts, they are of two types: (a) they add new information about the characters or context; or (b) they change the point of view of the text and thus expand it and open it up to a new interpretation.

Since these texts' genre is questioned from the outset, Gérard Genette's (1997) theory on textual transformations might aid our interpretation. According to Genette, when a narrative is transformed into the dramatic mode, there are several types of potential formal transformations that might occur. First, the texts would be subject to irregularities in the temporal order, which might include anachronisms or simply a temporal reshuffling. Between these three texts, some temporal transformations do occur. *Historia,* as the hypotext, is written as one long stream-of-consciousness-type narrative or monologue. The action seems to occur in one day, or even one hour, the length of the reading, since it involves one encounter between these friends, one conversation.

The transposition from *Historia* to *DC* adds narrative, dialogue, and action to the text and, in this way, transforms the temporal structure. The action in the narrative could not take place in one day. The events occur in Poroto, Leo, or Willy's past and present, and they also evoke their future. The bar scene is just one piece of *DC* and though it appears at the very beginning of the text, it is not necessarily the first event chronologically. In fact, it may occur after the final chapter of *DC,* upon Poroto's and Leo's return from exile (although that is not entirely clear) and it would seem to occur after Poroto's episode in medical school, which forms a later chapter. Most definitely, though, it occurs before the letter from a female admirer, which Poroto receives near the end of the *DC* text.

In *Nueva versión,* the temporal order is further transposed. The bar setting and the encounter between Poroto and Leo are similar to those of *Historia* and the beginning of *DC;* however, there are insertions in the *Nueva versión,* such as the initial Unidad 0, narrated by a Voice, which describes Poroto's encounter with his mother (this opening scene of *Nueva versión* appears near the end of *DC,* right after his letters to and from the female admirer). Unidad 1, a scene that reveals another significant temporal transposition, follows Unidad 0; in that scene the *parroquiano*'s internal monologue exposes his troubled relationship to his mother. These two pre-scenes, both excluded from *Historia* and the latter excluded from *DC,* alter the temporal structure of the text. The action in *Nueva versión* no longer occurs in one sitting and it moves the text beyond the lifetime of encounters between Poroto and his friends; the temporal structure, characterization, and actions of the Unidades 0 and 1 make the text more about Argentina and its citizens and less about these individuals, as I will show.

These temporal transpositions also affect the pace of the narration, signaling Genette's second type of transformation. The two dramatic texts are read/performed at a dizzying pace. In the reading, one would find it difficult to put down the text, since there are no natural breaks (especially in *Historia*). In the performance, spectators must turn their head from side to side quickly in order to "move" with the dialogue and the characters.

On the other hand, while *DC* has these characteristics of pacing in its beginning pages (the direct imitation of the *Historia* portion), in its later scenes, which work off the pre-text and supplement it, the pacing slows, as we read of Poroto's amorous adventures, his relationship to his father and mother, his encounter with Dr. Uriarte, the episodes with his uncle, his adventures as a medical student, and his final "flight" into exile. The chapters are subtitled to indicate their content and this also slows the pace of the narration.

In addition to the temporal transpositions, the shift in point of view is the most significant formal transposition that occurs within and between these texts. Genette argues that "narrative voice, who narrates, disappears entirely on stage . . . because the only dramatic viewpoint is that of the audience, who may, of course, direct and modulate their attention as they wish, but in a manner not susceptible to being programmed by the text" (1997, 280). Pavlovsky's strategies transform the point of view within each version and between them; thus showing how perspective flows from and between characters, narrators, and reader/spectator. I will closely examine these vacillating points of view because, as Boris Uspensky argues, "The structure of the artistic text may be described by investigating various points of view (different authorial positions from which the narration or description is conducted) and by investigating the relations between these points of view (their concurrence and nonconcurrence) and the possible shifts from one point of view to another, which in turn are connected with the study of the *function* of the different points of view in the text" (1973, 5). In Pavlovsky's texts the vacillating points of view function on both the dramatic and the ideological planes to transform the subject, content, and themes of the texts. For example, in *Historia,* third-person omniscient narration alternates with quasi-direct discourse. As I will show, this vacillation in point of view changes the protagonist from Poroto to Leo, who stands in for the reader/spectator. As Leo struggles to interpret Poroto (por-otro), the receptors, like Leo, also struggle to interpret their worlds. Analyzing the characters' reactions to their world (both their individual place in it and their reflections on events from their nation's past), the receptor learns important information about the relevance of those national events and their impact on Argentine citizens. Because the reader/spectator is now drawn into the text (Leo), the receptor reflects on his/her own reaction as well.

At first glance, the dialogues, the inner feelings of all characters, and the actions in *Historia* seem to be articulated by an omniscient and hyperperceptive narrator. This narrator describes every minute detail of the characters' movements, explains fragments of the friends' history, and documents their present encounter in the bar. The impersonal tone is supplemented by a stream-of-consciousness narration; sentences run together and there is no apparent "speaking" subject.

Centering on strategies of flight, the opening frames of *Historia* are recounted from a calculated, almost scientific perspective. The second paragraph introduces an interlocutor, but s/he too is unstable. "Each interlocutor was different and for each one alternative tactics were needed" (5). Poroto, the title character, finally emerges from within these first traces of a potential dialogue between the narrator (who is contemplating strategies of flight) and an unidentified interlocutor. It appears that the omniscient narrator will present, describe, and narrate the encounter between Poroto and his interlocutor(s) in a bar in Buenos Aires.

However, even though the omniscient narrator seems to be the prevailing voice in *Historia,* Pavlovsky plays with discursive strategies to question and change perspective in and on the text. Uspensky establishes that, on the phraseological plane, point of view can be determined and altered by changing the modes of discourse within the text. He argues that it is important to focus on examples of speech that are "neither direct nor indirect discourse, but quasi-direct discourse, a synthesis of both phenomena" (1973, 35). While most of the *Historia* text is presented from the point of view of the omniscient narrator, there are several instances in the text where the narrative mode shifts to a type of quasi-direct discourse. Uspensky defines this term as, "a phenomenon midway between direct speech and indirect speech, a phenomenon that permits transposition (by specific operations) into both direct and indirect speech" (36).

In *Historia* this is revealed when the third-person, omniscient narration converts to first-person monologue or dialogue in another voice, without the aid of quotation marks. At these times, this first-person perspective is probably not that of the narrator, and when the "voice" can be identified (and it is not always identifiable), it might be Poroto's or Leo's point of view. For example, after Poroto positions himself in his perfect seat by the door, the narrator recounts, "Suddenly (Poroto) felt the voice of Leo bursting in from behind: Poroto, dear Poroto over here! Come! Leo had seated himself at a back table and was having lunch" (7). In this instance, the narrator tells us what Poroto heard, and we assume that it is Leo who is calling Poroto over; however, there are no quotation marks separating the narrator's comments from those of Leo. Further on, though, the text does mark Leo's direct discourse through its use of quotes.

Leo's quasi-direct discourse is displayed in various forms: without any quotes, separated by quotation marks, or, sometimes, initiated by a quotation mark but not closed by one. Quasi-direct discourse is often juxtaposed with direct discourse in the text; thus marking it as different and intentional. Moreover, the alternating styles of discourse urge the receptor to pay closer attention to the text and thus reflect on the violence expressed in the passage and its effects on the protagonists. Since the quasi-direct discourse also changes the protagonist of the text, the new "narrator" becomes the victim of that violence. For example, as Leo and Poroto are conversing in the bar, the discourse changes suddenly from direct to quasi-direct:

—Poroto, dear Poroto I was so looking forward to seeing you
—Me too
—But you are so tight brother—so reserved I have to pull the words out of you with a corkscrew always so unexpressive like before what times!
I always remember the bomb do you remember I can never com-

> pletely forget about it—deep down it was a tragedy we didn't want to kill anyone they started fucking around wanting to check it out and it exploded on them . . . to hell with them for being idiots—to open a bomb you have to have the know-how . . . and they put in a lathe and they exploded . . . What amateurs! I was never so afraid in my life.
>
> An intense buzzing filled his head again. The memory of the bomb terrified him and he was on the brink of running but it would have been impossible to do so.
>
> (9)

The lines are intertwined; the first is most probably spoken by Leo (—Poroto, dear Poroto I was so looking forward to seeing you), although that is not clearly indicated in the text (why could it not be the narrator, or another bar patron?), and the second, "Me too" evidently answering the first, is uttered by Poroto. The quasi-direct discourse that follows, beginning with "But you are so tight brother" is assumed to be a continuation of Leo's speech; however, that is not clearly indicated. Again, the personal comments on Poroto's appearance and character, the reflections on the bomb, as well as the "intense buzzing that filled his head again," could indeed be expressed or thought by the narrator, Poroto, or Leo. All three utterances could be expressed in one narrative voice or a separate first-person narrator could express each one. The lines that follow this passage, "He had tried to erase the memory for years and suddenly he brought it back without warning, almost brutally, mercilessly, the buzzing in those moments didn't let him listen to Leo's words either" do seem to indicate that it is Leo who brought these terrible memories to Poroto, but there is confusion as to whether or not Leo actually expresses them, or if this is an interior monologue in Poroto's head (perhaps resulting from simply seeing Leo in the bar after twenty-two years).

Moreover, their discussion about the bombing, and their friend's suicide as a result of it, is followed by a quasi-direct discursive passage in which, again, it is difficult to determine who is speaking. Once again, it could be Poroto or Leo or the omniscient narrator. Moreover, because of *Historia*'s ambiguous discursive strategies, the omniscient narrator actually becomes an actor in the text, seemingly participating in Poroto and Leo's conversation. If that is the case, one could argue that there is yet a more removed omniscient narrator (maybe the author himself) overseeing the conversation and interactions of the three characters. It is possible that the following narration/dialogue could be in that twice-removed omniscient narrative voice as well or it could come from any of the three characters:

> When he killed himself *pause* you continued seeing each other *pause* how terrible you leave me speechless he was a sensational guy how he

> loved you how well you two got along how crazy Man he was from a Catholic family *pause* landowners from Buenos Aires province *pause* he was still married and the children *pause* how many did he have *pause* there are people who don't have the strength to live *pause*.
>
> You have no idea how much I cared about him—his eyes filled with tears—a high-class guy but so simple—so good-natured I remember when he invited us to the supermarket and bought us cold cuts do you remember—200 grams of salami 200 grams of stew meat 200 grams of curd 1/4 of Cuartirolo cheese we devoured everything . . . everything . . . every day . . .
>
> Are you crying Poroto? Tears are falling down your cheeks. I've never seen you cry Poroto. He began to observe with surprise that two big tears sprang from Leo's light blue eyes and were falling down his cheeks.
>
> (13–14)

It is impossible to determine who utters the above speech. Who are the "you continued seeing each other" for example? It could be Poroto and the dead man. Or it may have been Leo and the dead man (or Leo and Poroto). Furthermore, it is difficult to identify the speaking subject, the "I" of the rest of the monologue/dialogue. It is hard to determine who expresses, "you leave me speechless." It could be Poroto responding to Leo, or Leo himself, or even the narrator, reacting to the two men's conversation.

The most difficult ambiguity of the above passage, perhaps, revolves around the two men's reaction to their friend's death; who is crying and who asks about it. Does Leo or the narrator ask, "Are you crying Poroto? Tears are falling down your cheeks. I've never seen you cry Poroto." Furthermore, the juxtaposition of these ambiguous statements with the previous reference to the unknown man's suicide, as a result of a tragic bombing mistake in Argentina, focuses the attention on the word, "Porot(r)o" in the statements. In other words, "Estás llorando *por otro?* . . . Nunca te vi llorar *por otro*" (Are you crying for another [or through another]? I have never seen you cry for another [or through another])."[8] This emotional textual moment contrasts sharply with the cold, calculating tone of much of the text, and swings the emphasis from indifference to compassion and empathy. If it is not Poroto who is crying, but rather, another subject crying "por otro" ("for another" or "through another"), the reader/spectator questions who is the "you" that the text is addressing.[9]

In the following line, "He began to observe with surprise that two big tears sprang from Leo's light blue eyes and were falling down his cheeks" (14), again, it is hard to know who "began to observe" this. It could be Poroto. If so, then was he, too, crying or was Leo (or another) crying for another? Could it also be the omniscient narrator? If so, then a still outside narrative voice is describing that omniscient narrator's actions, and turns that omniscient narrator into a character in Pavlovsky's text. The prevalent quasi-direct discourse passages switch the emphasis from an outside narrator to the speaking subject(s) and at the same time, through the role of Leo, they move the reader/spectator into the text. As "Leo," "I read," I, too, am crying.

Since someone observes someone who sees tears streaming down Leo's cheeks, the receptor believes that Leo is crying. As Pavlovsky has possibly played with Poroto's name, so too has he played with Leo's name. *Leo,* "I read" in Spanish, stands in for the reader. The emphasis is on text, the text-making process, and interpretation, and therefore, through Leo, the reader is propelled into the prominent role of both interpreter and protagonist of this text, and within his/her new role, s/he too is deeply traumatized by the events described.

Leo has control over Poroto and thus, control over the text. Poroto recognizes Leo's control over him and the narrator remarks on this:

> The bathroom he thought the first thing he had to do was to get up from the table in the direction of the bathroom from the door of the bathroom he thought he could have a better view of the bar and upon returning to his table he would be able to control the situation, until now in the hands of his friend Leo, with more precision. The flight as preparation needed a minimum amount of control that with Leo seemed impossible given the irregular characteristics of his interventions.
>
> (11)

Poroto finds it impossible to move in the directions that he chooses because the reader has control. He had entered the bar, tried to choose the seat from which he could be in control of the outcome of the events, but Leo was always there first, even though Poroto had not seen him. Poroto's game of flight is played *por otro,* through another, in this case, Leo, who reads the main character's actions and (un)consciously controls them. Leo dismantles Poroto's tactics and thus affects the action of the text up to, but not including, the final moments. At every turn, Leo controls Poroto, until, perhaps, the end, when Poroto's unforeseen final escape happens, *but is not seen* by anyone.[10]

Leo is surprised by Poroto's final flight and, realizing its grave importance to the "story," he seeks to understand it. The reader must do the same. *Dirección contraria,* which absorbs the *Historia* intertext into it, now comes into play. *DC* works off the *Historia* pre-text and adds new information to it. This new information further transforms the receptor's role and also expands the text's themes, content, and context.

DC repeats the exact text of the Poroto bar scene but, in the pages that follow that scene, it continues the *Historia,* by unchronologically filling in the gaps in Poroto's and Willy's life stories. It includes characters not found in the pre-text and, although Leo is occasionally referred to in *DC* and has the same position in the opening (repeated) text, he does not appear in the rest of the novel. Willy, on the other hand, while only alluded to in *Historia,* becomes the protagonist of *DC,* thus opening the way for his larger role in the *Nueva versión.* In essence, at the beginning of the story, *DC* is a simple repetition, imitation, even plagiarism of the *Historia* text. As every word is the same, so are points of view, tone, and story content. Yet the rest of the *DC* text dialogues with its intertext and fills in the gaps in the story.

In his article on intertext and autotext, Lucien Dällenbach (1976) defines and outlines specific types of intertextuality by referring to Jean Ricardou's distinction between general intertextuality, or the intertextual rapport between texts by different authors, and restrictive intertextuality, the intertextual relationship between texts by one same author. In the *Poroto* texts, Pavlovsky definitely plays with both intertextual models, although here, I only examine Pavlovsky's unique use of restrictive intertextuality, because through it a new interpretation of self and nation emerges.

In addition to emphasizing restrictive intertextuality, the ways in which Pavlovsky connects these three texts points out both their external and internal intertextuality. Ricardou distinguishes between external intertextuality, understood as the relationship between one text and *another* text, and internal intertextuality, the relationship of a text with itself (Dällenbach 1976, 282). By actually placing his one text (*Historia*) inside the other (*DC*), Pavlovsky plays with these two modes of intertextuality and creates what Dällenbach calls a third form of intertextuality, called autotextuality. Autotextuality, or textual "mise en abyme," rather than just recognizing the intertextual relationship, places emphasis on the originality of text; it has a doubly reflective function that highlights and questions both the story and its structure and, at the same time, it dialogues with the text and serves as a theoretical device, "an apparatus of auto-interpretation" (1976, 282–84).

As Dällenbach argues, in order for mise en abyme to be present, "the work itself must *point up* the reflexion that is taking place; or, more precisely, the reflexion must become the subject of the reflexion" (1989, 17).[11] By repeating the entire *Historia* text as *the* text in the first part of *DC*, by putting it within a new, this time definitely narrative, context, and by giving the whole text a new name, Pavlovsky forces the reader to see the similarities between the two texts but acknowledge their difference(s). Questions of what (kind of) text we are reading and why (would the author do this) come immediately to mind.

Since the first twenty-eight pages of *DC* are a verbatim repetition of the entire *Historia* text, my analysis of *DC* will be limited to the rest of the novel, that is, the parts that differ from and expand upon the original text. *DC* continues after the "end" of *Historia* (although not chronologically), and those final fifty-three pages supplement the information of the pre-text and alter its point of view. Even though it seems like *Historia*'s omniscient narrator will continue the story, as the text moves on, receptors realize that just about every action described to them is a third- or fourth-hand account. For example, learning about Poroto's passion for soccer games, we read of a certain game that he and Leo attended, but the information comes to us, from Leo (who was at the game with Poroto but not present at the "time" of this telling), through Willy, to the narrator and, finally, to the reader (46). In another scene, an old woman tells Willy, who tells the narrator, who tells us of the words that Poroto whispered as he left from his retreat in San Cayetano Church (48). Still another chapter, narrating one of Poroto's work experiences, tells of how Poroto had given crossword puzzles to his boss, who then gave them to his girlfriend, who told the narrator, who tells us (52). Moreover, we learn of Poroto's father's strange character because Poroto told Willy, who told the narrator, who, in turn, informs us (54–55).

This distancing perspective, in which all information arrives at the receptor third- or fourth-hand, continues throughout *DC*. Ironically, however, even though the point of view changes between *Historia* (the beginning of the *DC* text) and the rest of the *DC* text, distancing is what ties the two texts together. The *Historia* text ends when Poroto mysteriously flees from the bar, unperceived by Leo and the rest of the patrons, and is seen/heard in the Plaza de Villa Devoto. The "original" version ends with, "Poor them! Poor them! Was what a young adolescent girl that crossed paths with Poroto heard him shout while he was passing by her" (*DC*, 41). This ending is a combination of the same type of quasi-direct discourse found throughout the *Historia* text and the narrative distancing that will form the backbone of the new *DC* text. "Poor them," presumably expressed by Poroto, but heard and repeated by the young girl who witnessed him in the plaza, has no quotation marks around it to separate it from the narrator's story or to mark it as a quote, yet it is evidently direct discourse. At the same time, these words, this text, come to the reader fourth-hand since no one directly witnessed Poroto's escape or saw him in the plaza afterward. The words come from Poroto, through the young girl, to the narrator, and, finally, to the reader, foreshadowing the extreme distancing, which is the core of the *DC* text.

The transposition of point of view, moving the text from the combination of omniscient narrator/quasi-direct discourse to extreme narrative distancing has several functions. First, it transforms the reader's perspective on the genre of the text, suggesting that this text is now "different"—it can no longer possibly be theater; it is now definitely narrative, a story being told, removed several times from the reader. *Historia* may have been theater and, if it was, then the reader would initially assume that *DC,* since it begins as the same text, should be theater too. But, as the story develops, it loses its dramatic essence and becomes the story of a story of a story: a purely intertextual narrative construction whose version depends on the teller. There is no longer the possibility of a direct connection between character/actor and reader/spectator. On the one hand, the reader becomes totally removed and distanced from the text; on the other, though, in an ironic and strange twist, the reader is essential, for it is s/he who will pass on the story, keep it moving along and create other versions. Maybe this is no longer theater, but, ironically, the reader, too, becomes an actor, otherwise Poroto's story would die. By distancing the reader from the narrated events, ironically, the author is bringing the reader into the text by creating a sense of intimacy. It is as if we were all "friends." We move from the initial bar scene, wondering what happened to Poroto. Then we, like the narrator, look over Poroto's girlfriend's shoulder as she reads the goodbye letter from her ex-lover, and we, too, try to understand why he broke up with her.

The differentiated role of the reader is a major way in which *DC* differs from *Historia,* and, as I will show later, this alters the perspective on and interpretation of nation within and between these texts. Leo as reader pulled receptor into *Historia* as an individual, first-person, singular character. In *DC,* the receptor/character is plural and collective. For example, before describing the strange behavior of Poroto's parents, the narrator begins, "*We all know* that there are situations in life that have left their marks. *We* also know that Poroto was an enemy of all reasoning that included the hermeneutic interpretive process about cause and effect" (54, my emphasis). "We," narrator and reader, know specific details about Poroto himself as well as about life in general. We, too, read this text and other life clues, and we interpret them. Even though Poroto is against this process of interpretation, the text(s) demand(s) that we participate and that we do it collectively.

The emphasis on this distanced, but at the same time collective and intimate, point of view serves another textual function in *DC;* it changes the protagonist of the text. Even though *DC* begins by incorporating the entire *Historia* text, and Leo/reader became the protagonist of that original text, the distanced point of view makes *DC* more about Willy than Poroto. Willy is obsessed with Poroto; he continuously tries to understand Poroto and to decipher his behavior.[12] In the first chapter after the *Historia* portion of *DC,* Serafina reads Poroto's good-bye letter. She is devastated and calls on Willy to help her interpret the letter (43). From this point on, Willy, who had been practically absent from *Historia,* becomes the protagonist. We learn of his sexual attraction toward Serafina and of his many attempts to interpret his friend Poroto's behavior. Willy, as the expert on Poroto, is the new focus of the text and he works to interpret Poroto and his life. This life, which had been read by Leo, is now being read by Willy and by all of us; receptors are called to work with Willy to interpret and understand Poroto.

The distancing and the protagonic switch from Poroto to Leo (reader) to Willy unite the original *Historia* text with the *DC* text and also have a tie to the *Nueva versión* that will come. For example, *DC* includes a letter from "an admirer" who was in the bar that day in the original text; it was the young woman of the young couple.[13] This young woman, a seemingly insignificant character in the original text, *grows* and takes on new life through her attempts to read and interpret Poroto. While Willy becomes the protagonist in *DC,* he is only so because he is a keen observer and interpreter of Poroto, "por otro," through another, and with us he is now committed to a collective understanding of the events that they all/we all experienced. The transformation of the readers' role in *DC* pulls the receptor more intimately into the text. The vacillation between the distancing (the third- or fourth-hand versions) and collective intimacy (the "we" know), functions like a Brechtian strategy, forcing receptors together to be aware of and committed to their role in interpreting and altering the events.

In *DC,* then, Willy takes over the text and, along with the receptor plays his dual role as character and interpreter. Both Willy and the waiter have minor roles in *Historia* and the latter is virtually absent from *DC.* Based on his "reading" of the two texts, however, Pavlovsky's friend, actor and director Norman Briski, propels Willy onto center stage in the *Nueva versión,* arguing, "For me, Willy is a narrator of this human phenomenon . . . The guy has consecrated his life to his friend, left his wife, everything, to become the waiter that serves Poroto" (Pavlovsky 2001, 185). Pavlovsky, too, who played the role of Willy in the staged *Nueva versión* maintains, "I embody the character of Willy the friend who is 'fascinated' by Poroto and who follows him everywhere because he believes in the philosophy created by Poroto: flight as a phenomenon of freedom . . . I disguise myself as a waiter so that Poroto does not see me, does not recognize me, and I explain to the audience that Poroto sits 'there,' that he does this or that, I explain his movements and his rhythmical transformations" (2001, 185–86). Their reading of Willy as protagonist comes through *Nueva versión*'s intertextual ties with the novel (*DC*), not the "play" *Historia,* since Willy is virtually absent from that original text.[14] Moreover, even though Briski intends to make Willy the protagonist of *Nueva versión,* Willy functions as actor, spectator, and protagonist but shares the stage with another narrator and, as we shall see, this split narrator's role and the role of other characters in the *Nueva versión* further move the text's focus from the individual to the collective nation.

Throughout the *Nueva versión,* Willy describes Poroto's, Leo's, the parroquiano's, the other bar patrons', and the spectators' actions, words, and thoughts. At given moments in this text, Willy observes, measures, calculates, and comments on these characters' body movements and mental processes, especially those of Poroto. He is equally adept at noticing behaviors as he is at analyzing those same behaviors. Several times, Willy narrates from inside Poroto's very head. He tells us of Poroto's obsessions and of the intense buzzing noise going on inside Poroto's mind. "The velocity of Leo's chewing seemed incredible (to Poroto) and the dialogue that the two had begun seemed very fast he had no awareness of what he was answering he was not listening to his own voice because his head seemed occupied by a very intense buzzing" (1999a, 34).

Willy, at times, is also the intermediary between characters, especially between Poroto and Leo. At the beginning of the Unidad 2, Willy serves Leo his steak and, "he goes to the table and shows Leo that Poroto has arrived" (29). Willy only speaks directly to the characters on a few occasions, but there are times when he laughs at them or laughs with them.[15] When he does talk to them, it is in his role as waiter. Noticing and narrating the exact position of Poroto's feet ("At that moment Poroto's right leg was 60 or 70 centimeters from his left leg—in contact through his feet with Leo's left leg"), Willy asks Poroto, "Are you going or staying?" (46). Assuming that Poroto's response indicates that he is staying, Willy cries out, "Two nice hot coffees with a little milk!" (47).

Willy also indicates that he had intervened in Poroto's past. Once, worried about Poroto's spasmodic movements, he had recommended that Poroto talk to his psychiatrist friend, Dr. Uriarte. He then narrates his version of the same encounter; he briefly recounts the episode that appears in the *Historia* and *DC* texts. Willy, then, is not just commenting on this single encounter between two friends; he, too, has an ongoing relationship with them.

Willy's interactions with Poroto, Leo, and the parroquiano are sometimes violent. Functioning as the director of the play as well, when he does not like the way Poroto is sitting, he physically moves his legs, as if Poroto were a mannequin (1999a, 45). Additionally, at the beginning of the *flan y dulce de leche* scene, Willy throws beer on the parroquiano's head (54), and he later grabs Poroto by the legs because he does not want to be reminded of the violence to which Poroto had formerly alluded.

Ironically, as the observer of Poroto's and the other characters' "show," Willy, too, is spectator. In Unidad 12:

> *Willy walks toward table 3 and sits down.*
> *Willy.* A young couple was observing [Poroto] smiling and they were interpreting Poroto's strange displacements as if they were part of some comic number and they were even looking around trying to discover some hidden video camera that might be filming the customers' reactions to Poroto's strange movements.
>
> (47–48)

As he watches these spectators watching Poroto's performance, the stage directions tell us that Willy, too, then, "(*looks under the table as if looking for some video camera. He looks out of the corner of his eye at Poroto and Leo, changes the rhythm of the monologue*). I observed Leo who was looking pensive with two coffees on the table and Poroto who was trying to avoid me" (1999a, 48). Willy, both actor and spectator in the play, watches them as they watch him and Poroto.

In the next scene, Willy continues to note Poroto's every move, and, at the same time, he comments on the spectators' point of view. Willy asserts, "(Poroto) turned 90 degrees entered into the bathroom. All of Poroto's movements always left his spectators with doubts" (48). In essence, he is reflecting on his own role as spectator and on spectatorship in general; he "sees" everything, but is still left with doubts.[16]

Willy is narrator/commentator, director, actor, and spectator in *Nueva versión.* Yet Willy is not the only narrative voice in this text; the didascalia function equally with Willy to show/describe/narrate actions, gestures, and movements of each character, including those of Willy and, as we have seen, the stage directions sometimes contradict Willy's point of view. As Willy narrates, the stage directions give us more detail; they tell us that Willy changes his costume and that "*He carries the chorizo steak to Leo. He goes to the customer's table and then to greet Poroto. He goes to table 4 and shows Leo that Poroto has arrived*" (29). The stage directions also describe Leo's actions (*Leo gets up* [29]) and Poroto's (*Poroto throws the plates* [35]). They indicate Willy's various movements and positions (*Willy is between Poroto and Leo next to the wall 'BAR'* [36]). The stage directions fill in the gaps in Willy's discourse, completing the pictures presented of all characters; they allow Willy to be an actor in the play and give the other characters more breadth as well.

Willy adds information, but also adds to the movement and sense of vertigo of the play through his different roles as narrator, actor, spectator, and critic in the *Nueva versión.* As narrator he follows the characters' dizzying routes from table to table, to the bar, to the bathroom, and through the revolving door out to the plaza of Villa Devoto. As actor, he himself moves from bar, to tables 2, 3, and 4, to the pulpit, to the bathroom, and to the revolving door. As spectator and critic, he sits at tables, leans against the bar, and stands with his back against the wall, watching the action. Willy's movements and changing positions are symbols of the readers'/spectators' roles in this play; we move around and through the text(s), changing points of view and participating in the vertiginous course that the writer, director, and actors are designing with us.

What the stage directions do not do, that Willy as narrator does, is describe or narrate from within the characters' minds. Nor do the stage directions interpret feelings; they only narrate the movements, gestures, and positions of the characters. Willy, on the other hand, tells us their feelings, their obsessions, and their whims. He reveals, for example, that Leo is crying, "He began to observe with surprise that two big tears sprang from Leo's light blue eyes and were falling down his cheeks" (43), and that Poroto, because he is preoccupied with his own position and his strategy of flight, has no interest in the content of his interlocutors' conversations, "His lack of interest in the content of the conversations was evident all his interest was concentrated on the movements of his departures" (31). At the same time, though, Willy also carries out a similar function to the stage directions; he describes his and the other characters' movements and gestures. Why not leave these details to the stage directions alone?

Willy's role combines what Uspensky terms both an external and an internal viewpoint on the psychological plane, while the stage directions remain exclusively from the external perspective (Uspensky 1973, 81). Because of the double emphasis on the external point of view (the stage directions and that portion of Willy's role), Poroto becomes a detached, puppetlike figure whose actions and sentiments are described from various perspectives, but with whom the audience is not even supposed to identify. Rather, they identify with Willy, and, like Willy at the end of the play, they set the revolving door in motion. The revolving door, unique to *Nueva versión,* as we will see, is a metaphor for both text and nation and it is Willy who is "caught" in it at the end of this *Nueva versión* of the play.

Uspensky suggests that, in performance, there is no distinction between the external and internal points of view and argues that "The distinction of points of view on the psychological level is important for different literary genres, except for drama" (99). He maintains that the only way to know a character's internal state is in the written play-text, through the stage directions. The unique role of Willy in Pavlovsky's *Nueva versión* shows how a stage performance might succeed in presenting an internal point of view through another character. Willy's multifaceted role as narrator, director, spectator, and actor gives the audience a more complete picture of Willy, Poroto, and Leo. Willy describes Poroto's actions and gestures, gets inside his head and describes his inner feelings and attitudes and the reasons for them. At the same time, he serves the characters and interacts with them; he is part of the performance too. Point of view is foregrounded through Willy, the didascalia, and the interlocutor's vacillating, chameleon-like role, and in this way, text and text-making, and interpretation, not dialogue, character, or action, are prioritized.

In addition, Willy "acts" like the waiter *before* he actually changes into his waiter's costume (29). Then, at the end of the play, Willy changes back into his original clothes (out of his waiter's costume) *before* telling Leo that he has to close the bar (62). These metatextual strategies demonstrate Willy's multifaceted role within the text and also urge receptors to question the theatrical frames and boundaries as well as the characters' and their own roles in the events. That questioning places spectator/reader in the same space and within a similar role with Willy and the others; receptors become the interpreters of their own and these characters' lives.

All characters in *Nueva versión* take on multiple roles, comment on each other's roles, and act as spectators to each others' performances. Leo, for example, becomes both El and Ella, two bar patrons who are supposedly observing Poroto and Leo's encounter, until Poroto takes over one of the voices and becomes El (32).[17] Willy tells how "Poroto always felt like a spectator of other people's dialogue" (35). From the outset, Poroto was "rehearsing" his act. As Willy tells us in Unidad 1, as soon as Poroto entered the bar, "He sat down and started to rehearse the hug he was going to give him and the necessary steps it would take to reach Leo" (29).[18]

Willy's multiple roles and the continuously changing perspectives of characters and spectators in the *Nueva versión* have an ideological function as well; they interrogate the boundaries of self and citizenship within the context of post–Dirty War Argentina. Characters are racing around, going through the motions of their lives, but are unable to experience them fully because of the trauma they have been through. This quotidian bar scene is overshadowed by the violence suggested in that one bombing event from some twenty years before this encounter. The different versions of the "play" are an attempt to come to terms with that event, symbolic of the whole Dirty War in Argentina. The three versions evolve in their presentation of the psychological state of characters and spectators in the aftermath of those events. *Historia,* through its focus on Leo, draws the reader into the text and posits an attempt to come to terms on an individual level. *DC* opens it up to a more collective experience and also shows how the events impact all these characters' full lives, not just this one encounter. Moreover, *DC* plays with the distancing and intimacy to force the "we" into an awareness of our own role in and reaction to the events. *Nueva versión,* on the other hand, shows that all characters are psychologically and emotionally traumatized.

In addition, the two scenes that open the *Nueva versión,* but are totally absent from the other two texts, further expand the meaning. Unidad 0 comes across like a dream. Labeled as Unit 0, the stage directions indicate that the tape-recorded voice is played as the spectators are entering the theater. Although it is part of the play, it is partially outside the text, outside of the frame of the script and the performance. The voice narrates a scene between Poroto and his mother: a Sunday afternoon in which, while the mother is cooking dinner, Poroto grabs a ladle from the drawer, waves it at his mother, and then throws it on the floor. Poroto then enters his mother's bedroom, sees her go into the bathroom, brushes off one of her sweaters with a clothes brush, jumps up and down, does three laps around the table, and runs out the door. This surrealist and absurd scene, though it may refer to one specific event from Poroto's past, alludes to a whole history of the relationship between Poroto and his mother and explains some of the psychological neuroses that the title character displays throughout all three versions.

While in Unidad 0, the Voice, an omniscient narrator, had exposed a tense relationship between Poroto and his mother, in Unidad 1, the parroquiano, in his own voice, expands on the violent maternal conflicts. This "dialogue" between the parroquiano and his mother stylistically imitates the quasi-direct discourse of *Historia,* and it foreshadows some negative traumatic effects of the street violence alluded to in the scenes of all three texts. The narrator of Unidad 1 elaborates on his extreme intimacy with his mother. But when he comes home one day agitated by the day's events, his mother knew something was wrong and insists that he talk about it. He refuses, she continues, and when she pushes him too far, a fight ensues in which he violently kills her (26–27). The rest of the passage expresses his grief and his guilt and his love/hate relationship with his mother and himself. Although her body is destroyed, he cannot kill her voice because she is the "voice of humanity" and it is as if, "I am speaking through humanity for you from your body my dear son" (28). This scene initiates the bar scene when Poroto enters looking for Leo yet, at first glance it seems totally disconnected from the scenes to come, only united because the parroquiano is also a patron of this bar. However, the mother's fragmented body is similar to the fragmentation of Leo and the others that I analyze in the next section; both fragmentations are due to absurd and extreme violence. Moreover, the physical and psychological fragmentation of all characters is produced by the violent street events that happened some twenty-five years before this encounter.

All three texts change their point of view; however, since in each case the goal is to interpret Poroto, his actions, his motivations, and his feelings, the narrative voice becomes the reader/spectator who cowrites the text with Pavlovsky through his/her own interpretation of it. *Historia*'s omniscient narrator cedes control of the text to Leo, reader and interlocutor, through the use of quasi-direct discourse. These examples of quasi-direct discourse, a conscious choice on the author's part, could be turned into direct discourse or indirect discourse by adding or eliminating quotation marks and directly affirming the speaker in each case. The fact that they are neither direct nor indirect places the text in between drama and narrative, but allows it to work in both spaces. The ambiguity brought forward by Pavlovsky's use of quasi-direct discourse serves a dual purpose: it forces the reader to focus on text and text-making and it takes significance away from Poroto, the individual, turning him into a collective entity. We are no longer hearing/seeing/reading about Poroto the person; he is transformed into Porot(r)o, seen through another, for another, by another. Moreover, the reader/spectator, who has become an actor and integral player in this collective script, interprets Poroto's adventures as those of all Argentines.

DC's extremely distanced perspective both alienates and includes the reader, who, like Willy, becomes obsessed with interpreting Poroto by piecing together the multiple episodes of his life. *DC* gives us a bigger piece of the story and suggests that the obsession with flight goes beyond Poroto's mere longing to escape from the bar that one day. Now that Poroto is no longer individual protagonist, I will show that the characters' desire for flight is both physical and psychological and it is provoked by the events that these characters evoke in the various versions.

Finally, while Willy had a virtually minor role in *Historia,* he takes on multiple roles in *Nueva versión;* he becomes the protagonist of the text, and is essential to the text-making process. Moreover, as Uspensky suggests, "on the level of phraseology a particular character emerges as the vehicle of the authorial point of view, while on the level of ideology he serves as its object" (1973, 102). As one of the vehicles of point of view, he seems to be a spokesperson for the "author" and this is probably the reason why Pavlovsky himself plays the part of Willy, not Poroto, in the staged version. The double emphasis on external point of view in *Nueva versión* allows the reader/spectator to sit with Willy and look for the hidden camera and then go back through the revolving door to attempt a clearer interpretation of "Poroto" and his nation.

Nation in the Poroto texts

In these works, narrator, protagonist, and point of view change from text to text, which has implications for both the genre of the text(s) and who articulates it/them. The relationship between the three versions goes beyond revision; rather than a revision from version to version, each version adds new information and changes the position and perspectives of characters and spectators. As the texts are transformed from a personal story about one man, Poroto, to a text about the reader and his/her interpretation, to a "play" that includes the receptor within the narrator's/protagonist's/author's perspective, so, too, does the speaking subject and, in this way, the text moves from a personal story to a national story. Whereas the earliest Poroto (*Historia*) text is about an individual's struggle to read and understand himself and his nation, the latest (*Nueva*) version presents a collective struggle for national identity and interpretation.

Through the language Pavlovsky chooses in each text, he marks the texts differently and thus expands the view of nation and its interpretations in each version. In this section I examine constructions of nation by looking closely at two linguistic signs, the body and the door, and how they differ in each text, in order to show how they redefine the national subject. These linguistic changes demonstrate how the earlier *Historia* version presents an individual interpretation of and response to nation whereas the later texts expand and open up that interpretation, positing a more collective national subject who is working through and working out the national fragmentation.

In his introduction to *DC,* Juan Carlos de Brasi highlights the importance of the body and its political symbolism, "There is no question about the body that is not, simultaneously, an answer—also political—that 'resists' the forces that try to embody it as one and [as] a unit of servitude—also voluntary" (1997, 11). Brasi sees in *DC,* "a metric of bodies" in the physical mobility, velocity, intensity, and agility of the bodies as "they cross the table and fall athletically on the other side" (12). Pavlovsky himself signals the importance of the body, most especially in his theories on acting as therapy and as an "aesthetics of multiplicity" (2001, 210–11). For Pavlovsky, the body of the actor displays the fragmentation within discourse itself. He emphasizes that "In the theater the body acquires the predominance: the word is my actor-being is body, body-word, word-body. It is difficult for any one of my texts not to be underscored with some corporeal attitude in some way. This gives me a style that I call the 'aesthetic of multiplicity'" (2001, 211).

The body in these three texts is presented as fragmented; however, that fragmentation moves from an individual distortion of Leo in *Historia* to a more collective fragmentation in the *Nueva versión.* Moreover, the body is delineated as the "national" body as descriptions of its fragmentation are framed by and enmeshed within both the discussions of what it means to be Argentine (the *flan* and *dulce de leche* scenes) and descriptions of the (real) bombing incident that happened around the years of the Argentine Dirty War. These three texts go beyond the multiple discourse/actor's body connection by showing that body as fragmented. In addition to the fragmentation created through the multiple discourses crossing/forming these texts, there is concrete corporeal fragmentation, displayed differently in each text. Movement, velocity, intensity, and agility are, no doubt, important in these works; however, the fragmented bodies come to symbolize individual and national alienation. The body fragments splattered throughout each text reveal both the mental and physical distress of the protagonists and, at the same time, they suggest regenerative, creative possibilities for text(s), individuals, and nation, relating subjectivity to what Kristeva (1977) would term *le sujet-en-procès* (the subject in process/on trial).

I propose that "text" for Pavlovsky is like Kristeva's *chora,* which she defines as a mobile receptacle of contradiction and movement in which the subject comes into being by working through identity conflicts between symbolic (social) and semiotic (instinctive, prelinguistic) forces. The *chora* is the site of a chaos that precedes subjectivity and is necessary to the process of "becoming."[19] Kristeva's theory refutes the possibility of the "sujet unaire," the whole, unified subject, and posits a split subject whose essence is "une multiplicité de rejets" (1977, 58). The "rejets" make of subjectivity an "affirmative negativity" and postulate subjectivity as a "teleology of becoming," a process constantly traversed by positive and negative flows that struggle through a type of schizophrenia within the being and both affirm and reject prelinguistic and social definitions of self. For Kristeva, a subject in process attacks all stasis within the unified subject as well as all ideological systems and social structures, and in this way introduces a new historicity that incorporates myths, rituals, and other symbolic systems of humanity to open them to both negative and positive interpretations. The subject "en procès" both puts itself on trial (one meaning of the French word "procès") and becomes (is in process). This self-examination and the processes that inform it allow the subject to detach itself from contemporary history or to open up readings of history to the same positive and negative forces underlying subjectivity.[20]

In *Historia,* Leo and Poroto seem separated and indifferent to each other's feelings and actions. After Leo reminds Poroto of the bomb incident from their past, an intense buzzing fills Poroto's head, and, because of it, he can no longer hear Leo's words. Leo's face becomes distorted in Poroto's mind and his body is separated from the words it is expressing: "the buzzing in those moments was not letting him listen to Leo's words either now he was only watching his mouth opening and closing his teeth yellowed by cigarettes and his arms and hands gesturing pompously accompanying a cold and serene discourse" (Pavlovsky 1996, 10). Leo's body is fragmented in Poroto's mind and that corporeal fragmentation accompanies his cold, serene account of the bombing.

The third-person omniscient narrator describes how Poroto sees Leo's mouth as separated from his words and from the rest of his body (his gesturing hands) (1996, 10). The narrator also remarks that the buzzing in Poroto's head and his detachment from Leo are attempts to erase and forget the past bombing incident and resultant deaths that Leo (or the narrator or Poroto's memory, as discussed above) had just brought up. The narrator explains, though, that, "For Poroto the bomb formed part of an event from reality and thus everything seemed blurry dreamlike—without passions or too many pains and intensities. The problem for Poroto was the 'departure' with Leo and the possibility of being able to flee austerely" (10).

Poroto's reaction to the "real" bombing incident is to try to escape to that "other" plane—fiction, madness, irreality. His problem, the narrator explains, is to be able to flee, to escape. Not only are the two characters separated from each other though; as Poroto becomes self-absorbed and obsesses about the potential means and position of his escape, he distorts Leo's image so that Leo becomes a fragmented body. Leo's fragmented body and Poroto's need to distance himself from his interlocutor alternate with memory fragments of the bombing incident and its aftermath and precise strategies for Poroto's escape. Poroto sees, in Leo's body, the pieces of the bombing victims, and even though *Historia* proposes that it was Leo who had "fled" after the bombing, we see that Poroto focuses on flight as well. This bombing, some twenty-two years before this encounter (the text was published in 1996), is a memory of the Argentine Dirty War years (1976–83).[21] With this text, Pavlovsky suggests that even those who remained in Argentina during the terrible years of the Dirty War found some strategy for flight through madness, fiction, or some other plane of irreality. This Dirty War era bombing psychologically impacts this reunion between Poroto (who stayed—although in *DC* we learn that he, too, left the country—but continuously invents strategies of flight) and his friend (who had left but returned), some twenty-two years after the incident. The earliest *Poroto* text was published in 1996; twenty-two years before that, 1974, is very close to the official start of that war, and as Luisa Valenzuela has suggested, strange things were happening. In *Historia,* then, Leo's physical fragmentation is played out in Poroto's mind—making both characters split subjects. The subjects' split self is related to the national split subject as the individual fragmentations alternate with the "pieces" of the bombing victims.

Some subtle differences in the bombing account in the *Nueva versión* provide more information on this incident and greater insight into individual and national consciousness. In all versions, memories of mother and bombing are evoked through the mention of "new Guernicas"; however, in *Nueva versión,* from the Unidad 20 to the Unidad 25, Leo, Poroto, and Willy fuse the bombing incident with their discussion of what it means to be Argentine, the "*queso* and *dulce,*" "*flan* and *dulce de leche*" scenes.[22] Leo had already brought up the bombing incident, Poroto had reacted to it by trying to flee, but Leo had caught him. In *Nueva versión,* Leo is no longer physically distorted, but the pieces of the bombing victims still remain. This time it is Willy, largely absent from *Historia,* who reacts to those fragmented bodies (in bold, my emphasis).

Leo. Why don't you like cheese with jam Poroto?
Willy comes out from behind the bathroom and goes toward Poroto, he takes him by the legs.
Willy. **I don't like to remember the fragmented bodies—how a body is fragmented into pieces—what remains after the explosion the horrible thing becomes meticulous to me I thought many times about the bodies they were three you remember . . .**

Unit 24
Leo. But the cheese with jam?
Where is the cheese with jam?
Where is it?
Poroto. Here it is.
Here is the cheese
Leo. And the jam.

(1999a, 59–60)

The fragmented bodies are sandwiched within the discussion of what it means to be Argentine, and this not only clearly locates those fragmented bodies at the site of the pre–Dirty War bombing, but also positions them within the Argentine, not just in Poroto's head or in Leo's fragmented body. Three bombing victims, three characters here who, some twenty-five years later (in this later text) are psychologically fragmented as a result of that national tragedy. Leo's physical distortion in *Historia* gives way to psychological fragmentation; even those "bodies that remained" are fragmented.

Through his texts, however, Pavlovsky proposes that the split national subject can also open itself up to creative possibilities. The further connection with the *Guernica* text identifies the fragmented bodies both with nation and with civil war. These are "new Guernicas," new ways to interpret the fragmented bodies and minds in an effort to survive and to define the Argentine. Willy continues:

Pieces of body in the air what happens with the blood
It must also explode . . .
Some beauty must exist
If it suddenly were to congeal

> Legs and arms pieces of face would exist
> Some harmony must have existed at some moment of
> the blast don't think of it as something living blown apart but rather as harmonic forms—new aesthetics—new Guernicas.
> If you think in shapes you can survive.
> The rigorous objective of thinking of the explosion as an aesthetic event would perhaps enable you to survive it.
>
> (1999a, 59)

These new aesthetic creations, these new texts, are a survival tactic—a way to move through a fragmented subjectivity toward a collective rebirth on another plane—and they are proof that the subject, like the text, is always in process.

Moreover, as mentioned above, Willy had been significantly absent from *Historia* and from the earliest pages of *DC.* Piecing the three texts together reveals that Willy was the only one of the three men to stay in Argentina during the Dirty War. The fact that Willy joins the conversation on what it means to be Argentine in *Nueva versión* and that it is clearly he who asks Poroto directly, "Aren't you Argentine then?" shows that he, too, is questioning what it means to be Argentine (55). In *Historia* Poroto affirms that he does not like to remember the fragmented bodies, but it is Willy in *Nueva versión* who articulates the terrifying memories, rejects them, and connects past with present.

As suggested above, recollections of the victims' destroyed bodies give way to reflections on what it means to be Argentine. In a seemingly absurd passage, the protagonists equate being Argentine with "flan" and "dulce de leche." This apparently innocent and ridiculous reflection allows them to iterate a weak and shaky Argentine national character. Willy confirms that "Everyone who has lived abroad asks me for it [cheese and jam]" and then, "He suddenly thought, THAT IS WHAT WE ARE: CHEESE AND JAM" (55). Poroto and Leo repeat and then modify his assertions; thus working through a definition of what it means to be Argentine. Poroto prefers to ally himself with a definition of Argentine as "flan y dulce de leche" (flan and caramel). Rather than identify himself with two poles, cheese with jam, he prefers the image of flan. When Leo asks him why he responds:

> *Leo.* Why flan?
> *Poroto.*: What does not flee is caught.
> *Leo.* Why caramel?
> *Poroto.* What is caught is torn apart.

Leo. What repulses me about flan is that it moves but it lets itself be eaten. It is weak.
Poroto. What
Leo. Flan
Poroto. At some point the grit was strong.
Flan cannot send arrows. It can only stop them.
The arrow is hostile—you have to know how to receive it and send it far away.

(60)

This text and the language they weave in it help them to work through definitions of the Argentine. The soft aspect of flan, the fact that it moves (symbolizing their constant desire for flight) but still allows itself to be eaten (symbolizing their inability to really escape), displays their self-image of Argentines as weak and incapable of resisting. Poroto tries to argue that the grit, the substance of the flan, was once firm, positing hope of strength at the heart of their character. But, according to their own self-image, they are like flan, incapable of stopping the hostile arrows and sending them away, constantly allowing themselves to be wounded.

All three texts present different articulations of national identity and work through these characters' image of themselves as Argentines. In each text, Poroto actually leaves, but the door through which he exits changes in each script. Each text emphasizes Poroto's desire for flight, his need to escape, and while in *Historia* and *Nueva versión* he does succeed in escaping, unperceived, from the bar, presumably to a plaza within Argentina, in *DC* Poroto actually leaves the country. The flights portray the protagonist's physical reaction to his situation, and additionally, they show his psychological need to flee. His perception of escape, and ultimately, exile, evolves between texts. Symbolically, the different kinds of doors in each text depict the state of the protagonist's entrapment or liberation.

The door, as a metaphor for escape, is different in each version. In *Historia,* Poroto is obsessed with fleeing, and to that end, his goal is to strategically position himself near the door of the bar in order to escape quickly and unperceived by Leo and the other patrons. When he initially fails to choose the seat nearest the door, because Leo arrives first, he continues to be obsessed with his position, but no longer worries about the actual door. In fact, the door seems to disappear; it is only important because it is Poroto's means for escape. While Poroto's position changes constantly, if not physically then certainly mentally, the door in *Historia* remains stable and unmoving, yet of primary symbolic importance in Poroto's mind.

The most notable reference to the door and its function in *DC,* on the other hand, occurs in a later chapter entitled "Pull and Push" in which Poroto shows the absurdity of language and reveals his and the texts' function: to question the signs and (re)interpret them. Because Poroto sees that the verb "tire" can mean both to pull and to push away (to throw away from your body), "Sometimes Poroto stopped at the bars' entrances for a long time." Confused over how to move the door, he gets stuck in his own possibilities for interpretation of himself and his situation. His role becomes one of exposing the situation; of urging the bar patrons, his interlocutors, to question the meaning around them. Because of Poroto's reactions, "Many people were beginning to think about other things in life that they did not question. The door stopped being a door, the obvious stopped being obvious, an order stopped being an order and a whole life was calling itself into question. That was Poroto's intrinsic value" (1997a, 79). Poroto's quirks, his apparent "schizophrenia," and his instability force his receptors to wake up and question what they had become accustomed to accept and obey.

Though Poroto is confused by the push and pull of the door in *DC* and this urges him and his receptors to question it and their position to it, in *Nueva versión* the door is in constant motion, never stable, for it is a revolving door. Characters get stuck in the revolving door, and it seems that Poroto makes his final, unperceived escape through it. The fact that it is revolving, though, indicates that there is the possibility of return through that same door and so the door becomes a metaphor for both a return from exile and a return from the psychological flight that citizens had to take to get through those difficult years.

As "*Willy goes to the revolving door and stays there,*" Leo and Poroto explain why they are discussing flan and dulce de leche as their national symbols. The revolving door is unique to the *Nueva versión* and, as such, like flan y dulce de leche, symbolizes the Argentine paradox. During the Dirty War and in its aftermath, all tried to leave in one way or another, through exile or through indifference, but no one succeeded. There is no escape from such traumatic history; it is a constant working through for the individual and national subjects "en procès."

Nueva versión expands the *Historia* version by focusing, not on the strategies for flight, but on the revolving door. The revolving door suggests movement, and not only Poroto, but also Leo and Willy spend time in it.[23] The ending does not change, although as in *Historia,* since Poroto's escape was "unperceived," it is not certain that he left through that door. Poroto still achieves his "final" flight and Willy still recounts Poroto's last words, once again narrated to him by "a young teenage girl" in the plaza. As the words, "Poor them" are repeated, Willy leaves through the revolving door, which then turns endlessly until the final blackout (1999a, 64). The revolving door of Argentines leaving and returning continues, but even those who remained are to be pitied ("poor them"), for they had fled emotionally and mentally through their indifference and fragmentation and still have not totally recovered. The revolving door is both symbolic of the real Argentines who came and went during the Proceso years, and it is a metaphor for the psychological state of all Argentines after those difficult years.

Moreover, Leo's distorted image, intermixed with the fragmented bodies of the bombing victims in *Historia,* is significantly absent from the *Nueva versión,* suggesting that the fragmented individual has given way to a fragmented collectivity and that the collective fragmented image can only be "cured" through the creation of a new "text," a new aesthetic. The fragmented bodies of the bombing victims led to flight, both physical and mental, and that metaphorical and real flight took place through the symbolic door. While all three texts are working through subjectivity there is a positive evolution in the process. The revolving door of the "new" text suggests that, even though they are sometimes caught in it, there is movement that, though sometimes in the wrong direction, is at least movement.

Pavlovsky's *Poroto* texts postulate movement through the door of interpretation and allow his own texts to function as that door. Aesthetic creation is a survival tactic, a way to move through a fragmented subjectivity. Thus, the progession in Pavlovsky's *Poroto* texts shows them as first, the history of an individual (survival) tactic (*Historia de una táctica*), then, a move in the opposite direction, a working through (*Dirección contraria*), and finally, a new way to survive (*Nueva versión para el teatro*).[24] The author and reader/spectator participate in Leo and Poroto's conversations and struggles and they, too, invent another plane, another aesthetic outlet through textuality, which can postulate a collective cure for a fragmented nation.

These three versions of *Poroto,* written by one author, are intentionally intertextual and, in many ways, they are attempts to write the same story that, in all cases, focuses on both the processes of (re)creating texts and those of (re)interpreting the Argentine. Even though Poroto is the title character of two of them and thus, seemingly, the protagonist of all three, Poroto is not really the protagonist in any of them. Text and subjectivity are the dual focus. Different points of view change and open up both the narrator and the protagonist of each text and make reading/spectatorship a collective experience. Moreover, the *Poroto* texts go beyond commenting on textual processes and interpretations, in them and their transformations Pavlovsky equates text-making with identity-making; Poroto, who exists, *por otro,* through another, is beginning to define himself and, in the end, is in control of his own departure as well as his own next move (the double meaning of the Spanish word, "partida"). Poroto is, thus, in the process of becoming the Argentine (text) that many receptors will interpret and experience.

Like Poroto, Pavlovsky's texts resist a fixed, critical approach. These three Pavlovsky works show how texts, like identity, are always fluid, in movement, unstable, but productive sites of creativity. In these texts the stage-space becomes the *chora,* an enlarged version of the interior of the protagonists' mind—confused, chaotic, always in motion, and incorporating positive and negative flows. The Poroto texts break all barriers and destroy all boundaries—linguistic, theatrical, narrative, and psychological—to show the violent effects of national trauma on the individual and collective sub-conscious and to present new, creative ways to overcome them.

RAFAEL SPREGELBURD'S *LA HEPTALOGÍA DE HIERONYMUS BOSCH: I, II, III*

Osvaldo Pellettieri divides his "theater of postmodern intertext" into two trends: "theater of resistance" and "theater of disintegration" and argues that "the proposal of these spectacular texts is that of taking postmodernism 'from within ourselves,' with our (own) limitations and perplexities, from what we could call 'our poverty,' and try to assimilate it into our identity" (2000, 19). Pellettieri postulates that, contrary to the "reflexive realism" of the previous decades, theater of resistance presents an ambiguous version of reality as a form of resistance against "official" culture (2000, 19). Theater of disintegration, on the other hand, does not rebel against or resist anything; it is an extension of the theater of the absurd and, as such, it exposes the nothingness of being. Pellettieri elaborates, "Theater of disintegration takes from the absurd the abstract idea of its theatrical language and the dissolution of the character as a psychological being—but it does not try to demonstrate anything, it believes that the meaning of the text, which is absolutely nonreferential, should be brought to light almost exclusively by the spectator" (2000, 20). The role of reader/spectator is paramount in interpreting the plays of disintegration, yet how does one interpret a play that is contradictory in both its form and its content? This is the subject of this section.

Theater of disintegration is profoundly pessimistic in that "this theater shows the disintegration of familial miscommunication, ferocious consumerism, gratuitous violence, the absence of love within 'postmodern cohabitation'; it is also intertextual with the social context" (Pellettieri 2000, 20). Unlike theater of resistance, this phase does not attempt to fight against societal malaise or political injustice, but rather displays them as hopeless, profound, and inevitable. Moreover, though Jorge Dubatti does not use the term "theater of disintegration," he explains how this new theatrical "system" attempts to portray Argentina and its place in the modern world. Dubatti argues:

> The new foundation of value, that implies a synchronization of cultural time of Argentina with the world, is no longer based on the belief in the process of the "advancement" of humanity toward achieving democratic and social equity and has down played or dispelled the myth of infinite progress, the value of "the new" as an instrument of questioning and "overcoming" the past, the universal process of secularization, the myth of human dominance over nature, the rationalist principle of "knowledge is power." The new foundation of value arouses the taking of many different positions that fluctuate between absolute rejection and uncritical acceptance.
>
> (2000, 8)

In theater of disintegration, the swing between absolute rejection and blind acceptance extends beyond culture and beyond the content; it is also manifested in the forms of the plays. The plays incorporate language and styles that both reject and embrace vanguard tendencies. Pellettieri suggests that these playwrights "are antivanguardists because they reject the basic preoccupation of the vanguard that is still present in the theater of resistance: that of creating a new art in an alternative society; but, denying the vanguard, they try to be the center of experimentation" (2000, 20). As theater of disintegration both negates and adheres to modern ideologies of society and culture, so too does it demonstrate ambivalence with regard to its own theatrical aesthetic.

Firmly rooted within this new Argentine theater of disintegration, Rafael Spregelburd's plays are marked by what Aisemberg and Libonati refer to as "a double auto-referentiality" because they relate both to his own dramaturgy and to the theatrical system to which it belongs (2000, 80), even while feigning to reject both. Moreover, most of his plays are highly intertextual, and as Aisemberg and Libonati argue, this high degree of intertextuality "is combined with other methods like the fragmentation of the story and the deconstruction of theatrical models" (80). While most critics agree that intertextuality is an increasingly predominant strategy in Argentine theater, few have analyzed how it functions dramatically and ideologically. Moreover, in works that thrive on attempting to be "nonreferential," why do playwrights choose to prioritize certain outside textual references in their own work? In this section I show how Spregelburd's plays employ other texts to both construct and deconstruct what Dubatti calls "epistemological metaphors of our current way of being in the world" (2000, 9). Additionally, I examine what that means for the Argentine nation at the end of the twentieth century and the beginning of a new one.

Rafael Spregelburd was born in Buenos Aires in 1970. His numerous plays have been published and/or performed, not only in Buenos Aires, but in many countries and languages around the world. In 1995, a first volume was published, which included *Destino de dos cosas o tres* (*Destiny of Two Things or Three*), *Cucha de almas* (*Dog House of Souls*), *Remanente de invierno* (*Remnant of Winter*), *La tiniebla* (*The Darkness*), and *Entretanto las grandes urbes* (*Meanwhile in the Big Cities*). These and other popular plays (*Raspando la cruz* [*Stealing the Cross*] and *Cuadro de asfixia* [*Scene of Asphyxiation*]) have received multiple awards such as the Primer Premio Nacional de Dramaturgia (*Destino de dos cosas o tres,* 1992), the Primer Premio Municipal de Dramaturgia de la Ciudad de Buenos Aires (*Cucha de almas,* 1997), the prestigious Premio Argentores (*Remanente de invierno,* 1996), and the equally laudable Premio GETEA (*La modestia,* 1999).[25]

Spregelburd is a multitalented dramatist, engaged in writing, directing, translating, and performing his own and other playwrights' works. His plays have been well received in Argentina, as well as in countries like France, Spain, Colombia, Portugal, Italy, the Netherlands, Chile, Venezuela, and Germany.[26] Spregelburd's critics continually emphasize the importance of language in his texts—language as a tool, as a theme, and as a game (Dubatti 2000, 15). Although language is important, however, it can be, as I explain above, both contradictory and nonreferential. Dubatti suggests that Spregelburd creates "a language that constructs reference but said reference does not possess a referenced 'reality'" (2000, 15).[27]

As Spregelburd's works play with language and recodify terms, they also often intentionally refer to other texts. His *Cuadro de asfixia,* based on Ray Bradbury's *Fahrenheit 451,* for example, incorporates Dostoyevsky, Kafka, and José Hernández as characters, literary models, actors, and texts-in-process. Moreover, the playwright himself suggests that *Cuadro de asfixia* uses these intertexts to portray and reflect upon memory as a way to rewrite the nation, postulating, "In a sad country in which memory is retractile, like a curled up bug, and amnesia cannot cure so many wounds. Ferocious amnesia, like a balsam that will pull us out of all of this, and will return to things their true value. Amnesia that obliges us to think about everything permanently, active amnesia that keeps the flesh and the senses wide awake. And alert. Here, in the country of drowsiness" (2000a, 8–9).

Similarly, in *Heptalogía de Hieronymus Bosch* (2000b), Rafael Spregelburd modernizes and extends the frame, structure, themes, and ambiguous messages of fifteenth-century Netherlands' painter Hieronymus Bosch's *The Tabletop of the Seven Deadly Sins* to both parody the earlier painting and to transplant its content to contemporary Argentina. In this section, I examine the first three works of Spregelburd's *Heptalogía: La inapetencia* (*Lack of Appetite*), *La extravagancia* (*Extravagance*), and *La modestia* (*Modesty*), to show the ways in which the playwright dramatizes and plays with his precursor text to portray contemporary Argentina, its values, and its place in the world. His incorporation of the fifteenth-century painting does more than propose a theme for his plays and it goes beyond evoking a dramatic style; it suggests an end of the century worldview which aids interpretation of Spregelburd's works and their cultural context.

Hieronymus Bosch's Tabletop of the Seven Deadly Sins

Spregelburd notes that the rare "tabletop" form of the Bosch painting demands an active attitude on the part of the spectator.[28] He suggests that "in the same way that Bosch's painting must be 'traveled around' to be seen," his plays cannot be seen as a whole, and so he suggests several possible ways to view them. Seven plays, seven sins, which, according to Spregelburd, "(Independent of each other but full of quotes like crossfire) they can be staged in one city in seven different theaters, or better yet: one can take advantage of the numerical coincidence and stage one play per day of the week. The order in which the spectator chooses to see them affects his/her worldview, and thus alters his/her particular view of each one of them" (2000b, 9). Reminiscent of Cortázar's revolutionary novel, *Rayuela* (*Hopscotch*), Spregelburd's proposed seven vignettes from Argentine life demand spectator participation to connect them to each other (beyond the mere reference to the *Heptalogía*), to decipher the language within each one of them, and to relate them to Bosch's fifteenth-century masterpiece and to contemporary Argentine culture.

The playwright himself initially links Bosch's intertext to his own modern world by stating that "my heptalogy is personal, and far from reflecting the anguish of the Middle Age man, it tries to give testimony to the fall of another order—the Modern, an order that we thought to be ours—formulating questions that accompany our own turbulence" (2000b, 7). But what are these questions about modern life that Spregelburd asks through his use of the Bosch intertext?

As noted above, Jorge Dubatti remarks, "Spregelburd's entire dramatic production is an investigation of language as origin of man's reality" (Spregelburd 2000b, back cover). The theatrical language that the dramatist chooses "translates" codes and contexts from one system to another. Through these texts Spregelburd is not only attempting to translate "some technical aspects of the painter," but he is also looking to translate "the language of intuitions, instincts, ideas, anticipated appearances, internal images, etc. . . . to a language that does not yet exist, but once the play is finished it will create all these interrelations between signs that constitute what we understand through language" (Spregelburd 2000b, 6).

To begin to decipher the language of these three complex plays and to connect them, beyond their titles, to Bosch's enigmatic *Tabletop of the Seven Deadly Sins,* I will first analyze that painting in detail. Probably created between 1475 and 1480, Bosch's painted *Tabletop* joins traditional religious iconography and themes of the Middle Ages with an almost postmodern, surrealist style and seemingly heretic and eschatological portrayal of the seven vices, which were said to lead to the demise of Christians during that period. Walter Gibson (1982) describes the painting as a "moral allegory" in which the "condition and fate of humanity are presented in a series of circular images." He further argues that "The central image, formed of concentric rings, represents the Eye of God, in whose pupil Christ emerges from his sarcophagus, displaying his wounds to the viewer. Around the pupil are inscribed the words 'Beware, Beware, God sees'; and just what God sees is mirrored in the outer ring of his eye, where the Seven Deadly Sins are enacted in lively little scenes taken from everyday life. The Latin name of each sin is clearly inscribed at the bottom" (1982, 33). As Gibson suggests, the labeling is superfluous, as the sins, Gluttony, Avarice, Envy, Anger, Pride, Lust, and Sloth, are obviously portrayed in each of the seven images around the central eye. The "little dramas," as Gibson calls them, are variously placed either in the Dutch countryside or "within well-constructed interiors filled with domestic details" (34).

Beyond the central eye and the representations of the seven sins, two other elements mark the painting: the message-bearing banderols at the top and bottom of the work and the four circles, one in each corner, representing Death, the Final Judgment, Heaven, and Hell. The top banderol reads, "For they are a nation void of counsel, neither is there any understanding in them. O that they were wise that they understood this, that they would consider their latter end." The lower scroll proclaims, "I will hide my face from them. I will see what their end shall be" (Gibson 1982, 36). Both inscribed texts come from the biblical book of Deuteronomy; while the top inscription reflects upon the follies of the nation, in the lower text the individual watches for the outcome of that national folly. The wheel-like arrangement of the composition as well as its religious content adheres to a medieval idea of "God spying on mankind from the sky" as a means of deterring sin (Gibson 1982, 37). Moreover, Bosch's work suggests a mirrorlike spiritual introspection, "wherein the viewer is confronted by his own soul disfigured by vice. At the same time, however, he beholds the remedy for this disfigurement in the image of Christ occupying the centre of the Eye" (Gibson 1982, 37).

Apparently, Bosch too used other intertexts to construct both the form and the content of his piece. Beyond the biblical references, Gibson notes similar themes and structures in Brant's *Ship of Fools,* Guillaume de Deguilleville's *The Pilgrimage of the Life of Man,* and a late fifteenth-century German woodcut, among other precursor texts. Moreover, Spregelburd is in good company in choosing Bosch's work as his intertext. It seems that Spain's Quevedo, as well, was fascinated with Bosch and his art. Whether Quevedo admired Bosch or condemned him remains questionable, but Bosch is one of the few artists whom Quevedo mentions by name in his literary works and, according to Helmut Heidenreich, he does so repeatedly (Snyder 1973, 160). Gibson believes that Bosch's painting "shows mankind given over to sin, completely unmindful of God's law and oblivious to the fate which he has prepared for them" (69). Nonetheless, there are other, more secular interpretations of Bosch's work. Basing their arguments on the little that is known about the artist's life, as well as on religious traditions of the time, other Bosch scholars present a different understanding of the *Seven Deadly Sins.*

Hieronymus Bosch seemed to be a religious man. In 1486, he was admitted to the prestigious Brotherhood of our Lady, a Catholic group that organized prayer meetings, distributed bread to the poor, presided over funeral ceremonies, and trained orchestras to perform in the cathedral. Interestingly, however, this organization also sponsored a theatrical company that staged all kinds of dramatic performances. The purpose of these performances was to calm and assure "God-fearing (and Satan-fearing) people, ridden with superstitions and obsessed by atavistic phobias stemming from the Dark Ages" (Delevoy 1960, 10). The plays, however, included farces, mystery plays, and pageants, as well as types of devil dances (ibid.).

In 1496, a foreign Jewish Christian man, Jacob van Almaengien, converted to Catholicism and joined the Brotherhood of Our Lady. Wilhelm Fraenger suggests that van Almaengien's foreign, formerly heretical viewpoint greatly influenced Bosch and his art. Based on this influence and supported by an analysis of the form and intention of the *Seven Deadly Sins,* Fraenger believes that every work of Bosch is "double-voiced," and "can be read either as a Christian-Catholic and traditionally devout or as Jewish-Christian and heretical" (1983, 270).[29]

A secular or "heretical" interpretation of the painting suggests that the central image is not that of God, but rather, "the tiny image in the 'apple of the eye,' the pupil, is believed to be man's self, his soul, a microcosm associated in a radiating relationship with the sun, the world-eye of the macrocosm" (Fraenger 1983, 270). Fraenger believes that the work functioned as an instruction guide for meditators. "By staring at the mirror reflection of his right eye in auto hypnotic concentration, the meditator strove to move beyond his ego-self and contemplate the world-self or sunlike god-self" (271). By walking around the *Tabletop* and staring at the inner self represented in the center and the earthly scenes of the seven panels, earthly life, not God, becomes the focus. Fraenger suggests, then, that this painting was "a psychagogic work designed to produce a spiritual catharsis in the viewer" (271).

In fact, the form of the painting confirms this "other" reading. According to Fraenger, the Church could not have commissioned this *Tabletop,* as there was no such thing as a "penitential table" in the Church of Bosch's time (268). The artistry and cabinetry of the piece suggest that it served as an "intimate center of spiritual exercises in everyday domestic life" (Fraenger 1983, 268). Moreover, the circle form often used by Bosch fosters meditation and spiritual concentration and is common to the mandala in Buddhist art. The circular form can also be connected to geometry, astronomy, and numerology.[30] The central image of the painting is made up of three circles: the outer circle of the wedges depicting the seven sins, the inner iris of the eye, and the innermost pupil. In the four corners of the table, outside the larger circle, lie the four circles of Death, Judgment,

Heaven, and Hell. "The whole work was contrived to suggest a ball, sphere, globe, microcosm of the universe" (Delevoy 1960, 24). Moreover, both the number seven and the circular shapes align it with the planets and their movement.[31] By following the *Tabletop*'s path to the right as the compositional center of each sin directs the viewer, the Table of Repentance becomes the *Table of Wisdom.*[32]

Even though the *Tabletop* seems to be understood from two apparently contradictory perspectives—within postmedieval Catholic tradition and from a secular, foreign, perhaps heretical point of view—Fraenger argues that the double pull of Bosch's *Tabletop* was not really contradictory. Extremely pious, devout Christians read it as a "primer of good churchly behavior," which included all the familiar images of their upbringing. A select few, however, allowed themselves to be pulled to a deeper, more mysterious level of understanding and spiritual concentration. "The resulting exalted feeling of being one of the elect disciples of a wisdom that seemed to offer a solution to the riddle of sin, death, and the beyond, and even to show the way to self-redemption, was the more unconstrained in that the new faith did not demand the repudiation of the old one" (294).

In this contradictory reading of Bosch's *Tabletop,* two points emerge that come to bear on my reading of Spregelburd's plays. First, as Fraenger suggests, Bosch's contact with the foreigner van Almaengien, is what ultimately impacted both his worldview and the creation of that painting. Fraenger argues, "The inflow of a powerful foreign influence had produced [an astounding rise in the thought level] in the hitherto locally constricted understanding of Bosch. Only a radical upheaval, a jolting loose from the normal framework of life, could so rapidly have transformed an unthinking copier of outdated clichés into the keen-eyed social satirist of the sinners' frieze, and such an upheaval could have been produced only by an 'alien'" (295). Similar to Bosch's painting, Spregelburd's plays comment on globalization and cultural imperialism, those "foreign" influences in contemporary Argentine culture. However, rather than speak against them, as one might have expected in theater of resistance, Spregelburd portrays them and their effect in a seemingly apathetic fashion; he notes their complex pull and invasion on the characters' condition as a matter of course, a necessary influence in today's world. What he seems to object to, however, is the way in which some citizens react to those foreign influences and invasions. His plays present apathy, disinterest, malaise, and overindulgence as the "sins" of our time.

Like Spregelburd, Bosch was an artist living between two conflicting times and, as such, he was an interpreter and prognostic of

Hieronymus Bosch (c.1450–1516). Consignment: COA0043083 (Position: 1) Seven Deadly Sins. Museo del Prado, Madrid, Spain. Photo Credit: Scala/Art Resources, NY

his moment. Delevoy suggests of Bosch that "placed at the crossroads of two Ages [Medieval and Renaissance], he illustrates a conflict of ideas, emotions, and tastes. Torn between hope and dark foreboding, between faith and doubt, his oeuvre may justly be regarded as a sign of the times, both fascinating and instructive" (1960, 18). Like Bosch's works, then, Spregelburd's plays are both fascinating and instructive because they are symbols of an artist caught between history and postmodernity, and they vividly portray the complexity of living in a global world of ever-changing boundaries and limitless configurations.

I suggest, then, that Spregelburd's plays use Bosch's painting to subvert the perspective on the world, as did Bosch. In other words, traditional interpretation of Bosch's *Tabletop* directs the viewer's attention to a worldview dictated by certain moral laws and shows how the viewer must be careful not to break those laws. Another perspective suggests that the individual is obsessed with him/herself and is caught in his own image within the world order. Spregelburd does not use Bosch's painting to extract and emphasize religious themes. Rather, Spregelburd's characters are those self-absorbed individuals trapped within themselves in a confusing, highly interconnected world. An analysis of the three plays, and the sections of the painting, the sins, that they parody, will shed light on the Argentine playwright's intentions and the form and functions of his plays.

Spregelburd includes a more recent interpretation of Bosch's *Seven Deadly Sins,* by Eduardo Del Estal, in the introduction to his 2000 publication of these three plays. Del Estal's ideas on Bosch highlight an interesting way to read and interpret Spregelburd's plays as well. Del Estal suggests that the *Tabletop* is "a cartography of madness" because it presents the fear of the possibility of a limited number of meanings (2000, 15). For life to continue, interpretation cannot be a closed system because "When each signifier comes to have one signified, that will be the end of the world" (Del Estal 2000, 19). Our times pose interesting questions because we know too much and we have too much. Excess is the cause for sin for as Del Estal argues, "If we pay attention to the nature of each of the seven sins we realize that each one consists of an excess of a natural activity" (2000, 17). The sins of Bosch's painting and in Bosch's time resulted from transgressing the boundaries of "normal," natural, and accepted behaviors through excess. Even though sin is not really part of our contemporary code, Bosch's themes hold true today for another important reason: they point out a problem in our time—we are a limitless world. Without limits and boundaries, excess is the norm, and desire is destroyed. "There must be transgression in order to have limits, and the limit, in so far as it is impassable, creates desire" (Del Estal 2000, 18). Without limits, desire is satiated and meaning is complete, but devoid of relevance, leading to death and "the end of the world."

The plays in his *Heptalogía I* are among the many works for which Spregelburd has received awards. The first play, *La inapetencia,* originally appeared in the October 1997 issue of the *Revista Teatro XXI* published by GETEA (Grupo de Estudios de Teatro Argentino e Iberoamericano). Jorge Dubatti calls the play "a parable of loss: Mrs. Perrotta is 'a mother that goes about losing everything,' metaphor for the human process of the 'loss' of reality" (2000, 15). In fact, though, Señora Perrotta does not really lose anything; she is caught in the nothingness of her existence, because she has no desire.

The play's five scenes depict the lack of communication between Señora Perrotta and her husband by dramatizing dialogues between them as well as scenes when Señora Perrotta describes their relationship to others. Each scene is presented in an absurdist fashion, highlighting both the lack of communication between the couple and the lack of meaning in their individual worldview and their life as a family. When it seems as if the couple might achieve communication around such serious topics as that of adopting a child (although we learn later that they already have one or more, that Señora Perrotta tries to sell her daughter to the gypsies, and that she has a strained relationship with her eldest son), thoughts of food get in their way.

The many references to food in the play, as well as the title itself, might lead the reader/spectator to immediately interpret *La inapetencia* (*Lack of Appetite*) as a representation of gluttony, one of the seven deadly sins depicted in Bosch's *Tabletop.* While food and, indeed, Señora Perrotta's obsession with it, are themes of the play, as Aisemberg and Libonati rightly suggest, the play is perhaps more about lust, than gluttony (2000, 81). In fact, Spregelburd condenses still a third sin into this piece, sloth, when Señora Perrotta remarks to her husband, "You should play some sport. Tennis, something. That is why you think so much. Because you don't do anything useful" (31). An examination of these three sins in the Bosch context and later in this play will help to show the ways in which Spregelburd subverts the Bosch context to write his own script on desire, decadence, and the postmodern nation.

Positioned at the top of the central eye, opposite anger, gluttony holds a predominant place on the Bosch *Tabletop.* Three pictures within the gluttony image symbolize both the enduring tradition of the sin and its injustice to society: a bloated glutton is stuffing himself at the table; his equally obese son approaches him wearing his father's shoes (symbolizing that he will follow in his father's sinful footsteps); and a scraggly, skinny beggar is only allowed a drink of water in spite of the abundance.

Ironically, gluttony and lust are connected even in Bosch's painting. His depiction of lust shows upper-class people amusing themselves in a half-open tent in an outside setting. The foods on a nearby table as well as the image of a poor man being brutally beaten with a large spoon connect the two sins. Fraenger suggests that "Bosch limited lust to the relatively refined pleasures of the table and of music, surrounding the courtly flirtation with delicacies and musical instruments." He further establishes that the spoon was a "symbol of illicit love in those days" and that a phallic-shaped bottle symbolizes the lustiness of the scene (1983, 274). The sloth scene in Bosch, on the other hand, shows a woman, a man sleeping in a chair, and a dog also sleeping and they represent the "mental state of dull lethargy in which energy flags and all vitality is extinguished" (Fraenger 1983, 274).

Beyond the title of *La inapetencia,* numerous references to eating and food exaggerate the play's connection to Bosch's gluttony. When the play opens Señora Perrotta and her husband are at the table where they "eat little or have finished eating" (25). Nonetheless, even though they seem to be full, at various points in the play one or the other will comment on their hunger. Often they cannot decide whether they are hungry or not:

> *Marido.* Aren't you still hungry? What did you say?
> *Sra. Perrotta.* I would eat a child of God.
> *Marido.* I can prepare some noodles. Or a little more omelette.
> *Sra. Perrotta.* No, forget it. I ate too much.
> *Marido.* Me too.
>
> (29)

Even though they vacillate between extreme hunger and fullness, their obsession with food and with eating is notable, as is the fact that they are never satisfied. In scene 4 the family is seated around a table but "no one is eating" (46–47). When their daughter Leila enters in scene 5, her mother asks her, "Did you eat anything?" When she replies, yes, rather than accepting her answer, her mother asks again. Later, the husband asks, "Did you eat? We could order some pizzas." (55). His wife later decides to order pizza, without acknowledging that her husband had already made the same suggestion.

Moreover, the couple wants children who can supply food for

them and who will feed them in their old age. The husband states that he wants children, "who give us food" (30) apparently forgetting that he already has a daughter and possibly two sons. In addition, they connect food, its excess, or its lack, with the nation and with the world.

> *Sra. Perrotta.* That is Yugoslavia, right?
> *Pause.*
> *Sra. Perrotta.* There are oranges.
> *Marido.* Mmh. How wonderful! Ex-Yugoslavia.
> *Sra. Perrotta.* Do you want some?
> *Marido.* No, no, that's okay. I'll buy myself a chocolate later.
>
> (29–30)

In scene 4, one of the scenes between Señora Perrotta and her friends, Romita remarks on an image she saw in the street: a man with a missing leg. She reacts to the man's loss, noting:

> He was missing a leg. It was impossible to look him in the eyes, I swear. And I could not stop doing it. What was impressive was not the lack of the leg in itself, the missing leg wasn't ugly, but rather the place from where the leg was missing. Do you understand? Not the lack, but the place, the borderline of the absence. The edge . . . It was not an unpunished absence. Nor honest. There are lacks that are more elegant. Won't you eat something? There are things that are lacking, there are hungry children, there is all that. I am not saying there isn't. But the stumps are ugly.
>
> (50)

Romita's reaction to the man's handicap is curious and strikes a contradictory note to the content of the dialogue in the rest of the play; while most of the play's characters have so much that they want for nothing and thus create new ways to sin, she seems indifferent to the man's missing leg, because there is so much want and need and greed in the world. Perhaps she is looking for some real limits in her life—limits between excess, satiation, and desire. Or maybe she is simply desensitized to this man's situation—living in her world as a glutton, with extravagant amounts of food and time to waste.

The dialogue with its rare juxtapositions reminds us of Bosch's image of gluttony itself. While the gluttonous man fills his face at the table and the woman continuously brings him food, the beggar symbolizes the world outside, haggard, thin, uncared for even when there is enough for everyone. Similarly, as the women in *La inapetencia* sit around the table filling their faces, they note the plight of the deformed man with amusement and indifference; no thoughts of feeding him occur to them. His handicap reminds them of hungry children, yet they ignore them as well.

Ironically, food becomes the only thing they can communicate about and the excess of conversation about food highlights the lack of communication in every other realm. Moreover, it is not just a lack of communication between husband and wife that is noted; Señora Perrotta has difficulty communicating with her friends in scene 4 and with the employees in the office in scene 2. The only scene where real communication seems to occur is the third scene where a gypsy reads Señora Perrotta's palm and the latter offers to give up her daughter because of what she learns about her daughter's future (that she will seek knowledge and have a mind of her own). Ironically, the gypsy admits to Señora Perrotta that he is deceiving her from the outset.

Obsession with and dialogue about food alternates with conversations about lust. In scene 2, Señora Perrotta searches for something to fill the lacks in her life: her lack of communication and empty relationships with her husband and her children. She admits to Sara, the employee she meets in the sadomasochist office, "I want to try hard sex, I want to be tied to a table and bitten in my sexual organs. I want to dress in leather and take hold of a whip. I want to discipline men and women, with and without pain. I have many fantasies about this" (38). Since she has no meaningful relationships, she obsesses over food and sex.

Even though Señora Perrotta seems to be in search of a more lustful life, she admits that she has really never practiced sadomasochism. "I don't know if I could spend a week there . . . I don't know . . . being the first time, maybe it would be better to spend a long weekend. Now in June there are two long weekends . . . Since during the week I work in schools. It is worth a try, isn't it?" (40). She is looking to try a more lustful life, to fill a void in her banal, monotonous existence. Her husband, on the other hand, is engaged in sadomasochistic acts, and in scene 5, as their daughter is preparing to go to Ex-Yugoslavia to help with the war and humanitarian efforts, her father returns home after a difficult day at work where he has been sodomized by two administrative coworkers. He is worn out and bleeding from the activity.

Gluttony and lust abound; the family and friends eat excessively and engage in sadomasochism. When they are not actually practicing these activities, they are talking and thinking about them. Bosch's sins are condensed in *La inapetencia,* and it is difficult to determine where one sin ends and the next begins. Sloth is also prevalently portrayed in the play. Beyond the comments cited above, there is a general attitude of apathy and laziness, which permeates the piece. At the end, for example, Señora Perrotta finally orders the pizza that both husband and wife had talked about during the entire last scene. In spite of their hunger, when the pizza arrives, no one moves toward the door.

> *The doorbell rings.*
> *Sra. Perrotta.* That must be the pizzas.
> *No one moves.*
> *Sra. Perrotta.* Who will answer it?
> *Silence. The bell rings again.*
> *Sra. Perrotta.* Ah, we could use the box as a napkin, then we won't have to get up to bring plates . . .
> *Sra. Perrotta.* (*The doorbell rings for the last time.*) Wow! What an appetite I have! (*Pause*) Who will answer the door? (*Blackout*).
> (62)

Not only are they too lazy to answer the door, but they are also too lazy to get up to get plates and napkins. Their slothfulness, however, is contrasted to their daughter's sense of duty, humanity, and industriousness.

Their daughter, Leila, is heading to Bosnia because there is a war going on and volunteers are needed. Leila has a visceral disgust of wars because, "Wars devastate the countryside where thousands of delicate and soft roses grow" (54). As a young idealist, she refuses to accept that the nation of Yugoslavia has ended, stating, "If we give up on it, it is the ex. If, on the other hand, we unite the forces of thousands of young people and go sow those roses that the tanks flatten, it is the great Yugoslavia, the homeland, the garden where I want my children to frolic" (56).

Her parents, on the other hand, see no relationship between Yugoslavia's fate and their own nation. Sra. Perrotta argues, "But that is there. That is Bosnia. Here it is different" (54). Leila cannot tolerate her parents' ignorance and apathy and she remarks, "I cannot tolerate it anymore . . . It is not 'ex' Yugoslavia. You are my ex-homeland, I ex-patriate myself, I spit on every plate of food you have given me, I am gathering my last things and I am leaving" (56). Rejecting her parents and her nation because of their indifference, their inactivity, and their apathy, she quickly packs her bags and prepares to leave her country.

Leila's parents' excessive vices, however, are also their undoing. Like in Bosch's painting, the punishment for the sins is contained within the "scenes from everyday life" showing how excess leads to moral decadence, a type of abulia.[33] In Spregelburd's play, for example, the *marido*'s bleeding "from his backside" is his punishment for his acts of lustfulness. As punishment for their gluttony, the couple cannot even move to the door to get their pizza at the end of the play. Their indifference leads their daughter to disown them. The punishment for their sins is their own excessiveness, compulsiveness, and self-absorption. They cannot move outside of themselves so they are forced to live with themselves. Similar to the existentialist view of Jean-Paul Sartre's *No Exit* where there is no escape from hell because we are forced to live with each other, in this play hell is also a self-made configuration.[34] Like existentialist works, Spregelburd's play seems to suggest that we create our own hell. Hell, if it exists, is a man-made place. There is no longer a divine God punishing us but rather we punish and have punished ourselves. We must take the blame for the world for it is through man's indifference that suffering exists.

Envy's Many Faces in *La extravagancia*

La extravagancia (*Extravagance*), directed by Rubén Szuchmacher, debuted on June 20, 1997, in the Sala Babilonia Theater in Buenos Aires and has had repeat performances in Madrid (1998) and Oviedo, Spain (1999) and Mexico City (2006). The play beautifully displays one of Spregelburd's most notable traits: his ability to create multiple characters using few actors. In *La extravagancia,* one actress plays all three sisters: María Socorro, María Brujas, and María Axila. The three sisters, arranged side by side onstage, take turns speaking, sometimes to an invisible sister or sometimes to the audience. As a writer, María Socorro, seated on the left, intertwines the creation of her novel, a love story between Frank and Dwight, with her concern for her own identity. Similarly, the other two sisters also wonder about their heritage. Apparently, their mother bore triplets but one died at birth. In an effort to recuperate their lost daughter, the parents adopted a daughter in the birth clinic, and thus brought home the girls, raising all three as if they were their legitimate children. The parents never revealed the truth to their daughters and destroyed all the birth papers and the clinic itself so that the girls would never know who among them was not the biological sister.

All three sisters are equally obsessed with their identity. María Axila, only shown through a television screen positioned between her two sisters, seems to be the most prominent figure, both because of her stage position in the center and because she is the most learned of the three. As the stage directions suggest, "When indicated, María Axila's text will be heard more loudly. Otherwise, the image of María Axila in the television program will not have audio, although her suggestive gesticulations will continue to allude to the extravagance already warned about in the title" (64). When her voice is not drowning out the others, her wild gestures, enlarged mouth, or pained expressions take the central focus. As a linguist, she continuously explains the formation of various phonemes and questions the relationship between words and their meaning.

The sister on the right, María Brujas, reveals to Socorro by telephone that their mother is dying of a strange, hereditary illness. Thus, the two biologically related sisters will soon die too. Ironically, each girl would rather die than discover that she is illegitimate, and as the play progresses, each sister fabricates symptoms pretending to be one of the ill, but real, sisters.

Rather than portraying the extravagance of the title, the play dramatizes the sin of envy which is symbolized by the bestiary image of the basilisk, a mythical, fantastic, reptilelike creature typically associated with envy (Spregelburd 2000b, 13). María Axila, the expert on language, opens *La extravagancia* with a speech about symbolism and meaning, in which she talks about the importance of both the salamander and the basilisk. "The basilisk is the animal that interests us most for the purposes of what we are going to describe. They said that he inspired fear, and that his gaze was capable of killing" (65). Like envy, the basilisk can kill with its gaze. Moreover, it is difficult to overcome and destroy, for as Axila suggests, "One could only kill a basilisk by approaching it walking backwards, following its foul-smelling gaze with a hand-held mirror. After killing it, the mirror had to be destroyed and its pieces buried far from the chicken coops" (65–66). Envy, like the basilisk, has gigantic dimensions; it is both deadly and difficult to destroy.

Envy, or the desire for others' traits, status, abilities, or situation is the opposite of the virtue of love or kindness. Bosch's painting of envy could appear remarkably serene; however, a closer look at envy reveals details that reinforce the sin and show how it affects many sectors. Envy is portrayed in each character in the envy image in Bosch's painting. According to Fraenger, the setting is a customhouse where the collector, envious of the rich man with the falcon, holds out a bone to (but withholds it from) two envious, and apparently hungry, dogs (although one of the dogs has a pile of bones in front of him, toward which the other dog looks longingly). Meanwhile, the man with the falcon is envious because another man is flirting with the collector's daughter in the left of the scene. On the right, a poor beggar is weighed down by a heavy sack. Fraenger suggests that the "intricate web of envy exposes the social gap between the rich and the poor" (1983, 274–75).

Envy and pride are linked together in this play because María Axila's description of the basilisk and its mythological powers and dimensions also associates it with another of Bosch's deadly sins: pride. As the basilisk can only be destroyed by looking at it through a mirror, so, too, in Bosch's *Tabletop,* the Devil's mirror destroys the vain woman in the *Soberbia* scene.[35] Spregelburd's play brings out the ridiculous aspect of excessive pride as well as envy, as each sister is so proud and yet so envious of the others that she would rather die than accept the possibility that she is the outcast.

Each sister displays her envy of the others differently. It is María Brujas who invents the story of the legitimate daughters' imminent death and telephones Socorro. Even though she has already placed the call, she insists that Socorro *call her* to learn the details. Her insecurity also leads her to accuse her parents of caring more about the others than about her.[36] So envious of the possibility that the "real" sisters might be dying, she cuts off her own hair and then leaves a message on her answering machine stating that she is deathly ill and suffering through chemotherapy. Finally, after learning that her sister has lumps under her arm, her jealousy leads her to acknowledge that "it is them, it is the two of them" before attempting to commit suicide by swallowing a bottle of nail polish remover (78).

María Socorro expresses her envy through her rage, suggesting yet another of Bosch's deadly sins: anger. Like Brujas she admits that she is lonely (83), but she reveals her true feelings toward her sisters when she says to Axila through the television screen, "And you too, you mute idiot! I only hope that you die before the two of us, and that you have a sophisticated wake and that your funeral is a parade of chaplains, and that it is far and that it rains!" (74). As a writer she realizes and expresses to the audience that she could arrange any of those possibilities because she is ultimately in control of this story. She affirms to the audience, "Yes, all that last part is filled with images, images that generate possibilities" (74). Moreover, her book comes as a result of both her envy and her anger at her sister and she admits, "That is to say, I use the irritation that my sister always provokes in me, I don't even know if she is my sister . . . that useless thing" (74). Interestingly, however, the writer's words are drowned out by the television, as "María Axila's text, whose beginning we have already listened to, superimposes itself over María Socorro's" (74).

Aisemberg and Libonati note the importance of television speech in Spregelburd's *Heptalogía.* María Axila's prominent position between the two sisters, the fact that her speech drowns out theirs and that she is an "expert" on everything from language to life, further displays the important impact of television in modern times. The sisters are envious of her knowledge and label her as the outcast. Nonetheless, though she never verbally expresses her envy, her pained expressions and the way in which she holds her breast and buries her hand in her armpits indicate that she, too, wants to belong.

The television, like the telephone, the only two objects onstage, highlights the lack of communication between the sisters. They never talk to each other, except through the television screen or the telephone. The sisters are incapable of communicating; on her television program, María Axila explains why this is so, stating, "there is no logical connection, and much less a natural one, between the sound of a word and its meaning" (67). Since there is no logical connection between words and meaning, communication is impossible.

Even though the possibility of communication is built upon an imperfect system, we continue to search for the truth and for meaning. As she begins to tell us her story, Socorro confirms that "what you are going to see is true," yet the myth of the truth is unraveled at every turn. As the sisters attempt to discover their origins, they know that their parents are lying to them. In addition, each sister lies to herself and to the others about her health, and thus about her own identity. Socorro reminds us, "the ultimate question of literature, of all literature, is: can we create a climate here inside, among ourselves, when it is raining outside?" (82). Literature is based on lies and so sometimes, the lies are much more interesting than the truth. What happens though when texts are intertwined, when one "story" has its roots in another that is connected to another ad infinitum? As is the case of *La extravagancia,* whose story is based on Chekhov's *Three Sisters* and perhaps other Russian stories noted within the play, all texts are intertextual, based on the lies created by others. Brujas admits that "the thing about the party at my home was a lie, it was another party that I had tape-recorded. The part about the chemotherapy treatment was a lie. Like it is a lie that the basilisk exists, that is mythology, and like it is a lie that its gaze alone is capable of killing" (84).

All this, however, was resolved in the Middle Ages, Axila reminds us in her first line of *La extravagancia* (65). Whether Bosch's sins were expressed by a devout Catholic or a heretic and whether his ideas came from the Church or from a foreign other, the painted images of the sins show how truth and fiction intersect. Though some believed in the power of the deadly sins, others, as we have seen, used the painting for purposes of Eastern meditation, ignoring its Catholic interpretation.

Moreover, once again, the punishment for the sin of envy is inscribed within the Bosch painting; the envious man is torn to pieces by dogs in the death medallion in the bottom left-hand corner of the *Tabletop* (Martin and Cinotti 1966, 87–88). In *La extravagancia,* however, the sisters punish themselves; not only are they isolated from each other and from their parents, but they also cannot live with themselves. Each sister would rather create suffering for herself than learn the truth. Once again, the truth and the search for it are paramount in Spregelburd; however, it is clear in *La extravagancia* that for these sisters the truth is meaningless; their envy and excessive pride ruin their life.

Nation in La inapetencia *and* La extravagancia

La inapetencia takes place in Argentina, though the only real reference to Argentina comes from Sara, the office worker in scene 2.[37] Although Argentina is only referenced once, Yugoslavia and Ex-Yugoslavia (Bosnia, Serbia) are mentioned several times, for that is Leila's destination. Outside of this context one might see very little relationship between the end of the twentieth-century Argentina and the Yugoslavian situation during the last twenty years; however, *La inapetencia* relates the two nations.

Leila admits that she is going to Bosnia because there is a war going on and they need volunteers. Señora Perrotta sees little connection between Bosnia and her country, and she reminds her daughter, "But that is there. That is Bosnia. Here is different" (54). Leila's response, "I cannot take anymore," would lead us to believe that she disagrees with her mother's interpretation. Leila does not see the war in Bosnia as so very different from what is going on in her nation.

Bosnia had been brought up earlier in the play. In scene 1 when Señora Perrotta and her husband's conversation over whether or not to adopt a child became tense, the husband reminds his wife that this tension is nothing like what is going on in Bosnia. He says, "Don't exaggerate. A couple should necessarily discuss certain things. It is normal. Even if they are painful, I mean. After all, we are talking about adopting a child and not about the war in Bosnia, right?" (27). He seems to recognize the troubling situation in that nation, yet he refuses to see any relationship between it and his own homeland. Moreover, Leila's father refuses to recognize Bosnia, the "modern" formation of that "nation," but rather he insists upon calling it the "ex-Yugoslavia" (29, 56). He is living in isolation and in a past, unrealistic, but utopian place, refusing to recognize both the turmoil and the fragmented nature of that or his own nation.

Why does Spregelburd choose to highlight the Yugoslavian/Bosnian/Serbian situation and to connect it to his own nation? Even though it would be difficult to say for sure, an examination of some of the key questions and issues surrounding former Yugoslavia might enlighten our reading of *La inapetencia.* According to James Gow, "the ambiguity over national self-determination in the Yugoslav context has peculiar features, but these are details which do no more than create emphasis—they do not make the Yugoslav case unique" (1974, 467). Ambiguity is certainly foregrounded in Spregelburd's play and equally so with regard to nation. Only a careful reading yields the Argentine context; far more mention is made of Bosnia/Yugoslavia than Argentina. Yet Señora Perrotta and her family are clearly Argentine, and their lethargy, passivity, gluttonous, lustful, and slothlike behaviors and attitudes are somehow caused by their national situation.

Leila rejects both her parents and her nation, stating, "You are my ex-homeland, I ex-patriate myself" (56). In his article on the Yugoslavian situation, Gow argues that "the security of the state depends upon making those within its borders feel that they belong" (473). Leila clearly feels like she does not belong in this family and in this nation. Events in Argentina during the past thirty years, ranging from the Dirty War, the forced national amnesia of the Menem years, and the economic crises that were building but exploded in the late nineties, have alienated a growing number of its citizens, especially the young (among whom Spregelburd, born in 1970, might be considered). As a result of Leila's alienation, she is rejecting her national family. Gow postulates that "In political reality, if not in international law, rejection of a political community by one group within it represents both the loss of legitimacy and the loss of sovereignty within that political community" (470–71). If the young do not believe in their nation, then that nation is illegitimate in their eyes.

Moreover, in rejecting her nation, Leila is rejecting its sovereignty and redefining the term. Gow argues, "if sovereignty is to mean anything, it means the inalienable right not to do what someone else wants" (471). In other words, ambiguity can be a useful tool of subversion and can help in the process of redefining nation. Gow further establishes, "it is plain that a clear understanding of these words with two meanings (sovereignty, self-determination, statehood, and security), including an awareness of their existence is required before the problems which arise from their ambiguities can be addressed" (475).

Spregelburd uses the Bosch painting and the Bosnian conflict to highlight the ambiguities of language, of texts, and of nation in an effort to recontextualize them. Gow postulates that "the possible impact of differing understandings is attested by the war in Yugoslavia" and that "the events in Yugoslavia have demonstrated what can happen when these concepts are not clearly understood by either the protagonists or those outside the conflict attempting to deal with it" (475). Yugoslavia/Bosnia and Argentina are not so very different. Misunderstanding, miscommunication, and misinterpretation have led to a divided nation and the alienation of its young citizens. The impact of these will be felt for years to come.

The question of legitimacy is the focus of *La extravagancia* as the three Marías strive to belong to their family. Belonging, though, means death for the two legitimate sisters. Since belonging to the family, that "questionable way of organizing bodies in space" (75), extinguishes life and causes the protagonists' illness, it is no wonder that their mother dies "against the foolish idea that a homeland exists" (85).

Both *La inapetencia* and *La extravagancia* include many characters that reject their family and their nation. Leila and the three Marías question their parents' actions and intentions and reject them. Because each character sees the nation as an extension of the family, they express similar negative attitudes toward their homeland. At the same time, however, all these characters long to belong, to fit into both their family and the nation. This difficult and even impossible situation is the location of citizens in our time; citizens are caught in a love-hate relationship with their homeland and search for belonging in a global world.

Although Spregelburd gives hints that he is writing about his Argentina he, like Bosch, is dramatizing a turn of the century mind-set, which does not speak of individual nations but rather of mankind or global citizens and their texts. The three Marías are each writing their own "story"; Brujas fabricates the "illness story," Socorro is writing the story of Dwight and Frank, and Axila retells the Ukranian story of the triplets as well as the myth of the basilisk, among other stories. Whether they wish to acknowledge it or not, their stories are necessarily intertwined, even though they are alienated from each other. The characters are the stories and yet, it is all one big story about life, about the search for truth, and about humanity. As the characters narrate their individual stories, all related intertextually to other stories from different times and places, they are analyzing themselves, each other, and their texts, thus highlighting their own metatextuality. As Patrice Pavis suggests:

> From now on, the representation of the real will not stop dematerializing, demotivating and destructuring itself into a more open text, where frontiers and differences between dramaturgy, writing and characters have become much more blurred, or even non-existent. For we are just about to move, even if the characters, so to speak, have not noticed it, to the level of metadiscourse—namely the possibility of saying, of knowing whether one is speaking the truth, of remaining silent. These are metadiscursive techniques which take place on the level of characters' statements, as on the level of a discursive mechanism, of textual indecisiveness, of the continuum of character/dramaturgy/textuality. (2000, 5)

Bosch's painting tells stories and, at the same time, promotes self-analysis; so, too, do *La inapetencia* and *La extravagancia* tell the stories of our times and promote a questioning of human essence, communication, and truth at the end of the twentieth century.

Cynthia Marsh argues that intertextuality is not only verbal but rather it can be manifested through nonverbal aspects such as setting, character hierarchies, and the utilization of space (1999, 602). A look at characters' behaviors and attitudes, the indirect or direct emphasis on the theme of sin and the labeling of them and their punishments, allows us to make a connection between the texts analyzed above and further expands upon the ideology of nation that each writer presents. The connection with Bosch's painting both circumscribes and expands readings of *La inapetencia* and *La extravagancia* because it allows the reader/spectator to focus on the details of the work—each individual character, the characters' immobility and passivity, their obsessions—while at the same time it frames it within the bigger picture of postmodernism and globalization.

Reading these Spregelburd plays against Bosch's painting brings out not only the vices and their inherent punishment, but it also modernizes them and presents them within a turn-of-the-century context. It is interesting to note that though they live in different times and distant places, Bosch and Spregelburd are both turn-of-the-century artists with similar worldviews. Living at the crossroads of two times must impact an artist's outlook. In his article on *Chekhov and the Philosophy of the Turn of the Century,* Ildiko Regeczi suggests that Chekhov's writing incorporates certain themes that are related to the religious philosophy of Lev Shestov. Regeczi argues, for example, that "very often Chekhov's heroes and the author himself admit their own inability to find their way and that they exist in a state of hopelessness" (1997, 388). This sense of hopelessness, though present in Spregelburd's writing, is reworked with a tinge of optimism. In spite of her gluttonous, lustful, and slothlike parents, Leila is moving forward, seeking a place where she is needed and can make a difference.

The quest for truth, however, is an ongoing process. Regeczi tells us, "the truth can be acquired (taking the word truth in the broadest possible sense) only individually. The truth, thus, is not its knowledge because it is obtainable only through an internal process. That is why a form which is considered to be suitable for communicating the truth cannot be direct or didactic" (391). In Spregelburd's plays individual characters are in constant pursuit of the truth and of a higher understanding. Señora Perrotta wishes to give Leila to the gypsies in *La inapetencia* because in her daughter's case, the gypsy tells her, "a thirst to know everything pulls her to search for more information" (44). Señora Perrotta, on the other hand, listens fully to the gypsy, and has no problem with the fact that the gypsy tells her upfront that he is lying.

> *A Gypsy.* I am warning you that they are lies.
> *Sra.* Perrotta. I know. I am going to pay you anyway.
> *A Gypsy.* Very well. What do you want to hear?
>
> (43)

Moreover, even though she knows that the gypsy is lying to her, she decides to give him her daughter because she does not like what she hears about her daughter's future.

In the other two plays, the theme of a search for truth is equally important; in *La extravagancia* the plot moves around the sisters' search for their true identity while in *La modestia*, as I will show, the characters' work to learn the manuscript's and the cassette's true meaning, true author, and true owner. The questioning of truth and lies, however, places greater emphasis on the writing. As mentioned above, while Socorro is writing her new story, Brujas reminds us that the sisters' story is based upon a Ukranian story about triplets, "three actresses stop working together after a long time of reaping success" (72). The three sisters follow their individual destinies until they are reunited in Moscow to bury their father. This twisted version of Chekhov's play *Three Sisters* allows us to reflect upon the importance of family and nation in *La extravagancia.*

In *Three Sisters,* the protagonists, Olga, Masha, and Irina are overcome by sadness over their father's and their mother's deaths. They mourn their parents' loss and realize that they, too, will die and be forgotten someday. When others affirm that they knew her mother and that she was "a fine woman," Masha replies, "Would you believe it, I am already beginning to forget her face. So people will not remember us either, . . . they will forget us" (1946, 105).

Since they have no work, Chekhov's three sisters wake up at seven and reflect upon their mundane life. Like other characters in the play, they wonder if "perhaps our age will be called a great one and remembered with respect. Now we have no torture chamber, no executions, no invasions, but at the same time how much unhappiness there is . . . The unhappiness which one observes now—there is so much of it , does indicate, however, that society has reached a certain moral level" (105). This same tone is present in *La extravagancia;* the three Marías are miserable, obsessed with their individual situation: so alone and yet so afraid of being alone. As Tchebutykin, the army doctor in Chekhov's play reveals, though, "You said just now, baron, that our age will be called great, but people are small all the same" (106).

The notion of belonging is paramount in both of these plays. As the Marías long to belong to their family, so too does María Axila, like Chekhov's sisters, reflect upon life in a larger community or town, especially in "small towns." She declares:

> If one only knew where her own tomb would be located upon her death, I cannot imagine the impression of walking around that place. Prowling like a cat. In small towns, single women never go outside certain geographical limits, and, inevitably, they know that they will rest forever on a piece of land that is as close as the bakery, or the bus station. But that happens in small towns, where life is simple, in the closed order of small towns. And I am talking about towns that don't know the sea, because there the case is completely different.
>
> (77)

The idea of community is expanded in the final words of *La extravagancia* when a voice, presumably that of the girls' mother, calls María Brujas to tell her that she is dying. As she takes her last breaths, the mother tells her daughter, "I am dying. That is to say, against the foolish idea that a homeland exists" (85). Belonging is an invented term and any sense of belonging to family, to community, to nation is just an illusion.

As Giovanni Buttafava suggests of Chekhov's *Three Sisters, La extravagancia* displays a violence that is inherent in human relationships (1990, 36). The monologue structure carried out by three supposedly different characters who should be talking to each other emphasizes the lack of communication and like "the Chekhovian dialogue, it often sounds like a dialogue between the deaf" (Buttafava 1990, 37). The structure of *La extravagancia* supports its theme, which is expressed by María Axila: "Why think that a family is the best way to organize bodies in space?" (71, 75). Questioning communication on every level, from its very linguistic origins, to the technology modern societies employ to "facilitate" it (television and telephone in the play), to the organization of social beings into family groups, the play presents an existentialist image of life in modern times.

Another turn-of-the-century theme in Chekhov, which holds true for Spregelburd as well, is that of loneliness and silence. Regeczi argues, "Loneliness appears in his [Chekhov's] works as a fundamental state of existence; silence is presented from an ironic point of view . . . Pauses have different roles in Chekhov's drama. Mostly they express the impossibility of finding a solution to the situation, helplessness or the refusal of verbal help. The heaviest and most tragic statements are regularly followed by pauses" (1997, 400).

Similarly, Spregelburd's plays are filled with intentional pauses that mark the lack of communication as well as emphasize isolation, silence, and loneliness. Señora Perrotta and her husband's conversation is sprinkled with pauses; each pause reveals a gap where the other person should have responded to his/her partner. Often, an unrelated statement emanating from the person who had just spoken follows the pause. For example:

> *Sra. Perrotta.* Well? What are you talking about?
> *Pause.*
> *Marido.* Okay, it seemed like a possible discussion.
> *Sra. Perrotta.* Yes.
> *Pause.*
> *Sra. Perrotta.* In Bosnia or Serbia?
> *Pause.*
> *Sra. Perrotta.* Excuse me. Then we agree and we can adopt.
> *Marido.* Yes.
> *Pause.*
> *Marido.* Aren't you still hungry? What did you say?
>
> (28–29)

The pauses give the receptor the sense that the conversation is going nowhere; they mark the total stagnation of dialogue and emphasize the isolation in which each character lives. Regeczi suggests that pauses also mark despair. "It is the only possible gesture of resignation . . . Pauses in the dramas are present to show the limits of rationalism, the ambiguity of logic and human speech" (400).

Regeczi argues, "Chekhov's characters are unable to get away from boredom" (400). Similarly, Spregelburd's characters are incapable of moving outside themselves and their narrow world; they are spinning around in their own hell, like Dante's characters. They are stuck in the circle of the seven deadly sins, revolving around the central eye, which, since they do not choose to examine themselves, they do not see.

Writing the nation in La modestia

La modestia, the longest and seemingly most complicated play of the first three pieces of *Heptalogía,* premiered in April 1999 at the San Martín Theater in Buenos Aires and was repeated at the Babilonia Theater in August of that year. Both the performance and the text have been honored; the former was selected for inclusion in the program of the Second Festival Internacional de Buenos Aires and for the November 1999 Festival de Otoño in Madrid, and the latter was chosen for a dramatic reading as part of the Series of Dramatic Readings under the New Argentine Dramaturgy in February and March 1999.

In their online review of the San Martín Theater performance, María Infante and Adriana Libonati declare that *La modestia* centers on ambivalence. "Today's individual continuously moves from one position to another, but that same individual is a consequence of the socio-political-cultural forces which comprise him/her at all times . . . A child of this time, *La modestia,* delights in ambivalence" (2000, 1).[38] Playing with the ambivalent position of people in an excessive world, people caught between their own desire and the impositions of social, political, and cultural forces upon them, the play shows how freedom itself is an ambiguous concept. Actually, all three plays demonstrate these postmodern characters' impossible positions in a world of excess and overload, and show how they, like the real people they represent, possess insufficient tools for interpreting the globalized world's meaning.[39]

Moreover, as Aisemberg and Libonati have remarked, "*La modestia* exhibits the high degree of intertextuality present in all the work of this author and, at the same time, it can be thought of as the condensation of his poetics and the solidifying of a more diaphanous sense relating to his earlier works" (2000, 81). Like Spregelburd's other works, this play intertextualizes Bosch's painting and Chekhov's style and themes; however, as Infante and Libonati note, *La modestia* also parodies television discourse, the detective genre, Argentine playwright Daniel Veronese's *El líquido táctil* (*The Tactile Liquid*), the Spanish Golden Age Comedy of Entanglement, and itself (2000). The critics even establish that "It could even be thought that the latticing of two stories [in *La modestia*] proposes an intertextual reading to the receptor, since each story is read against the other" (81). Replete with intertextual connections, *La modestia* is most fully understood by trying to understand the form and functions of some of these intertexts within the play.

Spregelburd's third play in the *Heptalogía, La modestia* presents tremendous challenges to even the most astute receptor, for how does one interpret a play where every sign—character, setting, object—contains multiple meanings? Each character in the play is that character (San Javier, María Fernanda, Angeles, Arturo) and another (Terzov, Leandra, Anja, Smederovo), but also connects to still other characters from other plays.[40] The two settings (María Fernanda's apartment in Buenos Aires in the first story and Anja's home in the second) transform into other settings: Arturo and Angeles's apartment and Smederovo's home, respectively. Moreover, every object has several meanings and uses as well, and, as we shall see, as the text recodifies an object, it moves the story forward by linking the two "plays," their settings, and their characters. Through these transformed objects, the two stories move forward, connect, and propose other stories.

Similarly, the play intertwines two stories: the tale of a dying Russian writer whose texts the other characters attempt to publish (for their own individual, mostly economic, reasons), and a more "modern" Argentine plot of infidelity and deceit. Like *La extravagancia,* the staging of *La modestia* is complicated since only four actors play eight characters, each actor performing a double role. The play progresses like a detective story on several levels: each plot searches for "evidence" (the missing manuscript pages in the past plot and an alleged cassette in the modern one); in both plots there is a search for the truth, and the whole play is a search for meaning, both of this play and of modern times. As the characters search for the missing items, so, too, do readers search for interpretative clues while they attempt to understand this and the other plays in the *Heptalogía.*

Spregelburd places many clues for interpretation right in the play itself, for as his character Anja suggests, "In a masterpiece, as they say, the first ten lines contain everything" (153). An interesting epigraph, taken from the *Canción en Esperanto de la Banda de Frontera,* initiates the first ten lines of *La modestia,* "In this way God punishes our excessive pride. In this way God punishes, ay mommy, our excessive pride in being a small nation" (89). The quote connects the play to Bosch's *Tabletop* by emphasizing the vice of pride and by connecting it to nation. The epigraph functions like the top scroll of the *Tabletop;* it orients the viewer to the sins and to the content of the work of art, and connects them to the nation. Moreover, the inscription on the top scroll of Bosch's *Tabletop,* "For they are a nation void of counsel, neither is there any understanding in them. Oh that they were wise, that they understood this, that they would consider their latter end" (Martin and Cinotti 1966, 87) presents a nation without leadership, without direction. *La modestia*'s epigraph ironically presents a similar image of a nation so excessively proud, yet complacent in its "smallness."

The epigraph, the title, and the characters' behaviors and words suggest that pride and the nation frame this play; however, other clues presented in the first ten lines further orient the receptor. San Javier enters a strange apartment and, although he has a key, he does not belong there. Moreover, the woman, whose apartment he enters (María Fernanda), does not belong there either; it is not her apartment but rather another apartment that she uses to conduct her extramarital affair with Arturo. As the play develops, the theme of who belongs where unfolds. The following scene of the modern story places San Javier in another apartment, equally foreign to both of them, since it belongs to Arturo and Angeles. Yet, because Arturo and Angeles have an estranged relationship and because Arturo is having an affair with María Fernanda, Arturo and Angeles do not seem to belong in their own space either. In the other story, a parallel questioning of who belongs where occurs. Anja announces to her husband Terzov that they will rent a room in their house to the foreigner, Smederovo. Most of the rest of that story, however, places Terzov (and later Anja) as "foreign" guests in Smederovo's house.

The stories of belonging, displacement, and the foreign other are also played out on another level in the two plays—in their discussions of immigrants and their role in the country. Throughout the modern play, the reader/spectator glimpses the actual situation of the nation through fragments of the characters' conversations, and these fragments suggest themes that connect this story to that of the Russian characters. For example, Angeles narrates the story of a Korean family that runs the kiosk down the street and explains why there are so many Koreans in Argentina:

> The Korean government signed an agreement with Argentina and sent them here. No one welcomed them. Of course, and now we chew the fat talking about the Italians, the Germans, the Polish that came on the boats . . . But these poor "Chinese" came by plane not by boat, and they have almond-shaped eyes . . . Then, they smell bad, they come to take our work, and now it turns out that they are thieves and they robbed your two thousand eight hundred dollars . . . No one welcomed them.

> What nationality is the name San Javier? I imagine that your family arrived in this country and could find a space. Space is what we have plenty of. But no: the Sung family literally "grows" inside the kiosk. No one talks to them, no one takes them out of there so that they can see something else, no one tells them how to get to Recoleta, for example. No one welcomed them. They left their homeland. They left their homes, their way of dressing. They left the land where they buried their dead. They left their docks empty, their tea houses, the gardens with ancient sculptures. They changed everything for a tiny kiosk, for a city where no one stops to talk to them.
>
> (171, 172)

Although she has mixed feelings about them, she defends the immigrants and criticizes Argentines' attitude toward them. She argues, "And how do you expect them to learn the language if no one talks to them?" (172). Her discussion of the many different immigrants and their negative image and treatment in Argentina leads San Javier to express his sympathy toward the Russians. Even though Angeles believes that they have higher status than the Koreans, San Javier notes that "Russia, everything it symbolized, impressive . . . a country that no longer exists" (174).

As Angeles reminds him, however, Russia no longer exists but because of all its writers, it remains great. She remarks, "But it is Russia, right? It is not Korea. Russia, with its nuclear tests, and its Red Square, and Tchaikovsky, and all those writers . . . Pushkin, Dostoyevsky, Chekhov . . ." (175). Nonetheless, Arturo argues that his wife is obsessed with the idea of immigration, "She is crazy. She is obsessed with that. She wonders how a whole country can 'move' inside another, and no one even cares" (175).

Angeles's view of foreigners represents her worldview and this is the impetus behind the "other" story, that of the foreigners. Nonetheless, in the foreigner's face she sees her own, for it is in her country where many different "foreign" countries have taken residence. Julia Kristeva affirms that "From heart pangs to first jabs, the foreigner's face forces us to display the secret manner in which we face the world, stare into all our faces, even the most familial, the most tightly knit communities" (1991, 4). The image of the foreigner, whose space now merges with her own, allows Angeles to reread the confusing and ever-changing boundaries between her space and their space, and to reevaluate the configuration of her nation.

But Angeles's obsession with the foreigner, perhaps, is indicative of still a deeper meaning. Kristeva questions, "Or should one recognize that one becomes a foreigner in another country because one is already a foreigner from within?" (1991, 14). These characters demonstrate displacement and alienation with regard to their nation; they are foreigners in their own land because they are strangers to themselves. Kristeva argues that "Every native feels himself to be more or less a foreigner in his 'own and proper' place, and that the metaphorical value of the word foreigner first leads the citizen to a feeling of discomfort as to his sexual, national, political, professional identity" (1991, 19).

While the Argentine story talks about the alien and alienated role of foreigners in Argentina and shows every Argentine to be a foreigner in his/her own land and thus a stranger to him/herself in this globalized world, the second story acts out the foreigners' problems by concretely entering into Anja, Terzov, Smederovo, and Leandra's life, a life of personal and economic hardships. Although Smederovo says he is a doctor, he will take any job in his desperation after he loses his position in a clinic; they fired him because he was a foreigner (189). Angeles had noted and obsessed over the discrimination toward and lack of support offered to immigrants; in this other story, both Terzov and Smederovo are the victims of that discrimination because they are foreigners.[41]

The discussions about foreigners in one play and Smederovo's discrimination experience in the other are followed by discussions in both texts about what it means to belong, reminiscent of the theme that the three Marías had begun in *La extravagancia.* María Fernanda, Angeles, Arturo, and San Javier talk about the proletariat. Who belongs to this class or to any group is their question (192–202). Finally, María Fernanda defines the homeland as "Five or six guys, like wounded puppies, with their arms hanging from slings" (200).

This modest, negative view of nation leads one to question the configuration of the modern nation in an age of open borders and great class hierarchy. What is a nation, this nation, if it is populated by citizens who do not belong to it or who feel like they do not belong to it? Since the end of the nineteenth century the question of the immigrant and the foreigner has been predominant in Argentine theater. Not one of these characters expresses ownership of or belonging to their nation, and their attitudes of alienation place them in desperate situations.

Moreover, this nation that the characters describe is sterile, in spite of its diversity. When Leandra first arrives here she plants flowers in pots because, "this land does not give anything" (122). The flower pot reappears at the end of the play when, as Leandra looks at the ruined house (it had been ruined by San Javier in the previous scene), she picks up the hammer (from that earlier scene) and "Suddenly she goes toward the table and destroys her pots filled with flowers. One by one, seizing the hammer with both hands, frenetically, she makes the fragile clay pots, the dry earth, the discolored petals, fly through the air" (249). The house is in ruins and so is the nation because an inadvertent series of events destroyed it. In scene 15 San Javier accidentally ruins the house while they are listening to Henryk Górecki's Concerto for the clavichord and string orchestra, opus 40 (another intertext):

> *San Javier has decided to leave, but obviously he must wait until the musical theme ends. He goes toward the back, where he hopes to remain unnoticed, and plays with one of those mantel decorations that consists of some pendulums with lined-up steel balls hanging down that produce a continuous swinging movement when you push the first ball in the series. With lamentable luck, the toy breaks, falling on a fish bowl that is on the lower shelf, that gives way, making the fish bowl and some books fall on an outlet. This produces a stupid domino effect that ends up, for example, in a short circuit, or in part of the masonry accidentally falling down. With mouths wide opened, everyone witnesses this rebellion of space, that has been tangibly destructive.*
>
> (230)[42]

San Javier destroys that one house, but that destruction infiltrates the house in the other play as well. In the final scene of *La modestia,* Leandra "observes the house in ruins," then she picks up the hammer and continues to destroy everything in her space (249). The sirens and explosions outside connect these destroyed houses with the space outside, the nation. The characters feel alienated from their surroundings and do not control their situation; because of this, they cannot stop destruction that continues to progress through the domino effect and has implications on all their houses, all their nations.

Language and Texts in La modestia

As mentioned above, *La modestia* poses the same difficulties of representation as *La extravagancia;* each actor plays two characters, one in each of the stories (Smederovo = Arturo; Leandra = María Fernanda; Terzov = San Javier; Anja Terezovna = Angeles). Every other scene continues the story; in-between scenes tell the second story.

In one story, San Javier, a stranger from out of town, mistakenly enters an apartment (though he had been given the key by Arturo) only to discover that he has walked into a doomed love triangle. Angeles's husband, Arturo, is having an affair with María Fernanda.

That story is alternated with that of Anja, wife of Terzov, who longs for her husband to be a writer so that they can become rich and famous. Since no editor has ever wanted to publish Terzov's works, Anja proposes that they pass off her father's manuscript as his. She contacts doctor Smederovo who diagnoses Terzov with tuberculosis and also agrees to find a publisher for the manuscript.

The scenes are linked by clues and signs such as cigarettes, the gun, knocks on the door, water, and the stove (in scene 7 María Fernanda burned her clothing on the stove and they threw water on her to put out the fire; in scene 8 Leandra enters wet and Terzov dries himself off from the rain on the stove). Even though in natural language these linguistic signs, these words, might have no connection whatsoever, the way in which they are used in the play helps form a dramatic unity and thus unites two seemingly disparate stories, times, and spaces.

Thematically, structurally, and linguistically, what happens in one scene of one story of *La modestia* impacts the other story. The text becomes a detective's game in which the receptor pieces together the clues that are connected within the play and which connect the two plays within the play.[43] What, in other contexts, might be considered an absurd play, takes on significance, and even the apparent lack of communication between characters and between the two stories, becomes, in this way, connected and overcharged with meaning. So many signs are linked, and as the characters transform into their other in a different story, so, too, do objects move from story to story, connecting the two sets of lives and changing the use and meaning of each object. The mysterious cassette (whose content is not made clear) that María Fernanda seems to possess takes on a similar function to that of the manuscript in the second story. The manuscript, who is writing it, what it is about, and its future (economic and fame-filled) fate and implications, becomes *the* story, and it makes writing *the* theme of *La modestia.* Many references to writing are interspersed within each of the two stories. Moreover, it could be argued that each story exists because a character from the other story is writing it.

Highlighting the writing process, the play also shows how texts necessarily evolve from each other and are linked to other texts. Terzov, Anja, and her father jointly write the manuscript in question but their texts have grown out of other texts: Chekhov's *Three Sisters* and *Uncle Vanya,* for example, and are also part of Spregelburd's play (which rewrites Bosch's *Tabletop*). Writing texts is an inevitable process of making infinite connections.

Texts and their intertextual links never die. Smederovo feverishly attempts to publish Terzov's writing and, even though he knows that Terzov is dying, he affirms, "We are not going to let him die" (164). Terzov will live through his writing, and, ironically, because of writing, the characters of the other story live as well. Leandra believes that the novel must be published because "this novel is more important than all of us. It no longer even matters if you don't get rich with it" (246).

Writing is important in the play not only because it is the essence of the play but also because it relates to the nation. In a way, these characters are writing about nation and writing the nation. Smederovo sees his role as the instigator and preserver of Terzov's (or the father's) writing. He remarks, "I want you to keep writing. Your literature is blood, and I must encourage you to bleed, we are all your literature; you have made our misfortunes worth the pain, you give name to our hymn, our agony, in *La Parranda.* In your prose, the shed blood of thousands of this land's children boils. And I am going to succeed; you will be the greatest writer, I swear to you" (111). Terzov himself recognizes that the reason he writes is to escape from the violence and terror of "his pueblo" and for this he chooses the luxury of writing:

> *Terzov.* Of course I am interested in comfort! I am interested in pleasure. I know that just a few kilometers from here, across that border, they kill each other by the hundreds and no one cares. I do not want to have anything to do with them, nor with their fanatical War. I am naturally inclined toward pleasure, and not just because it is simpler. Literature is a luxury! It must be! I need some comforts. With a gun in my hand and my village in flames I would only be able to write frivolous things. You have to know how to see. You have to choose. My tranquility is necessary so that those people's suffering takes on some beauty.
>
> *Smederovo.* Write then! Write that, what you just said!
>
> (164–65).

After Terzov dies, Smederovo plans to travel to Milan to attempt to publish the former's book, and he tries to convince Leandra to accompany him on the trip. She refuses, stating, "I am staying here. What would I do in Milan? Milan is not my homeland" (247). When Smederovo reminds her that this is not her country either, she replies, "Until now," implying that because of the events that have occurred, she now feels more at home in this nation than in any other.

Milan is not Leandra's nation and the manuscript does not belong to Smederovo; signs in *La modestia* are and are not what they pretend to be. As the signs change, they change the point of view or perspective in the text, and lead the receptor to the other story. For example, in scene 5, Angeles could not light the stove, and she smelled gas. In the following scene, Smederovo asks, "Don't you smell gas? And later Terzov asks Anja, "Did you explain to your younger sister (Irene) how the stove works?" (142–43). This same stove that singes María Fernanda, causing her to become soaked, warms the wet Terzov and Leandra in the other space. The stove, the gas, and the water have different, but important, roles in both stories and impact characters in both spaces, creating the same domino effect that ultimately caused the destruction of both houses and the nation.

Similarly, the revolver in María Fernanda's purse appears in both plays. In one space, Angeles, infuriated by her husband's affair with María Fernanda, removes the revolver from the purse and aims and fires it, first at her husband and then at María Fernanda. Because San Javier had already removed the bullets from the gun (219), Angeles is unable to kill anyone, not even herself (238–42). In the other story, however, Anja commits suicide with that same revolver, as had Masha in her story (244, 237). Had Terzov (San Javier) still been alive, he could have/would have saved her life, as San Javier had in the other play.

The evolving and transitioning objects in the texts alter the point of view with each transformation, changing the story, and the possibilities for interpreting it. As the Koreans/foreigners in Angeles's immigrant stories see things from one side of the kiosk and we see things from the other side, each object, every word is loaded with multiple meanings, creating new texts with each transformation. The artistic/dramatic function of intertextuality in this play is to show HOW texts are linked. Through certain words, certain transformed (by the author) signs, the two stories work off each other, explain each other, ask questions about each other, and enrich each other. In another context, these two plays would have no connection whatsoever, but their interwoven composition and the signs that they share connect them.

One of the many signs that connects them is the dollar and this has implications for both stories and, ideologically, on the nation(s) they represent.[44] After Angeles tries to kill her, María Fernanda reaches into Angeles's bathrobe (which María Fernanda has been wearing since the stove incident), and "takes out a little roll of dollars" (242). This sudden discovery of money contrasts to the excessive preoccupation with poverty, especially in the other story, a poverty that leads to the writing of these stories and the attempts to sell the manuscript.

Economic and capitalistic interests emerge in the first story as the characters discuss the class system in their nation and how they fit into it. Arturo notes that even though he is a lawyer, in his student days, "We liked to mingle with the people, we dressed like the people, we even used to go to the popular parties' committees, because that was where the PEOPLE were" (193). María Fernanda, on the other hand, wonders if she will ever cease being poor. "I do not know how many more years of my life I will continue being poor . . . The one who was a proletarian was my mother. Her whole life. She never had a dime. Clara and I were her capital, poor thing, her only capital in exclusively Marxist terms . . . not even a sewing machine, poor mom, only Clara and I" (193–94).

Economics dictate the actions of all characters in the second play as well. The story begins when Anja and Terzov decide to rent out a room in their home to a foreigner, as a way of earning the much-needed money to pay for Terzov's medical treatment. Anja sells her deceased father's bed as firewood to further aid their situation. In addition, economic preoccupations lead Anja to lie about the manuscript, passing her father's writing off as her husband's so that she might sell the work for economic gain. Similarly, Smederovo's own depleted economic condition, because he is a foreigner and has been unable to find work in his own field, compels him to try to sell Terzov's manuscript at all costs. Leandra reminds him, "We no longer have anything for lunch" (187) and when the manuscript continues to be unsuccessful he takes a job curing horses, not people, simply because they paid him (187). In addition, when Terzov refuses to cooperate with him regarding the manuscript, he reminds him that "We had an agreement . . . a brutal and economic agreement" (145).

Terzov continues to refute their lies and he refuses to play their game, telling his wife that "they do not want to help me. They want to become rich with your father's novel" (147). Nonetheless, when he himself looks for a job, he has great difficulty keeping it. When he is finally compensated for his work, the money is false. Leandra remarks with astonishment, "What is this? Who gave you this miserable thing? This bill came out of circulation two years ago" (181).

Smederovo recognizes that he did everything for money and that he had no regard for Terzov or Anja. Actual poverty and the fear of perpetual poverty force Smederovo, Leandra, and Anja to lie, to cheat, and to invent new stories.

> *Smederovo.* I wonder if we are only doing all this because we are motivated by the fear of being poor our whole lives.
>
> *Pause.*

Leandra.: I don't know. But we need courage to accept that we will always be poor.

(245)

Leandra believes that Anja accepted her poverty, but what she did not know is that Anja too was an imposter—attempting to rewrite a new story to escape from her impoverished life.

As mentioned above, words and objects evolve and are recodified in and through these plays and take on new functions between the texts. They serve as examples to show how texts are linked and transformed. Spregelburd's *La modestia* connects to Bosch's *Tabletop* and to certain Chekhov plays, among other intertexts. Spregelburd's style of transforming words and signs and linking them parallels the way in which he weaves these intertexts into his play(s). In addition, the changes in the texts and between them help to present his own worldview in *La modestia.*

The title of *La modestia* would indicate that this play connects to the "sin" of pride, since modesty is its opposite virtue. While pride does factor into the play, once again, Spregelburd condenses many vices into the lives and conduct of these sets of characters, among them, sloth, lust, wrath, greed, gluttony, and envy. As an example of how the sins are condensed and modernized, gluttony really means greed in this context. Little food is mentioned in the plays, yet, on two occasions Smederovo calls Anja "Glutton." He insults her with this capital sin because she is greedy and refuses to give him the manuscript. Yet, how can she or he be faulted for their greed, for it is only to put food on the table that they both want the manuscript?

Pride or the excessive belief in one's own abilities is considered the sin from which all others arise and, as Fraenger suggests, it is the gravest sin (275–77). In Bosch's painting pride is represented in a "doll-house" interior where a vain woman stares at herself in a mirror, held by the devil who wears the same headdress as she wears. An apple on the windowsill presents this woman as the "daughter of Eve." On the floor near her sits a jewel casket, which, when empty, will serve as her coffin (Fraenger 1983, 274).

Pride is prioritized in *La modestia* through the title (modesty is the opposite of pride), through the epigraph (which links it to nation), and through the various characters' excessive humility and modesty. In his opening notes, Spregelburd tells the reader that this play is about "Modesty, naturally. Modesty as a sin. The haughty and guilt-laden pleasure that is born from the desperate gesture of trying to be a little less than you are, with the intimate objective, perhaps, of paying off that infinite debt in comfortable payments" (2000b, 88).

From the outset the playwright warns the receptor that he has inverted this sign; the sin is its opposite.

As I have discussed, the epigraph ironically suggests that God punishes the nation for its excessive pride over its smallness, its lowly status in the world, its sense of inferiority. In other words, the nation is not proud at all, but rather, it is extremely modest and humble, and places itself in an inferior position within the world.

The characters' attitudes reinforce this excessive humility or modesty. Both Anja and Leandra admit that they have diminished their own stature and status to promote the grandeur of their husbands.

> *Anja.* I have undervalued myself. It was a process that took me awhile. And I do not think I even realized it was happening. I made myself small at his side because I thought he needed to shine. It is stupid, but I did it because I loved him. When he shined, finally, I began to believe that I deserved less than I had.
>
> (233)

Anja lowered herself to the point where she practically disappeared, so self-effacing was she. She affirms, "He is not to blame. The fault was mine, always. I became so small that I disappeared. It is my fault if life passes me by without seeing me" (236). For her part, Leandra is humbled by Anja's admissions, as her husband and his actions had already humbled her. She tries to convince Anja that Smederovo's intentions were good, stating, "My husband was noble, he believed in him, in his talent, and if this blind faith has been at a cost to you, I beg you to forgive him. It was the lesser sin anyway" (234).

The women's humility and modesty are punished, as is the sin of pride in Bosch's painting. On the *Tabletop,* pride is punished twice: both in its own representation (the devil's temptation and the presence of the casket) and in the hell image below (again the devil's mirror and the evil toad climbing on the woman's abdomen) (Martin and Cinotti 1966, 87–88). In *La modestia,* both women are punished for their excessive modesty; Anja loses her husband and then kills herself, while Leandra's husband abandons her to travel to Milan in a last attempt to publish the manuscript. Ironically, as he is packing to leave, he reminds her, "You are an intelligent woman. We are both intelligent people" to which she replies, "Don't be excessively proud" (243).

Whereas in the Middle Ages people were punished for being too proud, vain, or conceited, in modern times excessive modesty is the sin; Spregelburd's characters cannot succeed, cannot live, because they do not take pride in themselves. They view themselves as inferior and they place their nation in an inferior position as well.

All characters in *La modestia* suffer from their own lack of initiative (a version of sloth) and they take pride in nothing. Terzov does not want to participate in his wife's lie, so he refuses to continue writing or to attempt to publish his real texts. In the other story as well, characters are stuck in their love triangle and San Javier just stays on as the writer/witness, without acting to avoid the destruction.

With the plays of his *Heptalogía de Hieronymus Bosch I,* Rafael Spregelburd has succeeded in creating a truly postmodern play of disintegration. With these plays, Spregelburd models Bosch's and sometimes Chekhov's styles and themes in every way, while at the same time he questions them, subverts them, and tears them apart. Moreover, the ways in which he uses these intertexts give his plays a timeless quality since, in essence, Spregelburd is speaking of the same themes as his medieval and his nineteenth-century predecessors and is codifying them similarly. Like those artists, Spregelburd succeeds in vividly portraying the crisis and chaos of the turn of the century and suggests that the turn of the twenty-first century, these postmodern times, are not so different than the post-medieval era or the turn of the twentieth century. It is only in that thought that we can find comfort in his crisis-filled, absurdist works; life is cyclical and the ambivalence, insecurity, and excess that we experience in our world will once again pass.

Just when we think we have found *the* key to understanding Spregelburd's texts, like the characters in these stories, we realize that it is *a* key that opens *a* door (but it may be the *wrong* key to the *wrong* door, and furthermore, it does not belong to them or to us). The playwright cleverly transforms signs within his texts, so that each character, space, and object takes on multiple meanings. Moreover, these signs lead the reader/spectator to other texts, whose structures and/or themes further open up new possibilities for interpretation. As the cassette turns into the manuscript and San Javier transforms into the sickly Terzov, so too, does Anja's story change to Masha's (from Chekhov's *Three Sisters*). Similarly, the story of these characters turns into the story of the "foreigner/citizens" in the Argentine nation.

Although each play seems to replicate the theater of the absurd and apparently little communication takes place, the seemingly few references to nation exemplify notions of nation at the end of the twentieth century. Leila's discarding of her own nation/family and her desire to fight the Bosnian War in *La inapetencia* suggest that action is better than inaction. In an effort to escape the gluttony and sloth so ever-present in her family/nation, she chooses to jump into a war-torn, ill-defined nation. Her efforts to escape the excessive desire and consumerism of her family lead her to actively engage in creating her own idealistic model of a nation. Bosch's painting then allows Spregelburd to "paint" the apathy, gluttony, excessive desire, lust, and sloth of the turn of the century and to show that young people may tire of such blatant excess and turn to a more idealistic, but active, pursuit of nation. Rather than live in apathy and complacency, Leila's focus on Bosnia recognizes that nations are unstable and necessarily ever evolving; the only form of hope is to participate in that struggle.

La extravagancia exaggerates Bosch's vice of envy to question the notion of belonging and the fear of alienation that leads one to further alienate oneself. As the three Marías obsess over their identity, they choose illness and even death over isolation. Yet, their behavior and paranoia lead them to extreme isolation. Moreover, the work questions the basic social/political structures of family and nation as "healthy" ways to organize societies. María Axila questions, "Why do we think that a family is the best way to organize bodies in space?" (71). If the family is dysfunctional, then so is the nation, an idea that leads her mother to die at the end of the play, "against the foolish idea that a homeland exists" (85).

Finally, *La modestia* subverts pride's role in the world by showing the insecurity and extreme modesty that is destroying today's world. Because these characters do not believe in themselves, they are forced to live through others' stories. The stories lead to still more stories in an endless spiral of fiction that fails to lead them out of their poverty. Rather than empower them, their writing serves to bind them together and fuse them, leading to the destruction of their home and the ironic questioning of their belief in nation.

Spregelburd exploits the themes and style of Bosch's *Tabletop of the Seven Deadly Sins* to highlight the painting's double-voiced potential and its power as a tool of introspection, not its religious meaning. He subverts the painting's message to make it fit our postmodern times; rather than beginning with the nation (Bosch's top scroll) and ending with the individual (Bosch's bottom scroll stating, "I will hide my face from them, and I will see what their end shall be" [Fraenger 1983, 87]), Spregelburd's plays start with the individual at the root of the nation. These individuals do "hide their faces" through their apathy and their isolation and because of this their "nation" is ill-defined and "small."

James Snyder argues, "The inner world of Bosch is fraught with bizarre and alarming images of the pessimistic age of the Reformation to which Bosch belonged, presenting us with a world of extreme psychic instability on man's part in a landscape of violence and corruption . . . the society that Bosch depicts is three-fold in character: frenzied, violent, and hybrid . . . his people are caught racing in no particular direction toward no goal" (1973, 4). Spregelburd's postmodern world takes on similar characteristics, but his characters' apathetic reactions stand out against the frenzy, violence, and ever-changing chaos around them.

Interestingly enough, however, Ludwig von Baldass notes a deep pessimism in Bosch's work and argues that it portrays the "passive, not active, emotional tension . . . characteristic of the fifteenth century" (Snyder 1973, 76). Spregelburd's use of this intertext emphasizes that, in spite of the many changes in our world, modern people have not progressed very far in their emotional, psychological, or sociopolitical essence.

On the other hand, it is important to consider that both artists are playing with their audience, for Spregelburd's play is meant for performance. Von Baldass affirms similar strategies in Bosch's painting when he writes that "the tormented bodies in his pictures of Hell are not always represented as really suffering. They often seem mere actors pretending to be terror-stricken by a certain punishment . . . Bosch represents an age which had ceased to think 'in any but visual terms'" (Snyder 1973, 76). In Bosch's time art could vividly present the conflicts of life; Spregelburd's emphasis on the artistic pre-text serves to "paint" a more vivid picture of his world as well. Spregelburd's play and Bosch's painting are both artistic texts that know no boundaries. Whether Bosch's sinners are "performing" their sin and their punishment, or whether Spregelburd's actors are presenting still life scenes from everyday life depends on the perspective of the viewer.

As Aisemberg and Libonati have aptly noted, "In spite of the heterogeneity of materials that intervene in this textuality, the way in which these are structured is far from postmodern conceptions of the text as an encyclopedia of irrelevant quotations or as an indiscriminate amalgam of diverse texts. There is no eclecticism, but rather, on the contrary, [there is] a structural coherence in the way the intertextual links are brought together" (2000, 82). Ironically, the intertexts Spregelburd chooses and the way he weaves them into his plays expand communication between texts and receptor. The communication that he attempts to destroy in his dialogues is reopened through the various other texts he incorporates.

Osvaldo Pellettieri suggests that in spite of the marginalized status of Argentine theater, what stands out "is the ability of our theater to generate its own dynamic" (2000, 11). These Argentine plays creatively manipulate other texts within their own to present the reader/spectator with an unending textual labyrinth that spirals attention back to their own texts. At the same time, these intertexts redirect readings on the Argentine, suggesting that, through this new aesthetic, a new ideology of nation is emerging. As Pellettieri argues, "contemporary Argentine theater is only comprehensible through the set of texts that come before it and surround it" (23). By incorporating these preceding texts and surrounding texts into their plays and manipulating them accordingly, Pavlovsky and Spregelburd invent new texts and new ideologies of nation.

4
Cuba, Myth, and Transnational Revisions of Nation

> Freud's concept of the "narcissism of minor differences" . . . provides a way of understanding how easily that boundary that secures the cohesive limits of the western nation may imperceptibly turn into a contentious *internal* liminality that provides a place from which to speak both of, and as, the minority, the exilic, the marginal, and the emergent.
>
> —Homi K. Bhabha, *Nation and Narration,* 300

> To be a playwright in exile is . . . very difficult, but one has to live with what one has chosen, that is the only way of being. And, in the final analysis, as in the theater, it is the only possible truth.
>
> —Matías Montes Huidobro, *Ollantay Theater Magazine,* 44

READING "CUBA" THROUGH CUBAN THEATER HAS, PERHAPS, POSED more difficulties than defining any other nation through its theater at the end of the twentieth, beginning of the twenty-first century, largely because of the great number of playwrights writing outside of their national borders and, at the same time, because of the lack of freedom experienced by Cuban playwrights living on the island. As Cuban playwright and critic Matías Montes Huidobro affirms, "to do Cuban theater one can live anywhere" (1997a, 42). Until recently, though, Cuban theater written outside of Cuba was, for the most part, ignored.[1] Heidrun Adler argues however, that, after the political events of 1959, there emerged "two Cuban societies, [one] in Cuba and [another] in the United States" (Adler and Herr 1999b, 9). Her view on Cuban theater and nation proposes that there is "more uniting the two shores than separating them" (16).

Cuba and Cuban identity, from either space, are the themes of many plays written at the end of the twentieth century. Similarly, intertextuality has been an important tool to unravel confusing national discourses and sentiments in Cuban theater. Cuban playwrights have used other texts as allegories for their nation: as a way to speak out about the repressive political climate and textualize national ideology. Much in the way that seventeenth-century Mexican writer and dramatist Sor Juana Inés de la Cruz used religion to depict and bring forth the "American" while at the same time presenting subversive (in her case, feminist) intent, island playwrights, as far back as Virgilio Piñera and his 1940s classic, *Electra Garrigó,* have intertwined other texts into their plays both as diversion tactics, to avoid censorship, and as a way to vividly portray a national context. Outside the island, intertexts depict the conflicts and tensions of "life on the hyphen."[2]

Piñera's *Electra Garrigó* is only one of the many plays written on the island that has been staged in the United States. Beatriz Rizk argues that, in spite of the fact that in Miami "an ordinance exists on the books that prohibits providing public funds originating from taxpayers, to subsidize artists invited from the island," there is a plethora of "Cuban" works being staged in Miami and other parts of the United States (2000, 229). Among these, a large number are considered Cuban classics, and many of them intertextualize classical Greek texts, Afro-Cuban texts, or other Cuban texts.[3]

Piñera's *Electra Garrigó* rewrites the Greek tragedy *Electra* to show that "Like any mortal, the Cuban has a sense of the tragic" (Piñera 1960, 10). Nonetheless, as the playwright suggests, "We [Cubans] are tragic and comic at the same time" (10). The playwright uses intertextuality as a way to recontextualize the tragedy, to bring forth its presence in Cuban culture, and then to twist its implications, showing how that tragedy impacts Cuban culture at the time of the writing. Piñera affirms that his *Electra* "Is a very Cuban *Electra* and it takes place in the city of Havana" (37). The "new" text highlights this Cuban city and shows how "every city always has a perpetual monster" (Piñera 1960, 37).

As an example of intertextuality in more recent Cuban theater, Estorino's *Parece blanca (She Looks White)* (1994) uses the story of nineteenth-century Cuban novelist Cirilio Villaverde's *Cecilia Valdés,* to revise a national Cuban classic and to show the relevance of its themes of national identity at the end of the twentieth century. According to Graziella Pogolotti, "one of the greatest myths of Cuban culture serves as a pretext for Abelardo Estorino to propose an intense dialogue between history and destiny" (1999, 19). Estorino's incorporation of both a book, which he places on a lectern in the script, and the myth of Cecilia, the mulatta protagonist of Villaverde's epic story, shows how intertextuality can function on both the dramatic and ideological planes in theater. In essence, this revision of the Villaverde text evokes "a culture that has been growing throughout time to nourish a memory woven into the big story with an essential and intimate bond" (Pogolotti 1999, 20).

Another Estorino play, *Los mangos de Caín (Cain's Mangos)* (1964), rewrites both religious and artistic intertexts as a way to subvert national ideology and depict political and economic tensions within the Cuban nation. As Montes Huidobro argues, "every Civil War is a fight between brothers and one of the predominant figures has to be the biblical Cain" (1973, 387). In this play, the story of Cain and his brother Abel is mixed with the biblical story of Adam, Eve, and the serpent, not to comment on the religious texts or the state of religion in Cuba, but rather as a way to show post-Castro Cuba as a lost paradise and to reflect upon the limits of freedom (Montes Huidobro 1973, 389–90). As Montes Huidobro suggests, this is a clearly subversive work, "and so that there is no doubt about its Cubanness, Estorino gave Cain mangos, and nothing else, and the mangos give the work a strong local note" (1973, 400).

The three works I examine in this chapter use intertextuality to rewrite their nation by focusing on exile and its impact on the transnational Cuban community. In each of them I show how the playwrights choose other texts to show the tragedy of exile, to draw parallels between the intertext's or their authors' similar situations, and then to recontextualize their exiled status by breaking the imposed silence of the exiled through their new text. José Corrales and Manuel Pereiras's *Las hetairas habaneras: Una melotragedia cubana basada en Las troyanas de Eurípides* (*The Courtesans of Havana: A Cuban Melotragedy based on Euripides'* The Trojan Women) (1977) rewrites a Greek tragedy and also refers to Cuban literature, while Raúl de Cárdenas's *Un hombre al amanecer (A Man at Dawn)* (1988) and Pedro Monge's *Otra historia (Another (Hi)Story)* (1996) make similar statements by incorporating other Cuban texts into their work. As I discuss, all three of these plays recuperate silenced voices and through them, tell the other side of the Cuban Revolution story, protest against the exile's current situation, and invent a new medium, the New Cuban Dramaturgy, to empower the Cuban.

José Corrales and Manuel Pereiras's *Las hetairas habaneras: Una melotragedia cubana basada en Las troyanas de Eurípides*

The Cuban Revolution transformed the nation's history and initiated a search for the Cuban within and outside the island's borders.

Forced into exile, thousands of Cubans began to and continue to question both the future of their nation and their own relationship to it. Similarly, as Matías Montes Huidobro suggests, "Without proposing to do so, the Revolution creates an unplanned chapter in New Cuban Theater. The formative process of a new Cuban dramaturgy that develops outside of Cuba under very precarious circumstances is an outcome that deserves careful attention" (1997b, 103). Among the plays inspired by what some may consider the real-life tragedy of the Cuban Revolution, José Corrales and Manuel Pereiras's *Las hetairas habaneras: Una melotragedia cubana basada en Las troyanas de Eurípides* (*The Courtesans of Havana: A Cuban Melotragedy based on Euripides'* The Trojan Women),[4] stands out for many reasons; the play adeptly alternates rich poetic verses with melodic prose, vividly portrays the complex religious syncretism and political contradictions of Cuba and the Cuban, and skillfully intersperses humor and irony into the scope of an undeniable dramatic and political tragedy. Moreover, it does all this within an admittedly intertextual framework; as the title suggests Corrales and Pereiras's play "dialogues" with Euripides' classic, *The Trojan Women.*

This intertextual exchange connects the text to another time and tradition and to this specific Greek tragedy while at the same time locating the new text in Cuba, rather than ancient Greece. In his introduction to *Las hetairas habaneras,* José Escarpanter postulates it as a parody of Euripides' piece and argues that said parody is both aesthetic and political (1988, 6). He notes that the play "adheres to the most orthodox canons of the Athenian tragedy, both in the semantic and the formal aspects" listing various structural elements—such as the parallel characters, the function of the chorus, the poetic essence, and the role of music, song, and dance in the play—that model classic Greek style (6). On an ideological level, he sees that through intertextuality, the play "is later transformed into a ferocious diatribe against the regime that holds power in Cuba and concludes as a true tragedy" (Escarpanter 1988, 8–9). Escarpanter rightly sees multiple intertextualities in the play, noting its clear references to Virgilio Piñera's *Electra Garrigó* and the insertion of Alejo (Carpentier) into the text. While there is no doubt that this play parodies the Greek text and is a "ferocious diatribe" against Castro's Cuba, I believe that the intertextual link allows another reading of the Cuban text; by emphasizing some of the subtleties of the Greek text, Corrales and Pereiras's play takes the focus away from both the women and the war/revolution and replaces it with two other ideological concerns: the double loss of nation and its implications for the future.

My purpose here is to read the two plays together, highlighting their similarities and differences, to show how Corrales and Pereiras exploit the style, characters, setting, and themes of the Euripides text to postulate the double loss of the Cuban nation: first to an undesired government, that of Fidel Castro, and secondly, through exile. In the Cuban play as in the Greek tragedy the nation is ravaged and the women are forced into exile. Both texts present this second loss, the loss of nation through exile, as the greatest, and thus, not only is it a tragic theme in the two works, but the plays show how exile psychologically devastates the exiled and attempts to silence them. Reading the two texts together highlights exile in the second text and allows the receptor to react to the Cuban exile as the Trojan women reacted to theirs, thus heightening the tragedy and sense of loss. By understanding exile's impact on the banished Trojan women, readers/spectators of *Las hetairas habaneras* experience an intensified sense of doom over Cuba's and Cubans' seemingly parallel destiny. Once I have examined exile and its effect on women and nation in the two texts, I show two subtle changes in the Cuban text: the reaction of the gods and the fate of the child. These differences in the new text have both a dramatic and an ideological function; they present theater as a way of giving voice to the exiles and they postulate hope for the future of the nation through those voices.

Written in 415 BC, at the height of the Peloponnesian War, critics have read *The Trojan Women* in many ways: as "a passionate and poetic expression of the horror and futility and degradation of war at any time, but desperately urgent in its particular setting" (Hadas 1960, 173); or, as a play that prioritizes the effects of the fall of Troy on its female population, rather than on its "illustrious male warriors" (Morwood 2000, ix–x). As Escarpanter (1988) argues, *Las hetairas* could be read similarly; the text shows Menelao Garrigó's cruelty toward the women and his destruction of their family members and their life in the "house." Though both plays suggest that the war and the women are important, they are not really the focus; in both texts the women lament their house/nation's destruction and, more significantly, they despair over their forced exile.

The two plays center on the tragedy of one family, headed by a matriarch who has recently suffered tragic losses at the hands of Menelao Garrigó (Menelaus).[5] While the Greek mother's enemy comes from Sparta (outside her homeland), the Cuban mother's enemy, though outside her house, is a tyrant from within her own nation. In the Greek play the nation is destroyed from the outset, whereas in the Cuban text actual destruction does not come about until act 2. In act 1 the women are cautiously celebrating their good fortune over

Estrella's arrival to the house and the baby, Nicomedes', birth. Corrales and Pereiras masterfully create suspense in act 1 through the contradictory voices of the double chorus (Coro and Coralia), through religious syncretism, and through Iluminada's prophecies. In act 2, Diosdada, matriarch of the brothel, La Gloria (Hecuba, formerly queen of Troy), laments her misfortune because her husband, Primo (Priam), and her daughter, Alba (Polyxena), have been killed. Her other daughter, Iluminada (Cassandra), a woman with the gift of prophecy who had predicted and foreseen all the tragedy, is thought to be mad and will be forced to marry Agamemnon.[6]

Diosdada's son, Yayo (Hector) and her daughter-in-law, Carlota (Andromache) bore a son, Nicomedes (Axtyanax), who was to be the pride and hope of the Cuban brothel, La Gloria, where *Las hetairas habaneras* is set (Troy in the Greek text), for he was to carry on the lineage of Primo (Priam) and his family. In *The Trojan Women,* the boy is older; *Las hetairas habaneras* begins just after his birth, but by act 2 nine to ten years have passed and he is seen as a young boy. In both plays, this child symbolizes the future of the nation. However, the child's "punishment," different in each text, perhaps leaves room for some hope for the future in the Cuban play, as I will show. The severely maimed Nicomedes in *Las hetairas habaneras* symbolizes the difficult life of the Cuban exile. Although he is rendered mute and impotent, he is not killed completely as was his Greek intertextual ancestor.

As another vital character in the two plays, Estrella (Helen) may be seen as the cause of the destroyed nation, for it is because she has betrayed her former husband, Menelao, to be with Diosdada's son, that doom befalls them. The myth of Helen's great beauty is well known throughout Greek mythology. Morwood notes that "Helen's eyes were the stuff of legend" (2000, 140). In *The Trojan Women* Hecuba urges Menelaus to kill Helen but warns him not to be fooled by her great beauty. "I praise you, Menelaus, if you are going to kill your wife. But avoid seeing her in case she traps you with desire. She traps the eyes of men, she destroys cities, she burns homes. She casts such spells. I know her. So do you and those who have suffered" (Morwood 2000, 63).[7]

Estrella in the Cuban play has similar characteristics; she is extremely beautiful but here her beauty is specifically Cuban. Diosdada, Coralia, and Coro elaborate on her great beauty by stating, "She does not lack buttocks, she doesn't lack breasts. In her, nothing is superfluous, nothing is lacking . . . Yes, Estrella is perfect" (26). Moreover, the two choral voices, later repeated by Diosdada, identify Estrellas's beauty with nature, most notably with Cuba's "natural" attributes, by connecting her laughter to the breeze, her hair to the sky, her skin to the rain, and her walk to the sea (26–27). Earlier, Coralia had confirmed that she is, "The Star of this house, the Star of this Island" (26). She is, in essence, Cuban beauty, but, as Iluminada prophesies, "her star is one of bad luck" for soon, she will cause the great loss of nation for these women (27).

As Escarpanter (1988) notes, the chorus in Corrales and Pereiras's play follows a similar structure and has a parallel function to that of Euripides' tragedy. In both cases, it is a split voice, between Coro and Coralia in the Cuban version, and between the First-Half Chorus and the Second-Half Chorus in the latter, and its dual perspective on every situation creates dramatic tension. Moreover, in both plays the Chorus reveals the past, describes the action, fills in missing details, prophesies the future, and sympathizes with the women.

Menelao's role is similar in the two plays; however, it is interesting to note that in *The Trojan Women* he is the outside invader of Troy, whereas in *Las hetairas* not only is he a resident of the island but he has also often been a guest in the house of these women. In both plays the women fear him and also fear that they will be punished for Estrella's (Helen's) betrayal. Whereas in the Greek tragedy they loathe Helen for the doom she has brought to them, in the Cuban play most of the women admire Estrella and are intrigued by her, though they wonder how she could be happy after leaving her husband and daughters. Their doom comes, it seems, because they let Estrella into their house.

Moreover, they let in Menelao also. Even though the Cuban women fear Menelao, especially at the end of the play, Diosdada, like Hecuba, shares a relationship of mutual respect with him. Coralia reminds Diosdada, "but Menelao Garrigó is your friend" (25), to which the latter replies, "He is our friend and he continues to be so. He is a client and, what's more, he is a sensitive and intelligent man" (25). Throughout the text, though, the reader/spectator wonders whether this affection toward Menelao is genuine or if it is caused by fear and always expressed with a tongue-in-cheek type of irony. Nonetheless, both Iluminada and the deities blame the women for having let him and Estrella into their space.

As Escarpanter (1988) and Febles (1999) both suggest, in *Las hetairas habaneras* Menelao Garrigó symbolizes Fidel Castro. Coralia confirms that "Menelao is now our government, our entire government" (25). The women remember that they had promised him their support when they were fighting in the mountains and now they must be faithful to him. When he demands that they give up their religion, their homeland, their freedom, and their happiness, they agree to do so and place all their hope for the future in the doomed child, Nicomedes. In order to save that child, they rearticulate those promises to give up everything when Menelao forces them to. Humor and irony mark their empty words. On the one hand, the women confirm, "Menelao is the most macho man of all men" and state that they will renounce their saints, their ways of life, their happiness and their liberties (52–53). On the other hand, they tell Menelao that what they are accepting is, "Your contemptible arbitrariness, your filthy verbiage, your stench of death, your putrefaction, your plots, lies, and abuses" (54).

If Menelao is the government, then these women in La Gloria (The Glory) symbolize the Cuban people. Menelao tells the women that the past is over and "now is what matters" and in the present they will become the examples for the country. He warns, "You have to be controlled at all times, well controlled, or else the people will think that they can do the same. You are going to be the example" (48). Even though Menelao controls them and uses them as an example, ironically, he is impotent in Corrales and Pereiras's play and Estrella tells the women his secret. He is not the macho he pretends to be, but he does succeed in ruining their land and in forcing them into exile.

Critics of both *The Trojan Women* and *Las hetairas habaneras* have emphasized the war and the women; however, both plays subtly prioritize the nation and the tragedy of its double loss. The homeland's destruction causes tremendous grief in both texts. Even though the women have lost everything—family members and home(land)—they grieve most for the loss of their nation. Moreover, they lose their country twice: once because it has been ransacked, burned, and destroyed by the government, and finally, because they are forced into exile.

The opening stage directions of *The Trojan Women* highlight the ravaged city and the women who lament its loss, "in the background a great and rich city with ancient traditions is burning, and in the cold dawn a broken old woman, once queen of this city, is lying on the ground" (173). The settings in the two plays have many differences. Troy is burning from the outset, following its attack by the Spartans, whereas La Gloria is still intact until act 2. At the very beginning of *Las hetairas* the women are about to celebrate their good fortune over the arrival of Estrella, wife of Juan Alberto but former wife of Menelao Garrigó, and the birth of Nicomedes, "the boy-child of joy and salsa" (16). There is no note of happiness in the Euripides play. The Cuban play, on the other hand, begins on this happy note but that happiness is short-lived; Coro and Coralia foreshadow the imminent doom because of Estrella's infidelity.[8]

Hecuba's opening monologue laments the loss of country first, *before* she mourns her dead husband and children. "Up, unhappy woman! Lift your head and your neck from the ground! This is no longer Troy, we are no longer Troy's queen . . . What is there here that I do not mourn in misery? Country, children, husband—all are gone" (41). Later, as she lay mourning her grandson's tragic death, she again places her city first among her losses. Wondering who will bury the child, Hecuba cries, "No, it is I who shall bury your pitiable corpse, an old woman, who has lost her city and her children, giving burial to a mere boy" (71). In parallel manner, the Corrales and Pereiras protagonist mourns the devastation of her home and the destruction of her family members. Diosdada talks about the extreme beauty of Cuba and the sanctity of her home and feels betrayed because Menelao has destroyed it, lamenting, "The city is in ruins, as if dead . . . and now it is less than nothing" (57).

Evil invaders, one from outside Troy and the other who has been a guest in the Cuban "house," ruin both cities and in each case the gods react to the destruction and its causes. The roles of the gods in the two plays draw parallels between their predominant but different places in the two cultures (ancient Greece and Cuba) and their strong, but distinct reactions to the destruction of each nation. In *The Trojan Women* the Greek gods describe the events, both past and present, and appear to be friends of the Trojans.[9] Poseidon has a vested interest in Troy since he, along with Apollo, had built the city (Morwood 2000, 130). Because of the destruction, he chooses to leave Troy and join forces with Athena to punish the invaders as their ships set sail.[10] The gods, who clearly favor the Trojans, have a limited role in Euripides' tragedy. Poseidon and Athena open the play and plan to cause the Spartans' final defeat, although that is not part of the action of the play. Their role is to give background to the situation, as a type of chorus, and to establish sympathy for the women's plight.

The gods figure more significantly in *Las hetairas habaneras;* they symbolize the syncretism of Catholicism and Santería in Cuban culture, and they not only speak about the tragedy, but they weep for the country's loss and blame the women for it because they had let the invader into their house.[11] This syncretism is marked from the opening lines as the two choral voices, Coralia and Coro, announce the double blessings of Nicomedes' birth. Coralia affirms, "Diosdada's grandson will be in Glory as the only prince, the sole adored creature in the house, as the host is adored in the monstrance when it is exposed on the altar," while the Coro wishes that "May Elegua bless him and may the orishas [saints] of the Forest, all the saints, bless him" (18–19).[12]

Moreover, as part of her prophetic gift, Iluminada (The Enlightened One), not only reads the cards, but also the snail shells of Santería. Recognizing the priority of Santería over Catholicism in their house, Coralia remarks, "Throw the cards, or better yet, the snail shells, to Nicomedes" (21).

Not only do other characters embody the religious syncretism of the island, but also, the African goddess, Yemayá, and the Catholic San Roque, actively participate in the fate of the women as characters. Yemayá ends act 1, begins act 2, and plays an important role in establishing the Cuban space, in demonstrating faithfulness to the homeland, and in reacting to the actions and fate of the characters. At the end of act 1, as both Coro and Coralia let Menelao Garrigó into their house and praise him, the stage directions note that "*Yemayá has entered from behind and she places herself at center stage; as if on a throne, she looks at the courtesans scornfully and covers her face with an immense veil*" (30). She is ashamed of the women's betrayal because they have let Menelao and Estrella cause their ruin, and she scorns them. The women's actions so upset her that at the beginning of act 2, nine or ten years later, still positioned on the throne at center stage, Yemayá "*cries sorrowfully*" (31). When she hears the sound of African music she begins to take off some of her many veils, but when the music changes to a military march, "*Yemayá is irritated . . . and returns to the throne and again covers her face with a veil*" (31).

Whereas in the Greek text the gods punish the outside enemies, in the Cuban play Yemayá convinces San Roque that they should forget their past divisiveness and join forces to punish the courtesans for having let Menelao into their house. The African goddess designs the plan to mutilate Nicomedes, while the Catholic saint chooses to punish Estrella for bringing on the doom. Together, though, they plot to "hit these courtesans hard" (34). Ironically, as Menelao's secretary, Alejo, rips the child from his mother's arms, Coralia and the Coro pray to both the Afro-Cuban orishas and the Catholic saints who Menelao had wanted them to renounce (46).

In the Greek play, the gods take on an explanatory role and provide a sense of justice that allows receptors to be consoled, even as they are confronted by the great tragedy of the Trojan women. In other words, because Athena and Poseidon will rightly punish the Aegeans, receptors view the Greek tragedy as fair and just. While still feeling sorry for the poor women, at least the evil invaders will receive their punishment.

In the Cuban play, the two religious forces, so predominant but divided in Cuban culture, also join forces, but this time it is to punish the women/citizens themselves. The different role of the gods in the Cuban play suggests that the courtesans were ultimately the cause of their own destruction because they let Menelao into their house and they helped him defeat them and force them into exile. Yemayá is ashamed of the women's betrayal while San Roque, too, wants to teach them a lesson.[13] Both texts focus on the anguish of the citizens over the destruction and loss of their nation; however, in the Cuban text, the gods are also punishing the citizens for having let this destruction occur.

Beyond the destruction of nation, in both plays, the greatest tragedy is that the women are forced into exile. The Greek Hecuba laments, "O my sorrow! This is now the be-all and the end-all here of all my woes. I shall leave my fatherland, my city is being torched. Come, old legs, make what haste you can, however difficult it may prove, so that I can salute my wretched city" (73). In a dialogue with the chorus, the Trojan woman is distressed over the Achaean's plans to take her away. Hecuba notes that "the oarsmen are already moving toward the ships," the First-Half Chorus asks, "Alas, what are they planning? Are they now about to take me off over the sea from my fatherland?" Hecuba replies, "I do not know. I assume it means our ruin" (42–43). It is clear that Hecuba and the Trojan women fully identify with Troy and that exile is their ultimate punishment.

Later, Hecuba repeats, "Troy, unhappy Troy, you no longer exist. Unhappy too are those who leave you, both the living and the dead" (43). Because they are so closely identified with it, these women personify their homeland.[14] Their exile, their separation from the homeland, whether they are alive or dead, leads them to despair. The women go "weeping into exile," leaving behind their destroyed nation and their dead dreams (in the child Astyanax).

In like manner in the Cuban text the women are forced into exile. While it seems at first that it is only to the countryside, the end of the text shows that they will be taken to a place where they can no longer hear the birds or see the palm trees or taste mamey or papaya:

> *Coralia.* We are leaving the city, heading toward the countryside.
> *Diosdada.* But not to enjoy the sun, the palm trees, the breeze, but rather to hard and bewildering work. That is where we are heading.
> *Coralia.* They are taking us there, there, to suffer not only in body and soul but to try to hide our suffering . . . Because we will not even be

> able to hear the song of the birds . . . Because we will not be able to see flowers nor taste mamey and papaya. Because like the city, they have condemned us, you, me, all of us, to a sentence more terrible than death, because they have condemned us to emptiness, to not even being able to exclaim or say how much we suffer, because they have condemned us to be worms without consolation, without early-rising butterflies or gardens where they can fly and rest their thoughts, because they have condemned us to spend our life in hell, to hide within ourselves and forget, because they have condemned us to . . .
>
> *Alejo. (Enters and screams at the top of his lungs, interrupting Diosdada.)* SILENCE!
>
> (57–58)

The worst part of Menelao's takeover is that the homeland's citizens are forced into exile, made to leave their homeland. Destroyed and mutilated as it is, the fatherland has lost more because its citizens must leave. They are "worms" without consolation and these worms will be forced to live in hell in another nation.

Moreover, Diosdada and the other women are not even allowed to express their sadness; Diosdada cannot even finish her sentence, for Alejo interrupts her and demands silence (58). Alejo takes them away from their home violently and "in the most absolute of silences" (58). Their forced silence impedes their protests and intensifies their tragedy.

As the women are silenced, so, too, are the babies, yet their distinct treatment in the two plays suggests some optimism for the future in the Cuban tragedy. In Euripides' work, Menelaus' forces drop the child from a tower, thus breaking his neck and killing him. After his death, he is buried in the homeland before the rest are forced into exile. As a dead Trojan, the boy remains one with his homeland; however, his death destroys any hope for the nation. He will utter no protest and his compatriots will be distanced from him.

Nicomedes, in *Las hetairas habaneras,* however, suffers a different fate; Menelao Garrigó's men mutilate, rather than kill him. They blind him, rip out his tongue, and castrate him. Tragic though it is, he is not dead, but he is so mutilated that, as the chorus suggests, he lives like the island, "in the shadow of being nothing. Of being no one" (56). Diosdada, too, recognizes that her grandson, the boy-child of joy and salsa, *the Cuban,* "lives to never, ever bear fruit and to disappear on the margin of life. My grandson lives as if dead. They cut the dreams out of my grandson" (56). If Nicomedes had been the hope and joy for the future of La Gloria, this house, this island, he has been blinded, castrated, and rendered mute by the government.

Nicomedes' maiming has thwarted dreams for a fertile, productive, vocal, and active Cuban future. The chorus remarks, "They cut the nourishment of love and the beacon of my dreams out of your grandson. All is lost. The seed of mamey and avocado is lost. The barren tree will give no fruit. He will give no fruit, he is a tree without roots and without a trunk" (56). Coralia repeats this attitude of hopelessness and she and Diosdada see that Nicomedes' maiming symbolizes the city's ruin as well; Nicomedes and the city are one, and their ruin is the tragedy that this Cuban family must suffer.

> *Coralia.* We have lost everything, all that we loved most.
> *Diosdada.* We have even lost the Saints. We have lost everything, everything except life, but death is now our companion.
> *Diosdada.* The city is in ruins, as if dead.
> *Coralia.* This city that was everything.
> *Diosdada.* And that now is less than nothing.
> *Coro.* The city that was and no longer is. The cursed city of the gods. The now frenetic and vulgar city. The city now lost in disgust, in darkness. The city without dance and without song. The city without the splendor of years past. The city without laughter and the happy tapping of feet. The city that is now a hole.
>
> (57)

Corrales and Pereiras's Cuba, like Euripides' Troy, has been destroyed by Menelao/Fidel and his forces, stripped of its fame, and unwillingly purged of its citizens. Hecuba nostalgically remembers her homeland's past greatness as well and makes one last attempt to die in her homeland, even as it burns:

> O Troy, city that breathed forth greatness once among barbarians, soon you will be stripped of your famous name. They are burning you and leading us off from the land as slaves. O you gods! And yet why do I call upon the gods? They did not hear me in the past when I called to them. Come, let us run into the pyre. For it is best for me to die together with this my country as it burns.
>
> (73)

When she is unable to remain, she shakily walks away from her burning, collapsing homeland, to her exile, "a day when your life of slavery begins" (75).

In both Euripides' play and in *Las hetairas habaneras,* being forced to live in exile is seen as more tragic than the actual destruction of the nation. Whereas in *The Trojan Women,* the child is killed and denied the chance to suffer in exile, in *Las hetairas habaneras,*

Nicomedes will live his pathetic life in exile with the courtesans. As a Cuban child, the pride and joy of this house, Nicomedes had symbolized hope and happiness for Cuba and for the future Cuban nation. However, he, like the island under Menelao and the Cuban exiles forced from it, is maimed. Nicomedes is castrated, blinded, and his tongue is ripped from his mouth. Certainly, these are harsh punishments, and some might argue that living in such a deformed and violated state is a fate worse than death. Nonetheless, although Nicomedes will live a life of suffering, he will accompany the women to their exile. His punishment then becomes a symbol for Cuban exile: a tragic life where the Cuban protagonists are rendered mute and impotent regarding their own fate and that of their nation. However, even though Nicomedes cannot speak or reproduce, he is not dead, and this suggests some hope for the future. There is hope that, in his exile, through other means, he can partially recover his voice, gain some vision on his own position and that of his nation, and be productive in other ways.

It is no surprise that José Corrales and Manuel Pereiras would choose Euripides' tragedy to depict the double loss experienced by Cubans who once saw their freedom destroyed and were later forced to leave their homeland. According to James Morwood, "even Aristotle conceded that Euripides was the 'most tragic of poets'" (2000, xi). The function of tragedy, in the classic sense, was to produce catharsis. In *Las hetairas habaneras* everyone is crying, even the gods. The two lines of potential celebration that open the play quickly turn into an unraveling of one disaster after another. By the end of the play, the *hetairas* have lost everything, even their voice of protest. Diosdada's closing words express the tragic emptiness of the exile they will face, but before she can fully articulate the profound emotional impact of her loss, she is silenced by Alejo's final command, as Nicomedes had been silenced before her.

The Euripides intertext marks the two losses of nation in the Cuban play, but changes in the Cuban text suggest hope for the future if those who live in exile can recover their voice. Ironically, even though the courtesans are ordered to be silent and Nicomedes is rendered mute, the very writing of this play, and others like it, breaks that imposed silence by rewriting the tragedy, not only Euripides' but also that of the Cuban exiles. *Las hetairas habaneras* postulates that through "text(s)" playwrights can speak out against the status quo and reaffirm their place in (Cuban) history. In a memorial article entitled, "Reminiscence and Rambling: Regarding José Corrales as a Writer," published in the posthumous homage issue of *Ollantay Theater Magazine,* Corrales's longtime roommate and partner, Evan

Senreich, affirms that one of the most important aspects of Corrales that influenced all of his writing was his Cubanness. Senreich writes, "José was a man who loved the island of Cuba and its culture. Although he genuinely liked New York City, it was somehow never completely home to him . . . His feelings of alienation brought on by being in exile were constantly present until the day he died" (2003, 140). In that same article, Senreich quotes the playwright himself from a 1999 interview with a New York University doctoral student in which Corrales affirms, "I am Cuban, absolutely; the only thing I care about is Cuba . . . I'm Cuban. American I never was, and never will be. *Cuban American* is a thing that doesn't exist for me; it doesn't make sense" (140).

Like the Greek master before them, Corrales and Pereiras have created a dramatic testimony of the impact of the "war" on the (Cuban) nation and those forced to leave it. Both dramatically and ideologically, *Las hetairas habaneras* breaks the silence and creates a new dramatic form that allows Cuban exiles to recover their voice and write a new script for Cuba's future and their place in it.

Raúl de Cárdenas's *Un hombre al amanecer*

Raúl de Cárdenas's *Un hombre al amanecer* (*A Man at Dawn*) traces and reflects upon the life of Cuban writer and patriot José Martí by making him the only character and speaking voice(s) in the play. Winner of the 1989 Letras de Oro prize from the University of Miami, the workplaces Martí at the end of his life, upon his final return to Cuba after years of traveling the world and fighting, from exile, for Cuban independence, but it presents the writer/patriot's entire life through flashbacks. Even though Martí is the only character in the play, three dramatic strategies function to stage his life from multiple perspectives and, at the same time, to shift the thematic focus of the play from Martí and his life to an evaluation of what it means to be Cuban at the end of the twentieth century.

The playwright scripts *Un hombre al amanecer* to shed light on the life of one of the most interesting figures in Latin America and to inform the United States public about a character little known to them.[15] While this play does, indeed, teach about José Martí's life, the three strategies—the juxtaposition of past and present, the interweaving of four types of monologue, and the incorporation of Martí's own writings into the play—suggest that this dramatic text is not about Martí, but rather, about a writer's relationship with his nation.[16]

This section will examine the structure and content of *Un hombre al amanecer* to show how Cárdenas fuses multiple perspectives on the life and writings of José Martí to postulate a troubled relationship with his Cuban nation: a relationship that was as real for the nineteenth-century Cuban patriot as it is for the twentieth-century writer of the "new" Martí text. I will show how nation is defined through the various "voices" of the monologue and the excerpts from Martí's literary texts, postulating that, as Martí speaks through Cárdenas's text, but for himself, to himself, and by himself, so too does Cárdenas speak for himself and for Cuban exiles in general with multiple voices about his/their nation. Moreover, the way in which Cárdenas blends the past and "present" of Martí's life fuses a troubled Cuban past of a more recent time, that of Castro's revolution, with a patriot/writer's present attempt to come to terms with his place in and reaction to the nation he left.

Cuban patriot, martyr, and writer José Martí (1853–95) began writing shortly after the outbreak of the first Cuban war against Spain by editing and creating clandestine newspapers and pamphlets. One of his first published works, a dramatic poem entitled *Abdala,* which includes a protagonist who sacrifices his life to defend his homeland against oppressors, not only becomes autobiographic as Martí's life unfolds, but because of it, his other texts, and his revolutionary actions, he is detained, persecuted, and later exiled by the Spanish authorities in Cuba (Schulman 1994, 20).

Like Martí, Cárdenas's exile from Cuba in 1961 deeply impacted him. He writes, "My departure from Cuba, after the debut of my one-act play *La Palangana* [*The Washbasin*] in 1961, managed to paralyze my dramatic production for more than ten years" (Gónzalez-Pérez 1999, 141). Nonetheless, Cárdenas is author of many plays including *La muerte de Rosendo (The Death of Rosendo)* (1986), *Al ayer no se le dice adiós (You Can't Say Good-bye to Yesterday)* (1986), *Las Carbonell de la Calle Obispo (The Carbonell Girls of Bishop Street)* (1986–87), *Aquí no se baila el danzón (No Cuban Dancing Here), Dile a Fragancia que yo la quiero (Tell Fragancia That I Love Her), El Barbero de Mantilla (The Barber of Mantilla)* (1987), *Las sombras no se olvidan (Shadows Don't Forget)* (1989), *Recuerdos de familia (Family Memories)* (1988), *Sucedió en La Habana (It Happened in Havana)* (1987), and *Los hijos de Ochún (The Children of Oshun)* (1994).

Cárdenas is not the first Cuban playwright to dramatize the life and works of a nineteenth-century Cuban writer in an effort to revise and unveil history, nor is he the first to draw parallels between the selected writer's and his own condition as expatriated citizen and writer. In her article in *Ollantay Theater Magazine,* Beatriz Rizk shows how both Abelardo Estorino (*La dolorosa historia del amor secreto de don José Jacinto Milanés* [*The Painful Story of Mr. Jose Jacinto Milanes's Secret Love*], 1974) and Abilio Estévez (*La verdadera culpa de Juan Clemente Zenea* [*Juan Clemente Zenea's True Guilt*], 1986) blend textual fragments from a century ago with the "author's present moment in the late twentieth century" to "underscore the continuing relevance of the discussions surrounding the word-concepts 'fatherland,' 'liberty,' 'insularity,' and 'exile'" (1998, 123–24).[17] Cárdenas's play follows a similar structure by including a variety of intertexts from one selected author, however, monologue, the blending of past and present, intertextuality, and the prioritizing of theater over the other intertexts (suggested both by the primary role of Martí's play *Abdala* among the intertexts and the primacy of metatheatrical devices), control the point of view in the play and shift the thematic emphasis.

Un hombre al amanecer charts the biographical course of Martí's life—his years in Spain, Mexico, Guatemala, New York, and Cuba—and dramatizes his relationships with his Cuban friends, his parents, his female lovers, his children, and Generals Máximo Gómez and Antonio Maceo, with whom Martí had met several times in an effort to free Cuba from Spain.[18] Cárdenas succeeds in depicting the broad scope of Martí's life and in evoking great movement onstage through Martí's memories, even though the play all takes place in one twenty-four-hour period, in one location, and the protagonist never moves out of the space nor does any other character enter it.

Cárdenas accomplishes this through the intricate way in which he weaves the many "different voices" of monologue. According to Heidrun Adler, paradoxically, "monologue is the oldest and, at the same time, the most modern, theatrical convention" (1999a, 125). Different from dialogue, the monologue structure "is totally determined by the dialectics between visible and imaginary presence . . . The dramatis personae is alone, there on the stage, and s/he addresses a hypostatic reality converted into an interlocutor to which s/he surrenders him/herself completely." Because there is no dialogue partner, "the social medium comes completely alive." When a dialogue partner is present, the social context is based on each one of the specific interactions between characters, but "only monologue is capable of transforming the general, or rather, the totality of the social medium in which the dramatic character moves, into a valid interlocutor" (Adler 1999a, 126).

In Latin America where, according to Adler, three out of every ten plays published during the past twenty years are monologues, the technique becomes a framework that promotes communication, not alienation. Adler outlines four types of monologues in Latin American theater: dialogue with one or more offstage characters who are invisible to spectators but whose voices can be heard; dialogue with the audience who is assigned a concrete role; dialogue with imaginary voices, hallucinations, or personified objects; and interior monologue, a form of auto-analysis with an imaginary other (1999a, 127–34). As we shall see, Cárdenas incorporates all of Adler's monologue strategies into his play, although Adler's final three points are prioritized since on only a few occasions is there a voice, a tape recording, music, or an expression uttered from offstage. The use of monologue expands the point of view and shifts the focus from the presumed subject of the play (Martí) to his images of and relationship to his nation. As the protagonist "dialogues" with each different partner (with the audience, with imaginary, but real, historical people, or with himself, through his reflections, his memories, his writings during the play, and the Martí intertexts included by Cárdenas), Cuba and his relationship to it change.

Cárdenas weaves the four types of monologue in such a way that at times the protagonist is talking to himself, then he will turn to the audience and say something or turn toward an imaginary character to carry on a conversation with him/her. Martí, however, is the only speaking character, though at one point in the text, a voice is heard from offstage, calling his name and accusing him of the crime for which he will be executed (50). The different types of monologues create motion within the text; they move the text through Martí's life historically, they direct the audience through the places of Martí's travels and exile, and they focus attention to an imaginary entrance on the part of each invisible interlocutor. This feigned movement allows an entire lifetime to be represented in one single day and also creates the sense that this text is not about this one day or this one life, but rather about an entire nation and its relationship to its citizens, in and from any space. In this way, the monologue transports character and spectators through space and time and, as a result, transforms discourse and the message behind it.

The protagonist speaks the opening lines of the play with his back to the audience. In that initial monologue, he expresses an overwhelming inner agitation that cannot be calmed, even by the beauty and tranquillity of Cuba, and he reveals his turmoil even while he is in his beloved homeland.[19] Nevertheless, as he turns to the audience, his attitude changes and suggests that Cuba, and only sweet Cuba, can calm him. To the audience he reveals that, even though he is about to be killed for his revolutionary ideals, "There is no longer any sadness breaking my heart. Only the sweetness of my Cuba, goddess of my anguish and my dreams. I exist now soaked by the rain of her clouds. The leaves of her trees caress me, the thorns that I find in the brushland tickle me, I taste the troubled water of her rivers on my hands. The years spent in the most painful of exiles now erase themselves from my mind" (8). The contradiction between what he expresses to himself and what he reveals to the audience suggests his ambivalence and tremendous inner turmoil with regard to his nation. He so wants to love Cuba and to be calmed by his homeland, but in his soul he feels deeply disturbed about his nation.

The change in attitude when he speaks to the audience highlights the self-analytical stance of the earlier passage. Adler notes that when a monologue is between a protagonist and an imaginary other and when it takes on a self-analytical tone, "the monologue serves to elaborate memories and thus to find the truth itself" (1999a, 132). This type of monologue uses personal memories as well as free associations and allusions to the political, social, or historical context to provide a background through which the protagonist can present him/herself (Adler 1999a, 132). In this way, the monologue can express the subject position of the protagonist and, in this case, it highlights Martí's ambivalence vis-à-vis his nation.

Beyond the revelation of his inner struggle to come to terms with Cuba and his relationship to it, often, when Martí talks to himself, he nostalgically elaborates memories of "his Cuba." With every return to his island and every memory of it, Martí describes the fragrance, beauty, and mythical essence of the Cuba he loves.[20] In *Un hombre al amanecer,* Martí's passion for his nation is as pronounced as his constant discovery of it. Everywhere he goes, both within and outside the island, he is surprised by the newness of the nation that unfolds before him. On a trip with his father to the provinces he says, "For the first time, my land was opening like a flower, the unknown Cuba that I could only imagine on the streets of Havana. The green fields, infinite. The haughty palm trees. The small hamlets full of humble and good-natured people. The morning goldfinch, and the mockingbird, that in the summer months, would frantically attack the ripe fruit" (13). Martí's words expose two conflicting relationships; he deeply loves a rapturous, exotic, mythical Cuba, yet he is tormented both by his estrangement from the island and by the political events occurring within "his" Cuba.

Adler argues that a conversation with imaginary characters is the most common form of monologue (1999a, 130); this is also recurrent in Cárdenas's text. As in Adler's analysis of Beatriz Mosquera's *Vio-*

leta Parra y sus voces (Violeta Parra and Her Voices), in *Un hombre al amanecer,* "the monologue is not accompanied by any action. It is self-critical, a posteriori justification and explanation, a reflexion out loud that leads to a recognition of the need to gain its own argumentation in order to be able to overcome socially programmed feelings of guilt" (130). Similarly, beyond the "dialogues" with himself and with the audience, Martí's conversations with imaginary others allow him to work through those conflicting relationships and the difficult events that mar his ties with the Cuban nation.

Among the imaginary characters with whom Martí dialogues in the text, his father takes on an important role as critic of his son's writings and revolutionary activities. He converses with his mother, as well, and the two parents, though never seen, become the antitheses of each other. While his father is critical of every aspect of his son's life, José sees his mother as supportive, sweet, tender, and understanding of him and his ways. These two conflicting perspectives toward the protagonist and his role with regard to the nation parallel Martí's own conflicting views on nation and his relationship to it.

Martí also has conversations with his friend, Fermín, and through these the reader/spectator experiences the roots of their intimate relationship, which, interestingly enough, begins in Cuba but has strong connections with the United States. In fact, Martí's very first conversation with his friend centers on the United States as the two friends discuss the classic book *Uncle Tom's Cabin.* By referring to that North American classic, Martí is able to present his ideas on the injustice of slavery and the need to defend freedom and to expand upon the North American problem by relating it to Cuba. Beyond presenting a sociopolitical stance, however, the protagonist links Cuba and the United States on a more personal level as well. At one point he reminds Fermín about their plans to go to the park to watch the North American boats and then he turns to the audience to tell them that "In this way a friendship that would last a lifetime was being cemented" (16). Is he only referring to his friendship with Fermín or could the protagonist/author be alluding to his friendship with North America: a "personal" friendship that will, indeed, be cemented and last a lifetime (through his exile there) because of the situation in "his" Cuba?

Even though *Un hombre al amanecer* is a monologue, the protagonist talks to different types of characters and presents distinct information to each of them. He also reacts to noises and a call from offstage. In most of the play, however, the protagonist is talking to the audience. In those sequences he reveals his thoughts about nation and gives details about individual events in his life and the people who impacted him most by presenting and reenacting scenes from his life. When Martí talks to the audience, he expects them to listen to him and to understand both his life and his inner feelings. As mentioned above, when Martí turns to the audience in the opening scene, his attitude about Cuba seems to change. The apparent contradiction between what Martí expresses to himself (that his soul is in turmoil and not even Cuba can console him) and what he tells to the audience (that his return to Cuba erases all those years of pain), is notable as it reveals a man who continues to struggle with his relationship to his nation. In this way, Cárdenas juxtaposes two types of monologue to present a more complete and complex image of his protagonist and as a means of controlling that image and the audience's view of it. In her analysis of monologue in other Latin American plays, Heidrun Adler confirms that a protagonist, "through monologue, gains control over time and space, that is to say, s/he gains the power to manipulate truth and lies, dreams and reality" (1999a, 129).

Martí uses the audience to present his side of the story, and it is clear that he expects the audience to agree with him, even when others do not. For example, when Martí tries to convince a schoolmate to join his revolutionary cause and take arms against Spain, he turns to the audience to tell them that the classmate, "went away furious, defeated by his own rage, without wanting to understand the meaning of my words" (15). This revelation indicates that the audience is presumably complicit with Martí's cause, otherwise, the protagonist would have needed to defend himself as a result of his friend's abrupt departure or he might not have exposed that information to the audience. Martí's statement to the audience assumes that the audience understood the meaning of his words and that the classmate is the odd man out.

Besides manipulating the audience's view of José Martí and presenting him as a sympathetic character, Cárdenas's text blends the past and the present in some of the monologues, provoking the audience to question the time frame and context to which the play refers. As the protagonist reminisces, the verbs often vacillate between past and present tenses, suggesting that both nineteenth-century protagonist and contemporary author/audience share similar feelings about Cuba. At the beginning of act 2, the protagonist must once again leave his homeland, and he expresses his sadness to the audience by stating, "Havana **welcomed** me in all its sad splendor. In this land that ***is*** still not mine I **found** only visible fatigue" (42).[21] The alternation between past- and present-tense verbs might indicate a slippage between the point of view of the protagonist and that of the playwright. As Boris Uspensky argues, verbs in different tenses within one discourse may reveal a change in temporal position and authorial point of view. Uspensky affirms, "The narrator may change his positions, borrowing the time sense of first one character, then another—or he may assume his own temporal position and use his own authorial time, which may not coincide with the individual time sense of any of the characters. Different combinations of characters' temporal positions and authorial time determine the degree of complexity of the compositional structure of the work" (1973, 66). This vacillation between past and present verb forms occurs repeatedly when the protagonist reminisces about his nation. The character remarks:

> Our struggle **had** not **been** halted, it **was** only covered in the fog that history sometimes forces on noble causes. The new generation of Cubans **was** preparing itself to be reborn and to be worthy of its homeland. The truth ***is,*** and it ***is*** very sad, that liberty might have been obtained if we **had** not **been distracted** by our own misery and passion, in the egotism of feeling ourselves weak and miserable and in search of a caress to soothe our feelings. ***I feel*** guilty. I **looked** for excuses to justify my pain and ***it hurts now. It hurts*** deeply.
>
> (43)

Here, an outside voice (that of the playwright himself?) expresses his current guilt and pain over the loss of nation, over the lack of freedom in his relationship to his homeland, and over his tormented feelings because of what went on in the past.

To better direct the war for independence from exile, Martí moves to the United States and this act, too, evokes tormented images of the patriot's relationship to his nation. Once again the verbs the protagonist expresses vacillate between past and present tense. "What ***is*** this torment that constantly ***burns*** my insides? How am I to respond to my duty as father and husband? Where am I to find the place that Cuba ***has*** designated for me? The conflict **divided** my heart like Solomon's knife, but I **was** not as wise" (52). From his exile in the United States, the protagonist wonders, in the present tense, what his role is in relationship to Cuba. The same conflict that divided Martí's heart weighs heavily on the "present" soul as well.

Like Beatriz Mosquera's protagonist analyzed by Adler, Cárdenas's protagonist sometimes uses his monologues as a way to work through his, and perhaps the author's, guilt. In speaking with Carmita, one of his lovers (perhaps his most important because she seems to understand his love for Cuba more than anyone), Martí queries, "What ***can*** we do, Carmita? What ***can*** we do? I ***feel*** guilty. Maybe we **ought to have waited** a little longer. The impatience in my heart ***is*** great, but I ***cannot*** win this battle alone" (54). The switch between past- and present-tense verbs and the unclear references to the battle, past and present, suggest that the author himself is still waging this battle and that, rather than referring to a concrete, external battle, it is a patriotic battle within his soul.

Nonetheless, the present author/patriot is determined to win this battle. In a conversation directed to the audience and interrupted by a Martí poem expressing the patriot's resignation with regard to Cuba, once again the change in verb tenses postulates a switch in narrative position within the monologue. The protagonist states, "My duty **was** already more clear and defined than ever. All that roaming through the lands of America **had taught** me that if Cubans really **wanted** liberty for their island they **had** to fight alone. Alone!! . . . This time ***we are going to*** triumph" (56–57).

The juxtaposition and confusion between past and present verb forms continues through to the end of the play. As Martí is about to join forces with Generals Gómez and Antonio and declare war on his nation to free it, the protagonist remarks, "I **recalled** the War. My responsibility ***begins*** rather than ends with it. For me, the homeland ***will*** never be triumph, but rather agony and duty. My blood ***is*** already boiling . . . For me the hour ***is*** now!" (70). The protagonist (writer?) clearly expresses here that as he evoked the war (of the past) he knows his present responsibilities and feelings.

Since there is only one character in Cárdenas's play, the playwright uses many strategies to insert and affirm his own authorial point of view with regard to nation. Beyond monologue and the vacillation between past- and present-tense verbs, the Martí intertexts and the way they are woven into the play further shift the focus of the text from Martí's to Cárdenas's perspective on nation. Martí's actual texts are often alternated with the author's text (the protagonist's words that this author has written), making it difficult to distinguish between the two. Moreover, although the intertexts are taken from many Martí sources (essays, letters, *Versos sencillos, Versos libres,* and his theater) the predominance of his play *Abdala,* the many references to theater in Cárdenas's play, and the primary role of the audience as interlocutor, suggest a self-consciousness about theater in general and about this play in particular as a way to stage the relationship of a writer with his nation.

Writing, then, takes on heightened significance in the play from the outset. The opening stage directions emphasize Martí's papers, books, and diary in the middle of this open-air camp in Dos Ríos, Cuba, and also indicate that "The entire text that appears within quotation marks is José Martí's original text: verses, speeches, letters, all of which have been adapted to give more credence to the character" (7). The playwright admits, however, that "this material has been used freely, adjusting it and editing it to fit the needs of the work" (7). Writing, the text, Martí's texts, are all in process here; even though the playwright attempts to recreate Martí and his voice(s), he is admittedly editing Martí's texts as he goes and recreating his own version of them.

The many juxtapositions of Martí's literary texts with the protagonist's words (Cárdenas's text) further highlight the similarities between the nineteenth-century patriot's view of nation and that of our writer. The protagonist himself knows that "I will not be the last, I am sure, to write about these cruelties as long as a force exists that is strangling Cuba, no matter what its name or ideological condition might be" (28). Recognizing that others will come after him who will write about the "cruelties of a force that strangles Cuba," the protagonist then begins to write Martí's own words, quotes from Martí's writings about nation, which are heard on a tape recorder offstage, "(HE THINKS AND WRITES. A VOICE IS HEARD WHILE HE WRITES—Tape recording): 'Let me think that you still do not know: that in this land there is still honor . . . Return for your honor' " (29).

Even though the Martí quote refers to his nation's colonization by Spain and his own anguish because of his and his nation's lack of freedom, Martí the fictional character's announcement that others will write this after him, juxtaposed with the "real" Martí's words, highlights the multiple voices here—Martí's and Cárdenas's—and postulates Cárdenas as one of those "other" writers. Cárdenas's text, then, echoes Martí's, once again suggesting that the playwright's views on nation also parallel those of the nineteenth-century patriot's.

Other excerpts from Martí's texts explain his views on patriotism. At one point, the protagonist turns to the public and in Martí's words defines what it means to be a foreigner, "I was convinced that I was not 'a foreigner in Mexico, or outside of Mexico. True foreigners are the enemies of decency and of the people's moral code; they are those who, instead of lending useful and honorable support to their homeland, discredit her' " (36). Martí did not consider himself a foreigner because he was an honorable person who upheld the values of his homeland in and from any space. As Martí did not consider himself a foreigner in Mexico or outside of it, Cárdenas is not a foreigner in the United States; he, like Martí, is Cuban in any space, lending honor to his homeland and defending it values.

Often, Cárdenas includes fragments of quotes from Martí's actual texts within a line in which the protagonist gives the verse a new context. The protagonist contextualizes the Martí verse that follows it, for example, by initiating it with the words, "For me, for all of us, 'the homeland will never be triumph, but rather agony and duty'" (58). The interspersing of Martí intertexts alongside the "new" Martí's (protagonist's) words ("For me, for all of us"), rewrites the sentiment of the nineteenth-century verses, giving them a broader and more contemporary context.

At the end of the play, Cárdenas interweaves quotes and fragments from Martí's letters to General Gómez with his protagonist's own words, once again modernizing the context and reinterpreting Martí's writing to apply them to the current struggle for Cuban identity. Speaking with the imaginary general, Martí affirms, "If we allow ourselves to be governed by only one authority, 'What guaranty can we have that public freedoms might be better respected tomorrow?'" (62). The juxtaposition of the new text with the past text as well as the question that directs the ideology on liberty to a tomorrow or future time, broadens the meaning; that tomorrow that José Martí evoked, is the author's present time.

The structure of the rest of this conversation remains the same: intertextual fragments alongside and within the new text, past-juxtaposed with present- and future-tense verbs. The protagonist continues, "'the homeland does not belong to anyone, and if it does belong to someone, it will belong, and only in spirit, to whomever serves it with the greatest generosity and intelligence,' . . . Consider me what you will, but the Republic does not belong to one person, but to everyone" (62). The protagonist, through Martí's real text, reflects upon the essence of his nation; however, the protagonist, in his own (Cárdenas's) words, includes himself and his contemporaries within that ideology of nation.[22]

Even though Cárdenas incorporates fragments of many different Martí texts, theater, both Martí's and his own, is his primary focus. The different types of monologue expand the message of this play and switch the thematic focus from Martí to Cárdenas's relationship to his nation. Most of the time, Martí talks to the audience. Adler argues that "the character that acts alone on the stage with the help of the spectator's fantasy can make the realm of his/her closed life come alive, s/he can travel through time and space and fulfill and even transform his/her identity" (1999a, 133).[23]

In *Un hombre al amanecer* the audience is the primary interlocutor and this metatheatrical strategy is one way in which theater and its important function in shedding light on nation is foregrounded.

During his conversations with the audience, Martí reveals important information about himself and his relationship to his nation. Beyond the awareness of an involved and complicit public, however, the protagonist views the history of his nation as drama, as well. To the audience he says that "The bloody Ten Year drama began to unfold" (18). Soon after, he turns to his parents and "DIALOGUES, leave me, mother, leave me. I don't have to deceive you or lie to you. 'I have no fear of the public (audience) and it matters little to me whether they idolize me or mock me'" (19).[24] Is this latter quote, in which he talks about his relationship with the audience, taken from Martí's own texts? Or is this protagonist responding to the current audience reaction to the views he had just expressed to them? In either case the protagonist compares the history of his nation to a play and, at the same time, is conscious of his role in that play. As Martí and other historical figures are judged by their audience, so, too, is this protagonist aware of his role and that of his audience.

The metatheatrical elements in Cárdenas's play, however, go beyond a self-awareness of character, audience, and theater's roles in history and with regard to individual and nation; the play also foregrounds Martí's theater in order to rescript its style and message. In the first stage directions Cárdenas writes that "The last poem is taken from the play, *Abdala.* In it the word 'Nubia' has replaced 'Cuba' to achieve the appropriate effect on the ending of the work" (7). Notably, Martí's play is an intertext throughout most of Cárdenas's play, not just at the end.

The excerpt Cárdenas includes is a direct quote from Martí's *Abdala,* a play that was published in the only issue of *La patria libre (The Free Homeland),* the Cuban newspaper that the character Martí had just referred to in his monologue, and which he and Fermín had founded. Printed on October 23, 1869, *Abdala: Escrito expresamente para la patria (Abdala: Written Especially for the Homeland),* is a dramatic poem praising and honoring Cuba.[25] In the Martí play, the protagonist Abdala leaves his mother to fight to free his homeland from the foreign oppressors. The first excerpt that Cárdenas includes comes from Abdala's dialogue with his mother, in which the son explains to her his intense love for his homeland.

> Love for the homeland, mother
> Is not the ridiculous love for the land,
> Nor for the grass that our plants press down upon;
> It is the invincible hatred towards whoever oppresses it,
> It is the eternal loathing of whoever attacks it.
> And such love awakens in our breast

> The world of memories that calls us
> Back to life, when blood,
> Flows with anguish from the wounded soul.
> The image of the love that consoles us
> and the placid memories that it protects!
>
> (Cárdenas 1991, 19)

In the following passage in Martí's "real" text, however, the mother questions the greatness of her son's love of nation and she asks, "And is that love greater than that which your mother awakens in your breast?" Abdala responds to her with the question, "Perhaps you believe that there is something more sublime than the homeland?" (21). The quote from *Abdala* that Cárdenas includes shows the love/hate relationship of the patriot to his nation. His soul is in turmoil, filled with passion and anguish flowing as from an open wound, juxtaposed with a love that consoles the patriot as well. What Cárdenas chooses to omit from the Martí intertext, however, is the assertion that, in spite of the inner battle that patriotism wages, love for the nation is greater and more sublime than any love.

In fact, love for his nation is greater than love of any woman and Cárdenas proves this in his depiction of Martí's amorous relationships. Once again, he uses the theater to do this. Cárdenas includes excerpts from Martí's comedy, *Amor con amor se paga (Love is Paid for with Love)* to reveal his love affair with Concha Padilla, the actress in his play. From offstage, Concha's tape-recorded voice recites the final verses of that play. Those verses, directed to the audience of Martí's "real" play, reflect on the nature of patriotism, love, and exile and both the writer's and the actor's role in facing them. The real Martí wrote and this Martí hears:

> Sit, love, forgive
> With your natural goodness;
> If it is bad, the will
> Of the actor and poet will improve it.
> A person without a homeland
> in which to live can give nothing better,
> neither a woman to die for,
> nor the pride to try,
> he suffers, vacillates, and flatters himself
> imagining that at least among good audiences
> love is paid for with love.
>
> (39)

These plays and Cárdenas's play demonstrate the intense love that the playwright feels toward his nation. Even though the writer has many female lovers, Cuba is his primary passion. When he is in exile in Mexico, for example, he fills the emptiness in this soul by beginning a relationship with Rosario. Nonetheless, the protagonist turns to the audience and admits that "The sweetest hours of my life I have spent in the arms of a woman. Only this island that has the name of a woman can steal the passion from my heart" (37). The island is foremost in his thoughts and first among his lovers.

Both his third lover and his fourth lover emerge in and through his theater, yet the protagonist feels guilty because he uses these women as substitutes for the nation he cannot be part of. Curiously, his guilt comes forth not because he is using the women, but rather because he feels like he is slighting his nation. He expresses, "So far from Cuba at that moment, preoccupied with selfish and sensual love affairs, I felt guilty" (40).

The protagonist affirms that Cuba is for him, "like a desirous, amorous woman." He further extends the lover/nation metaphor by quoting from Martí's texts, "That Cuba, desolate, may turn its eyes to us . . . The palm trees are girlfriends that wait and we have to place justice as high as the palm trees . . . And let us place this formula of triumphant love around the star on the new flag!" (63–64).

The excerpts from Martí's plays serve a dual purpose; they reinforce Martí's passion for his lost nation by making that nation his most beloved lover and they show how theater can, has, and does portray, intensify, and dramatize texts, history, and ideologies. The other included fragments of Martí's texts serve to refocus the plot of Cárdenas's play; it is no longer Martí's Cuba that is being dramatized, but rather Cárdenas's. A close examination of the protagonist's words reveals how Cárdenas subtly changes the time frame of the text. Martí turns to the audience and says, "In my heart the emptiness of a distant Cuba . . . that of the warm and sunny mornings, that of the fresh and fragrant flowers, that of the emerald green sea and the white foamy waves, that of the beaches of fine sand, that of the fields of sweet sugarcane. My Cuba! The Cuba that was shuddering again before a *new* crime" (my emphasis, 30). Is this *new* crime that of Fidel Castro's revolution and the resultant exile of our writer?

At another moment, the protagonist reflects on the future of Cuba postulating that it is time to dry the tears and stop Cuba's weeping. Again, he speaks in the protagonist/writer's words, but mentions the real Martí poem, *Cuba llora (Cuba Cries).* The alternation between Cárdenas's text and Martí's fuses past with present and shows how relevant Martí's words are to Cuba's current situation:

> (*LIKE AN ORATOR, FROM HIS BALCONY*) This is the flag of the future Republic of Cuba. From that Cuba that cries over the mothers

> stripped of their children, and in the children torn from the breast of the homeland. "Cuba cries" and her tears soak the tombs of our dead, and the streets and the cities, and the fields and the sown ground. "Cuba cries" and her tears are the redemptive rain that revives a pure flower in the soul of patriots for tomorrow.
>
> (31)

According to Ivan A. Schulman, Martí's life and writings embraced a return to the past while at the same time they intuited a perception of a renewed present and future. For Martí, Schulman suggests, "to modernize does not imply burying the past, but rather bringing it back to life in an original, individual, and creative way" (1994, 17). In like manner, Raúl de Cárdenas employs Martí's life and his writings, both to pay homage to a Cuban past and, at the same time, to rewrite and relive that national history in an original way. The (con)-fusion between Martí's texts and Cárdenas's text, and between past and present, suggests a blurred boundary between the two writers and their texts. As writers they both represent the Cuban nation and express their relationship to it from their exiled position and through their texts.

Along with the alternating past/present points of view, the various types of monologue in *Un hombre al amanecer* narrate a complex life in many voices and from diverse spaces and create movement where there is none. The voices of the monologue further serve to expose the protagonist/writer's conflicting feelings about his nation. Adler suggests that, sometimes, "in monologue (a protagonist) also speaks without any disguise" (1999a, 129). At times, when Cárdenas's protagonist is speaking to himself he reveals his innermost self, as if we are witnessing and hearing the true José Martí. What is interesting, however, is that at these times we are NOT reading Martí's writings, but rather those of Cárdenas; this is highlighted because those words are juxtaposed to actual Martí quotes. Cárdenas succeeds in making Martí live, through Cárdenas's own writing, which combined with the actual Martí texts, transports the message to the present time and new Cuban spaces. In Cárdenas's play, as in Martí's real life, the exiled patriot returns to Cuba, if only metaphorically. The protagonist describes his love, his nation, and knows that, even when he is far away, he belongs to his homeland.

Moreover, the metatheatrical strategies—the self-consciousness of the protagonist about theater (talking to the audience, his spectator role at some theatrical performances) and the predominance of Martí's theatrical text, *Abdala,* among the intertexts—further emphasize theater as a means to portray the nation and speak about it.

Abdala's protagonist loves his nation above all even though he has many questions about nation and his relationship to it; that Martí play dramatizes the playwright's true love for his nation and its protagonist performs his inner struggles over his own national identity. In similar fashion, Raúl de Cárdenas writes *Un hombre al amanecer,* a patriotic play whose protagonist loves his nation above all and is willing to die for his Cuba.

Un hombre al amanecer does not just write the story of José Martí facing the Cuban dawn on the day of his death; the man at dawn is Cárdenas, a Cuban exile who is at the dawn of understanding his tormented relationship with his beloved homeland. Filled with turmoil, he, like his protagonist, learns that "This is the way to make war against the country that gave us life but that strangles us as if it had been transformed from mother into blind tyrant" (9). Nonetheless, that dawn of understanding also includes a new inner peace and acceptance of the exile's position with regard to his nation. Like the protagonist, the writer realizes that, even when he is far away from it, he belongs to his Cuba and loves it above all else.

Beatriz Rizk suggests that, according to Carlos Rincón, modern and postmodern authors may employ "intertextual procedures" to express a desire for continuity or its opposite, a desire for discontinuity (1998, 126). In *Un hombre al amanecer* both contradictory desires are at work; on the one hand, the play is about Martí's inner struggle to come to terms with his relationship to his nation. Cárdenas shows Martí's turmoil as noble and worthy of his heroic essence. On the other hand, Cárdenas's play raises more questions than it answers, not about Martí, but about the essence of patriotism. What did Martí gain by his loyalty? Should one put patriotism above all else? And what does the nation give in return? In this way, intertextuality posits a rupture or discontinuity in the view of history and nation that are presented. This play allows Cárdenas to explore some of his own ambivalent and tormented feelings about his nation and his national identity while at the same time expressing his unquestionable love for *his* Cuba.

Even though, as Matías Montes Huidobro postulates, "it is easier to accept the official (hi)story and to reproduce it in accordance with the official reports . . . the true (hi)story can only be written by opposition, including at the cost of never being performed" (1997a, 42–43). Cárdenas includes these oppositions within his play and represents history and the story from multiple points of view through the monologue and intertextual fragments he incorporates; in doing so, he also explores the essence of being a Cuban exile today.

As E. J. Westlake reminds us, theater is a poignant way to represent nation and national sentiment (1998). By fusing two plays, two writer's words on nation, and by narrating those texts in a monologue that, through that one voice, represents a complex historical relationship with that nation and raises contemporary questions about it, Raúl de Cárdenas dramatizes Cuba's history and Cuba's contemporary situation and their impact on Cubans both on the island and outside of it.

Pedro Monge's *Otra historia*

> Someone who's been uprooted, exiled, has no country. Our country exists only in our memory, but we need something beyond memory if we're to achieve happiness. We have no homeland, so we have to invent it over and over again.
>
> —Reinaldo Arenas, cited in Isabel Alvarez Borland, *Cuban-American Literature of Exile: From Person to Persona,* 1

In 1961, Cuban playwright Pedro Monge Rafuls embarked on what he has since called, "the saddest exile that has been lived, not only in Cuba, but in all the Americas, a misunderstood and reproachful exile" (González-Pérez 1999, 49).[26] This exile continues to mark him personally and professionally. Through intertextuality, his *Otra historia (Another (Hi)Story)* (1996) dramatizes exile's impact on Cubans and presents the process of reconstructing identity and nationality after exile.[27] The play demonstrates the conflicts and difficulties of life in exile and, at the same time, searches for a new image of the exiled self and its relationship to nation.

Otra historia presents a unique perspective on exile by suggesting through its title and in its script that behind the main story lies another story. Both stories encompass love triangles; in one case, womanizing protagonist José Luis struggles with his ambivalent sexual feelings toward Marina, his female lover, while in the other, this same protagonist confronts his vacillating emotions toward his homosexual lover, Marquito. Teresa, a scheming and admittedly loose woman, who forms the third angle of each triangle, threatens both love stories. Feigning loyal friendship with Marina and romantic interest in Marquito, Teresa plots to create her own romance with José Luis. The two parallel, but doomed, love triangles foreground José Luis's sexual identity conflict. These two frustrated love triangles, however, are not the only stories that Pedro Monge wants to tell, nor are they the main ones; *Otra historia* also reveals the relationship of a Cuban exile with himself and his culture. This third triangle—exiled person/inner self/Cuban culture—is exposed through an intertextual relationship with another Cuban text, Lydia Cabrera's 1954 *El monte (The Forest).*

Monge's play makes explicit its indebtedness to *El monte* many times throughout the text. First, the stage directions prior to act 1 indicate that "The work is deeply indebted to *El monte* by Lydia Cabrera" (Monge 1999, 52). Second, two footnotes in act 1 cite exact page numbers in *El monte* where one would find descriptions of the rituals that the characters perform in Monge's play. Third, the final scene takes place in *el Monte,* and though it is a replica of the sacred Forest described by Cabrera in *El monte, Otra historia*'s Forest is in New Jersey. In this sacred space, Monge's characters participate in an Afro-Cuban religious cleansing ceremony, similar to those described in *El monte.*

Monge uses Cabrera's text both directly, as mentioned above, and indirectly in *Otra historia.* From the outset he expresses gratitude for Cabrera's text, yet he acknowledges the differences between his text and the precursor text, thus inferring that his intended use of *El monte* is not simply to establish a dialogue between the two texts.[28] As John Kronik suggests, intertextuality is "no longer a formalized contract between two distinguished and distinguishable parties but a wide-ranging instrument of relevance retrieval whose function is the accrual rather than the immediate exchange of knowledge" (Brownlow and Kronik 1998, 12). In the case of *Otra historia,* Monge reveals this one intertextual reference and names it, but its inclusion in the text goes beyond direct mention, specific footnotes, page references, or cited ceremonies; Pedro Monge's use of Cabrera's text serves specific functions, as I will show, and highlights two important elements: Afro-Cuban culture and its relationship to the Cuban exile experience.[29] Once again, intertextuality expands the text's message and opens new paths for its interpretation.

That Monge incorporates Afro-Cuban gods, rituals, and the power of Santería into his play is not a novelty in itself. According to Linares-Ocanto, even though Afro-Cuban religious themes did not enter Cuban theater until the twentieth century, by the 1960s their inclusion had become prevalent. As a consequence of the Cuban Revolution, authors highlighted the marginalized sectors of Cuba and used Afro-Cuban religious elements in their works to render more explicit portrayals of sexual and amorous relationships (2000, 43). Monge, too, uses the Yoruba gods to show the tensions in both heterosexual and homosexual relationships; however, his play brings Afro-Cuban cultural beliefs and conflicts to the exiles in the United States. By using Cabrera's text and focusing on the differences between the two texts, Monge's play restructures the marginality of the

Afro-Cuban within Cuba and makes the Cuban exile experience in the United States parallel to it. In other words, Monge's text becomes a treatise on marginality and on trying to make a home in a new land.

Polly Hodge writes of the great number of plays in recent years that dramatize or refer to other literary texts and proposes that intertextuality can function at various levels in theater (1999, 97–98). Intertextuality in Monge's *Otra historia* does indeed function in all the ways postulated by Hodge; (1) it pays homage to Cabrera and her text and highlights their importance within Cuban culture and (2) it functions as a metatheatrical mechanism, as we shall see. Most significantly, in this case though, intertextuality serves "as a mode of transmitting a social or cultural commentary from a histrionic perspective" (Hodge 1999, 98). My purpose here is to examine how *Otra historia* communicates with Cabrera's text and why this is important.[30] What is the function of *El monte* as an intertext in Monge's *Otra historia?*

Monge's characters are involved in three conflictive love/hate triangles: José Luis/Marina/Teresa, José Luis/Marquito/Teresa, and José Luis/self/Afro-Cuban culture. From the outset, José Luis struggles with his relationships, which these triangles represent. On the one hand, he loves Marina and recognizes her devotion to him. When he is with her, he is happy, yet he feels torn by his homosexual feelings toward Marquito. Neither José Luis nor Marina suspect that Teresa is trying to break them apart, hence they both trust and confide in her.

In the second triangle, Marquito patiently waits for José Luis to accept their homosexual relationship. When his lover comes to him, he serves him, prepares food for him, and comforts him. He is jealous of José Luis's affair with Marina, but believes that his love for José will eventually secure their relationship. Marquito enters a bar looking for José Luis and there he meets Teresa. She notes "something strange about Marquito. A man does not behave like that. Teresa suspects something but does not know what it is" (64). Teresa's suspicions of Marquito's homosexuality raise doubts about José Luis's potential to be her heterosexual lover.

José Luis's relationship with his *padrino* (godfather) and the gods of Santería marks the third triangle. The godfather's apartment is the space of the gods and the former spends his days reading the shells and coconuts of Santería. He constantly urges José Luis to mend his ways and to go to the "Forest" to be cleansed of his sins. As the Santero in the play, the godfather becomes possessed by Changó, the predominant god in Santería. There are also indications in the text that José Luis himself is Changó. On the one hand, José Luis tries to completely disconnect from such old Cuban values, but on the other, he is the very embodiment of Changó's spirit. Like Changó, he dominates the feminine, is a fighter, and is the god of passion. José Luis, with his three potential lovers, is like Changó, who, according to Cabrera, "is an incorrigible womanizer" (1992, 226).

Monge's text frequently compares José Luis with Changó, and similarly, José Luis's three lovers also have the characteristics of some of Changó's most important lovers: Oba, Oyá, and Oshún.[31] Marina could symbolize Oba, as she is, in Cuba (but not in Africa) the first and legitimate wife of Changó. According to Jorge and Isabel Castellanos, "Oba is pretty, industrious, and madly in love with Changó" (1992, 48). In parallel fashion, in Monge's story, "Marina lives in her own little world, a world in which José Luis rules even when he is not there" (64). He is like a god to her. Moreover, she and José had originally met at a *tambor* where, after their meeting, an orisha or saint had predicted their black future together (67–68).[32]

The black future comes about largely because of Teresa's intervention, paralleling the structure of Oyá's revenge in Yoruba tradition. Jealous of Oba and Changó's relationship, Oyá pretends to befriend Oba to take revenge on the lovers (Castellanos 1992, 48–49). Teresa's revenge follows the model of Oyá's; in Afro-Cuban myth, Oyá pretends to befriend Oba and advises her to disfigure herself so that Changó will stay with her. When Oba does so, Changó leaves her because of her self-mutilation (Castellanos 1992, 48–49). Like Oyá in Lucumí myth, Teresa "is revolutionary, valiant, and connected with death" (Castellanos 1992, 46). Even though Teresa does not advise Marina to cut off her ear to save her relationship, Cabrera's descriptions of Oyá fit Monge's character Teresa and her plot to take revenge on Marina and José Luis.

Perhaps the most unlikely but interesting symbolism in Monge's story is the parallel between Marquito and Oshún, the goddess of sensuality and fertility. As the most venerated goddess, the beloved patron of the island, she is "beautiful, happy, charming and flirtatious, but sometimes she is wretched and tattered" (Castellanos 1992, 49–51) and she ultimately saves Changó from Oyá. Even though Marquito is a man, Monge ties him with the goddess Oshún throughout the play by calling him Oshún's son (85, 86). Moreover, in ironic support of homosexuality, even the godfather advises José Luis to go to the Forest to cleanse himself with a goat, the animal of Oshún,[33] and then, giving Marquito a necklace of Oshún to protect him (87), he instructs him to wear the necklace and to give a necklace of Changó to José Luis. In the final scene of the play, Oshún dresses Marquito as a goat (88).

Like Elegua, "the god of the way" the godfather reads José Luis's shells and forecasts his destiny with regard to his sexual, spiritual, and national identity.[34] The "santero" sends José Luis to the Forest, "el Monte," in New Jersey, where the play ends and where he, accompanied by Marquito, fulfills his cleansing. Similar to the ceremony described by Cabrera (1992, 15), the two lovers bring all the material offerings the godfather had suggested and they leave them at the base of the trees that represent the orishas or saints. An elaborate, all-night choreography follows in which the gods prepare the two sexually active lovers as their sacrifice. The ritual, including a necklace ceremony and a cleansing with a goat,[35] reminds readers and spectators of José Luis's earlier dream in which Marina had come to the Forest and violently killed him, Teresa, and Marquito. An open ending, in which all characters are simultaneously laughing, screaming, and braying like goats, leaves receptors wondering whether or not José Luis's dream repeats itself or if there is another possible destiny for these star-crossed, exiled lovers in New York.

The ending in the Monte and other intertextual references to Cabrera's text *El monte* go beyond direct dialogue between precursor text and text; through intertext Monge's play evokes Santería as an essential but problematic element within Cuban culture. As Lydia Cabrera posits, "We will not get very far into Cuban life, without encountering this African presence that does not manifest itself exclusively in skin coloration" (Castellanos 1992, 5). El Monte, transplanted to New Jersey, allows the playwright to tell another story: that of exiled Cubans living in New York City and their troubled relationship to Cuban culture. As these exiles nostalgically compare their new life in New York with their memories of Cuba, it is apparent that their personal identity issues are overshadowed by their problematic relationship with their homeland.

In the first scene with José Luis, for example, Marina reminds her lover, "You told me at the beginning that I was the woman with whom you wanted to live outside of Cuba, far from Placetas . . . that life in New York is very lonely" (56). In another scene Marquito reminds José Luis that "the neighbors don't even know that you are here and if they know it, they don't care what happens here inside or there outside . . . This is New York and not a small town" (61). Earlier, Marquito had accused José Luis of living in two worlds without confronting either, "A person who lives in two worlds without facing either one has to learn the difference" (61). While his comment was explicitly referring to José's dual sexual identity, the later reference to living in New York, and not a small town in Cuba, brings it to a different level. José Luis, like Changó himself, "took up the path of exile" (Cabrera 1992, 230). In fact, all characters, except for the godfather, recognize that New York is different from Cuba and this is reflected in their vacillating feelings toward Santería and toward each other.

Monge intertextualizes *El monte* to portray the nostalgia and inner conflict of Cubans in exile. The characters' love/hate relationships with Santería and with each other highlight their ambivalence toward both their old and new cultures.[36] Monge's play focuses on the *story* of Cuban identity as not just one story, but *multiple stories.* In intertwining the interpersonal stories with the stories of cultural struggles suffered by the characters, Monge's play reads like a *patakíe* or Afro-Cuban narration, which, in this case, explains some of the basic feelings and tensions within the Cuban exile community. According to the Castellanos, the *patakíes* are not just works of fiction, but rather, "they construct a complete reality; the deepest, most primordial and ultimate truth" (1992, 64). Functioning like a *pataki̇́e* in a new context, Monge's play, through its emphasis on the stories (his characters', his own, Cabrera's, other stories), explores some fundamentals of the Cuban exile community in the United States: their preoccupation with the myths of Cuba and their identity conflicts, living in a new space.

The emphasis on the story, the stories, and the other story, also places emphasis on the reader/viewer/listener or receptor of those stories. Monge's use of Cabrera's text and his intricate subversion of it direct his message to a specific receptor: Cubans in exile. As Juan Villegas notes, "every cultural practice demands the potential receptor's competence to decipher its message" (2000, 30). As Monge's characters try to make sense of their relationships with each other and with their culture, so, too, must exiles come to terms with their new situation. As the first and foremost authority on Afro-Cuban religions and rituals, *El monte* is a treatise on how the marginalized fit within Cuban culture. Cabrera maintains that one cannot understand Cuban life without understanding the African presence (Castellanos 1992, 5). Through the integration and transformation of this intertext in his play, Monge questions what it means to be Cuban and, at the same time, proposes a new way of reading/interpreting the "Cuban" within the context of the exiled experience.

Additionally, Monge's style models Cabrera's. Lydia Cabrera proposes that her work is unscientific and that it includes digressions, explanations, repetitions, and contradictions from Afro-Cuban informants (the marginalized community itself) (1992, 7). Similar to Cabrera's text, in Monge's *Otra historia,* the Afro-Cuban orishas speak through and with the Cuban characters in New York and New Jersey, and the spirit of the "old" culture lives on in exiled Cubans. Monge's use of *El monte* as intertext affirms the Cuban, even in a different space, and reveals the internal conflicts of being Cuban in the diaspora. Positing more than just a literary style for his play, however, Monge's choice of intertext reveals the dramatic nature of *El monte* as well, by highlighting the inherently visual elements of Cabrera's text. There is no denying the theatrical potential of *El monte;* Lydia Cabrera's text is a profoundly pictorial and visual anthropological and literary study of the Afro-Cuban presence and its importance within Cuban culture. As Monge's play is "another story," so, too, is Cabrera's narration an unrealized dramatic text. As Polly Hodge suggests, "the use of intertexts is understood as a metatheatrical mechanism. In other words, every text is theater given the right circumstances" (1999, 104). Through intertextuality, then, both texts grow and create new knowledge with an energized and unique reciprocal relationship that, in this case, fuses two spaces (Cuba and America), different races (the African presence within Cuban culture), and multiple time periods.[37] The dramatic nature of both texts, rendered more apparent through intertextuality, brings to life their mutual message of marginality and rebellion.

The marginality and rebellion displayed by Monge's characters is further emphasized through intertextuality by connecting the authors of the two texts; Cabrera, too, was a Cuban exile. She had completed *El monte* while still in Cuba, but most of her publications were written from her exile in the United States. She left Cuba in 1959 during the Cuban Revolution, and never returned. She is considered one of the foremost Cuban exile writers.

Exile marks the writing of both Cabrera and Monge and, as Eduardo Galeano suggests, "exile sows doubts and raises issues not necessarily faced by those who live far away by choice" (1992, 143). As Monge explores the doubts and questions raised by exile, he searches for a new definition of nation through *Otra historia* and its intertextual connections. Intertextuality, here, moves the text beyond a direct reflection on Santería and its importance or marginality within Cuban culture; it posits that very marginality as the cornerstone of the exile experience. As Santería was once marginal in Cuban culture, so now are exiles in the diaspora struggling with marginality in their relationship to the Cuban nation.

At the same time, Monge uses Santería and the intertextual references to *El monte* to attempt to reinvent his nation and to protest exile. Jorge and Isabel Castellanos see that "These African laws obviously constitute an act of cultural resistance on the part of the recently arrived toward the overwhelming ethnocentric pressure and the obligation of radical absorption into the dominant group" (1992, 11). Like the newly arrived African slaves in Cuba who brought out their orishas and the *patakíes* about them as a form of protest, Monge uses intertextuality to inscribe protest into his play. His play reveals the conflicts of another "new arrival" in another space, the Cuban exile in the United States, and provides a place to work through the difficult questions of the transplanted nation. In this way, Pedro Monge uses intertextuality to establish a new process of communication within a new context. Monge's play employs intertextuality for both its dramatic function (to recreate a marginal text, which then in turn can textualize the very marginality of the exile experience) and its ideological signification (to reflect on the meaning of being Cuban in any space). Juan Villegas affirms this dual function of intertextuality and maintains that "what is important, in many cases, is to ask oneself why a certain text or element of a text is reutilized by other authors in different historical circumstances" (2000, 102). Monge writes a play that both rebels against the exile experience, and, at the same time, attempts to make sense of that experience.

Jonathan Culler suggests that intertextuality, in "bringing to bear one body of discourse on another" can release energy, allowing the text/s and the relationships between them to become objects of knowledge (1976, 1395). This dual textual energy, referred to by both Culler and Hodge (106), empowers Monge's play and opens up the many love/hate relationships in the story and in the stories behind the story. The love/hate relationship between text and precursor text is paralleled in Monge's text by José Luis's love/hate relationships with Marina, with Marquito, with Santería and therefore with himself and his exiled place with regard to nation.

Ernest Renan theorized that "A nation is a soul, a spiritual principle. Two things, which in truth are but one, constitute this soul or spiritual principle. One lies in the past, one in the present. One is the possession in common of a rich legacy of memories; the other is present-day consent, the desire to live together, the will to perpetuate the value of the heritage that one has received in an undivided form" (1882, 19). As Monge shows, these ideas still hold true today. *El monte* helps Pedro Monge depict some of the marginalized memories of the Cuban past that form the background of his story, but his desire to build the consent to perpetuate his Cuba in the diaspora is part of the other story.

Finally, Monge's *Otra historia* is a visual validation of the exile experience. As Amy Kaminsky suggests, "Exile is, as much as anything, a spatial phenomenon" (1999, xiv). It is a process of movement and change, which can only be interpreted through spatial metaphors (Kaminsky 1999, xvi). The playwright fuses space and intertextuality in *Otra historia* to reaffirm the Cuban in his characters and in himself. Through theater, Pedro Monge explores Cuba and the Cuban in the diaspora and shows the struggle to reinvent self and nation in exile.

These three Cuban plays rewrite exile as a difficult and tragic experience that attempts to silence Cuban voices. These texts, however, empower those voices by rewriting the scripts, both those of the precursor texts and those of history, nation, and national identity. The texts of the New Cuban Dramaturgy reinvent the Cuban and, at the same time, create their own place in Latin American theater history. Each play shows how Cubans, living in the diaspora, can rewrite the national script and give voice to their once silenced identity.

Conclusion: Performance and National Myths

> The nation is not an already accomplished, perfected idea, much less a reality . . . it remains to be put together in agreement with the contemporary demands.
>
> —Julia Kristeva, *Nations without Nationalism,* 40

> The patrimony exists as a political force insofar as it is dramatized.
>
> —Néstor García Canclini, *Hybrid Cultures,* 109

THE LISTSERV THAT WAS CREATED FOLLOWING THE FIFTH CONFERence on Latin American Theater Today held at the University of Kansas in April 2003 brought innovative and interesting topics to the forefront and initiated a new kind of dialogue between Latin American theater theorists and practitioners.[1] As the most modern kind of "text," this electronic source is also intertextual, weaving past texts into its fabric to create relevant and vibrant discourse and produce fresh takes on plays, their performances, their texts, their contexts, and their future. Two topics that emerged from the list discussion, translation and transnationalism in theater, became the focal points of the Sixth Conference on Latin American Theater Today in 2005.[2] My book continues some of the conversations that were begun there. While translation certainly connotes the transcription of a text into another language, translation can also refer to the crossing over between media: a play-text into its script or into its many performances. Theater theorists have argued that each performance is in itself a translation, an interaction or intersection between the dramatist's, director's, and/or actors' interpretations of a text.

Similarly, as I have shown, past texts and contexts can also be rescripted by playwrights, and their meanings are transformed and transposed through the way in which they are incorporated into a new text. Intertextuality manipulates both the texts, past and present, and our interpretation of them. Sharon Magnarelli shows us, for example, how through Maruxa Vilalta's rescripting of historical and religious texts, "the playwright herself has 'translated' Saint Jerome's texts as well as our visual image of him, not only from one language to another but also from one medium to another" (1998, 28). Intertexts can be reworked and "translated" to create a new script. These multiple levels of translation—intertext to text, text to script, script to performance—have implications on the ways texts are interpreted and on the ways they in turn "perform" their nation.

Benedict Anderson argues that "nationalism has to be understood by aligning it, not with self-consciously held political ideologies, but with the large cultural systems that preceded it, out of which—as well as against which—it came into being" (2003, 12). As nationalism and subconscious images of nation have emerged from other preceding cultural scripts, so too do texts emerge through, with, and against other texts. Anderson further suggests that it was, in fact, the dissemination of writing, through the invention of print media, that fostered the rise of consciousness about nations and citizens' places in them. He postulates that, in the early days of nationalism, "print languages laid the bases for national consciousness" because "they created unified fields of exchange," they "gave fixity to languages" of power, and they let people know how many others were like them (44–46). By controlling the "texts," national images were manipulated and structured by those who regulated the discourses of power. Even today we can see that in a global world, where nations are constantly vying for what is theirs, s/he who controls the text, controls the image of nation.

On the listserv and in recent conferences, transnationalism and theater has also elicited important discussion, and it, too, can be linked to translation. Stuart Day suggests that "given a broad definition of translation—(re)rendering—this theme could encompass many additional, interesting topics that share the prefix 'trans': transculturation, transgender, transnational."[3] With this book, I hope to add to that important conversation by showing how different nations can be "imagined" through intertextuality and by articulating that the border spaces between and within texts are sites for that creative, and collective, reconfiguration. I believe these intertexts and their manipulation within the plays show that "the production of knowledge is always a collective effort, a series of back-and-forth conversations that produce multiple results" (Taylor 2003, xx).

My book examines plays that deliberately rescript other past texts within the boundaries of their own and I have suggested that, in the cases studied, this translation or transposition of one text into another reveals new imagined communities that have national implications. I have analyzed plays that intertextualize different kinds of texts—

other plays, narratives, paintings, songs, newspaper articles, religious texts, themselves—to show the diverse potential of sources and the numerous ways in which they might be rewritten within a playtext. In an attempt to limit this study, I have selected plays from four Latin American nations out of many possible others, but know that I could find countless examples of this national reconfiguring through intertexts in other national theaters.

This textual reconfiguring of the "national" may make one question the future of any concept of nation. Yet as Julia Kristeva argues, "beyond the opening of borders and the economic and even political integrations that are taking place within Europe and throughout the world, the nation is and shall long remain a persistent although modifiable entity" (1993, 5). In spite of globalization, transnationalism, transformations, and tensions with regard to the geographical, political, and social configurations of nations in the twenty-first century, there is something about nation and nationalism that is here to stay. Although this "something" undoubtedly exists, it is extremely difficult to pinpoint and define. As these plays prove, there is a subconscious pull to nationalism, even in its ever-evolving form, which compels citizens to affirm a sense of belonging to their nation, in spite of outside, invasive, or imperialistic influences, and in spite of or because of their estrangement from it. These plays are an attempt to portray the subconscious pull surrounding nation for, as Kristeva suggests, "a nation is a language act" and therefore, only language can carry out the necessary integration of what nation means from inside and outside its borders (1993, 44, 68). People need nation because it appeals to both their historical circumstances and their unconscious desires (Kristeva 1993, 67).[4] Because artistic texts can capture both the history and the subconscious desires or flows through their artistic language, past texts can be manipulated within a new (con)text to express new views on history and nation and to express subconscious desires in the new text.

Kristeva's image of nation, which she locates on the boundary between the semiotic flows of the subconscious and the praxis of the symbolic sphere, is perhaps parallel to what Benedict Anderson postulates as the space of the "meanwhile." He believes that the "conception of simultaneity" is "of such fundamental importance that, without taking it fully into account, we will find it difficult to probe the obscure genesis of nationalism" (2003, 24). Anderson shows how, in eighteenth-century Europe, both the novel and the newspaper "provided the technical means for 're-presenting' the *kind* of imagined community that is the nation" (25).

Words, language, and the texts they create, then, represent and embody both the subconscious flows and the symbolic structuring of the modern nation. By controlling them and manipulating them, writers and readers can maneuver them to fit their own vision. In this book, though, I am not talking about just any words or just any texts; I am specifying theatrical texts. Why manipulate other words, someone else's language and already scripted texts in plays? Why is *performing* the nation so important?

In Anderson's study, he argues that during the transition from sacred/medieval communities to the modern nation, "we are faced with a world in which the figuring of imagined reality was overwhelmingly visual and aural" (22–23). Today, as well, we live in a visual and aural world where television, video games, computer screens, neon lights, and music dominate our every interaction. Theater is able to capture the verbal and render it visual. It can take a "text," as I have shown, whether an ancient poem, a song, an old story, or a painting, and turn it into a visual image of our postmodern, global, and/or local experience.

Latin American theater critic Leonardo Azparren Giménez seems to agree when he affirms that "the theatrical word is visual" and "theatricality resides in the theatrical word" (2005, 23, 25). Moreover, he argues, "the theatrical word is fictional and refers to the imaginary" (23). The idea that the theatrical word evokes a visual image that opens the door to imagination reminds us both of Anderson's nations as *imagined* communities and of Usigli's emphasis on imagination in all renditions of dramatic (anti)history.

According to Azparren Giménez, "Dramatic action lies *within* the verbal exchange that produces and is produced by the conflict" (26). This can mean that, when an intertext is a large part of that verbal exchange or is the background of it, it can manipulate the dramatic action as well as transform or transmit an ideological component. This is because of the importance of what Azparren Giménez calls "the hidden connections." He argues that "the hidden connections are in all processes of theatrical discursive practice and they are the keys to understanding the meaning of the interaction of the textual and staged conflict . . . Therefore, approaching the hidden connections exposes a primordial task" (28). The "hidden connections" evoke the importance of the subtext in theater. According to Patrice Pavis, "the subtext . . . comments on and controls the totality of dramatic production. It imposes itself on the audience more or less simply and lets them foresee an unexpressed perspective of the discourse, a 'pressure behind the words'" (Azparren Giménez 2005, 29).

Beyond the visual and subtextual powers of theatrical words, theater is also important to this project because, as Diana Taylor argues, "not everyone comes to 'culture' or modernity through writing . . . it is imperative to keep reexamining the relationships between embodied performance and the production of knowledge" (2003, xviii). Even though I have highlighted the written articulations of the intertexts in these plays, and they might "play out" differently in their performances, it is important to recognize that, as Anne Ubersfeld reminds us, performance is intrinsic to the play-script, for plays are meant to be performed. In addition, Taylor highlights that "performances function as vital acts of transfer, transmitting social knowledge, memory, and a sense of identity through reiterated, or what Richard Schechner has called, 'twice-behaved behavior'" (2003, 2–3).

Moreover, "from Aristotle through Shakespeare and Calderón de la Barca, through Artaud and Grotowski and into the present," performance embodies the idea that it "distills a 'truer' truth than life" (Taylor 2003, 4). Nonetheless, not all theater is imitation of reality; performance hovers between mimesis and pure fiction. I believe that this is why intertextuality works so well in theater; from the outset the intertext points out that this is a text, this is a performance of a text. An intertextual reference pulls receptors into a "contract" that forces them to enter into the layers of artistic construction to evaluate their real and/or fictional content. Taylor reminds us that "representation, even with its verb to *represent,* conjures up notions of mimesis, of a break between the 'real' and its representation, that performance and perform have so productively complicated" (14). Like theater, intertextuality also struggles with this "anxiety of influence" in its battle between prioritizing the old text or the new text, *the* text or a (re)presentation of the text.

In addition, incorporating other texts into a play-text creates a type of "interpreter's utopia," that idyllic border space described by Echeverría in his theory on the Malinche and her role in the conquest. This border space within texts and between texts is an open space that the "new" writer and his/her reader fill with meaning by replacing the meaning of the pre-text with a new one, which is somehow extracted in the intermediary or border space where the texts merge. García Canclini affirms that in our time borders are paramount, since "all cultures are border cultures," hybridizations, and he argues, "thus cultures lose the exclusive relation with their territory, but gain in communication and knowledge" (1990, 261). However, understanding these new hybrid configurations within the world and finding one's place in them demands what García Canclini calls "a new optic" (Rojas 2002, 65). Mario Rojas affirms that globalization demands this "new way of viewing . . . Confronted with this sweeping globalization, in accordance with Grüner, it is necessary to create 'narratives of resistance and reconstruction of our own identity.' The theatrical text, like any other cultural text . . . should be used as a type of national allegory that seeks to redefine the contour of this identity, lost or hijacked by imperial domination" (65). Different ways of seeing also expose, as George Yúdice points out, that "performative force is experienced differently in different societies . . . there is no one performative style, and certainly, not a *national* performative style" (2003, 43). Out of these distinct performative styles emerges "a politics of disidentification," which "enables one to maneuver within identity only by reframing it" (Yúdice 2003, 57). The hidden connections within theatrical texts and the subconscious flows within and about Latin American nations have not only given theater a new and powerful role, that of performing those border spaces, but they have also created a theater that is exclusively Latin American. Mario Rojas affirms, "A new theatrical syncretism, which combines theatrical codes from different geographic and cultural sources with vernacular codes to create new ways of theatrically representing the social and cultural processes that Latin American societies experience, has been produced in Latin America . . . and this new syncretism cannot be interpreted purely as exoticism . . . nor as a decorative baroque form. It is not born in Europe but rather in Latin America" (2002, 67–68). Even when it chooses to "dialogue" with other texts, Latin American theater no longer needs to look to the "other" to express itself; by looking within its own textual and national border spaces and by recognizing its own syncretic image it empowers and creates its own essence.

The ground gained, however, does not come without concessions. As García Canclini reminds us, "postmodern visuality . . . is the staging of a double loss: of the script and of the author" (1990, 243). The disappearance of the script means that the great narratives that used to order and hierarchize are now questioned. However, in this loss lie new creative possibilities, not only because it allows writers and receptors to rewrite the script, but also because in those revisions something of everything remains and, at the same time, is destroyed. The postmodern text lies in those interstices between texts for, according to García Canclini, "postmodernism is not a style but the tumultuous co-presence of all styles, the place where chapters in the history of art and folklore are crossed with each other and with the new cultural technologies" (1990, 244). The performance of this border space allows for a more personal "translation" of the nation, which incorporates the individual, the collective, the (post)modern, and the historical but, at the same time, leaves room for an endlessly "imagined" community.

These texts show that "the place from which several thousand Latin American artists write, paint, or compose music is no longer the city in which they spent their infancy, nor the one they have lived in for several years, but rather a hybrid place in which the places really lived are crossed" (García Canclini 1990, 242). The Cuban nation, imagined from exile then, is just as "real" as Malinche's Mexico. Similarly, Hieronymus Bosch's heretic spirituality can postulate a worldview that is parallel to that of Spregelburd's turn of the twenty-first century malaise in Argentina.

Rewriting the intertexts into their own script allows these playwrights to revise their national story and reimagine their community. Intertexts help them to define and articulate the subconscious, semiotic flows of their space, the "meanwhile," by manipulating the hidden connections behind the texts' words. In this way, the words that make up both their texts and their nations become their own. They become the master of their own narrative, which, rewritten in the new theatrical script allows them to perform their nation on their own stage.

Notes

Introduction

1. All translations are mine unless otherwise noted.

2. It is interesting to note that Barthes connects his idea of the distancing of the author to Bertoldt Brecht's theory of distancing in theater (1994, 493).

3. Gérard Genette, as well, views "the relationship between the text and its reader as one that is more socialized, more openly contractual, and pertaining to a conscious and organized pragmatics" (1997, 9). The reader's role is crucial to any discussion of intertextuality and its functions in a text.

4. Gérard Genette maintains that, for Riffaterre, "the intertext is the perception, by the reader, of the relationship between a work and others that have either preceded or followed it." In other words, Riffaterre marks intertextuality as "the mechanism specific to literary reading" and states "it alone produces significance" (Genette 1997, 2).

5. Kristeva sees in the term "rejet" a Hegelian type of "affirmative negativity" or a "productive dissolution" (1977, 63). In *Le sujet en procès* [*The Subject in Process/On Trial*] (1977), she affirms, "If it is destructive, a death impulse, the 'rejet' is the very mechanism of the release of tension, of life, tending toward a state of equalizing the tension, of inertia and of death, it perpetuates tension and life" (71). She further elaborates, "The 'rejet' reconstitutes real objects, or rather it is the condition of the creation of new objects: in this sense, it reinvents the real and resemioticizes it" (75).

6. Morgan confirms that quotation is the most explicit kind of intertextuality, while allusion is the most implicit or unmarked. "Plagiarism falls in between these two poles as an unmarked but wholesale textual borrowing" (1989, 267).

7. Genette's fifth type of transtextuality, architextuality, is the "most abstract and most implicit of all," because it includes, "the entire set of general or transcendent categories—types of discourse, modes of enunciation, literary genres—from which emerges each singular text" (1997, 4,1). He does not elaborate on architextuality in *Palimpsests,* since "transtextuality," his fourth category, "goes beyond, and at the same time subsumes, architextuality, along with some other types of transtextual relationships" (1).

8. Morgan attempts to define Levi-Strauss's theory of "bricolage" by establishing that, "the *bricoleur* is the native mind itelf, which thinks about problems and their solutions 'mythically,' or in terms of a 'closed' set of 'tools and materials' ordered into values by a 'finite' set of rules. Although the *bricoleur* does not invent his own terms and operations but works with those already provided by the indigenous culture, the closure of *bricolage,* or its very systematicity, permits a potentially infinite number of messages to be generated from the same sign-objects" (1989, 252).

9. The full quotation from Gladhart's text is, "Performance is intrinsically

contingent and unstable, and citational in the widest sense that is, citing not only the (a) text, but social norms, gender roles, cultural in-jokes, and historical narratives" (2000, 14). The continuation of this quote hints at the necessary and multidimensional intertextuality inherent in theatrical performance.

10. For an excellent synthesis and summary of the history of theories of intertextuality, see Judith Still and Michael Worton's introduction (Worton and Still 1990, 1–44).

11. Borges's narrator writes of Menard, "He did not want to compose another Quixote—which is easy—but rather *The Quixote.* Useless to add that he never confronted a mechanical transcription of the original; he was not intending to copy it. His admirable ambition was to produce some pages that corresponded—word for word and line by line—with those of Miguel de Cervantes" (1977, 49). He continues, "Cervantes's text and Menard's are verbally identical, but the second is almost infinitely richer. (More ambiguous, his detractors will say; but the ambiguity is a richness)" (44).

12. Hodge affirms that intertextuality is metatheatrical because it shows that "any text is theater given the right circumstances" (1999, 104). It is important to recognize that, at the same time, the converse may be true—all theater also has some narrative qualities. The degree to which intertextuality aids in blurring distinctions between genres, while complex, may lend new meaning to the text in question.

13. In his article on the reasons behind the breakup of the former Yugoslavia, James Gow reflects on "the problematics of sovereignty, self-determination, statehood and security—the four S-words which have returned with a vengeance on the European scene, but which have significant global echoes. These are all words which can have different uses or meanings, depending on the user and the context. What they are taken to mean will depend on the interpretation, either explicit, or implicit, of another word replete with ambiguity: nation" (1974, 456).

14. In fact, many of the prominent political figures of the time were also major playwrights. Argentine political leader, Bartolomé Mitre (1821–1906) wrote the play "Cuatro épocas," in which he attacked nineteenth-century dictator Juan Manuel de Rosas. Peruvian military leader Manuel Ascenso Segura's plays (1805–71) criticized military adventures and satirized women's domineering role in Peruvian society, while Chilean president Bernardo O'Higgins was responsible for constructing the first National Theater in Chile in 1818. Cuban patriot José Martí and Venezuelan lettered diplomat Andrés Bello were also prominent playwrights.

15. For some examples of how theater functioned in different countries during those years, see George Woodyard and Leon F. Lyday, *Dramatists in Revolt* (Austin: University of Texas Press, 1976); Severino Joao Albuquerque, *Violent Acts* (Detroit: Wayne State University Press, 1991); David William Foster, *Violence in Argentine Literature: Cultural Responses to Tyranny* (Columbia: University of Missouri Press, 1995); Jean Graham-Jones, *Exorcising History: Argentine Theater Under Dictatorship* (Lewisburg, PA: Bucknell University Press, 2002); Amalia Gladhart, *The Leper in Blue: Coercive Performance and the Contemporary Latin American Theater* (Chapel Hill: University of North Carolina Press, 2000); Priscilla Meléndez, *La dramaturgia hispanoamericana contemporánea: Teatro y autoconciencia* (Madrid: Pliegos, 1990); among others.

16. Anderson elaborates, "It is imagined because the members of even the smallest nation will never know most of their fellow members, meet them or even hear of them, yet in the minds of each lives the image of their communion . . . The nation is imagined as limited because even the largest of them . . . has finite, if

elastic boundaries, beyond which lie other nations . . . It is imagined as sovereign because the concept was born in an age in which Enlightenment and Revolution were destroying the legitimacy of the divinely-ordained, hierarchical dynastic realm" (2003, 6–7).

Chapter 1. Unraveling National Threads

The quotation in the epigraph does not appear in the published version of the journal.

1. For an excellent synthesis of Mexico's political crisis from 1968 to 1997, see Jacqueline E. Bixler's article, "Power Plays and the Mexican Crisis" (1999, 83–99). Bixler notes that Tlatelolco in 1968 "marks not only the beginning of what is commonly referred to as 'La crisis,' but also growing distrust of the PRI that had controlled the country since the late 1920s" (84). She further explains how the crisis developed and intensified during the 1980s and 1990s, until July 6, 1997, which she calls the "pivotal point" in Mexican politics because "Opposition parties won control of the lower house of the National Congress for the first time since 1929. In the same elections, a non-PRI candidate, Cuauhtémoc Cárdenas of the PRD, wrested the Mexico City mayor's office from the PRI by a vote of 47% to 26%" (92). These transformations in the Mexican political system, after more than seventy years of rule by the Institutional Revolutionary Party, came to a head in 2000 with the presidential victory of PAN candidate Vicente Fox.

2. On the negative side, Armando Partida Tayzan writes that, in spite of what he would label five or six prolific and productive generations of dramatists coexisting in contemporary Mexico, "the social panorama has been economically and ideologically dominated by conservative forces, as much within state power structures as within the business environment; only now they are conditioned by the rules of the market economy, following the process established by world globalization" (2000, 159).

3. In an interview with Stuart Day, the playwright comments on the origin of his name and especially emphasizes his literary destiny. He remarks that on a bookshelf in his grandfather's ranch his mother "discovered Victor Hugo and decided to give me that name, condemning me to writing" (2005, 21). According to Frank Dauster, "At the end of the seventies authors of the so-called New Dramaturgy appear in Mexico. There are important differences between them but they all bear the mark of the profound uneasiness that overwhelms the country since the massacre of Tlatelolco" (1998, 88).

4. In her article on hyperrealism in Rascón Banda's plays, Myra S. Gann describes what she means by the term in Rascón Banda's case. Frank Dauster quotes Gann here stating that Rascón Banda "brings the fourth wall of naturalism back to us . . . Language is more transcription than invention; antecedents and explanations of events remain outside, unless they appear in a totally natural way . . . In general and above all, he tries to hide theatrical devices (that are there anyway, of course, but more hidden than in other works)" (1998, 88). Bixler and Day confirm that critics "have dedicated many pages to debating whether Victor Hugo's style is documental realism, hyperrealism, poetic realism, or simply realism but, when all is said and done, that debate does not explain the success that his theater has had, especially in recent years" (2005, 18). For a detailed list and description of most of Rascón Banda's plays, see Dauster (1998, 88–93).

5. In her article on *Volver a Santa Rosa,* Beatriz Rodas notes similarities be-

tween these narrative texts and Rascón Banda's theater. She highlights that, even though the language is simple, some of the stories are filled with linguistic games. She also remarks on the author's capacity to narrate simple, everyday political and social events in such a way as to awaken the reader's sensitivity. Moreover, Rascón Banda's treatment of suspense allows simple stories to "leave us with that magic of well-told stories" (1998, 82–86). The same holds true of his theater.

6. Cypess affirms, "The other element of importance for the paradigm is the supposed opportunity of an encounter between La Malinche and an Indian suitor. Although she appears to be accepting the possibility of an Indian mate, her actions in effect reject him. Her renunciation of the Amerindian male is perhaps the most serious of the charges that cling to her image; it becomes a metaphoric act signifying the repudiation of the native in favor of the foreign. Her role as a mistress to Cortés and her marriage to Juan Jaramillo provide further substantiation of the paradigmatic behavior called *malinchismo* today" (1991, 35).

7. Stuart Day (2004, 2005), Laurietz Seda (2005), and Daniel Meyran (2004) discuss the controversy surrounding the staging of *La Malinche,* the tension between the text and its performance, and the effects of these on the playwright. Day highlights the conflicts between Rascón Banda and his director Johann Kresnik and notes the less than enthusiastic reaction of the critics (2004, 123). In his interview with Day, Rascón Banda expresses the importance of this work to his life stating, "My theatrical life is divided between before and after *La Malinche.* I lost friends, directors, actors and very famous, high level playwrights who rejected my product, and I felt rejected because they did not understand" (Day 2005, 31). Seda says that "the work has been classified in Mexico as one of the most controversial in recent years" (2005, 92), and Meyran affirms that its staging "caused a scandal" (2004, 52). Seda examines "Race and Social Class in the Context of the Processes of Globalization in *La Malinche* de Víctor Hugo Rascón Banda" and also affirms that the play "depicts a Mexican nation threatened by globalization (understood as Americanization)" (2005, 100).

8. Bixler and Day signal *la traición* [betrayal, treason, treachery] as Rascón Banda's most prevalent theme. They affirm that "In Victor Hugo's theater, we are all, in some way, thieves and traitors, even the audience or, at least we are unconscious accomplices in a system where the goal is to survive, be that as it may" (2005, 19).

9. Since this part of the scene is actually a metatheatrical performance, it may be Young Malinche who is condemning Cortés, although that is not specifically spelled out.

10. George Woodyard confirms that the work's "impetus inexorably turns toward the disintegration of the present-day Mexican nation, due to two imperatives: the Free Trade Agreement and the conflict produced by the Zapatistas in Chiapas" (2004, 72).

11. Laurietz Seda comments on the metatheatrical nature of the performance when she recalls that "by actually putting the spectators in the representatives' curule chairs, he obliges them to reflect on their responsibility for the historic past and for the country's present events. At the same time, it suggests that they have in their hands the possibility of changing the reins and the destiny of the nation" (2005, 95–96).

12. After describing and condemning the conquest, the lyrics highlight that "Today, in the heart of the twentieth century white men keep coming here and we open our houses up to them and we call them our friends. But if an Indian arrives, weary from walking the hills, we humiliate him and look at him like he is a

stranger in his own land" (20). As both Octavio Paz and Sandra Cypess have argued, malinchismo continues to plague Mexican society.

13. Even the very word "la lengua," used so often to describe Malinche and her role throughout history, has multiple translations. It could mean "tongue," "language," or "source" among other possibilities and it could have positive or negative connotations depending on the context.

14. As we shall see in the following pages, the 1994 Chiapas Revolution, among other contemporary indigenous uprisings, continues to disrupt any image of a unified Mexico.

15. León-Portilla affirms, "There are two documented sources that permit us to approach this composition by Aquiauhtzin in its original version in Nahuatl as well as to analyze the circumstances in which it was formally presented." He goes on to describe those two sources, the "four folios toward the end of the *Cantares mexicanos*" and the "*Seventh Relation* of Chimalpahin" (1992, 258).

16. According to Molly Moore of the *Washington Post* Foreign Service, the Chiapas conflict intensified in December 1997, "when a paramilitary-style group, supported by members of the ruling Institutional Revolutionary Party attacked the mountainside village of Acteal and massacred 45 people" (1998, 2). In Rascón Banda's scene 8, "the Massacre of Acteal," actors, dressed as "average people, outside of their role" sing "The Ballad of Acteal," a song that describes the violent attack on them by the PRI and elaborates on the effects of the violence on its innocent victims. The song's verses suggest that this type of massacre is but a continuous phase of violence in Mexico's history, questioning, "Why Dear God of Heaven, do you send us such misfortune?" (51).

17. Fox displayed the other Mexican icon, the Virgin of Guadalupe, on his campaign banner. Before elected president, he vowed to "respect the right to life, reduce the Church's taxes, promote the opening of centers to spread religious doctrine and officially recognize the education provided by parochial schools" ("Mexico Elections," 2000). Fox has also maintained hostile relations with the Chiapas revolutionaries. According to the EFE News Services, Marcos expressed his disappointment that "we have not obtained any positive response and, in fact, there have been some openly negative insinuations" from the Fox government. Also, Marcos has "accused the Mexican army of profiting from bootleg liquor and prostitution in Chiapas" ("Mexico-Chiapas," 2001, 1–2).

18. The subtitle of the first chapter, *Viento primero: El de arriba* [*The First Wind: The One from Above*], reads, "That tells how the supreme government was moved by the Indians' poverty in Chiapas and thought it good to provide the society with hotels, jails, barracks, and a military airport. And it also tells how the beast feeds on the blood of this town and other unhappy and unfortunate events" (Marcos 1994, 1).

19. Marcos affirms that "Outside the indigenous peasants of Ocosingo, Oxchuc, Huixtán, Chilón, Yajalón, Sabanilla, Salto de Agua, Palenque, Altamirano, Margaritas, San Cristóbal, San Andrés y Cancuc, dance in front of a gigantic image of Zapata painted by one of them; they recite poems, sing, and have their say" (1994, 11).

20. In her famous article on Sor Juana Inés de la Cruz's *Respuesta a Sor Filotea,* Josefina Ludmer affirms that in the repetition of "no" throughout the text, the seventeenth-century nun empowers herself. Ludmer argues, "and that is where she sets up her chain of negations: not to tell, to say that she does not know, not to publish, not to dedicate herself to the sacred. In this double gesture she combines the acceptance of her subaltern place (women must keep their mouths shut), and

her trick: to not say but to know, or to say that she doesn't know when she knows, or to say the opposite of what she knows. This trick of the weak that here separates the field of speaking (the law of the other) from the field of knowing (my law) combines, like all strategies of resistance, submission and acceptance of the place assigned by the other, with antagonism and confrontation, retreat from collaboration" (1984, 51–52).

21. In a couple of cases, the sources were not referenced totally correctly; Carlos Fuentes's article, "Después del neoliberalismo" [After Neoliberalism] was not printed on April 10, 1998, as Rascón Banda indicates, but rather on April 20 of that same year. Moreover, having searched extensively for David Márquez Ayala's article, "La extranjerización bancaria" [Bank foreignization] in the April 10, 1998, *La jornada,* to date I have been unable to locate this intertext.

22. There are numerous intentional anachronisms in the play. In scene 18, for example, Cortés tortures Cuauhtémoc and "They submit them to tortures used by today's Mexican police." The stage directions then concretely list some of those modern torture methods. "El pocito [head submersed in barrels of water]. El tehuacanazo [mineral water shaken up their nose]. Cigar burns on their body. Electric shocks on their genitals" (81). The anachronisms connect past to present, display some of the idiosyncrasies of the present, and add some humor to the performance of the past.

23. Stuart Day argues that "this image of the tourists on stage during the conquest of Mexico connotes the tunnel vision of gold-crazed soldiers (sixteenth-century Spaniards) and modern-day venture capitalists from the United States; the conflation of Spanish and U.S. predators underscores the greed of a new generation of unwanted predators" (2004, 125).

24. Seda also postures Malinche as a "ser fronterizo" [border being] in this play arguing that "The Malinche, as a border site in this work by Rascón Banda, functions as a complex, multidimensional, and contradictory sign in which both the cultural values and the History of Mexico are transformed, constructed, destroyed, reinvented, and rearticulated" (2005, 102).

25. Magnarelli gives an excellent bibliography of Vilalta's theater and lists both publication and performance dates. In addition, she notes the many awards that Vilalta has received for her theater (1998, 36–37).

26. While *1910* does not portray the life of a saint or religious figure, as do the other works I mention, it does incorporate the same meticulously researched presentation of history as the plays about religious figures.

27. There are, of course, some exceptions to this in contemporary Mexican theater. Rascón Banda's *La Malinche,* as we have seen, has some twenty-two characters while Ximena Escalante's *Fedra y otras griegas* [*Phaedre and Other Greek Women*] contains twenty-seven and Flavio González Mello's *Obra para próceres y comparsas* [*Work for Illustrious People and Extras*] includes some twenty-nine plus an undefined number of soldiers, policemen, and lepers. For the most part, though, Mexican plays still adhere to the minimal cast, for obvious staging and economic reasons.

28. The Ignatian writings she includes are his *Autobiography* and the *Spiritual Exercises,* taken from *Obras de San Ignacio de Loyola* [*The Works of Saint Ignatius of Loyola*]. Among the historical and contemporary texts are famous books explaining the history and philosophy of the Jesuits by Peter Kolvenbach, Jean Lacouture, Albert Longchamp, Marcel Bataillon, Pablo López de Lara, Roberto Martialay, and Martin Malachi, among others. She includes many important "historical" texts on contemporary Spain and the Spanish civil war, such as those writ-

ten by Salvador de Madariaga, Pietro Nennï, Herbert S. Southworth, and Hugh Thomas. Nonetheless, as I show, *En blanco y negro* is not necessarily about the Spanish civil war or about contemporary Spain. Because of the way in which Vilalta presents history and historical texts throughout this play, the important articles written by her father during a time of political crisis take on heightened meaning. The articles defend the young Catalonian men for their revolutionary actions and criticize Franco for persecuting and condemning them to death.

29. During that battle Ignatius was wounded in his right leg, and although the French apparently tried to help him they were incapable of giving him the medical attention he deserved. Thus, he lived with the leg injury his entire life. Vilalta's play refers to this injury several times and affirms that the Saint Ignatius character walks with a limp.

30. According to George E. Ganss, S.J., an exercitant is "a person who sincerely desires to discover how he or she can please and serve God best, and who for about thirty days can withdraw from ordinary occupations (whence arose the name 'retreat') in order to make the four to five contemplations a day, alone with God in complete solitude" (1992, 4).

31. Footnote 3 of scene 1 directs us to the description of Ignatius found on page 171 of the book *Jesuitas* by Jean Lacouture but immediately the playwright reminds us that Lacouture's words were taken from the essayist Andrés Suárez who, in turn, is referring to an earlier painting of Ignatius done by Luis de Morales. She also affirms that in describing this saint she (and the journalist and we) also has (have) other texts in mind, like "the portrait painted by Alonso Sánchez Coello in 1585, whose copy is found in the Jesuit residence in Huesca, and can be seen on the cover of *Iñigo de Loyola* by Roberto Martialay" (129–30). This, and other footnotes that refer to her intertextual sources emphasize that everything is a text and that all texts are connected in our collective and individual imaginations.

32. Another connection between this scene and the Don Quixote text is the questioning of Ignacio's sanity. The journalist says, "You are definitely crazy." Ignacio replies, "Blessed madness that allowed me to come pay homage to my lady" (45). Later in the scene the journalist says, "It is curious, you no longer seem crazy. Even though there is no worse madman than he who we take for sane" (46).

33. According to Geoffrey Cubitt (1993), "The Society of Jesus had rapidly established itself as the most famous and most controversial of the militant forces of Counter-Reformation, and the activities of its members as teachers, as missionaries, and as confessors had kept it in the forefront of religious and ecclesiastical conflict throughout the seventeenth century" (19). Because of this controversy and the complex times in which the Jesuits gained power, the Jesuit orders, "driven successfully from Portugal (1759), from France (1764), from Spain, Naples, and Sicily (1767), the Society of Jesus had finally been dissolved, supposedly 'forever,' by Pope Clement XIV in 1774" (Cubitt 1993, 19). Nonetheless, Cubitt argues, "Pope Pius VII re-established the Society of Jesus throughout Christendom. Constitutionally and organizationally, the revived order was the replica of its predecessor" (19–20).

34. The end of the scene pokes fun at the saint in another way and also highlights a more modern tone. When the journalist asks Ignacio why it took him so long to accept the position, they begin a conversation about scruples:

Ignacio. I said it in front of everyone. I did not consider myself worthy.
Journalist. I cannot understand the reason for such scruples.
Ignacio. Don't you know what scruples are?

Journalist. In my profession everything happens at the same time; there is no time for doubts.
Ignacio. Pitiful.
Journalist. If I had scruples, I would not be able to do anything.
Ignacio. Or maybe you would do much more.

(85)

35. "Which woman was in the convalescing Iñigo's thoughts, has not been able to be discovered with certainty. The hypotheses proposed up until now are reduced to three main possibilities: the Lady Germana de Foix, niece of Louis XII of France and the second wife of Ferdinand the Catholic, who died in 1516; second, Catalina, Charles V's sister, born in 1507, who in 1525 married Don Juan III, king of Portugal; third, Leonor, older sister of the Emperor and of Catalina, married first to Manuel, king of Portugal, and then to Francis I of France. The three hypotheses present serious difficulties. Germana de Foix and Leonor of Hapsburg were married at the time of Iñigo's fantasies; Catalina was only fourteen or fifteen years old. As Saint Ignatius kept absolutely reserved on this point, it will be difficult to clear up this mystery" (140).

36. In his article "La función de la imaginación en las *Coronas* de Rodolfo Usigli" [The Function of Imagination in the *Corona* Trilogy of Rodolfo Usigli], Roberto R. Rodríguez maintains that "in the 'anti-historical' trilogy of the *Coronas,* Usigli makes use of some elements created through artistic imagination to extract from those works a subjective, creative, and personal interpretation of the historical facts of Mexico" (1977, 44). Rodríguez shows, for example, how Usigli uses dreams or Carlota's madness to "incorporate the past" and to rework it into the present, and thus postulate a new interpretation of history. Vilalta uses her footnotes and other intertextual references in the same manner.

37. These footnotes would clearly work much differently in a performance of *En blanco y negro* than they do in the script. Nonetheless, an astute director could include visual or verbal references to them in the performance. The intertextual references could not be eliminated from the performance without totally changing the meaning and structure of this play.

Chapter 2. Traders or Traitors

1. As William Anseume suggests, many of Rengifo's plays have a revolutionary impulse that is "applied to a possible conquest of political power on the part of the left (in many ways it is a thought similar to the political project of our current ruler, Hugo Chávez)" (2002, 60).

2. While most critics laud Rengifo for his political and social activism in the theater and consider his great influence on Venezuelan national theater, William Anseume argues that Rengifo was simply a product of his time—a playwright largely imitating Bertolt Brecht's vision of the theater. Anseume writes, "In the political sense, Rengifo's theater responds to a marked reality of its moment, too circumstantial, and its ideological projection in dramaturgy and later theater is very vague. Undoubtedly, this Caracas author takes up Brechtian theater at a time when it causes a social commotion in the middle class and/or the bourgeoisie of Latin America" (59).

3. Nelson Osorio T. in *Hispamerica* (1992) suggests that there are three types of characters in *Las torres y el viento* and in possibly all of Rengifo's petroleum

plays: (1) those who are active agents of domination but devoid of humane qualities; (2) those who are passive and do not fight against the agents of domination; and (3) those who fight and continue living even after they are supposed to be dead (86). These characters symbolize three types of Venezuelan responses to imperialism. Rengifo's Faust rewrite, as I will show, suggests a fourth, more active, living reaction to the domination.

4. *El rey de los Araguatos* was inspired by César Rengifo's dramatic "mural" of the Federal Wars in Venezuela (1859–63). In fact, Caballero attributes his vision of theater as a generator of class-consciousness to masters such as Rengifo, Gilberto Pinto, and Luis Márquez Páez, among others. Caballero's first play was staged by El Nuevo Grupo under the direction of Luis Español (e-mail interview with playwright, January 2002).

5. In an article in *Ollantay Theater Magazine,* Carman Mannarino calls *Una pequeña ayuda de mis amigos,* "one of the best works of the decade" (21). This issue also publishes the script of one of Caballero's most recent plays *Desiertos del paraíso* [*Deserts of Paradise*] (2002, 195–227).

6. According to Tabuas, "Enormous lines of spectators at the ticket window, an auditorium filled with a euphoric audience, sold out performances, dozens of young people outside clamoring with desire to see the play; these are all a reflection of the success of Néstor Caballero in writing this work" (1991, 966).

7. With background music from *Jesus Christ Superstar*, Fidel Castro plays psychologist to government agent Gilberto, who is dressed as a guerrilla. During the session Gilberto vents his anger and hatred toward Alvaro, his English professor "friend" who stole every one of his girlfriends and is now having an affair with Gilberto's wife.

8. According to Judith Ewell, "The cult of María Lionza differed from many of the rural and folk traditions in its strength and its ability to thrive also in urban Venezuela. Based on the legend of an Indian girl who became protector of animals and nature, the cult's principal sanctuary was near Chivacoa in the state of Lara. Shamans or mediums of the cult would fall into a trance, often induced partly by smoking cigars. They used their magic to solve personal problems or to cure illnesses among cult members. María Lionza was often portrayed as a beautiful young woman who rode on the back of a tapir" (1984, 33–34).

9. The stage directions read, "*Sulay finishes what she is doing. La Chata gets up and both she and the cameraman like the rest of the members of the team, continue filming as if they were in their place. Sulay and Chata walk toward each other and meet in a neutral zone where they can see Saturno*" (1030).

10. "With a Little Help from My Friends," © 1967 Sony/ATV Tunes LLC. All rights administered by Sony/ATV Music Publishing, 8 Music Square West, Nashville, TN 37203. All rights reserved. Used by permission.

11. Even though the Beatles were a British group, Caballero uses this song to reflect on United States imperialism in Venezuela. This becomes apparent, as I will show, in the way he uses the intertext in the play and in the characters' many references to the United States. Although the song is by a British group, it was re-recorded and reappropriated by many other cultures. Beatles songs were extremely popular in the United States as well.

12. Even after one sexual interlude, Sulay says to Alvaro, "It was delightful, wasn't it, my love?" Alvaro replies to her, not in Spanish but in English, the language of his betrayal, "Very, very good," signaling his deception (991).

13. Gilberto humiliates and infuriates Sulay at the hippies' reunion she tries to organize when he mocks her by telling her that there is a group of people upstairs

waiting for her. He says, "Sulay! Sulay! Look, upstairs there's a crowd with placards! All hippies! They are looking for you! They are applauding you, Sulay! Come on! What's the matter! Hurry! Hurry! They are looking for you, Sulay!" (1040–41). No one comes to her reunion.

14. A former minister in Rafael Caldera's government and presidential candidate in 1982, contemporary journalist Teodoro Petkoff (2000) suggests that Venezuelans have been and continue to be (under President Hugo Chávez), unfamiliar with their history, and that this allows them to be exploited and manipulated. He writes, "The way Chavez narrates history (falsifying and exploiting Bolivar's myth) is infantile but, without a doubt, it is directed toward an audience that does not know history, that is hearing it told for the first time—because it is the first time that there is a president in Venezuela that is dedicated to talking about our history—but, unfortunately, this audience is being educated in a totally adulterated version of the history of Venezuela, for purely instrumental purposes" (74).

15. After calling Sulay "fat" and insulting Alvaro and his profession, Gilberto sarcastically criticizes Saturno's homosexuality. "Saturno or Loly. By what name do the faggots know you? Ah? What name did you give when they took you prisoner for being a drag queen in a raid? (*Imitating Saturno.*) An artistic name: Loly. (*Like him.*) You have your file in the police station for being a faggot" (1042).

16. Chata is also violated by Gilberto. After she intimately confesses to him that she had failed in her attempt to make love to Tigre, Gilberto forces himself on her sexually in the street/park. Ironically, as he fixes his pants, he tells her that he did it in the name of friendship (1001).

17. Act 2 opens in Tigre's garage in 1969 with, "*Lying down, covered by a sheet, two human figures that we cannot make out.*" We later discover that Tigre and Saturno had slept together. Tigre, however, denies it when he says, (*Interrupting him. He gets up. Violent.*) "Nothing! We are nothing! We're not shit, Saturno! Did you hear me? Nothing happened here. I don't remember anything! Nothing!" (1021). Tigre also tries to strangle Saturno (1019).

18. Caballero affirms that he lived in a commune with Sulay in the sixties and that he was infatuated with her. Like his play's character, his friend Sulay was "the busiest and most experienced little girl in the neighborhood" (e-mail interview with author, January 2002).

19. The author, too, maintains that indigenous cultures coexist alongside the foreign and national interests, but the former are felt more passionately in Venezuela than North American concerns. He determines, "If Anglo-Saxon culture produced musical compositions like those of Jimmy Hendrix and Janis Joplin, here in Latin America, we were vibrating in a more visceral way with Atahualpa Yupanki and Violeta Parra. It was in this way that we passionately displaced those Bob Dylan ballads with those of Venezuelan singer Alí Primera or the Chilean Victor Jara" (e-mail interview, January 2002).

20. At the turn of the twentieth century, United States' protection was preferable to Venezuela than British or German invasion. According to Ewell, "The nearly inevitable favorite protector (of Venezuela) was the United States, which presented less of an immediate threat than neighboring Great Britain" (1984, 29–30). Ewell also argues that additional political problems, such as the English-German-Italian blockade of 1902–3, further compelled Venezuelan leaders to seek U.S. assistance and protection (34).

21. *Sulay:* At the root of the attacks against the installation of General Motors . . .
Tigre: Sears.
Sulay: And the American Embassy.

Tigre: The police and the National Guard reinforced their protection of such important enterprises.

(982)

22. Ewell states, "For if much of the resentment and envy was directed toward the three dominant oil companies—Shell, Gulf and Standard—it increasingly became directed toward the Venezuelan government which catered to the foreigners more carefully than to Venezuelans" (62).

23. Marcos Pérez Jiménez, who ruled Venezuela from 1952–58, was tried for his government's crimes during the 1960s. Ironically, he was only convicted of minor financial crimes. According to Ewell, "in the wake of the violence and economic problems of the 1960s, the vote for Pérez may have represented a nostalgia for the mythological stability and prosperity of the 1950s" (1984, 166).

24. Venezuela lies across the dangerous Bocano fault system, which extends from the Táchira depression at the Colombia-Venezuela border to the Caribbean coast of Venezuela, within the Mérida Andes and along the eastern foothills of the Sierra de Aroa (http://io.ingrm.it/sfit/Bocono_1996.html). This fault forms the backbone of the Venezuelan Andes and several large historical earthquakes have been attributed to it (http://home.hiroshima-u.ac.jp/kojiok/QR/sawop.htm). The July 1967 earthquake (6.7 magnitude) referred to in Caballero's play left 300 dead and 2,000 people injured. Earthquakes and other environmental disasters (mudslides, floods) are a national concern. According to the National Science Foundation, geologists warn that Caracas is due for another major earthquake within the next ten years (http://www.reliefweb.int/w/rwb.nsf).

25. Though tensions within Venezuela and between Venezuela and the United States remain extremely high, things have changed under President Hugo Chávez, who does not have a "friendly" relationship with the United States, especially under U.S. president George W. Bush. Ironically, however, the lack of U.S. political support toward Venezuela has not reduced U.S. economic imperialism in that Latin American country. U.S. control of Venezuelan oil and the power wielded by U.S. companies in Venezuela remains a significant problem for the Chávez government and for the citizens of Venezuela.

26. Alvaro also avoids another thorny situation, but in doing so he perhaps causes more violence in the end. He had noticed that Gilberto was wearing a pistol, but pretends not to see it. If he had acknowledged it, he may have avoided the violent fate of Sulay at Gilberto's hands at the end of the play (986).

Chapter 3. Texts without Exit

1. Pavlovsky first "discovered" psychodrama while working with children on group therapy when he realized that "The children spontaneously begin to make up stories and to dramatize them" (1985, 30). He began theorizing the concept in the early 1960s when he traveled to New York to study with Moreno, the father of psychodrama. In 1963 Pavlovsky helped found the Asociación Argentina de Psicodrama to train professionals in the technique.

2. For interesting studies on Pavlovsky's many plays, see articles and books by Jacqueline Bixler (1994), Jean Graham-Jones (2000), George Woodyard (1997), Alfonso de Toro (2001), Jorge Dubatti (1997), and Diana Taylor (1997, 2003), among others.

3. For an interesting discussion of the evolution of and the intertextual connec-

tions in *Rojos globos rojos*, see George Woodyard (1997) and also Jorge Dubatti's introduction (Pavlovsky 1997, 25–30).

4. Jorge Dubatti points out the strong connection between Pavlovsky and Samuel Beckett and refers us to Laura Linzuain and Mariana Theiler's study on Beckett's *Waiting for Godot* as intertext for *Somos* and *La espera trágica* [*The Tragic Wait*]. In the introduction to Pavlovsky's *Obras completas,* Dubatti suggests that *El señor Galíndez* has intertextual ties with Harold Pinter's *El montaplatos* [*The Dumbwaiter*], which the playwright had seen in New York in 1963 (1997).

5. To add to the ambiguity of the work, the title of *Poroto: Historia de una táctica* could be translated in many different ways. First, there's the play on the word *Poroto,* which, as I will discuss, could simply be the name of the character or could refer to the Spanish *por otro,* for another, through another, or by another. The double meaning of *historia,* history or story, adds an additional layer of potential confusion. Finally, *una táctica* could be translated as tactic or strategy.

6. The play was directed by Norman Briski and featured Briski, Pavlovsky, Susy Evans, and Elvira Onetto. The first clue that Poroto was NOT the protagonist was that Pavlovsky played Willy, the friend and waiter, not Poroto. For a more complete description of this staging, see Alfonso de Toro's article (2001, 104).

7. In an effort to avoid confusion and redundance as I move between these three texts, I will refer to each one by a portion of its title: *Historia* for *Poroto: Historia de una táctica; Nueva* for *Poroto: Nueva versión para el teatro;* and *DC* for *Dirección contraria.*

8. Juan Carlos de Brasi discusses the potential play on the words, Poroto and por otro, in his introduction to *Dirección contraria* (1997, 8).

9. The cold calculated tone and the quasi-direct discourse are important and effective tools in the performance as well. In the performance, the characters express their lines hastily, at a rapid pace, so spectators do not see anyone in particular crying.

10. In another attempt by Poroto to escape to the bathroom, Leo unwittingly anticipates and impedes Poroto's actions by placing his right hand on top of Poroto's. "With this movement of his (Leo's) right hand on top of his (Poroto's) left hand, Leo had dismantled his first important tactical movement: because the departure toward the bathroom did not in any way represent the playing out of the ending but rather an important tactical movement because it allowed him to momentarily leave the radius of action of his interlocutor" (12). Not only does Poroto enlarge the importance of Leo's control of his hand, "It seemed that his whole being was his left hand and that there was no Poroto beyond his hand" (12), but he also sees himself reflected in Leo's face "everything came about through the observation that Poroto could deduce from Leo's face" (13). Poroto is controlled by Leo's image of him.

11. Dällenbach borrows this term from André Gide and elaborates on its meaning. "The *mise en abyme,* as a means by which the work turns back on itself, appears to be a kind of reflexion; its essential property is that it brings out the meaning and form of the work . . . it gets its name from a heraldic device that Gide no doubt discovered in 1891" (1989, 8).

12. Willy never actually appears in *Historia.* The only reference to him is with regard to the Dr. Uriarte scene; it was Willy who had introduced Poroto to his friend Uriarte. The encounter between Poroto and Uriarte destroys the friendship between Willy and his doctor friend.

13. Of course, the inclusion of this letter puts the question of "time" in *DC* at the forefront. When does the "initial" bar scene take place? It must take place

during the novel but before this letter, yet it is at the beginning of *DC* and perhaps after Poroto's flight to Greenland, in the final scene. The episodes from Poroto's life are not in chronological order.

14. Willy has a very minor role in the original *Poroto Historia* text. The omniscient narrator tells us that, "Sometimes Willy—a doctor friend of Poroto from his adolescence who was a bit worried by his strange movements and disappearances—sent him to consult a psychiatrist friend" (1996, 18). Willy is then referred to, in this flashback scene only, through the omniscient narrator. Willy does not appear in the space of the text, rather, the narrator recounts Willy's conversation with Dr. Uriarte (the psychologist friend) about Poroto. In other words, through Dr. Uriarte's conversations with Willy, interpreted by the omniscient narrator, we have another reading of Poroto's strange behaviors. This distancing proves that this text is not about Poroto, but rather about the reading. In other words, the interpretations porot(r)o—by, through, for another—are more important than the character himself.

15. After Leo recounts some of Poroto's youthful amorous adventures, "the three of them [Leo, Poroto, Willy] laugh" (45). Later, Willy reacts to Poroto's use of the word "polvo" [powder] by laughing at him (1999a, 51).

16. Willy's role as spectator is quite well developed, but oscillates with his role as narrator/commentator. After listening to (and watching) Poroto's monologue about his father (this monologue is much longer and more developed in *DC*), Willy "laughs" and says, "Bravo, bravo!" but then notes that "Upon finishing his last sentences . . . a bravo was heard coming from the teenagers' table" (51).

17. In *DC* this same dialogue is repeated by Poroto's parents, rather than the nebulous "El" and "Ella" of *Nueva versión.*

18. Ironically, the emphasis on rehearsing is even greater in *Historia.* Perhaps this is because the *Nueva versión* is the "real" theatrical show?

19. For Kristeva, the *chora* "designates a mobile receptacle of blending, of contradiction, and of movement, corresponding to the mother and necessary to the functioning of nature before the teleological intervention of God; the *chora* is a uterus or a wet nurse in which the elements are without identity or reason. The *chora* is the site of a *chaos* that *is formed* and *comes into being* prior to composition as far back as the first measurable body" (1977, 57).

20. "A subject *en procès* attacks all stasis of a unified subject. It also attacks closed ideological systems (religions), as well as structures of social domination (the state), and accomplishes a revolution that can be distinct or, until now, unaware that the socialist and communist revolution is not its 'utopic' or 'anarchic' moment, but rather designates its blindness to the very process that sustains it. This 'schizophrenic' process of avant-guard practice introduces a new historicity, a 'monumental history' crossing myths, rituals, symbolic systems of humanity by declaring itself detached from contemporary history or by following that contemporary history to open it toward the process of the negativity that is its driving force" (1977, 61).

21. *Nueva versión* was published three years after *Historia,* in 1999, hence the change from twenty-two to twenty-five years in the two texts. In this way, Pavlovsky indicates that he is referring to a specific bombing incident during those years.

22. In Argentina, *queso y dulce* is soft cheese with a fruit-compote-type topping, sometimes made of guava jelly or quince preserve. I am translating it as cheese with jam for the sake of economy. *Flan* is a custardlike dessert enjoyed in most Spanish-speaking countries. *Dulce de leche* is a caramel-type confection, which can be found in many Argentine desserts such as cookies, pudding, ice cream, and candy. Because flan is so widely understood, I maintain the Spanish.

23. At some point each of the characters is stuck in the revolving door. "*Poroto goes toward the revolving door and leaves the bar. Then, Poroto returns.*" (40). "*Willy goes to the revolving door and stays there*" (60). (This occurs in the middle of the flan y dulce scene.) "*Willy goes out from the door toward the bathroom and leans on the wall. Poroto comes down from the table, passes through the revolving door, turns behind the bathroom and leaves. He enters the BAR again and lights a fuse*" (61). Then, Leo "*gets down from the bar, turns through the revolving door and leaves the bar*" (61). "*Leo appears through the revolving door and goes toward the fuse that Poroto lit. Leo returned to his table and dozed—maybe hoping for the arrival of Poroto*" (62).

24. The "middle" text, *Dirección contraria,* shows the necessary psychological back and forth between the forces of (national) subjectivity and, contrary to what the title postulates (the opposite direction), the text really does move forward in terms of textual information and subject definition.

25. *La modestia* has received numerous awards besides the Premio GETEA, including the Premio Municipal Trinidad Guevara, the Terna del Premio Florencio Sánchez (given by the Casa del Teatro, 2000), and the Premio Diario Clarín (1999).

26. The fifth play in the *Heptalogy, La estupidez* [*Stupidity*], was commissioned by El Deutsches Schauspielhaus in Germany in 2000 and has received many awards, such as the prestigious Premio Tirso de Molina (2003), the PremioTeatro del Mundo for dramaturgy, direction, and music (2003), the Premio GETEA for Best Actress (2003), and the Premio del Espectador for dramaturgy and direction (2003). In spite of its (three hours and twenty minutes) length, it has been extremely well received by audiences around the world. In May and November 2006, Spregelburd had his U.S. debut with an English translation of *El Pánico* [*Panic*], the fifth play in his *Heptalogy.* The work was translated and performed in New York City through BAIT (Buenos Aires in Translation).

27. Dubatti explains how "Spregelburd breaks with one of the most powerful traditions of the national theater, realism; his characters are no longer what they say they are. They speak, they tell stories, they reflect on their 'past' and their 'present,' but truthfully everything is reduced to constructions of language without connection to a shared 'reality.' There is no other reality but language. The greatest disturbance in Spregelburd's plays stems from his ability to show that behind language there is no reality nor human substance possible, that language is an illusion of reference. Language 'constructs' reality, but only a linguistic reality that always results in self-reference" (2000, 15).

28. The painting's current placement on a crowded wall in the Prado museum destroys the "tabletop" intention of the painting since viewers cannot walk around it.

29. Delevoy also suggests that the *Seven Deadly Sins* was probably painted just after Bosch's marriage, in the early stage of his artistic career. He associates it with a "phase of doubt" in Bosch's life (1960, 21).

30. Fraenger shows that the *Seven Deadly Sins* is based on the numbers four and seven and he explains the significance of the 128 rays radiating from the pupil of the eye stating that 128 is both the "number of the Messiah" and that it can be broken down into a "Pythagorean perfect" number (1983, 277).

31. Fraenger argues that in seven days the moon wanes and grows to a half-moon and after seven more it becomes full. Within the next seven days it then shrinks again to a half-moon and in seven more to a sickle. He declares that "In purely spiritual things the number seven has the qualities of immobility and unchangeability, but it also exercises great far-reaching power over sensorily per-

ceived things through the movement of the planets in their orbits, which influences everything on earth, and through the cycling of the moon" (1983, 277).

32. Fraenger suggests that "the seven [sin] segments have one common principle: their compositional center of gravity, their dramatic and moral focal point, is always located in the right-hand corner—so consistently that the regular rightward swing of the rhythm compels the viewer to walk around the table in that direction" (273).

33. It is interesting to note that the writers of Spain's Generation of 1898 also described and depicted a similar type of abulia at the end of the last century. Writers like Pío Baroja, Azorín, and Unamuno portrayed a similar societal malaise related to Schopenhauer and Nietzsche's philosophies.

34. In an enlightening article, "Chekhov and the Philosophy of the Turn of the Century," Ildiko Regeczi argues that turn-of-the-century religious philosopher Lev Shestov, with whose belief system Chekhov seems to have adhered, was "somebody who 'understands' others but is not able to accept them" (1997, 388). Aisemberg and Libonati (2000) suggest that Spregelburd is greatly influenced by Chekhov and it would appear that both Chekhov and Spregelburd would fall into this category. Spregelburd has an astute albeit pessimistic perception of the world; however, his characters have great difficulty coexisting with each other.

35. In the *Seven Deadly Sins* image of pride, a vain woman admires her new hat but an extravagantly bonneted demon holds out the mirror to her from behind a cupboard.

36. "I am not Brujas . . . I recently spoke with her . . . No, it doesn't matter. I already realized that you are more concerned about her than about me. I am no fool" (72).

37. Sara tells Señora Perrotta that she lives in the outskirts (of Buenos Aires) on the road to Ezeiza (airport).

38. The Web address is http://www.spregelburd.com.ar/web/index.html.

39. Infante and Libonati affirm that in *La modestia,* "The alternation between past and present is thereby converted into a device to point out the breaking of the space that affects the society of this time, a society that enjoys an excess of symbols and suffers from insufficiencies in interpreting them" (2000, 1).

40. For example, María Fernanda is but another one of the "Marías" from Spregelburd's *La extravagancia.* She too has another sister named María and she tells Arturo, "I was born afterward. But it is true that there is a fixation on having three daughters and naming them all María María María" (195). On the other hand, Anja connects to Masha, both the protagonist of her/Terzov's/her father's manuscript and one of Chekhov's *Three Sisters.* Anja embodies many of those characters' personality traits, her depression for example, and she suffers a parallel fate. In addition, it would be impossible to ignore the similarity between these characters and those of Chekhov's *Uncle Vanya:* the disillusioned Uncle Vanya (Smederovo) who recognizes both his own failures and those of the sickly Professor Serebryakov, the writer (Terzov). Everyone seems to recognize his failed attempts at writing but continues to allow the professor to play his game and continue writing.

41. Terzov also attempts to get many jobs but is let go quickly both because of his illness and because he is foreign.

42. It is interesting to note a similar blast that destroys Román and Claudia's house at the end of Argentine playwright Jacobo Langsner's *Locos de contento.* In both plays, the destruction of the home is out of the characters' control and symbolizes the protagonists' feelings of helplessness and desperation with regard to their nation and the world they live in.

43. The receptor as "detective" or "knowing sleuth" is reminiscent of Riffaterre's definition of the reader's role in intertextuality (Morgan 1989, 262–65).

44. In their Web review of the performance, María Infante and Adriana Libonati note that the premiere of *La modestia* in the San Martín Theater in Buenos Aires used, "a basic reference of world cultural capital. The imposition of an economically globalized model has repercussions on the cultural sphere, and it is because of this that rules and traditions tend to modify themselves, to adapt to the established order, but also to offer the resistance that is fundamental for the identity of nations" (2000, paragraph 1).

Chapter 4. Cuba, Myth, and Transnational Revisions

1. In the introduction to *De las dos orillas: Teatro cubano,* Heidrun Adler argues that Rine Leal was the first critic to document the exclusion of exiled Cubans from Cuban theater and to suggest that Cuban American theater should be seen as a "part of our own." Adler further points out that, until the publication of *De las dos orillas,* there was only one anthology of Cuban theater that included plays written by Cubans both in and outside Cuba (Adler y Herr 1999b, 9–10).

2. In *Life on the Hyphen: The Cuban-American Way,* Gustavo Pérez Firmat analyzes the "destiny of the 1.5 generation," those born in Cuba who spent their childhood and adolescence in the United States, and he affirms that it is one thing to be Cuban in America and another to be Cuban American (1994, 3–4).

3. Examples of some of these are works such as Pedro Torriente's *Delirio habanero* [*Havana Delirium*], which contains intertextual references of Celia Cruz and Benny Moré. Beatriz Rizk notes the intertextual success of this work, remarking that it succeeded in "achieving very rich intertextual levels since each movement, each basic sign, each verbal inflection corresponded to similar ones in the exiled Cuban community for which it was being performed" (2000, 232). Other examples include Abilio Estévez's *Perla Marina* [*Marine Pearl*] and *Santa Cecilia: Ceremonia para una actriz desesperada* [*Saint Cecilia: Ceremony for a Desperate Actress*], Alberto Pedro Torriente's *Manteca* [*Lard*], José Triana's *Medea en el espejo* [*Medea in the Mirror*], and Antón Arrufat's *Los siete contra Tebas* [*The Seven Against Thebes*] (Rizk 2000).

4. Born in Guanabacoa, Cuba, in 1937, José Corrales studied at the Academia de Arte Dramático in Havana and soon after began his career as playwright, actor, director, and poet. Disenchanted with the Castro regime and the revolutionary process, Corrales fled into exile to New York in 1965, where he remained until he died of Parkinson's disease and cancer on May 7, 2002, at the age of 64. With more than twenty plays and several books of poetry to his credit, in 2001 Corrales received the Palma Espinada Award, an award given annually by the Los Angeles Cuban American Institute of Culture to the most notable artists in exile. Corrales's most well-known dramatic works include *Un vals de Chopin* [*A Chopin Waltz*] (1967, 1998), *Juana Machete: La muerte en bicicleta* [*Juana Machete: Death on a Bicycle*] (1978), *El vestido rojo* [*The Red Dress*] (1998), and *Las hetairas habaneras* [*The Courtesans of Havana*] (1980), written in collaboration with Manuel Pereiras. For more information on José Corrales's life and works, see the special issue of *Ollantay Theater Magazine* (volume 11, no. 21) dedicated to him and to playwright Manuel Martín Jr., posthumously. Manuel Pereiras García was born in 1950 in Cifuentes, Cuba. His family went into exile in the United States in 1963. In 1977, he received his first NYSCA grant to write a bilingual children's musical

production, *The Butterfly Cazador,* which he cowrote with Corrales. In 1980, he cofounded, with José Corrales, the Stonewall Repertory Theater. He has written over fifty plays, among them, *Holy Night.*

5. The parallel Greek character is noted in parentheses.

6. In the Cuban text, Iluminada is dragged off and insulted by Alejo, Menelao Garrigó's secretary. She returns briefly in act 3, possessed by the Afro-Cuban gods and dancing to African music, to predict the final acts of destruction upon the house: Estrella's betrayal and Nicomedes' future maiming.

7. All quotes from *The Trojan Women* are taken from Morwood's edition (2000).

8. After Coralia's opening lines forecasting "joyful times" in Diosdada's house, La Gloria, the Chorus responds, "What is happening is so delightful to my ears that it frightens me." Coralia then also acknowledges her premature good wishes by stating, "You are afraid because happiness is not a resident of this house" (13).

9. Morwood affirms, "Euripides makes Poseidon a friend of the Trojans. In Homer's *Iliad* he is their uncompromising enemy" (2000, 130).

10. Poseidon agrees that he will "whip up the Aegean Sea" as the Spartans set sail, for "The mortal who sacks cities and temples and tombs, the holy places of the dead is a fool. Having given them to desolation, he himself meets destruction in time to come" (Morwood 2000, 40–41).

11. Febles reads the character Alejo as yet a third religious voice in the play. He writes:

> The first (Saint Roque) exemplifies bourgeois Catholicism while the second (Yemayá) personifies the Yoruba cult that fuses with the official religiosity to produce a polisemic ritualism, since each image, each symbol is interpreted according to the circumstance. Finally, Alejo—that problematic lackey that clumsily mimics the political behavior of the novelist Alejo Carpentier—suggests another religious will: the secularism based on the absolute admiration of the tyrant, that is converted on stage into a new deity which is exalted by means of grotesque names ("well-hung," "horse") and the profane prayer.
>
> (1999, 84)

12. The very name of the mother, Diosdada [Given by God], has Catholic religious connotations as does the place where they live, La Gloria [Glory].

13. San Roque calls them, "Foolish women. You'll pay for this" (33).

14. Critics have remarked on the close identification between these Trojan women and their homeland. Barlow notes that "It is as if Troy is also one of the suffering Trojan women" (Morwood 2000, 132).

15. At the end of the edition of *Un hombre al amanecer* published by the North-South Center of the University of Miami, the editor writes, "According to the author, he wrote *A Man at Dawn* 'because José Martí is one of the most interesting Latin American figures and possibly one of the least well known in the United States'" (1991, 74).

16. Many other Cárdenas plays also incorporate intertextuality as a means of refocusing or reinforcing his message. In the introduction to his *Los hijos de Ochún* in González-Pérez's book, Cárdenas affirms his attraction to classic Greek theater and also discusses his interest in the Afro-Cuban sources that he uses as the basis for *Los hijos de Ochún* (González-Pérez 1999, 142).

17. Rizk lists a number of other Cuban plays that prioritize intertextuality in an effort to demonstrate the instability and unraveling of perspectives on history. Besides those mentioned earlier, she cites Joel Cano's *Timeball,* Abilio Estévez's

Santa Cecilia: Ceremonia para una actriz (also a monologue), and Alberto Sarraín's *Yarini* (1998, 124–29).

18. On June 14, 2003, the Bilingual Foundation of the Arts sponsored a staged reading of *Un hombre al amanecer* in Los Angeles.

19. (*With his back to the audience*) "Who could fall asleep! Neither the hammock, nor the night, nor the freshness of the dewdrops can calm this agitation that I feel overflowing" (8).

20. On one remembered return the protagonist says, "Under the name of Julián Pérez, attracted by instinct and nostalgia, I took a boat that was headed to Havana. My Havana. (*BRIEF PAUSE*) When I arrived, the city was sleeping. The lights of the Port were beginning to wake up, and in my heart, the memories. The absence. The quarries. The fragrance of its moonlit nights and its patios of jasmine and gardenias. The narrow streets and the bustle of carts and carriages . . . My Havana. When I arrived, dawn was breaking" (41).

21. The bold letters and the italics are my emphasis; past-tense forms are highlighted in bold plain text and present-tense verbs are in bold italics.

22. This slippage between the intertext and the present text, that is, Martí's and Cárdenas's mixed voices in the play-script as shown in the previous section, would probably not be noticed by spectators viewing the performance, unless the director chose to highlight it in some unique dramatic way. Nonetheless, this juxtaposition of present text with intertext is a powerful addition to the character Martí's monologue, in that it reinforces a heightened awareness of both texts as texts and, at the same time, it emphasizes Cárdenas's authorial voice alongside that of Martí's, giving Cárdenas his rightful place as an important Cuban writer in exile.

23. Adler's (1999a) study analyzes these monologue strategies exclusively within the scope of Latin American theater written by women. She writes, "Therefore monologue presents itself as a form of representation to show that feminine subjectivity for which it is fighting: women speak, they give themselves voice, they show themselves alone on the stage, they put themselves on stage and, over and above the argumentation of their personal situation, seen from their own perspective, they exhort the dialogue." Adler ends by questioning, "Is monologue a theatrical realization of gender studies?" (133). I agree with the theorist's discussion of the form and function of the monologue in Latin American plays written by women, although I hope to have shown how some of these strategies can be applied to discussions on monologue by other "marginalized" (exiled?) playwrights.

24. I believe that Cárdenas is playing with the double meaning of the Spanish word "público." In a different context, this could be translated as simply "public"; however, in the context of a play and the theater, the word "público" can also refer to the audience.

25. This subtitle is taken from the title of Martí's play. In that text, as Cárdenas notes, Cuba is called Nubia.

26. Pedro Monge was born in Central Zaza, Placetas, Cuba, in 1943, and escaped from Cuba by boat in 1961, shortly after Castro's takeover. After brief stays in Honduras and Colombia, he moved to the United States, first living in Chicago and later moving to New York City, where he remains until this day. Author of numerous plays and founder of *Ollantay Theater Magazine,* he has been an award recipient (Very Special Arts Award, 1991), has served on the board of the National Endowment for the Arts, and has presented his works at international festivals.

27. To date Pedro Monge has written several plays, mostly published in anthologies of Cuban American literature. Along with *Nadie se va del todo* in Rine Leal, ed., *Teatro: Cinco autores cubanos* (Jackson Heights, NY: Ollantay Press, 1991),

109–58, his works include, *Trash* and *Otra historia*, in Armando González-Pérez, ed., *Presencia negra: Teatro cubano de la diáspora* (Madrid: Editorial Betania, 1999); *Se ruega puntualidad* (Jackson Heights, New York: Ollantay Press, 1997); *Recordando a mamá: Antología de teatro breve hispanoamericano,* ed. María Mercedes Jaramillo and Mario Yepes (Medellín, Colombia: Editorial Universidad de Antioquiía, 1997); *Momentos*, an as yet unpublished work that includes five short, previously performed plays, and *www.solucióndecuervos.com,* an unpublished work written in March 2005.

28. Monge writes, "The work is deeply indebted to *The Forest* by Lydia Cabrera, but it should be announced in the program that the reality of Santería ritual has not been maintained, neither in the magic, nor in the reading of the snail shells and especially not of the coconuts. The differences between the Law of Ocha and the Conga Law have also not been taken into account" (1999, 52).

29. It is important to note that Monge includes many other intertexts in *Otra historia.* Among these are the dedication to José Triana, epigraphic quotes from José Martí, José Corrales, and Abdallah Al-Baraduni, and the song *Antología de Caricias,* played in a bar scene in act I. It is beyond the scope of this book to examine all of Monge's intertexts, but I suggest that all of them would back the same thesis: that beyond the story of sexual identity conflict the intertexts reveal another story—that of Cuban exiles struggling to find themselves and their relationship to Cuban culture from the diaspora.

30. Hodge maintains that the key question in examining intertextuality is to determine, "How does the present text communicate with the anterior texts, the intertexts, and what meaning does this dialogue bear in the cultural sphere of the present moment?" (1999, 100).

31. In Santería there is some confusion as gods and goddesses switch identities, and as their roles vary from oral tradition to oral tradition, from African stories to Cuban renditions. The Castellanos affirm that "The geneology of the African gods is very complicated and often contradictory" (1992, 29). In *Otra historia,* as well, characters may symbolize one or another god or goddess depending on one's perspective.

32. According to Jorge and Isabel Castellanos, a *tambor* is a religious ceremony in the laws of Santería. They affirm, "The rites of initiation, as well as the sacrifices and possessions or spiritual trances, so frequent in the ceremonies called *guemileres, bembés* or *tambores,* are particularly important" (1992, 17).

33. Surprised by this, the godfather rereads the coconuts to confirm (57–58).

34. According to the Castellanos's, "Elegua can be old or a child and it is he who opens and closes the paths to man" (1992, 30). The padrino serves to help José Luis find his path in this new culture.

35. The Castellanos confirm that "The first initiation ceremony of the Law of Ocha is the imposition of the necklaces" (89).

36. The padrino seems to be the only character that does not waiver in his traditional beliefs. José Luis is as ambivalent about his relationship to the Afro-Cuban gods as he is about both of his sexual relationships. He continues to visit his godfather to ask for advice and ultimately does go to the Forest to perform the cleansing ritual even though he denies that he believes in Santería. Marquito, too, repeats, "I am not a believer." Nevertheless, he agrees to accompany José Luis to the Monte and is adamant in stating that the cleansing should be done according to the rules. Marina, as well, vacillates in her beliefs. She loves José Luis in spite of the warnings of their doomed relationship given to her by the gods at their initial meeting. She has an altar in her apartment and prays to Changó and Papá Elegua, yet, when she learns of José Luis's homosexual relationship, she destroys her altar.

37. Polly Hodge suggests that "The fusion of energy between the intertext and the present text is seen precisely in the dialogue between the past and a present moment" (1999, 106). Monge's use of Cabrera's text in *Otra historia* also posits a connection with a Cuban past and, at the same time, proposes a more "present-centered" reading of the Cuban.

Conclusion

1. Organized by George Woodyard, editor of *Latin American Theater Review,* these conferences, which began in 1982, are an important meeting ground for Latin American theater critics, playwrights, theorists, actors, and directors from all over the world. The conferences include paper presentations, panel discussions, and round tables, as well as several live performances of Latin American plays. Thanks to the efforts of Professor Woodyard, his former students, and a committee of experts in the field who held a round table during the final day of the 2003 conference, the conference will continue to be held on a regular basis at different universities around the United States and the world. Stuart Day of the University of Kansas created and oversees this listserv.

2. This important conference was organized and hosted by Professor Laurietz Seda of the University of Connecticut. The conference included more than one hundred academic paper presentations, several dramatic readings, multiple workshops on selected topics in Latin American theater, daily round tables featuring a total of some fifteen Latin American playwrights, book expositions of the latest publications in the field, and nine live performances, some of which were created specifically for this conference.

3. E-mail to Latin American Theatre Today listserv, May 27, 2003.

4. Elaborating on the formation of the modern nation and its relationship to the word, Kristeva discusses former French president Charles de Gaulle's success in reinventing and fortifying France for its people. She argues that de Gaulle defined the "domain of the political," which he situated "on the boundary between *unconscious desires* for identity and power (that religion and psychology are fighting over) and *circumstances* (that are ruled by laws, force, diplomacy, and inevitably, economics . . .) . . . Conceived in such a manner, the political became concretized during the twentieth century in the idea of nation" (1993, 67).

References

Adler, Heidrun. 1999a. "¡Háblame! La técnica del monólogo." In Adler and Röttger 1999c, 125–34.

Adler, Heidrun, and Adrián Herr, eds. 1999b. *De las dos orillas: Teatro cubano.* Frankfurt am Main: Vervuert; Madrid: Iberoamericana.

Adler, Heidrun, and Kati Röttger, eds. 1999c. *Performance, Pathos, Política de los Sexos: Teatro postcolonial de autoras latinoamericanas.* Frankfurt am Main: Vervuert; Madrid: Iberoamericana.

Adler, Heidrun, and Jaime Chabaud, eds. 2004. *Un viaje sin fin: Teatro mexicano hoy.* Frankfurt am Main: Vervuert; Madrid: Iberoamericana.

Aisemberg, Alicia, and Adriana Libonati. 2000. "La dramaturgia emergente en Buenos Aires (1990–2000)." In Pellettieri 2000, 77–88.

Allen, Graham. 2000. *Intertextuality.* London & New York: Routledge.

Altman, Charles F. 1981. "Intratextual Rewriting: Textuality as Language Formation." In *The Sign in Music and Literature,* ed. Wendy Steiner, 39–51. Austin: Univ. of Texas.

Alvarez Borland, Isabel. 1998. *Cuban-American Literature of Exile: From Person to Persona.* Charlottesville: Univ. Press of Virginia.

Anderson, Benedict. 2003. *Imagined Communities: Reflections on the Origins and Spread of Nationalism.* Great Britain: Verso.

Anseume, William. 2002. "César Rengifo: ¿Paradigma del teatro político venezolano?" *Ollantay Theater Magazine* 10 (19): 58–64.

Aulakh, Preet S., and Michael G. Schechter, eds. 2000. *Rethinking Globalization(s): From Corporate Transnationalism to Local Interventions.* New York: St. Martin's Press.

Azar, Héctor. 1997. "Prólogo." In Vilalta 1997, 8–12.

Azparren Giménez, Leonardo. 2005. "Esbozo de una teoría del análisis crítico del discurso teatral." *Gestos: Teoría y Práctica del Teatro Hispánico* 39 (April): 13–37.

Bablé, Pepe. 2001. "De globalización y teatro latinoamericano." In *Discursos teatrales en los albores del siglo XI,* ed. Juan Villegas, 236–38. Irvine: Gestos.

Bakhtin, M. M. 1981. *The Dialogic Imagination.* Trans. Caryl Emerson and Michael Holquist. Austin: Univ. of Texas Press.

Bangert, William V., S.J. 1972. *A History of the Society of Jesus.* St. Louis: Institute of Jesuit Sources.

Barthes, Roland. 1994. *Oeuvres complètes.* Tome II. Paris: Editions du Seuil.

BBC Monitoring Original Source. 1996a. "Armed Group Attacks Peasants in Chiapas State." *La Jornada,* Mexico City (Internet version), May 6, http://infoweb.newsbank.com.

———. 1996b. "Army Increases Presence in Tezonapa Mountain Range." *La Jornada,* Mexico City (Internet version), August 22. http://infoweb.newsbank.com.

———. 1996c. "Subcommander Marcos Sends Open Letter to People's Revolutionary Army." *La Jornada,* Mexico City (Internet version), September 3, http://infoweb.newsbank.com.

Bello, Andrés. 1979. "Venezuela consolada." In *Obra literaria,* ed. Pedro Grases, 4–14. Caracas, Venezuela: Biblioteca Ayacucho.

Bhabha, Homi K., ed. 1990. *Nation and Narration.* London: Routledge.

———. 1994. *The Location of Culture.* London: Routledge.

Bixler, Jacqueline. 1994. "Signs of Absence in Pavlovsky's 'Teatro de la Memoria'." *Latin American Theatre Review* 28.1 (Fall): 17–30.

———. 1997. "The Postmodernization of History in the Theatre of Sabina Berman." *Latin American Theatre Review* 30.2 (Spring): 45–60.

———. 1999. "Power Plays and the Mexican Crisis: The Recent Theatre of Sabina Berman." In Adler and Röttger 1999c, 83–99.

Bixler, Jacqueline, and Stuart A. Day. 2005. *El teatro de Rascón Banda: Voces en el umbral.* Mexico, D.F.: Escenología, A.C.

Bloom, Harold. 1973. *The Anxiety of Influence.* New York: Oxford Univ. Press.

Borges, Jorge Luis. 1977. "Pierre Menard, autor del Quijote." In *Laberintos,* 35–47. Buenos Aires: Editorial Joraci.

Brasi, Juan Carlos de. 1997. "Métrica intensa." In Pavlovsky 1997a, 5–12.

Brennan, Timothy. 1990. "The National Longing for Form." In Bhabha 1990, 44–70.

Brownlow, Jeanne P., and John W. Kronik, eds. 1998. *Intertextual Pursuits: Literary Mediations in Modern Spanish Narrative.* Lewisburg, PA: Bucknell Univ. Press.

Burgess, Ronald D. 1997. "Five Summers of Mexican Theatre." *Latin American Theatre Review* 30.2 (Spring): 61–71.

Buttafava, Giovanni. 1990. "Anton Chejov y Las tres hermanas." *Primer acto* 232:32–37.

Caballero, Néstor. 1991. "Con una pequeña ayuda de mis amigos." In *Teatro venezolano contemporáneo: Antología,* coordinador Orlando Rodríguez B., 974–1047. Spain: Fondo de Cultura Económica.

Cabrera, Lydia. 1992. *El monte: Igbo-finda, ewe orisha, vititi nfinda.* Miami, FL: Ediciones universal.

Cárdenas, Raúl de. 1991. *Un hombre al amanecer.* Miami: Univ. of Miami.

Castellanos, Jorge, and Isabel Castellanos. 1992. *Cultura afrocubana: Las religiones y las lenguas.* Miami: Ediciones universal.

Castillo, Susana D. 1980. *El desarraigo en el teatro venezolano.* Caracas: Editorial Ateneo de Caracas.

Chekov, Anton. 1946. *Nine Plays of Chekov.* New York: Grosset & Dunlap.

Compton, Timothy G. 2001. "Mexico City Theatre (Spring 2000)." *Latin American Theatre Review* 34.2 (Spring): 153–62.

Corrales, José, and Manuel Pereiras. 1988. *Las hetairas habaneras: Una melotragedia cubana basada en Las troyanas de Eurípides.* Honolulu, HI: Editorial Persona.

Cubitt, Geoffrey. 1993. *The Jesuit Myth: Conspiracy Theory and Politics in Nineteenth–Century France.* Oxford: Clarendon Press.

Culler, Jonathan. 1976. "Presupposition and Intertextuality." *MLN* 91:1380–96.

Cypess, Sandra Messinger. 1991. *La Malinche in Mexican Literature: From History to Myth.* Austin: Univ. of Texas Press.

Dällenbach, Lucien. 1976. "Intertexte et autotexte." *Poétique: Revue de théorie et d'analyse littéraire* 2:282–96.

———. 1989. *The Mirror in the Text.* Trans. Jeremy Whiteley and Emma Hughes. Chicago: Univ. of Chicago Press.

Dauster, Frank. 1996. "The Spanish American Theatre of the Nineteenth Century." In *The Cambridge History of Latin American Literature,* ed. Roberto González Echeverría and Enrique Pupo-Walker, vol. 1, 536–55. New York: Cambridge Univ. Press.

———. 1998. "Víctor Hugo Rascón Banda y el nuevo realismo." *Revista de literatura mexicana contemporánea* 3.7 (January): 88–93.

Day, Stuart. 2004. *Staging Politics in Mexico: The Road to Neoliberalism.* Lewisburg, PA: Bucknell Univ. Press.

———. 2005. "En sus propias palabras: Víctor Hugo Rascón Banda." In Bixler and Day 2005, 21–32.

Del Estal, Eduardo. 2000. "'La tabla de los pecados' del Bosco." In Spregelburd 2000b, 11–19.

Delevoy, Robert L. 1960. *Bosch.* Trans. Stuart Gilbert. Lausanne: Editions d'Art Albert Skira.

Dubatti, Jorge, ed. 1997. *Teatro, postmodernidad y política en Eduardo Pavlovsky.* Uruguay: Ediciones Búsqueda de Ayllú.

———. "Prólogo." 2000. *Teatro argentino: Luis Cano, Cecilia Propato, Alfredo Rosenbaum, Rafael Spregelburd, Alejandro Tantanian, y Daniel Veronese,* 2–21. Buenos Aires: Libros de Tierra Firme.

During, Simon. 1990. "Literature—Nationalism's Other? The Case for Revision." In Bhabha 1990, 138–53.

Eagleton, Terry, Fredric Jameson, and Edward W. Said. 1990. *Nationalism, Colonialism, and Literature.* Minneapolis: Univ. of Minnesota Press.

Echeverría, Bolívar. 1994. "Malintzin, la lengua." In *La Malinche, sus padres y sus hijos,* ed. Margo Glantz, 129–38. Mexico: UNAM.

Escarpanter, José A. 1988. "*Las Hetairas Habaneras:* Una parodia cubana." In Corrales and Pereiras 1988, 5–9.

Ewell, Judith. 1984. *Venezuela: A Century of Change.* California: Stanford Univ. Press.

Febles, Jorge. 1999. "De la desazón de los 70 al prurito reconciliador de los 90: Revolución (y contrarrevolución?) en cinco piezas del exilio cubano." In Adler and Herr 1999b, 77–96.

Fraenger, Wilhelm. 1983. *Hieronymus Bosch.* New York: G. P. Putnam's Sons.

Frow, John. 1990. "Intertextuality and Ontology." In Worton and Still 1990, 45–55.

Fuentes, Carlos. 1998. "Después del neoliberalismo." *Reforma* online, April 20. http://busquedas.gruporeforma.com.

Galeano, Eduardo. 1992. *We Say No.* Trans. Mark Fried and Others. New York: W.W. Norton.

Gann, Myra S. 1991. "El teatro de Víctor Hugo Rascón Banda: Hiperrealismo y destino." *Latin American Theatre Review* 25.1 (Fall): 77–88.

Ganss, George E., S.J. 1992. *The Spiritual Exercises of Saint Ignatius.* Chicago: Loyola Univ. Press.

García Canclini, Néstor. 1990. *Hybrid Cultures: Strategies for Entering and Leaving Modernity.* Trans. Christopher L. Chiappari and Silvia L. López. Minneapolis: Univ. of Minnesota Press.

———. 2001. *Consumers and Citizens: Globalization and Multicultural Conflicts.* Trans. George Yúdice. Minneapolis: Univ. of Minnesota Press.

Garibay K., Angel María. 1953. *Historia de la literatura náhuatl.* Mexico: Editorial Porrúa.

Garza, Adolfo. 2000. "Mexico Candidates Take On Corruption in 2000 Polls." *Reuters News Service,* January 5. http://infoweb.newsbank.com.

Genette, Gérard. 1997. *Palimpsests: Literature in the Second Degree.* Trans. Channa Newman and Claude Doubinsky. Lincoln: Univ. of Nebraska Press.

Gibson, Walter S. 1982. *Hieronymus Bosch.* New York and Toronto: Oxford Univ. Press.

Giella, Miguel Angel. 1998. "El teatro como refracción: *Poroto* de Eduardo Pavlovsky." In *Tendencias críticas en el teatro,* ed. Osvaldo Pellettieri, 145–52. Buenos Aires: Galerna.

Giles, Paul. 2003. "Transnationalism and Classic American Literature." *PMLA* 118.1 (January): 62–77.

Gladhart, Amalia. 2000. *The Leper in Blue: Coercive Performance and the Contemporary Latin American Theater.* Chapel Hill: Univ. of North Carolina Press.

Glantz, Margo, ed. 1994. *La Malinche, sus padres y sus hijos.* Mexico: UNAM.

González-Casanova, Henrique. 1997. "Es Ignacio y es Chiapas." In Vilalta 1997, 13–15.

González-Pérez, Armando. 1999. *Presencia negra: Teatro cubano de la diáspora.* Madrid: Editorial Betanía.

Good, Carl, ed. 2001. "Introduction to Special Issue on Mexico in Transition: Art, Culture, Politics." *Discourse: Journal for Theoretical Studies in Media and Culture* 23.2 (Spring), online, http://www.sip.uiuc.edu/discourse/23.2.htm.

Gow, James. 1974. "Serbian Nationalism and the Hissssing Ssssnake in the International Order: Whose Sovereignty? Which Nation?" *SEER* 72.3 (July): 456–76.

Graham-Jones, Jean. 2000. *Exorcising History: Argentine Theater under Dictatorship.* Lewisburg: Bucknell Univ. Press.

Guibert, Joseph, S.J. 1972. *The Jesuits: Their Spiritual Doctrine and Practice.* Trans. William J. Young, S.J. St. Louis: Institute of Jesuit Sources.

Hadas, Moses. 1960. "Introduction." In *Ten Plays,* by Euripides, Trans. Moses Hadas and John McLean, vii–xix. Bantam Books.

Hodge, Polly. 1999. "El teatro y la intertextualidad." In *Propuestas escénicas de fin de siglo: FIT 1998,* ed. Juan Villegas, 97–108. Saline, MI: McNaughton & Gunn.

Holzapfel, Tamara. 1981. "The Theater of Maruxa Vilalta: A Triumph of Versatility." *Latin American Theatre Review* 14.2 (Spring): 11–18.

Infante, María, and Adriana Libonati. 2000. "La estética de la contradicción: A propósito de *La modestia* de Rafael Spregelburd." Online, http://www.spregelburd.com.ar/web/index.html.

Jameson, Fredric, and Masao Miyoshi, eds. 1998. *The Cultures of Globalization.* Durham, NC: Duke Univ. Press.

Jezierski, Karin. 1986. *Un pueblo pinta su historia: El muralismo en Venezuela.* Venezuela: Cuadernos Lagoven.

Kaminsky, Amy K. 1999. *After Exile: Writing the Latin American Diaspora.* Minneapolis: Univ. of Minnesota Press.

Kristeva, Julia. 1977. "Le sujet en procès." *Polylogue.* Paris: Editions du Seuil, 55–106.

———. 1984. *Revolution in Poetic Language.* Trans. Margaret Waller. New York: Columbia Univ. Press.

———. 1991. *Strangers to Ourselves.* Trans. Leon S. Roudiez. New York: Columbia Univ. Press.

———. 1993. *Nations without Nationalism.* Trans. Leon S. Roudiez. New York: Columbia Univ. Press.

Kronik, John. 1977. "Usigli's *El gesticulador* and the Fiction of Truth." *Latin American Theatre Review* 11.1 (Fall): 5–16.

Larson, Catherine, and Margarita Vargas, eds. 1998. *Latin American Women Dramatists: Theater, Texts, and Theories.* Bloomington and Indianapolis: Indiana Univ. Press.

León-Portilla, Miguel. 1961. *Visión de los vencidos: Relaciones indígenas de la Conquista.* Mexico: UNAM.

———. 1992. *Fifteen Poets of the Aztec World.* Norman and London: Univ. of Oklahoma Press.

Linares-Ocanto, Luis. 2000. "Los dioses en sí mismos: Lo afrocubano en *Requiem por Yarini* de Carlos Felipe." *Latin American Theatre Review* 33.2 (Spring): 43–52.

Ludmer, Josefina. 1984. "Tretas del debil." In *La sárten por el mango,* ed. Patricia Elena González and Eliana Ortega, 47–54. Río Piedras, Puerto Rico Ediciones Horacán.

Magnarelli, Sharon. 1987. "Contenido y forma en la obra de Maruxa Vilalta." Trans. Carlos David Malfavón. *Plural: Revista cultural de Excelsior* 16.12 (September): 77–78.

———. 1998. "Maruxa Vilalta: *Una voz en el desierto.*" In Larson and Vargas 1998, 23–40.

Mannarino, Carmen. 2002. "Influencia extranjera en un teatro distinto." *Ollantay Theater Magazine* 10 (19): 14–23.

Marcos, Subcommandant I. 1994. "Chiapas: El sureste en dos vientos, una tormenta y una profecía." *Departamento de Prensa y Propaganda, EZLN,* January, http://www.ezln.org/documentos/1994/199208xx.es.htm.

Marsh, Cynthia. 1999. "Gor'kii and Chekhov: A Dialogue of Text and Performance." *Slavonic and East European Review* 77.4 (October): 601–19.

Martí, José. 1940. *Teatro: Abdala; Obras completas de Martí.* Director, Gonzalo de Quesada y Miranda, vol. 27: 9–26. La Habana, Cuba: Editorial Trópico.

Martin, Gregory, and Mia Cinotti. 1966. *The Complete Paintings of Bosch.* New York: Harry N. Abrams.

Meléndez, Priscilla. 1990. *La dramaturgia hispanoamericana contemporánea: Teatro y autoconciencia.* Madrid: Pliegos.

———. 1996. "Co(s)mic Conquest in Sabina Berman's *Aguila o sol.*" In *Perspectives on Contemporary Spanish American Theatre,* ed. Frank Dauster, 19–36. Lewisburg, PA: Bucknell Univ. Press.

Meyran, Daniel. 2004. "Representar el pasado es repasar el presente o Las recuperaciones del mundo precolombino y colonial en el teatro mexicano contemporáneo." In Adler and Chabaud 2004, 43–55.

"Mexico-Chiapas: Zapatista Leader Prepared to Lay Down Arms for Genuine Peace." 2001. *EFE News Services online,* January 8, http://infoweb.newsbank.com.

"Mexico Elections: Fox asks for Support from Mexican Catholics." 2000. *EFE News Services online,* May 7, http://infoweb.newsbank.com.

Monge Rafuls, Pedro R. 1999. "Otra historia." In *Presencia negra: Teatro cubano de la diáspora,* ed. Armando González-Pérez, 51–94. Madrid: Betania.

Montes Huidobro, Matías. 1973. *Persona, vida y máscara en el teatro cubano.* Miami, FL: Ediciones Universal.

———. 1997a. "Escribir teatro en el exilio." *Ollantay Theater Magazine* 5 (2): 41–44.

———. 1997b "La voz del otro en el teatro cubano contemporáneo." In *El teatro y su mundo: Estudios sobre el teatro iberoamericano y argentino,* ed. Osvaldo Pellettieri, 99–107. Buenos Aires: Ediciones Galerna.

Moore, Molly. 1998. "Mexico, Zapatista Rebels Open First Talks Since '96." *Washington Post* online, section A, page A 14, November 21, http://infoweb.newsbank.com.

Moreno, Iani del. 1996. "*Jesucristo entre nosotros* de Maruxa Vilalta." *Revista de literatura Mexicana contemporánea* 2 (4): 82–87.

Morgan, Thaïs. 1989. "The Space of Intertextuality." In *Intertextuality and Contemporary American Fiction,* ed. Patrick O'Donnell and Robert Con Davis, 239–79. Baltimore and London: Johns Hopkins Univ. Press.

Morwood, James, trans. and ed. 2000. *Euripides: Hecuba, The Trojan Women, Andromache.* New York: Oxford Univ. Press.

Mujica, Jesús. 1991. *César Rengifo: A viva voz.* Caracas, Venezuela: Fundarte.

Naim, Moises. 2001. "The Venezuelan Story: Revisiting the Conventional Wisdom." *Carnegie Endowment for International Peace,* http://www.ceip.org/files/publications/VenezuelanStory.asp.

Nigro, Kirsten. 1987. "On Reading and Responding to (Latin American) Playtexts." *Gestos* 2.4 (November): 101–13.

O'Malley, John W. 1990. "Some Distinctive Characteristics of Jesuit Spirituality in the Sixteenth Century." In *Jesuit Spirituality,* ed. John W. O'Malley, John W. Padberg, and Vincent T. O'Keefe, 1–20. Chicago: Loyola Univ. Press.

Osorio T., Nelson. 1992. "La alucinación del petróleo en una obra de César Rengifo." *Hispamerica: Revista de Literatura* 21.63 (December): 81–87.

Pavis, Patrice. 2000. "Ivanov: The Invention of a Negative Dramaturgy." In *The*

Cambridge Companion to Chekhov, ed. Vera Gottlieb and Paul Allain, 70–79. New York: Cambridge Univ. Press.

Pavlovsky, Eduardo. 1982. *Proceso creador: Terapia y existencia.* Uruguay: Ediciones Búsqueda de Ayllú.

Pavlovsky, Eduardo, Carlos Martínez Bouquet, and Fidel Moccio. 1985. *Psicodrama: Cuándo y por qué dramatizar.* Buenos Aires: Ediciones Búsqueda.

Pavlovsky, Eduardo. 1987. "Las identidades fragmentadas." *Grupal* 5 (October): 29–32.

———. 1996. *Poroto: Historia de una táctica.* Uruguay: Ediciones Búsqueda de Ayllú.

———. 1997a. *Dirección contraria.* Concepción de Uruguay: Ediciones Búsqueda de Ayllú.

———. 1997b. "Estética de la multiplicidad, Concepciones de la producción de subjetividad en mi teatro." In *Postmodernidad y postcolonialidad,* ed. Alfonso de Toro, 205–32. Frankfurt am Main: Vervuert; Madrid: Iberoamericana.

———. 1997c. *Teatro Completo I.* Buenos Aires: Atuel.

———. 1999a. *Poroto: Nueva versión para el teatro.* Buenos Aires: Galerna.

———. 1999b. *Textos balbuceantes.* Buenos Aires: Ediciones Teatro Vivo.

Pavlosky, Eduardo, and Jorge Dubatti. 2001. *La ética del cuerpo: Nuevas conversaciones con Jorge Dubatti.* Buenos Aires: Atuel.

Paz, Octavio. 1959. *El laberinto de la soledad.* Mexico: Fondo de Cultura Económica.

Pellettieri, Osvaldo, ed. 2000. *El teatro del año 2000.* Buenos Aires: Galerna.

Pérez Firmat, Gustavo. 1994. *Life on the Hyphen: The Cuban-American Way.* Austin: Univ. of Texas Press.

Petkoff, Teodoro. 2000. *La Venezuela de Chávez: Una segunda opinión.* Caracas, Venezuela: Grijalbo, S.A.

Piñera, Virgilio. 1960. *Teatro completo.* La Habana: Ediciones R.

Pogolotti, Graziella. 1999. "Mostrar lo invisible." In Adler and Herr 1999b, 19–27.

Proaño-Gómez, Lola. 2001. "Miradas a la globalización desde la escena latinoamericana." In *Discursos teatrales en los albores del siglo XXI,* ed. Juan Villegas, 57–75. Irvine, CA: Gestos.

Quackenbush, L. H. 1974. "Cuestión de vida y muerte: Tres dramas existenciales." *Latin American Theatre Review* 8.1 (Fall): 49–56.

Rascón Banda, Víctor Hugo. 2000. *La Malinche.* Mexico: Plaza & Janés.

Regéczi, Ildikó. 1997. "Chekhov and the Philosophy of the Turn of the Century: Chekhov and Shestov." *Studia Slavica Hung* 42 (3–4): 387–400.

Renan, Ernest. 1882. "What is a Nation?" Trans. Martin Thom. In Bhabha 1990, 8–22.

Rengifo, César. 1977. "El raudal de los muertos cansados." In *Teatro: César Rengifo,* ed. María del Carmen Pérez, 302–50. La Habana, Cuba: Casa de las Américas.

———. 1977. "Las torres y el viento." In *Teatro: César Rengifo,* ed. María del Carmen Pérez, 351–419. La Habana, Cuba: Casa de las Américas.

———. 1978. *Pintores venezolanos.* Ed. Ratto-Ciarlo, José. Madrid: Editorial Mediterráneo.

———. 1979. *Un fausto anda por la avenida.* Caracas, Venezuela: Fundarte.

———. 1989. *Obras: Artículos y ensayos.* Tomo VI. Mérida: Editorial Venezolana C.A.

Riffaterre, Michael. 1990. "Compulsory Reader Response: The Intertextual Drive." In Worton and Still 1990, 56–78.

Rizk, Beatriz J. 1998. "History as a Recurrent Rhythm in Late Twentieth-Century Cuban Theater." *Ollantay Theater Magazine* 6 (11): 122–31.

———. 2000. "Miami: Meca del exilio cubano y escenario medido aunque efervescente." *Latin American Theatre Review* 34.1 (Fall): 229–46.

Rodas, Beatriz. 1998. "*Volver a Santa Rosa* de Víctor Hugo Rascón Banda." *Revista de literatura mexicana contemporánea* 4.9 (October): 82–86.

Rodríguez, Roberto R. 1977. "La función de la imaginación en las *Coronas* de Rodolfo Usigli." *Latin American Theatre Review* 10.2 (Spring): 37–44.

Rojas, Mario A. 2002. "Interculturalismo y multiculturalismo y nuevas tendencias del teatro latinoamericano actual." In *Imagen del teatro,* ed. Osvaldo Pellettieri, 63–73. Buenos Aires: Galerna.

Rose, William, ed. and trans. 1925. *The History of the Damnable Life and Deserved Death of Doctor John Faustus.* London: George Routledge & Sons, Ltd.

Salcedo, Hugo. 1997. "¿Existe un nuevo teatro en México?" *Latin American Theatre Review* 30.1 (Fall): 85–89.

Schulman, Ivan A., ed. 1994. *José, Martí: Ismaelillo, Versos libres, Versos sencillos.* Madrid: Ediciones Cátedra, S.A.

Seda, Laurietz. 2005. "Etnia y clase social en el contexto de los procesos de la globalización en *La Malinche* de Víctor Hugo Rascón Banda." In Bixler and Day 2005, 91–102.

Senreich, Evan. 2003. "Reminiscence and Rambling Regarding José Corrales as a Writer." *Ollantay Theater Magazine* 11, no. 21: 137–40.

Smith, Michael Peter, and Luis Eduardo Guarnizo, eds. 1998. *Transnationalism from Below.* New Brunswick and London: Transaction Publishers.

Snyder, James, ed. 1973. *Bosch in Perspective.* NJ: Prentice-Hall.

Solórzano, Carlos. 1985. "El teatro de Maruxa Vilalta." *Latin American Theatre Review* 18.2 (Spring): 83–87.

———. 2002. "Prólogo." In Vilalta 2002, 11–14.

Sosa, Marcela B., and Graciela Balestino de Adamo. 1997. "Reescritura y teatro latinoamericano." In *El teatro y su mundo: Estudios sobro teatro iberoamericano y argentino,* ed. Osvaldo Pellettieri, 135–43. Buenos Aires: Galerna.

Spregelburd, Rafael. 2000a. *Cuadro de asfixia.* Buenos Aires: Ediciones Teatro Vivo.

———. 2000b. *Heptalogía de Hieronymus Bosch I, II, III: La inapetencia, La extravagancia, La modestia.* Buenos Aires: Adriana Hidalgo editora.

Suárez-Radillo, Carlos Miguel. 1972. "Vigencia de la realidad venezolana en el teatro de César Rengifo." *Latin American Theatre Review* 5.2 (Spring): 51–61.

Tabuas, Mireya. 1991. "Introduction to *Con una pequeña ayuda de mis amigos.*" In *Teatro venezolano contemporáneo: Antología,* coordinador Orlando Rodríguez B., 965–70. Spain: Fondo de Cultura Económica.

Tavira, Luis de. 1992. "El teatro histórico en la trilogía antihistórica de Rodolfo Usigli." In *Rodolfo Usigli: Ciudadano del teatro, Memoria de los homenajes a Rodolfo Usigli, 1990–1991,* 79–85. Mexico: Instituto Nacional de Bellas Artes.

———. 2002. Introduction. In Vilalta 2002, 137.

Taylor, Diana. 1997. *Disappearing Acts: Spectacles of Gender and Nationalism in Argentina's "Dirty War."* Durham and London: Duke Univ. Press.

———. 2003. *The Archive and the Repertoire: Performing Cultural Memory in the Americas.* Durham and London: Duke Univ. Press.

Tayzan, Armando Partida. 1997. "Aspectos formales en la escritura dramática mexicana." *Latin American Theatre Review* 30.1 (Fall): 91–97.

———. 1998. *Dramaturgos mexicanos, 1970–1990: Bibliografía crítica.* Mexico: Instituto Nacional de Bellas Artes.

———. 2000. "La dramaturgia mexicana de los noventa." *Latin American Theatre Review* 34.1 (Fall): 143–60.

Toro, Alfonso de. 2001. "El teatro *menor* postmoderno de Eduardo Pavlovsky o el 'Borges/Bacon' del teatro: De la periferia al centro." *Gestos* 31 (April): 99–110.

Ubersfeld, Anne. 1999. *Reading Theatre.* Trans. Frank Collins. Toronto: Univ. of Toronto Press.

Usigli, Rodolfo. 1965. "Primer Prólogo" and "Segundo Prólogo." *Corona de Luz.* Mexico: Fondo de Cultura Económica.

Uspensky, Boris. 1973. *A Poetics of Composition.* Trans. Valentina Zavarin and Susan Wittig. Berkeley: Univ. of California Press.

Versényi, Adam. 1993. *Theatre in Latin America: Religion, Politics, and Culture from Cortés to the 1980s.* Great Britain: Cambridge Univ. Press.

Vertovec, Steven, and Robin Cohen, eds. 1999. *Migration, Diasporas and Transnationalism.* Cheltenham, UK and Northampton, MA: Edward Elgar Publishing Ltd.

Vidal, Hernán. 1991. "Notion of Otherness within the Framework of National Identity." *Gestos* 11 (April): 27–44.

Vilalta, Maruxa. 1997. *En blanco y negro: Ignacio y los jesuitas.* Mexico: Fondo de Cultura Económica.

———. 2002. *1910 y tres obras más.* Mexico: CONACULTA.

Villegas, Juan. 2000. *Para la interpretación del teatro como construcción visual.* Irvine, CA: Ediciones de Gestos.

Westlake, E. J. 1998. "Performing the Nation in Manuel Galich's *El tren amarillo.*" *Latin American Theatre Review* 31.2 (Spring): 107–17.

Woodyard, George, and Leon Lyday. 1976. *Dramatists in Revolt: The New Latin American Theater.* Austin: Univ. of Texas Press.

Woodyard, George. 1997. "*Rojos Globos Rojos* de Pavlovsky: Intertextualidad y aspectos posmodernistas." In *El teatro y su mundo: Estudios sobre teatro iberoamericano y argentino,* ed. Osvaldo Pellettieri, 239–46. Buenos Aires: Editorial Galerna.

———. 2004. "Tres damas históricas de Víctor Hugo Rascón Banda." In Adler and Chabaud 2004, 65–79.

Worton, Michael, and Judith Still. 1990. *Intertextuality: Theories and Practices.* England: Manchester Univ. Press.

Yúdice, George. 2001. "From Hybridity to Policy: For a Purposeful Cultural Studies." In García Canclini 2001, ix–xxxviii.

———. 2003. *The Expediency of Culture: Uses of Culture in the Global Era.* Durham and London: Duke Univ. Press.

Index